30 to 90 (at Roans Pr
left
about 6-7 miles, left
9.5 miles to left onto 10
108 to 103 (left) at stop sign
103 to house about 3/4 mile
past creek bridge

Assembly

BOOKS BY JOHN O'HARA

JOHN O'HARA

ASSEMBLY

My task, which I am trying to achieve, is, by the power of the written word, to make you feel—it is, before all, to make you see. That—and no more. And it is everything.   JOSEPH CONRAD

RANDOM HOUSE • NEW YORK

to
WOLCOTT GIBBS
(March 15, 1902—August 16, 1958)
"Many fetes"

Contents

Foreword

All but three or four of these stories were written during the summer of 1960. I wrote most of them in two sittings of about three hours apiece, and it was some of the most joyful writing I have ever done. The pleasure was in finding that after eleven years of not writing short stories, I could begin again and do it better; and the joy was in discovering that at fifty-five, and in spite of aches in spine and tendons, I had an apparently inexhaustible urge to express an unlimited supply of short story ideas. No writing has ever come more easily to me, and I say that notwithstanding the fact that I have always been a natural writer. It is not to be inferred by the layman or the tyro author that because the writing looks easy, or because I say it came easily, hard work was not involved. The hard work is half the fun (the other half, of course, is in the contemplation of the finished product). There may be as many as a dozen persons in the world who are able to detect the techniques employed, and they will understand what I mean by the fun of the hard work. They will know right away, while I could write a long book on techniques that the layman would not, and should not, bother to read. How do you start a paragraph? What is a character's first speech? When is a homely detail valuable? What is good dialog?

If you are an author, and not just a writer, you keep learning all the time. Today, for instance, I was thinking about dialog, listening to dialog of some characters in my mind's ear, and I learned for the first time in my life that almost no woman who has gone beyond the eighth grade ever calls a fifty-cent piece a half-a-dollar. A male author, writing dialog carelessly, might easily have a female character say "half-a-dollar" because it sounded vernacularly right to him. But it would be wrong, it would harm his characterization, and he would never know why. Hard creative work is filled with hundreds of such hazards, and the author of prose can't go back to Bacon or Blake to see how *they'd* have done it.

During the years I was not writing short stories I was occasionally invited by magazine editors to excerpt passages from my novels which the editors thought would "stand up" as short stories. I never did. I am a great believer in the creative flow, that once you have commenced the writing of a novel, all that follows is part of that novel. In spite of digressions and interruptions, a novel is continuous and should not be capsulized or "digested" or even synopsized, unless the synopsis is clearly labeled as such. (I allowed a novel of mine to be "digested" and I promise not to let that happen again.) By the same token it is artistically wrong to take a passage out of a book and present it as a short story, no matter how it is labeled. The short story is such a different art form that an author simply must not have the same approach to a novel that he has to the short story. The author must say to himself that this is to be a short story; he must say it over and over again so that he conditions himself and disciplines himself before setting words down on paper, until the habit of thinking in short story terms is re-formed. Obviously he must make all the words count, obviously he must set space limits ahead of time. But at the time he is preparing himself to compress, he must also bear in mind the fact that this may be the only thing of his that some reader will ever read. In other words, the artistic conscience must be functioning. The author may write rapidly, and I do, but let it not be inferred that I "dash them off." The way I feel about writing, which is practically a religious feeling, would not permit me to "dash off" a story. And there is another aspect to it: the *work* of writing is fun, and without the work the writing is not fun, pleasure, or a joy.

Nowadays I get letters from students who are the sons and daughters of men and women who read my early short stories when they first came out. Thus, without realizing it, I was writing for posterity, and posterity is here. I hope that the students who read these stories will have posterity of their own, but these stories were not written for them. In a real, literal sense they were written for my own pleasure.

JOHN O'HARA

Quogue, Long Island
Summer, 1961

Assembly

Mrs. Stratton of Oak Knoll

As was their nightly custom, Evan Reese and his wife Georgia finished their small chores and took their seats to watch the eleven o'clock news program on the television. Evan Reese's chore was to put the backgammon men in place for the next night's game; Georgia's was to remove the coffee tray to the kitchen. Evan Reese now lit his pipe, Georgia lit a cigarette, and they sat patiently through the preliminary commercial announcements. "And now the news," said the announcer.

"Do tell," said Georgia, stroking the head of their Airedale.

Evan Reese smiled. His wife had given up her letters of protest to the newspaper editorial pages against the length and number of commercials, but she always made some small audible comment when the man said, "And now the news."

"Quiet, please," said Evan Reese.

"A four-engine bomber on a routine training flight over the Rocky—" the announcer began. At that moment the dog growled and the Reeses' doorbell rang.

Evan Reese frowned and looked at his wife, and they said, together: "Who could that be?" and Georgia Reese added, "At this hour?"

"You pay attention to the news, I'll see who it is," said Evan Reese. He switched on the carriage lamps at the front door and the floodlight that illuminated the driveway. He peeked through the draperies and saw, in the driveway, a large black limousine. He held the dog by the collar and opened the door.

A middle-aged man in chauffeur's livery raised his hand in a semi-military salute. "Stratton residence?" he said.

"No, this isn't the Stratton residence. You have the wrong house."

"This is Ridge Road and West Branch Lane, isn't it?" said the chauffeur.

"Yes it is, but if you'll notice there's a driveway across the road, with a sign that says Oak Knoll. That's the entrance to Mrs. Stratton's place."

"Sorry, I didn't see no sign."

"It's there in plain sight," said Evan Reese.

"What the hell's the delay?" The voice came from inside the limousine, and Evan Reese could make out a man's hatless head but little more. The Airedale barked once.

"I'll leave the floodlight on and you can turn around—and you can tell your employer to mind his manners."

"I'll tell him a lot more when I get my tip," said the chauffeur. "I don't work for him, I work for the rental company. He only hired this car, and believe me, I'll never drive him again."

"Is he drunk? He sounds it."

"Drunk? He was drunk when I called for him. The Racquet Club."

"New York, or Philadelphia?"

"New York. Well, sorry to trouble you, Mister."

"That's all right. Hope you get a big tip. Goodnight."

"Goodnight, sir, and thanks again." The chauffeur saluted, and Evan Reese closed the door, watching through the draperies until the limousine was out of his driveway.

"A drunken man calling on Mrs. Stratton. Obviously with the intention of spending the night, since it's a hired car. Now we have something on her."

"I guess it must be that son."

"No, I'd rather think it was some gigolo she sent for."

"She's a little old for that. Did you get a look at him?"

"I can give you a perfect description. Black patent leather hair, waxed moustache, and a gold bracelet . . . No, I didn't really see him. Would her son belong to the Racquet Club?"

"Oh, at least. You can look him up in the Social Register."

"Where is it?"

"It's in my sewing-room, by the telephone."

"Too much trouble," said Evan Reese. "Anything in the news?"

"I wasn't listening very carefully, I was overcome with curiosity about who'd call on us at eleven o'clock at night."

"Mrs. Stratton's drunken son, I guess. Now the next time she writes us one of her neighborly notes about our dog, we can come back at her."

"Oh, Ev, that was ten years ago."

"Well, it's still the only time we ever heard from her. Ten years and she never came to call on you. I think I *will* look up the son. By the telephone?"

"On the lower shelf of the little table."

Evan Reese obtained the book and returned to the library. "Now then," he said. "Stratton, there *she* is. Mrs. Francis, Oak Knoll, High Ridge, New Jersey. Phone number 7-1415. Ah, yes, here he is. Francis A., Junior, 640 East Eighty-third. R for Racquet, B for Brook, K for Knickerbocker, H-37. Harvard, '37. That would make him about forty-five years old. Oh, and here's one. Stratton, Mrs. Virginia C., Virginia Daniels, and under her name another Virginia, at Foxcroft, and another Francis, at St. Mark's. There we have the whole story, the whole tragic story of the drunken mama's-boy, coming home to see mama because the boys at the club were mean to him."

"It may not be that at all."

"I'll bet it's close to it. Now let's see if he's in *Who's Who?*" said Evan Reese. He took down a volume and opened it. "Nope. I didn't think he would be. I formed my impression of him when he barked at the driver of that car. Driver was a polite, decent-looking fellow. Probably very efficient, too, except for not seeing the Oak Knoll sign. *Say,* that's interesting."

"Why?"

"Wouldn't you think that Stratton would know where his mother lived? Maybe he was asleep, or so drunk—no, he wasn't that drunk. And he wasn't asleep. Maybe it isn't her son after all. But I think it is. Do you know what I think, Georgia?"

"What?"

"I think we have a mystery on our hands."

"Well, you puzzle it out, I'm retiring. I have all sorts of things to do tomorrow, and don't forget. We have Bob and Jennie for dinner tomorrow night."

"God, is tomorrow Wednesday? Well, at least they're coming here. We don't have to go out."

"If you stay up reading, don't fall asleep in your chair or your arm'll get stiff again and you won't be able to work."

This was a bit of caution she gave him about once a week. He was miserable when his arm hurt and he could not paint, especially when he was painting well, and more especially when he was finishing the last of his pictures for a one-man show in the spring. It was not only his habit of falling asleep in his chair that made his arm sore, nor was he telling the truth when he blamed the weather. He had bursitis, he knew it and she knew it, but they pretended he was in perfect health. He—they—would not admit that he was sixty years old and already a victim of the painter's occupational disease. He refused to see a doctor, to confirm what he had long suspected, to submit to treatment that was never wholly successful. "The minute I hear myself snoring, I'll come to bed," he said.

"Goodnight, dear," she said.

"Goodnight, Pussycat," he said. He put her hand to his cheek and kissed it, and she left him. The dog stretched out on the rug and dozed.

Evan Reese turned the television to a different channel and for an hour or so watched a lovely British movie that he knew by heart, having seen it at least ten times. He did not have to follow the plot, which was nothing much to begin with and concerned the refusal of some Scotsmen in a remote village to pay their taxes until the government promised them a new road. Evan Reese could share the Scotsmen's feelings toward London; he could sing "Men of Harlech" in the Welsh, although he had never been to the land of his fathers; but he knew the movie so well that he could pick up the story anywhere along the way, and there was no suspense in it for him. The charm of it was in the characters and the acting and in the verisimilitude of the exteriors and interiors—the laird had a forty-year-old

Rolls-Royce station wagon instead of the 1960 Cadillac that Hollywood would have considered suitable for a laird. The house in which the laird lived was not too unlike Evan Reese's; built to last, furnished for comfort, a warm shelter whether the winds came down from Canada or from the North Sea.

The movie came to its happy ending and Evan Reese turned off the television. At the cessation of the sound, Mike, the Airedale, raised his head, expecting to be let out. "Just you hold it now till I finish my pipe," said Evan Reese. The dog wagged his tail to indicate that he knew he was being addressed, and Evan Reese reached down and scratched the animal's head. "I think you must be getting old, too," said Evan Reese. "You're not the watchdog you used to be. You never heard Mr. Stratton's car."

The dog again wagged his tail.

"Well, you're twelve years old," said Evan Reese. "And that's supposed to be the equivalent of eighty-four human years. You're a good boy."

At the words "good boy" the dog got to his feet and began to back out of the room, keeping his eyes on the master.

"All right," said Evan Reese, and opened the front door and let the dog run into the darkness. It was not his custom to turn on the floodlights for Mike, and in the moonless, starless night he noticed that Mrs. Stratton's house was lit up on two stories. The shades were drawn, but there was light behind them, and he could not recall ever having seen light in the house at such a late hour. It was past midnight. As his eyes became accustomed to the darkness he began to see smoke issuing forth from one of the chimneys on the Stratton roof, and he wondered what could be going on, what scene was taking place between the widow and her son. A happy reunion? He thought not.

Evan Reese whistled softly for his dog, which responded to the signal, and man and dog returned to the warm house. "Snow tomorrow, for sure," said Evan Reese. "I can feel it in my bones." He saw that the dog was curling up on his piece of carpet in the library, and he now retired for his own rest.

Bob and Jennie Hewitt were fourth-generation residents of High Ridge. She as an amateur painter and he as president of the local bank had been the Reeses' first acquaintances in the town and the friendship between the two couples had become a pleasant one. The men were the same age, the women were only two years apart, and when Bob Hewitt got over the first shock of discovering that he was somewhat less conservative than a man who earned a good living as a painter, the weekly dinner-and-bridge was instituted and had continued. A running score was kept, and at the end of their October-through-May season never more than $50 changed hands.

"Bob, get Evan to tell you about the visitor he had last night," said Jennie Hewitt. "Go on, Evan. He'd be interested. I think it's fascinating."

"Well, with that build-up, who was it, Ev? Brigitte Bardot?" said Bob Hewitt.

"Not quite," said Evan Reese, and related the events of the previous night.

Bob Hewitt was a good listener, and at the end of Evan's report he said: "Well, you have him pegged about right. Frank Stratton is a mama's-boy and a heavy drinker. Did you see him around today?"

"No. I looked for him, but there was no sign of him."

"The last time he did this, came home to mama, was before you moved to High Ridge. It was when his wife left him. He came home then, under almost the same circumstances. Drunk, and in a hired car. But the next day the old lady sent him packing. Banished him. She didn't want him around, or that was the story. Jennie, you tell that part."

"I'm dying to," said Jennie Hewitt. "And I'm dying to know if she lets him stay this time. What happened before was that Mrs. Stratton was furious because Frank did what everybody always said he'd do. Come home to mother at the first sign of trouble. And there *was* trouble. It even got in the papers, a little bit. You see, Frank is—well it was *in* the *papers*, so I might as well say it. Frank is a fairy."

"Well, don't say it that positively, Jennie. After all, he did marry and he had two children." Bob Hewitt spoke sardonically.

"But what was he arrested for?"

"*He* wasn't arrested. The other fellow was arrested for beating him up and stealing money and stuff. You've got it all mixed up."

"Well then you tell it," said Jennie Hewitt.

"There isn't much else to tell. He was beaten up by a young serviceman that he met in a bar, and the police found Frank's wallet and cigarette case on him. Stupid. You'd think he'd have got rid of such incriminating evidence, but as I recall it the soldier tried to sell the cigarette case in some bar on Eighth Avenue and the bartender tipped off the military police. Then the New York cops went to Frank's apartment and found him lying in a pool of blood, and that was how the story got out. You had to read between the lines—"

"Oh, Bob. Between the lines. They couldn't have been more explicit."

"No, maybe not, but there was no charge preferred against Frank. That's where you're giving the Reeses the wrong impression."

"I was trying to give them the right impression. Ev, Georgia, what would you think if you read that story in the newspapers?"

"I'd be inclined to think that Mr. Stratton was very indiscreet, not to say impulsive," said Evan Reese.

"I'd say he got what was coming to him," said Georgia Reese. "Picking up soldiers in a bar."

"And you'd be right, and his mother was furious," said Jennie Hewitt. "She told him to go right back to New York and face it out. Brazen it out, I'd call it. But she was right, as it turned out. He did go back to New York, and went right on seeing people and of course nobody could come up and say to him point-blank, 'Were you a fairy with that soldier?' And after while people began to say well maybe the soldier *did* follow him to his apartment and try to rob him. In other words, people sort of gave him the benefit of the doubt. That was his version to the police."

"Maybe it was true," said Evan Reese. "When I was a young man living in Greenwich Village there were certain reprehensible characters who made a living by blackmailing older men. They'd see a man getting drunk in a speakeasy and they'd get in a taxi with him or follow him home, and then threaten to expose him if he didn't shell out. Some of those men were certainly guilty, or at least vulnerable, but I wonder how many were innocent. I knew a sculptor who paid blackmail for years because he got drunk with a male model and he could never actually remember whether he'd made passes at him or not. My friend, the sculptor, was of course vulnerable. He was bisexual. He said to me more than once, 'Reese, I honestly don't know. Maybe I did.' "

"What ever happened to him?" said Jennie Hewitt.

"My friend? He gave up. He became very successful, made a lot of money, and one day when the young bum came around for his cheque, my friend told him to go to hell. 'You can't blackmail me any more,' he said. 'I've stopped denying it or pretending I'm anything else, so get out.' "

"How delightful," said Jennie Hewitt.

"Not really," said Georgia Reese. "He later hanged himself. He was genuinely in love with a girl, and she wouldn't have him."

"I guess the old Greenwich Village must have been quite a place, Ev?" said Bob Hewitt.

"It doesn't sound much different today, only worse," said Georgia.

"We had some gifted people," said Evan Reese. "Real talent. Once in a while a genius, or very close to it. Anyway, real artists. First-rate writers, some of the best. But now all I ever hear about is an occasional saxophone player. You see, we worked. We did a lot of talking, and a great deal of drinking and sleeping around, but we also worked. Now we don't hear much about work down there. Talk, yes. Drinking and sleeping around, and dope. But they don't seem to know how to paint or write."

"I never liked the Village," said Georgia. "You never did anything really good till you got out of it."

"Oh, yes, I did some good things, but I never did anything first-rate till I was past forty anyhow, so the Village did me no harm. And I did work."

"Well, this isn't very interesting to the Hewitts. We were talking about this Stratton man."

"And I wouldn't waste any pity on him," said Jennie. "Unfortunately, Bob and I weren't surprised when that happened, the beating and so on."

"No, it's one of those small-town secrets that only a few people think they're in on, but it was pretty generally known, I guess," said Bob Hewitt. "When did we first hear about it?"

"When did we first hear about it? Why, that time—"

"That time he had that friend home from college. You're right. The maid quit because Frank brought a friend home from college and—"

"Lorna. Lorna Parton."

"Lorna walked in to clean the drawing-room and there was the friend sitting at the piano, stark naked at nine o'clock in the morning. Went right on playing, too."

"Where was Stratton?" said Evan Reese.

"Oh, I don't know where he was, probably upstairs sleeping off a hangover," said Bob Hewitt. "But the friend went right on playing, even when Mrs. Stratton came in to remonstrate with him. What was it he said to her?"

"He was the boldest thing I ever heard of. He finished playing whatever it was, regardless of her saying *Mister* Jones, or whatever his name was. He came to the end of the piece and then he turned to her and said: 'Do you play?' You know, as though he expected her to join him in a duet."

"No more friends home from Harvard," said Bob Hewitt.

"What do you *mean?* No more *Frank.* She told him she didn't want him to come home at all," said Jennie Hewitt.

"That's right," said her husband. "She wouldn't have him in the house, not even at Christmas."

"Till he announced his engagement. And even then she wouldn't go to the wedding. She stayed home on some pretext or other. She never actually met Frank's wife till the first grandchild was born, and then she couldn't do enough for them. She adored the grandchildren, and they used to all four of them come visit her."

"The money," said Bob Hewitt.

"Oh, yes. She gave Frank's wife a hundred thousand dollars when each grandchild was born, *and* a trust fund for the children."

"And changed her will."

"And changed her will so that Frank gets nothing, not a penny. He gets what is it?"

"A thousand a month while she's alive. Twelve thousand a year. Then when she dies, nothing. It all goes into a trust fund for the grandchildren."

"And the ex-wife gets the income as long as she doesn't remarry. If she remarries, it all goes into the children's trusts."

"And that's our neighbor?" said Evan Reese. "I had no idea she was so rich."

"*Rich?* At one time she owned this whole mountain, or her husband did. You've never been in that house, have you?" said Bob Hewitt.

"I've never even had a good look at it from the outside. The trees and the hedges," said Evan Reese.

"Tell them about the downstairs," said Bob Hewitt.

"Tell us about the whole house," said Georgia Reese.

"Well, you knew that Frank had an older sister," said Jennie. "Bernice. She was my age."

"No, we never heard about a sister," said Georgia Reese.

"Oh, yes. Bernice, about twelve years older than Frank. I went there a lot when we were children and until Bernice eloped, at seventeen. Mrs. Stratton would send the car to my house—"

"A Rolls, needless to say," said Bob Hewitt. "Limousine when the weather was bad, and a touring car when it was good."

"I was one of the girls that Bernice was allowed to play

with, but she never came to my house except to things like birthday parties. I always had to go to her house, but of course I didn't mind."

"The house, the house," said Bob Hewitt.

"But later I want to know about the daughter," said Georgia Reese.

"So do I," said her husband.

"First let her describe the house," said Bob Hewitt.

"Well, it's so long since I've been inside it that now it's almost unbelievable, although I'm told it hasn't been changed much. The main hall was two stories high, with at one end stained glass windows, imported from Italy, and they went all the way up to the second floor. On the right as you went in, a small reception room, then next to that, the drawing-room, where Frank's friend played the piano, and off that the music-room, as it was called. That was all done in white and gold and those two rooms were where we danced when they had their big parties. On the other side of the hall, the big dining room, easily room enough for, oh, sixty people. The library, lined with books all the way up to the ceiling with one of those ladders on a track like the old-time shoe stores. Two huge fireplaces. When I was little I could stand erect in the fireplaces. And a smaller room that had been Mr. Stratton's office, although they called it a study. I remember he had a stock ticker in that room, although I didn't know what it was then. They changed it after he died. On that side of the house was an enclosed porch, and on the other side, opening off the drawing-room, the conservatory. And I wouldn't attempt to describe the furniture. The dining-room chairs, high-back armchairs, brocaded, of course, and I'll bet the table weighed a ton. The paintings, you *must* have a look at them somehow, Ev. There's a Gainsborough in the main hall. A Van Dyke, a Rubens—"

"Yes, yes," said Bob Hewitt. "But don't start telling all about the paintings. Just give them the general idea. For instance, the pipe organ."

"They had a pipe organ, that was in the main hall, with the console on the first landing. They used to have an organist from Philadelphia with the wonderful name of Thunder, he'd come and give recitals once a year. Henry Thunder, a famous organist he was. And on Easter they always had a big crowd for lunch and then they'd have one of the local organists play."

"The only house in this part of the State with a pipe organ. And I'll bet no other house had something else they had. A barber chair. A real barber chair in Mr. Stratton's dressing-room."

"Sunken bathtubs?" said Georgia Reese.

"No, I guess the house was built too early for that. The tubs were iron, but had wood all around them. Encased in wood with mother-of-pearl inlaid. I remember when they added an elevator. We were absolutely forbidden to ride in it, probably because of several experiences when we got stuck in the dumb-waiter."

"Ev, this will impress you," said Bob Hewitt. "They had their own road-roller. A steam road-roller, with a little whistle. They used to lend it to the township, but it belonged to them. I suppose at one time they had around eight hundred acres. Now it's dwindled down to, oh, I think she has no more than twenty acres now, but I think I remember the figure eight hundred. This house that you're in, this used to be occupied by a cousin of Old Man Stratton's."

"Yes, I heard that when I bought it," said Evan Reese.

"They owned all these houses on Ridge Road and rented them out to relatives and retired couples for practically nothing. I don't think there was a house within a mile of the Strattons' that they didn't own. Not that there were so many houses in those days. This section wasn't started to be built up till the Thirties," said Bob Hewitt.

"Where did Stratton's money come from?" said Evan Reese.

"In two words, Wall Street. Railroad stocks, land out west, coal mines in Pennsylvania and West Virginia. He didn't make it all himself, by any means. His father was in with Jim Fisk and Dan Drew and Gould, that crowd, but not as a very big operator. Enough to leave old Frank Senior a nice fortune, and Frank had brains. He may not have been the most honest man in the world, by present-day standards, but he stayed out of trouble. He married late in life. The present Mrs. Stratton, the old lady, was about nineteen or twenty and he was in his forties when they got married. He was well in his fifties when the present Frank was born."

"Who was she?" said Georgia Reese.

"She was a High Ridge girl, born here. She was a Crowder. The Crowders weren't immensely wealthy, but they were well fixed and got around in New York society. Oh, she had plenty to offer. She was a good-looking girl."

"She was a handsome young woman," said Jennie Hewitt. "I can remember her very well. Beautiful bone structure and quite sexy-looking."

"When did he die?" said Evan Reese.

"Let me see now, in the late Twenties. He was eighty or close to it when he died," said Bob Hewitt.

"And that was when she became a recluse?" said Georgia Reese.

"Before that. Mr. Stratton was paralyzed and they practically never left Oak Knoll after that."

"Just lived there in solitary splendor?" said Evan Reese.

"Solitary splendor!" said Jennie Hewitt. "Splendor, but not solitary. They had Phillips, the majordomo. Pierre, the chauffeur. Tripp, the coachman, and a colored groom. A head gardener whose name I forget, and as many as five or six other gardeners. Mrs. Phillips, the cook. A full-time waitress. Three or four chambermaids. Mrs. Stratton's personal maid, Alice. A tweeny."

"What's a tweeny?" said Georgia Reese.

"A tweeny is a sort of a cook's helper and not quite a regular maid. In-between."

"I never heard of it," said Georgia Reese.

"It's English, and I understand that the butler has certain privileges there. *Droit de seigneur,* you know, although I don't think Phillips claimed his. How many is that?"

"About seventeen or eighteen," said Bob Hewitt. "And you didn't include the handyman-carpenter, the night watchman, or people like the old boy's secretary, O'Neill, or nurses for the children."

"Well, twenty or so. So it was splendor, Ev, but not solitary," said Jennie Hewitt.

"No, and you left out Madigan, the superintendent, and a lot of these people had husbands and wives living on the place, but not what you might call staff," said Bob Hewitt.

"Where did they put them all?" said Georgia Reese.

"Oh, some lived in the big house, some over the garage and the carriage-house," said Jennie Hewitt.

"I had no idea we were so close to such grandeur," said Evan Reese.

"Grandeur is right," said Bob Hewitt. "They even had their own buttons for the servants' livery. An oak, of course, and if you looked carefully, the letter 'S' in the foliage."

"No coat of arms?" said Georgia Reese.

"I never saw one," said Bob Hewitt. "In spite of everything we've told you, the old boy wasn't much for show. He had the very best of everything, mind you. Cars and horses, and paintings by famous artists. But when he took the train to New York, he rode in the day coach. He had a pass, of course. And when he got to Jersey City, his private car was probably sitting there on a siding. For a man as rich as he was, he lived very inconspicuously. Take for instance, living here. This was never like Tuxedo or one of your Long Island communities. Nothing fashionable about High Ridge."

"That's true," said his wife. "And they never had a yacht or a racing stable or any of those things."

"Don't disillusion me," said Evan Reese. "I was beginning to feel that some of the grandeur would rub off on me."

"I'm afraid there isn't much of it left," said Bob Hewitt. "My father told me one time how much it cost Stratton to whitewash all the post-and-rail at Oak Knoll. You know, my father was in the building supply business. Brick and lumber, cement and paint. So he knew pretty well what Stratton spent. Stratton was my Dad's best customer, year in, year out. We—

my Dad, that is—supplied the trap rock for Stratton's roads. Stratton put me through college, if you want to look at it that way. But I'll tell you one thing. Madigan, the superintendent, never had any chance to knock down a little graft. You'd always see that 'S' on the upper right-hand corner of every bill, which meant that Stratton had seen it before okaying payment. If Stratton caught a man stealing or even cheating a little bit, the fellow'd be on the next train out of here, bag and baggage, with orders to never return to High Ridge."

"The result was there was very little cheating," said Jennie Hewitt. "And they all knew they had a good thing. They were well paid, and they didn't have to eat slop or live in broken-down shacks."

"Yes, the Strattons paid their help a little more than the going rate because this was such an out-of-the-way place," said Bob Hewitt. "And he was a great believer in education. For instance, Phillips's son graduated from Johns Hopkins with an M.D. degree, and practices medicine out in California somewhere. Quite a few of the kids on the place went to college with Stratton's help."

"Anybody that wanted to, if his mother or father had been with the Strattons long enough. Ten years, I think it was," said Jennie Hewitt.

"The boy that wanted to go to Harvard," said Bob Hewitt.

"Oh, yes. Pierre, the chauffeur, had a son that was the same age as Frank Stratton, and the boy decided he wanted to go to Harvard. So Pierre told Mrs. Stratton his son wanted to go to college and would she lend him—"

"Four thousand dollars," said Bob Hewitt.

"Four thousand dollars," said his wife. "Pierre didn't want to touch his savings account, and Mrs. Stratton could take the money out of his salary. 'Why of course,' she said. She'd be *glad* to help. And what college was Joseph going to? 'Harvard,' said Pierre."

"That cooked it," said Bob Hewitt.

"She said no. 'But Madame is sending her own son to Harvard,' said Pierre. 'Precisely,' said Madame. Then of course Pierre, being a Frenchman, caught on. So Joseph went to Dartmouth."

"She was no fool," said Bob Hewitt. "Frank and his naked piano-players, classmates of her chauffeur's son."

"I'm dying to know about Bernice, the sister," said Georgia Reese.

"Shall we forget about bridge tonight?" said Evan Reese. "I'd rather hear about my neighbors. Ten years. Might as well have been living in an apartment house in New York. There you don't expect to know your neighbors."

"I'm perfectly willing, if you'd care to hear about them," said Jennie Hewitt. "You never heard of Bunnie Stratton?"

"I don't think so," said Georgia Reese.

"Madcap Bunnie Stratton? That's what she was called by the newspapers. Madcap Bunnie Stratton."

"She made up for all the publicity her father didn't get," said Bob Hewitt.

"Notoriety, you mean. Not just publicity. She was a regular F. Scott Fitzgerald heroine," said Jennie Hewitt.

"Which one?" said Evan Reese.

"Which one?" said Jennie Hewitt. "Why—I don't know which *one*."

"The reason I asked, Fitzgerald's heroines weren't madcaps," said Evan Reese.

"Well, I always thought they were," said Jennie Hewitt.

"No. Here's another example of the picture versus the printed word. People tend to think of John Held's girls when they hear Fitzgerald's name. But Fitzgerald's heroines, at least the ones I remember, were totally unlike the Held girls. Do you remember Daisy, in *The Great Gatsby*? She wasn't a Held girl. And Nicole, in *Tender Is the Night*. The very thought of John Held doing a picture of that tragic figure is repellent to me."

"Ev, I'm afraid you're a little too literal-minded. When I said an F. Scott Fitzgerald heroine I might as well admit I never read a word he wrote. And I *was* thinking of the John Held Junior drawings."

"Then call her a John Held Junior girl, but don't call her a Fitzgerald heroine. Give the artist his due, and don't distort what the author wrote."

"Oh, come on, Ev," said Bob Hewitt.

"No, now don't you protest before you think," said Evan Reese. "If I came into your bank and tried to tell you that a share of stock was a bond, you'd correct me damn quickly. Well, this happens to be something *I* know about. For years I've been hearing and reading people talking about John Held's girls and Fitzgerald's, as though they were one and the same thing. They just simply weren't. From the literary point of view, one of the worst things that ever happened to Fitzgerald was the simultaneous popularity of John Held's drawings. Those damn editorial writers were largely to blame. Who would want to take Fitzgerald seriously if all they ever knew about him was that he wrote about those John Held girls? Held was a very good satirist, and he didn't *want* his girls to be taken seriously. Of course Fitzgerald was partly to blame. He called one book *Flappers and Philosophers,* and in the public mind the flapper was the John Held girl. Actually, of course, Fitzgerald and Held and the editorial writers were all misusing the word flapper. A flapper was English slang, and it meant a society girl who had made her debut and hadn't found a husband. On the shelf, they used to say. It wasn't an eighteen-year-old girl with flopping galoshes."

"Well, according to your definition, Ev, Bernice was never a flapper, but according to mine she was," said Jennie Hewitt. "She was a sort of a John Held girl. One of the first to bob her hair and smoke in public and all the rest of it. And she didn't even make her debut."

"And *that* was a party we were looking forward to," said Bob Hewitt. "The plans."

"They started planning that party I don't know how many years ahead," said Jennie. "She was to have a New York party, but her real party was going to be here, June 1921, it was supposed to be. A thousand invitations. Mrs. Stratton hired a secretary just for that party, and she came to work over a year ahead of time. Special trains were going to leave Jersey City and Philadelphia."

"Art Hickman," said her husband.

"Art Hickman, Ted Lewis, and Markel's orchestra."

"The club," said Bob Hewitt.

"They engaged the whole club for the weekend, a year in advance, and every available hotel room for miles around. Not including families like my family and Bob's that offered to put up guests."

"Sherry. Louis Sherry."

"You can imagine the preparations Sherry's would have had to make. A thousand guests, extra servants and musicians. Supper and breakfast. Dinner before the party and luncheon at the club the next day."

"What about liquor?" said Evan Reese. "We had Prohibition by that time."

"I don't know what they were going to do about liquor. We had Prohibition, but not much enforcement then. They wouldn't have had any trouble. The stuff was coming in from Rum Row and Canada, and you can be sure Stratton would have had the best, not just Jersey Lightning."

"What was Jersey Lightning?" said Georgia Reese.

"Applejack. What we drank instead of corn liquor. They served it over the bar in every country hotel, and it wasn't bad. It had the desired effect."

"But they never had this party?" said Georgia Reese.

"No," said Jennie Hewitt. "Bunnie eloped. Don't either of you remember that? Bunnie Stratton and Jack Boyle?"

"Oh, hell," said Evan Reese. "Of course I remember now. Jack Boyle, the baseball player. Played first base for the New York Giants, and one of the first All-Americans Fordham ever had. But I'd forgotten *her* name. How did they ever get together?"

"They weren't together very long," said Jennie Hewitt. "Less than a year. Jack was a lifeguard at Belmar."

"Belmar?" said Georgia Reese.

"Belmar-by-the-Sea. A summer resort we used to go to in

those days. Bob's family went there and so did mine, and quite a few of the *nicer* Irish."

"Which didn't include Jack's family. Jack was a hell of a good athlete and a handsome son of a gun, but let's face it, they weren't the lace-curtain Irish. Jack was from Jersey City, and his father was a watch repairman for the Jersey Central. White-collar, but not lace-curtain."

"We'll come to that," said Jennie Hewitt. "Anyway, Bunnie was allowed to spend a whole week with me at Belmar, the summer of 1919. She'd never swam in the ocean before, in spite of all their money, and I can't give you any better proof of how strictly *I* was brought up than by telling you that the Strattons allowed Bunnie to visit me. And a whole *week*. Six days too long."

"She took one look at Jack Boyle," said Bob Hewitt.

"And he at her. One day was too long. Love at first sight if there ever was a case of it," said Jennie Hewitt.

"Your father," said her husband.

"My father told Jack that if he didn't stop hanging around our house he'd have him fired, and Jack told my father to go straight to hell and he *was* fired. So then he had nothing to lose, and he saw Bunnie every day and every night."

"She was sixteen then?" said Georgia Reese.

"Sixteen. Jack was about twenty-one."

"Older than that, Jennie," said Bob Hewitt. "He'd been overseas in the war. He was a good twenty-three or four."

"Well, whatever. My parents were afraid to tell Mr. and Mrs. Stratton, and hoped it would blow over, but Jack went back to Fordham and that year Bunnie was at Spence and they managed to see each other."

"Then Boyle quit Fordham and went with the Giants," said Bob Hewitt.

"Now I remember. Sure. Boyle eloped, and McGraw fired him," said Evan Reese.

"But *I* don't know any of this, so go on, Jennie," said Georgia Reese.

"Well, her family of course were outraged, but so were his.

They were Catholic and Bunnie and Jack had been married by a justice of the peace, in Greenwich, Connecticut. So the Boyles wouldn't have anything to do with Jack. Wouldn't let him in the house. And the only thing Jack could do was play baseball."

"But as I remember it, he did," said Evan Reese. "He played for some team in the International League, Binghamton or one of those teams."

"It *was* Binghamton," said Bob Hewitt.

"But they didn't pay him much, and Bunnie was pregnant. Mr. Stratton sent a lawyer to talk to Bunnie, but Jack wouldn't let him see her."

"Wouldn't let him *see* her?" said Bob Hewitt. "He was arrested for giving the lawyer a punch in the nose, and he told him that was what Mr. Stratton could expect, too, if he ever came around."

"Bunnie adored her father," said Jennie Hewitt. "And he did come to see her in Binghamton, while Jack was away, and he persuaded her to come home with him, knowing that Jack would follow her."

"*Thinking* that Jack would follow her. Mr. Stratton *wanted* Jack to follow her. I know that. And he wanted to give Jack a job. But he didn't know Jack Boyle. That fierce Irish pride, I guess. When Boyle got back to Binghamton and read Bunnie's letter, he quit baseball and Bunnie never heard from him again. Never. Not a word, not a line."

"What happened to him?" said Georgia Reese.

"He drifted around for a while, and then joined the Army. He'd been a lieutenant, but he enlisted as a private. I think you had to enlist for seven years then. Anyway, when he got out he became a bootlegger with some of his old friends in Jersey City. He's still alive. Frank Hague got him a job on the Hudson County payroll. Inspector of something or other. The last I heard he was a sort of an organizer for one of the labor unions."

"And what happened to her?" said Georgia Reese.

"Oh, plenty," said Jennie Hewitt. "She didn't have the baby.

Whether she lost it or they got her an abortion, I don't know. The latter, I suspect, because after she divorced Jack and married the Englishman she had two children, one of which the Englishman refused to take the credit for."

"When you say the Englishman, you mean the first Englishman," said Bob Hewitt. "She married two Englishmen. The Army officer, and the writer."

"Yes, but the writer was an Australian, and if he was a writer, nobody ever heard of anything he wrote," said Jennie Hewitt. "Except bad cheques. I always understood that the first Englishman, the *English*man, was quite attractive and very much in love with Bunnie. He resigned from the Army to marry her, and I guess he took all he could stand."

"What happened to her two children?" said Georgia Reese.

"The first was killed in the war, North Africa. The second was a girl," said Jennie Hewitt. "I heard that she got married during the war, but what's happened to her since I have no idea."

"And where is Bunnie herself?" said Georgia Reese.

"Majorca, surrounded by pansies and Lesbians of all nationalities. She has enough to live on and supply wine and gin for her hangers-on. She's a countess. She picked up an Italian along the way. There's some doubt about the title, or not so much about the title as her right to it. She married her Italian on a steamship, or so she says. But if she wants to call herself countess, none of her present friends are going to object. The count is over seventy and feeble-minded. I haven't seen or heard from Bunnie in over twenty years. We saw her once, briefly, in London before the war. But a friend of ours looked her up in Majorca and she said Bunnie refuses to speak English because all her little boys and girls are Italian or Spanish or French. When we saw her in London we could hardly understand her, she was so English. But not any more. She's had her face lifted a couple of times and she wears oversize sunglasses and big floppy hats, never goes out in the daylight, and her house is lit by candles. I wonder what she thinks."

"Yes," said Georgia Reese.

"You know. People like you and I, Georgia. Let's face it, we live a lot on our memories. We love our grandchildren and these two nice old things that we're stuck with—"

"Oh, thanks," said Bob Hewitt.

"But my life would be very empty without my memories, the good times we had, *and* the bad, and the old sentimental recollections. Think of what our life would be like without them. And yet I don't suppose Bunnie ever gives a thought to Jack Boyle and those days."

"Probably not," said Georgia Reese.

"Or the Englishman, or the Australian. Or the dear-knows how many lovers she had. I imagine she shuts all that out and just goes on from day to day, as though one part of her brain had been removed."

"Let me give you the other side of the coin," said Evan Reese.

"All right, Ev," said Jennie Hewitt.

"What about Mrs. Stratton, who has nothing *but* memories?"

Jennie Hewitt nodded. "Yes, that's a pretty horrible thought, too."

They were all silent for a moment, then Georgia Reese spoke. "They must suffocate her, her memories."

"Yes, who has it worse? The mother remembering everything, or the daughter remembering nothing?" said Bob Hewitt.

"Why, Robert Morris Hewitt, you're almost poetic tonight," said his wife.

"I have my moments," said Bob Hewitt. "I get in the same rut everybody gets in, and I take the old lady for granted. But every once in a while I have to talk to her on the phone, about bank business, and when she calls me Robert, I feel as though I were just starting out and she was old Queen Mary. The most personal she ever gets is to say 'Good morning, Robert,' and 'Thank you, Robert.' She never asks about Jennie or our children or grandchildren. These are business calls. But she's quite an old gal, to be able to make me feel like a fumbling assistant paying teller at my age. I don't really give a damn what Bunnie thinks, if she thinks anything. But I often wonder about the old lady in that house, the money going, the place shrinking a little every year. From eight hundred acres to twenty in a little over one generation. And the God damn futile mess that her two children have made of their lives. That was a beautiful woman once, Mrs. Stratton. I remember one time twenty-five or thirty years ago, I happened to be walking up Fifth Avenue and she was twenty or thirty feet ahead of me. She was alone. But as I followed her I couldn't help noticing how the people coming in her direction would automatically fall out of the way. Just looking at her, they'd make way for her. I never forgot that."

"I wish she hadn't written that letter about the dog," said Evan Reese. "The only communication we ever had from her."

"What did the letter say?" said Jennie Hewitt.

"Well, it was ten years ago, and I can't quote it verbatim, but to the effect that Airedales were known as one-man dogs and ours had snapped at somebody on her place."

"I know why she sent that letter," said Jennie Hewitt. "Ten years ago? Ten years ago her grandchildren used to come here a lot."

"Then why didn't she say so?" said Evan Reese.

"Oh, that wasn't her way," said Jennie Hewitt. "Nothing dramatic or appealing to your better nature. Or sentimental about children. She was simply stating the facts about Airedales, impersonally. She wouldn't dream of mentioning her grandchildren. That would be a show of weakness on her part, inviting familiarity."

"That's true, Ev," said Bob Hewitt. "She approved of you, or you never would have got this house. She probably knew your work, and for all I know, she may even own one of your paintings."

"No, I know where all my paintings are."

"In any event, you were okayed as a purchaser and a neighbor, but that's as far as she'd ever go. Like she wouldn't call on Georgia, not because she wanted to be rude to Georgia, but because she didn't want Georgia to return the call. I see her household bills, you know, and as far as I know, she hasn't had anyone for dinner in at least ten years. At least. She buys a lot of books, and she has four television sets in the house. But for instance, she hasn't bought a bottle of liquor or wine since before Pearl Harbor. She smokes a lot of cigarettes. Camels. That was the only thing she asked for during the war, was a regular supply of Camels. And I got them for her because she never cheated on gas rationing, or shoe coupons or any of those things, and it would have been easy for her to. Technically, Oak Knoll was a farm, and there was a lot of funny business by so-called farmers then."

"I'm going to have to see this woman. That's all there is to it," said Evan Reese.

"Make it accidental," said Bob Hewitt. "Don't let her see you coming up the driveway, or she'll hide in the closet."

"Not hide," said Jennie Hewitt. "She just won't be at home."

"Well, that's what I meant. Ev knows that. And it's nothing personal. I've known her all my life, and I handle a lot of her business and talk to her over the phone, but I never go to her house, even when there are papers to sign. I send my secretary, who happens to be a notary public."

"Oh, I'll make it accidental," said Evan Reese.

"And make it soon," said Jennie Hewitt. "She's over eighty."

"Yes, and *I'm* over sixty," said Evan Reese.

The Hewitts' car was covered with snow when the time came for them to depart. "I missed the weather report," said Bob Hewitt. "Was this expected?"

"Ev expected it," said Georgia Reese.

"Look at Mike," said Bob Hewitt. "He doesn't want to go out in it. Come on, Jen. Goodnight, Reeses, thanks for a pleasant evening. And I didn't lose any money."

"Have you got snow tires?" said Georgia Reese.

"We'll be all right. Bob's careful."

"I'd feel better if you'd call us when you get home," said Georgia Reese.

"All right, as soon as we get home, but don't worry. It hasn't had a chance to freeze," said Jennie Hewitt.

For a little while Evan Reese stood at the window, looking out at the new winter scene under the floodlight. "I can think of three men that I'd like to see do that. Maxfield Parrish. George Luks, and Charles Sheeler. And Salvador Dali, that makes four. Each of them had his own special blue, and none of them would see it the way I do."

"How are you going to do it?" said his wife.

"I'm not going to attempt it. When I finish this picture I'm not going to paint anything for at least six months."

"I wasn't talking about your painting. How are you going about meeting Mrs. Stratton?"

"Is that what I was thinking about, Georgie?"

"That's my guess. Whenever you're really thinking about painting, you don't talk about it."

"It must be fun to guess. Well, you're right, this time. I'm not always thinking about something else when I talk about painting, but this time I was. With that son staying there she's not going to be very receptive, less so than usual. But then isn't that just the time to make a sortie, when she's least pre-pared for it?"

"Sounds mean."

"I am above meanness. However, I'm not above curiosity, and believe me, I'm damn curious. Instead of a rather dull, cranky, faceless old woman, our neighbor turns out to be— well, Jack Boyle's first mother-in-law. Boyle to me was one of the really interesting baseball players. Much more interesting really than if he'd stayed in the game and been as good as your fellow Georgian, Mr. Tyrus Raymond Cobb. And he might have been almost as good as Cobb. Potentially he was, they all said. Maybe he'd have been better. But I've always been interested in the near-misses. Understandably. I'm one myself."

"Now, now," said his wife.

"Well, you know how I feel about my work, so the hell with that. But Boyle was a near-miss, and in her way, so is Mrs. Stratton. She was never one of the famous hostesses, or mistresses, or philanthropists, and yet she could have been any of those things. Or all three. Or any two. I never even heard of her as a great beauty."

"You never heard of her husband, either."

"Yes, I did. He was a well-known millionaire, but I forgot all about him many years ago, and never connected him with the woman we bought this house from. When I was young and living in Paris and the Village, I knew the names of the millionaires. If a millionaire bought one of our pictures our prices went way up, overnight. If one of us sold a picture to Jules Bache for a thousand dollars, that was ever so much better than getting a thousand dollars from someone with less money. The inconspicuous fellow, the art-lover that happened to like your picture, and happened to have a thousand dollars—that was nice. But that kind of a sale was usually considered a lucky accident. On the other hand, if someone like Bache shelled out a thousand bucks, we never sold another picture for that little. We didn't have to. Writers have the same experience. I'm sure that William Faulkner and Ernest Hemingway got big prices for pieces that they would have sold for fifty dollars when they first wrote them. And that's as it should be. Faulkner is a great artist, and all his work is extremely valuable, whether it's his best work or his worst. The mere fact that he wrote it makes it valuable, because there is only one Faulkner. Fortunately, people believe that about painters. Look at Pablo Picasso."

"Look at Evan Reese," said his wife.

"Yes. You'll never starve, as long as you have enough of my pictures lying around," he said. "A snowscape! Tomorrow morning. I shall take my little camp stool and some of the tools of my trade, and do some sketches."

"No."

"I'll bundle up good and warm. I'll go up West Branch Road, where I can be seen from the big house. We'll *try* that anyway."

"So that's what you were thinking?" said Georgia Reese.

"Well—yes," said her husband. Bob Hewitt telephoned, and the Reeses retired for the night.

In the morning Evan Reese put on hunting socks, heavy shoes and six-buckle arctics; tweed suit and sweaters; sheepskin reefer and cap with earlaps. He carried his camp stool, large sketch pad, and a vacuum bottle of coffee, and established a vantage point in the middle of the West Branch Road, which had not yet been visited by the township snow-plow. He made several quick sketches of the valley, then paused to take a few sips of the coffee. He screwed the cap back on the bottle and resumed sketching, aware that he was about to have company.

"Do you mind if I watch?" said his visitor. Evan Reese recognized the voice from the limousine, the same harshness but now without petulance. The harshness was of the kind that is usually attributed to whiskey-drinking.

"Why, no," said Evan Reese. "If you'd like to see what effect cold weather has on fingers. My name is Reese."

"Oh, I know. My name is Frank Stratton. My mother's a neighbor of yours."

"Of course."

"I won't talk any more. Don't let me interrupt."

Evan Reese quickly finished the sketch he had begun, turned over the page and started another. "Do you know anything about this kind of work?"

"Not a thing."

"Well, then I'll explain what I'm doing. This is what I call my shorthand. My notes. As you see, I didn't try to do that barn or that farmhouse in any detail. The silo. The pigpen. I've lived here ten years and I know all that. But as I sketch— now here for instance, I'll do this clump of trees. Ten years from now, twenty years from now, if I'm alive, I'll be able to look at this sketch and remember what I don't want to forget, which is the metallic white of the snowdrifts over there to the right, as it looks at half past ten, Eastern Standard Time. There. That's enough. My fingers are getting clumsy with the cold. Would you like a spot of coffee?"

"I was going to suggest that you come back to the house and have a cup with me."

"Thank you very much, but I think I've done enough walking. I'm headed for home. But you're obviously out for exercise. Would you like to come down with me and have a cup of coffee at my house? Do you like hot cinnamon buns? That's what I'm going to have."

"I haven't had one since I was ten years old. Sure, if it's all right?"

"Of course it is. Here, you're a young fellow. I'll give you this stool to carry, and you'll feel as if you earned your cinnamon bun."

"Fine."

"I'm not going to do this again, till I get one of those electric hand-warmers. You know the ones I mean, in the Abercrombie catalog?"

"Let me send you one when I go back to New York."

"All right. I'll trade you. One of these sketches for a hand-warmer."

"Oh, no, Mr. Reese. I get much too much the best of that deal."

"I suggested it, so it's satisfactory to me."

"Well—okay. But if you're going to be generous, will you put your initials on it?"

"When we get to my house," said Evan Reese. "You know, it's God damn cold up here. That kitchen's going to feel good."

They entered the house through the kitchen door, unbuckling their arctics and leaving them inside the storm door. "Georgia, I have a customer for a hot cinnamon bun. This is Mr. Stratton, our neighbor's son. Mr. Stratton, my wife."

"How do you do, Mr. Stratton. Come in and get warm. Just put your things any old place. It's nice to have a visitor. You take coffee?"

"I'd love some coffee."

"And I dunk," said Evan Reese. "The molasses sticks to my teeth if I don't dunk. A good cold slice of butter, dunk just a little so the butter doesn't melt, and then enjoy yourself. And don't count the calories."

"I never count the calories," said Stratton. "I'm glad to see you've kept this kitchen just the way it used to be. I used to come here when I was a boy. My cousins lived in this house, and they had a cook that made apple butter."

"Apple butter," said Evan Reese. "Let's get some, Georgia?"

"All right. I'll put it down."

"Did you ever eat apple butter on fried scrapple?" said Stratton.

"Never heard of it, but I don't know why it wouldn't be delicious," said Evan Reese. "But scrapple is no good any more. We tried it, and it isn't the same. I'm a Pennsylvanian, and I got some to introduce it to my wife, but it just wasn't right."

"No, I didn't care for it," said Georgia Reese.

"It's a long time since I've had scrapple. Or fried mush with molasses."

"I had that for breakfast every morning before I went to school," said Evan Reese. "Or mush-milk. Corn meal mush in a soup dish, with milk and sugar."

"That's why children are so nervous these days. They go to school without breakfast, half the time," said Georgia Reese. "They might as well start the day with a cigarette and a Coke, the kind of breakfasts they eat nowadays. Have you got children, Mr. Stratton?"

"I have two. A boy and a girl, and I know what you mean." Stratton looked about him. "You *have* made some changes. Do you use the big range at all?"

"Hardly ever from about the first of April to November," said Georgia Reese. "But beginning around Thanksgiving I use it. I like to cook on it, and there's nothing like it for heating the kitchen."

"Please don't ever get rid of it. You have bottled gas, I suppose? Oh, now I see. You have all the new things in what used to be the laundry. Your electric icebox. This is the dishwasher? Electric iron. *That's* how you did it. You have the old kitchen, but you have the modern conveniences. You see, we didn't have bottled gas in my day, and I can remember when we had our own electricity. We had a Delco plant, for Oak Knoll and the nearest houses like this one." He got up and went to a cabinet and opened a drawer. "Oh, look. You still have it." He took from the drawer a removable hand-grip for the laundry irons. "Where are the irons? Have you still got them?"

"Where they always were. Keep looking," said Georgia Reese.

"They should be—*there* they are." On a brick ledge beside the coal range were half a dozen laundry irons. He clamped the grip on one of them. "See, I remember how it works. My sister used to love to iron. I have an older sister. She lives abroad now, but I can remember coming down here with her when I was just a small boy, and she loved to help my cousin in the kitchen. Have you ever been to Majorca, Mr. Reese?"

"No."

"That's where my sister lives. She's a good deal older than I am. But she loved this house. She was very domestic, considering. I mean she's been married a lot and lives an odd sort of life. Oh, well . . . You have all those wonderful canisters. The spices and coffee and sugar. This table used to be covered with blue-and-white checkered oilcloth. I see you like it better without the cover."

He asked to see the rest of the house, and they showed him around. He enjoyed himself in simple fashion, admiring the Reeses' possessions, exclaiming delightedly on recognizing items that had been in the house when he knew it. His delight was strange, coming from a man of middle age who carried the scars of dissipation in face and figure. His sweater and tweed jacket fitted him tightly; the jacket sleeves were a little short, indicating that he had put on weight in shoulders and arms since the jacket was made. The fat sloped down from his temples and his original features were hidden in the puffy veined cheeks. He was just under six feet tall, the same height as Evan Reese, but beside Reese he appeared chubby. Reese, mentally carving away the excess flesh, saw a sensitive man enlarded in the person Stratton had made of himself. And yet as Stratton's visit extended to an hour, Evan Reese found that he was liking the man, pitying him, and hoping that he would remain as he now saw him. No matter what his intelligence told him—which was that Frank Stratton was a committed voluptuary, beyond redemption—Evan Reese wanted to postpone the reversion, and to do so he prolonged Stratton's visit.

"I'm having an exhibition in February," said Evan Reese. "How would you like to have a preview?"

"I'd be delighted, on condition that you won't hold it against me if I say anything stupid," said Stratton. "Where do you work?"

"You remember the potting-shed your cousin used to have? I turned it into a studio. It looks small, but it has as much space as some studios I've had in New York. I'm very pleased with it. I put in skylights and a linoleum floor, and that's about all I had to do. We won't be there very long, however. The only heat is from two electric heaters, and they're so murderously expensive, I never turn them on except when I'm working. So put your coat on."

Evan Reese put on his reefer, Stratton put on his trench coat and they went to the studio. It was a strictly utilitarian one-room house, containing canvases of various sizes in profusion; easels and paint tubes, brushes, knives and palettes and paint-stained rags; one damaged leather chair, several camp chairs and stools, and a bridge table on which lay a couple of large metal ash trays and a half-filled pipe rack. There were two naked electric bulbs hanging from the ceiling. "You see what I mean by cold," said Evan Reese. He turned one of the two spigots of a kitchen sink, and water came forth. "Not frozen," said Evan Reese. "But I'm going to have to get that snow shoveled off the skylight."

"Maybe I can do it. Have you got a ladder?"

"Thanks, but there'll be a fellow along some time today. A sort of a handy man. He'll be out to put the chains on my tires and maybe he might even clear the driveway, if he's in the mood. One of those local characters. I don't like to make suggestions to him, because he always says, 'Mr. Reese, I got it all planned out, now you just let me do it my way.' And he's usually right. He wants to make sure that I understand, you see, that he knows this property better than I do."

"Oh, I guess that's Charley Cooper."

"That's who it is, all right. But he's Mr. Cooper to me. Well, here are thirty-nine pictures, and on the big easel is the fortieth. All sizes. They're the ones I'm going to show in February. My last exhibition was six years ago, and these are all pictures I've done since about—well, since I chose the ones for my 1954 show. These aren't all I've done, of course. I often have three going at a time, and always two. Now for instance, here is a house in Rhode Island, Saunderstown. While I was painting this I was also painting—where is it, now? Here it is, this young lady. Pretty, isn't she?"

"Lovely."

"She talked a blue streak and smoked one cigarette after another. She was very stimulating company, and a very relaxing change from the job of doing that house. This is Spithead, Bermuda. This is a still life done right here in two days, actually in about six hours. But this son of a bitch, this took me three months before I got it right. Same size picture, and apparently just another still life. Same number of objects, just about. But why do you suppose this one took six hours, and this one three months?"

"Just answering for myself, you probably felt like painting when you did the quick one, and were getting fed up when you did the other."

"You've hit it on the nose. My wife and I'd been abroad and I hadn't had a brush in my hand for over two weeks, and we got home and I came right here and started painting without even taking my hat off. Literally. But this one, the one that took me three months, it wasn't because I was fed up with painting. No. You see, I'd seen a picture I didn't like, in Dublin. Had a quick glance at it and dismissed it from my mind, or so I thought. Then one day I arranged some fruit in a bowl and set a table for two. Plates, knives and forks, and began to paint. I worked on that damn thing, I thought about it, I had dreams about it. And then one morning, just before I woke up, I had a dream that I was painting this picture and someone kept getting in my way, standing in front of the table and obstructing my view. And do you know what I decided it was? It was the artist who had painted that picture in Dublin. I didn't know the artist's name or whether it was a man or a woman, but I was unconsciously plagiarizing him, or her. So I went right on and deliberately plagiarized, as much as I could remember of that ugly picture in Dublin, and when I finished it it was about as unlike the original as a picture could be. If you look on the back, I don't always give names to my pictures, but this is one called Plagiarism."

"Fascinating," said Stratton. "And they're not at all alike?"

"Yes, they are alike. A layman would say right away that the two pictures had been painted by the same man, but an expert, another painter or a first-rate dealer or an art historian, would know right away that the two pictures couldn't possibly have been painted by the same man. If I get a good price for this picture I'm going to track down the Dublin picture and buy it. It was a terrible, terrible picture, but it was that artist's masterpiece. The son of a bitch got something in there, in his picture, that offended and irritated me, and it was good. And *he* wouldn't be able to tell me what it was. He wouldn't know it was there. I'm sure of that, because he was such a bad, mediocre painter for the rest of the picture, that he couldn't possibly know what was good. Now that, of course, poses a problem in ethics."

"How so?"

"Well, I could buy his picture, pay a good price for it if he still owns it, which I don't doubt. But then what do I do? Do I tell him that I, a pretty well-known painter, have bought his picture and thereby encourage him? Or do I keep quiet? Or do I buy it and tell him the truth, that he's a bad painter and try to discourage him? Tell him to quit while he's ahead?"

"I really don't know."

"There's still another alternative. I can destroy *my* picture. But I can't, because I know it's good."

"Maybe you ought to find out all about the painter before you decide."

"That's the humanitarian approach, and I've rejected it. I

don't want to know about this painter. If it's a he or a she, a
dilettante, a half-taught amateur, a poor struggling bog-trot-
ter. Art is cruel, and in this problem I represent art. This
painter will never do anything good. Never."

"He did once, Mr. Reese."

Evan Reese laughed. "Damn it, Stratton, you've touched me
where I'm vulnerable. I can't *be* art, with a capital A. A genius
would be ruthless. A genius would do what it's only my inclination to do."

"A man that makes a mistake usually gets a second chance.
I think a man that does something good ought to, too."

"Well, apparently that's what I've decided. I had all this
out with myself a dozen times, and never done a thing. So I
probably won't do anything."

"And the Dublin artist did inspire a good picture."

"Oh, naturally I keep telling myself that," said Evan Reese.
"Hello, dear?" Georgia Reese entered the studio.

"Mr. Stratton is wanted on the telephone," said Georgia
Reese.

"Wanted on the telephone?" said Stratton.

"I'll show you," said Georgia Reese. "And you come in, Ev.
You've been out here long enough."

Evan and Georgia Reese waited in noncommittal silence in
the kitchen while Stratton was answering the telephone in the
library. He returned shortly, smiling. "That was my mother. She
was afraid I might have fallen in the snow and broken my
leg."

"How did she know you were here?" said Georgia Reese.

"That's funny. How did she? I never thought to ask her."

"I imagine she was going to try every house in the neighborhood before sending out a scouting expedition," said Evan
Reese.

"That's probably it. Well, it's been a very interesting morning, at least for me," said Stratton. "Thank you very much for
the coffee and the cinnamon buns, Mrs. Reese. And, Mr. Reese,
may I remind you that we made a deal?" He obviously was
about to leave.

"Here's your sketch. I'll expect the hand-warmer any day now." Evan Reese had written: "To Frank Stratton, Oak Knoll, November 1960. Faithfully, Evan Reese."

"I'll have it framed. Maybe I'll become an art collector."

"I'm all for that, if you have the money," said Evan Reese.

"That's very dubious, but many thanks. Goodbye."

"Nice to've seen you," said Evan Reese.

The Reeses watched him trudging up the hill in the snow.

"That's going to take it out of him," said Evan Reese. "He's in terrible physical condition."

"His manners aren't any too good, either," said Georgia Reese. "Not even a mention of our coming to his mother's."

"How did she seem over the phone?"

"She didn't ask for him. It was a maid with an Irish brogue."

"We'll be invited, don't think we won't," he said.

"Why are you so sure all of a sudden?"

"Why am I so sure? Because he's going to want to come back here, and he can't very well do that without inviting us to his house *sometime.*"

"And why is he going to be so anxious to come back here? Were you at your most fascinating?"

"Yes, I was at my most fascinating, and you were nice to him, and he likes this house. He isn't very bright, and he isn't much of a man. But he isn't the pig I thought he was. He *has* good manners, and when I told him about the Dublin still life I liked his reactions. Decent. Honorable. Also, he isn't an art-phony. People with a bit of pansy in them are apt to be art-phonies. One thing you've got to say for the Zuleika Dobson school, they aren't art-phonies."

"That's my school."

"I know it is. Someone brought up as rich as Stratton was shouldn't have to be phony about anything, but unfortunately you get just as much bullshit about art from the rich as you do from everybody else. I wish I knew something about the ballet. I'd try this fellow out on the ballet and see if he goes phony there. Why don't *you* know something about the ballet?"

"Because for thirty-one years I've been your cook and mis-

tress, and nursemaid and mother of your children, and haven't
had time to get culture."

"Well, I'll accept that excuse. But don't let it happen again.
Telephone. Probably Joel Channing wanting to know when he
can see the pictures. Tell him I've gone skiing." He followed
her slowly to the library and listened to her side of the conversation.

"Yes it is," she said. "Oh, yes . . . This afternoon? Well,
I'd have to ask my husband and call you back. He's working
and I can't disturb him, but he'll be in for lunch any minute
. . . I hope so, too. And thank you for calling."

"The old lady?" said Evan Reese.

"Could we come in for tea this afternoon about five. So
bland. You might think we'd moved here yesterday."

"Maybe from her viewpoint it *was* yesterday."

"Do you want me to say we'll go?"

"Yes, what's the use of pretending? She'd see through that,"
said Evan Reese. "And as Jennie pointed out, the time is
getting short."

A few minutes before five that afternoon the Reeses' door-
bell rang. Evan Reese recognized the man at the door, Elwood
Blawen, who had a farm on West Branch Road. "Hello, Mr.
Blawen. Come in."

"No thanks. I came to fetch you to Mrs. Stratton's," said
Blawen. He pointed to an old jeep with a winter top.

"How did that happen?"

"How did that happen? Why, she just called me up and said
I was to go fetch you at five o'clock in my jeep. Wasn't any
more to it than that. But I *imagine* she figured'd take a jeep to
get you there, and she's pretty near right. You'd never get up
the hill in your car, 'specially without chains. No Charley
Cooper, I see."

"No, he must be counting on all this to melt away."

"Charley's all right once he gets working, but I never saw
such a man for putting things off. Deliberating, he always
calls it. But there's other names for it, too. Good afternoon,
Mizz Reese."

"Mr. Blawen. You going to be our transportation?"

"Looks that way. She's all cleaned out inside," said Blawen. "I even got a heater in there for you."

"Not just for us, I hope," said Georgia Reese.

"Oh, no. If you mean did I put it in special." He smiled. "Oh, no. Those days are gone forever. But mind you, I seen the day when the Stratton family *would* do a thing like that. Why, they tell me she used to have a man come all the way from Philadelphia just to play a few tunes on the organ." He lowered his voice. "Paid him five—hundred—dollars." They got in the jeep. "Five hundred dollars, just to play a few tunes on the pipe organ. One time they had Woodrow Wilson here for Sunday dinner. The President of the United States. And old Stratton wasn't even a Democrat. But him and Wilson were acquainted with one another outside of politics. Oh, yes, there was always something going on around here in those days. Twenty-eight people on the payroll, sometimes more."

"You don't work for Mrs. Stratton, do you?" said Evan Reese.

"Only when she has something special and I can spare the time. Like today, she knows I have my jeep, so she phoned and said would I call for you and Mizz Reese. I always try to accommodate her if I can. Never been here before, have you?"

"No, but how did you know that?" said Evan Reese.

"How did I know that? Just took a good guess. She don't have many visitors. She only got twenty acres left out of what used to be eight hundred, and I guess she feels hemmed in. Here we are."

"Thank you very much," said Evan Reese.

"Oh, I'll be here when you come out," said Blawen.

"How long will *we* be here?" said Evan Reese.

"Well, maybe that's not for me to say, but not more'n a half an hour."

Frank Stratton came out to greet them. "I heard the jeep," he said. "I'm so glad you could come."

A maid took their things and Frank Stratton showed the way to the library. Mrs. Stratton turned from gazing into the fireplace, but she did not rise. Her left hand clutched the silver mounting of a highly polished walnut walking stick. She was obviously very feeble.

"Mother, this is Mr. and Mrs. Reese."

"Good afternoon. I'm glad you could come," said Mrs. Stratton. "Did you have a nice ride in Elwood Blawen's hideous conveyance? But it does do the trick, doesn't it?"

"My first ride in a jeep," said Georgia Reese.

"And you, Mr. Reese? Your first ride in a jeep too?" said the old lady.

"Oh, no. I did some painting for the Navy during the war, and I rode in a lot of jeeps."

"What kind of painting? Camouflage?" said Mrs. Stratton.

"No. I did some pictures of the landings at Iwo Jima, in 1945."

"Photography?"

"No. Paintings."

"*Painting?*" she said. "But wouldn't photography be much more accurate? I don't understand."

"There's no lens wide enough to take in the whole scene, so we did some sketches and the painting came later."

"And weren't you frightened?"

"I was on a big ship. It was noisy, but you don't mind it so much if you have something to do."

"How far away were you?"

"Three or four miles, most of the time."

"But that's close enough to be dangerous, isn't it?"

"Yes. But not much more dangerous than it is around here during the deer season."

"Oh, come now, Mr. Reese," said the old lady. "Did you approve of this undertaking, Mrs. Reese?"

"Yes. My husband wanted to do it very much," said Georgia Reese.

"Frank, will you ring, please?" said the old lady. "And you believe in supporting your husband in such matters? Well, I must say so do I. Division of authority only leads to confusion." She pronounced her words so slowly that they seemed to be shaking during utterance, but plainly her speech was not keeping up with her thought. "My son tells me you are preparing for an exhibition. February, did he say?"

"The last week in February," said Evan Reese.

"We'll have some tea and then Frank can show you some of my husband's purchases. They should all be in museums, but I can't bear to part with them. Not because I appreciate their merit. I don't. But I'd miss them. They're all spoken for, or I'd give one or two of them to private people. I'm not at all sure that a museum is the right place for a painting. How do you feel about that, Mr. Reese?"

"Most good pictures should be in museums," said Evan Reese.

"Then we don't agree. Do you paint to have your pictures in museums?"

"No one ever asked me that before. In fact, I never asked myself. Do I paint to have my pictures in museums? No. I paint to satisfy my need to paint, and in the hope that one person will see a picture and like it well enough to buy it. Preferably somone who can afford to pay a lot."

"I got an original Evan Reese for the price of a hand-warmer."

"What's that about a hand-warmer, my dear?"

"Mr. Reese and I made a trade. He gave me a sketch, and I'm giving him an electric hand-warmer."

"That isn't why I'm giving you the sketch, Mr. Stratton. I'm giving you the sketch because you impulsively offered to give me the hand-warmer."

"Mrs. Reese, would you with your steady young hands . . ." The old lady directed the maid with the tea things to place them in front of Georgia Reese. "Not very strong for me, please. One lump. No cream or lemon. Frank, will you take Mr. Reese on a very brief tour, but don't be gone long, as I have to leave our guests."

Evan Reese followed Stratton into the great hall and inspected the Gainsborough, the Van Dyke, and the Rubens, devoting about one minute to each picture, but making no comment. After each picture he looked at Stratton, and after the Rubens he said: "Very interesting. Now I think we ought to go back."

"Yes. You can come again and have a longer look," said Stratton.

In the library the old lady looked at Evan Reese. "Very interesting, don't you think, Mr. Reese?" she said.

"Very."

"I thought you'd find them so. Now, I'm afraid you'll have to excuse me." She got to her feet. "Thank you for coming, and now you understand why I haven't been more hospitable before. Mr. Reese, I'm sure *you* understand?"

"I do indeed, Madam," said Evan Reese. "Perfectly."

The old lady took the maid's arm and left them.

"Would you have time to see some more of the house?" said Stratton.

"Oh, I'd—" Georgia Reese began.

"Not today, thanks," said Evan Reese, quickly and emphatically. "But ask us again, will you? Or come in for a cup of coffee tomorrow. I'll have some heat in the studio, and we can have our coffee there."

The Reeses were returned to their house, and Evan Reese, taking his accustomed chair in the library, lit his pipe and stretched out his legs.

"Why did you rush us away? I wanted to see the rest of the house."

"We'll be seeing the rest of the house. And why am I sure? Well, I was sure before and I'm just as sure now. I also know why the old lady never invited us before."

"Obviously because she's so helpless and didn't want to be seen," said Georgia Reese.

Evan Reese shook his head. "You didn't get that little by-play between her and me, at the end."

"No. I thought she was being old-lady flirtatious. A by-play?"

"Yes. She and I understood each other. Do you know why we were never invited to her house? I'll tell you. Because I'm a painter. And there isn't a painter in the world over twenty-five years old that wouldn't know right away that the Rubens, the Van Dyke and the Gainsborough are all fakes. And the son doesn't know it. The Gainsborough is in Pasadena, California. The Rubens is owned by a man named Lee, in Chicago. And the Van Dyke is owned by the Spencer family, in Newport. Mrs. Stratton hasn't owned either of the originals since long before the war. I wonder if she has any jewelry that her heirs presumptive are counting on. If so, I'll bet it's all paste."

"But how do you get rid of three old masters without any publicity?"

"You do it through a dealer, who arranges a private sale, and you make sure that the picture isn't bought for a museum. You sell to people who have the money and want the pictures, but don't want the publicity. There are still a few people in this country who can pay a hundred and fifty thousand for a picture for their own private enjoyment. I imagine that a condition of the sales was that there should be no public announcement, and a reputable dealer would keep quiet."

"But Bob Hewitt knows all about her financial condition."

"No he doesn't. He talks big, but Bob only knows about her account in his bank. She probably deals with some firm like the United States Trust, in New York. Bob handles the grocery bills, but I'll bet you he's never had anything to do with her securities."

"I wonder what made her change her mind, and let you in the house?"

"Well, she knows what we're like after ten years, and I think she trusts us. But of course it also has something to do with her son's visit. We'll know when she gets ready to tell us."

"She's very feeble."

"But she's a fighter."

In the morning Evan Reese was in his studio, intent on his painting, and he was irritated when Stratton knocked on the door. "Come—in," said Evan Reese. He had his pipe in his clenched teeth and he knew he sounded fierce, but Stratton's interruption was unwelcome.

"Is it too early for a cinnamon bun?" said Stratton. "I can come back, or maybe you'd like to be left alone."

"Oh, that's all right," said Evan Reese. Stratton was almost pathetic in his desire for company. "Have a seat and I'll be with you in about two minutes."

"I'll be perfectly quiet."

"You can talk. I don't mind, if you don't mind getting delayed answers."

"You've got it nice and warm in here today."

"Yes, the electric heaters."

"With the heat on it's a very pleasant room. Cozy," said Stratton. "You must like it here."

"I do," said Evan Reese. "I can work any place, but I've done more work in this little shack than anywhere else. And I've become attached to it. Probably in more ways than one."

Stratton was silent for a moment, and Evan Reese glanced at him quickly.

"What was I thinking?" said Stratton. "I was thinking about how you can hold the pipe in your mouth and go on talking and painting. The English do that. You see them riding along on bicycles, both hands on the handlebars and never taking their pipes out of their mouths."

"But I'm not English. I'm Welsh."

"Of course. Of course," said Stratton apologetically. Then, as though to make up for his mistake, he said: "You made a great hit with my mother."

"She made a great hit with me."

"You know, Mother knows a lot more about you than you might think."

"There isn't a hell of a lot to know," said Evan Reese. "Unless you want to argue that there's a hell of a lot to know about everybody. But there's nothing very spectacular about me. I've never had much personal publicity."

"That isn't the kind of thing I meant anyway. Mother doesn't care for that sort of thing, either. But she's studied you."

"Has she? I don't see how. I never met her before yesterday."

"I'll show you how," said Stratton. He stood up and went to a window. "Would you like to see how?"

"Just one second," said Evan Reese. He pressed his thumb on the canvas, put down his brush and palette, wiped his hands with a rag, and took his pipe out of his mouth. "Okay. Through for the morning."

"Well, you see the bay window on the second floor of Mother's house?"

"Indeed I do. I've often envied her that view."

"That's where she sits. And do you know what she has there? A telescope."

"I would too, if I had that bay window. And that's how she studies me?"

Stratton nodded. "You, and Mrs. Reese, and God knows how many others. People think of Mother as an old lady all alone in her mountain fastness. Actually she's an old busybody."

"In Pennsylvania a busybody is an arrangement of mirrors. You see them on second-story window-sills. You can see who's walking on the sidewalk to the right or left of your house, or ringing the doorbell, without opening the window."

"I've heard of them. At least I've seen them mentioned in novels without quite knowing what they were. But Mother's the other kind. The human kind."

"Oh, indeed she is. Very human. That's why I like her."

"Oh, you like her? I'm glad you like her. She's had a very tough life, at least the second half of it. My father was ill, and between me and my sister, we didn't give her much to be thankful for. I suppose you may have read about my sister, or heard about her."

"A little."

"A little is enough, and that goes for me, too, if you know anything about me, and I'm sure you do. People talk. People gossip."

"Yes. They do," said Evan Reese. "Shall we go over to the kitchen?"

"You'd rather I didn't talk about myself?"

"Oh, you're wrong. But there's coffee in the kitchen, and a place to sit."

"You don't *mind* if I talk?"

"Not a bit. I just thought we'd be more comfortable in the house."

"Oh, fine. You see, Mr. Reese, I know what people say about me, and they have every right to. But I always think that artistic people and writers take a different point of view. More tolerant, if you know what I mean."

"I don't know that they're really more tolerant, but they have to pretend to be."

"Well, that's almost as good. It's better than being avoided. I'm not going to be a pest, honestly I'm not. But I felt right away that you were someone I could talk to. I could tell that you'd heard about me. I always can. But you didn't try to get rid of me first thing, the way so many do."

"Let's have some coffee, and a cinnamon bun."

Stratton's face was transformed, from middle-aged voluptuary's to trusting boy's. "Yes, let's," he said.

Georgia and Evan Reese, jointly present, restrained Stratton from further candor, if that had been his inclination; but he stayed an hour and the conversation was easy and obviously enjoyable to him. "I hate to leave you two," he said. "But Mother likes me to be prompt. By the way, Mr. Reese, it's perfectly all right to tell Mrs. Reese about the telescope."

"Oh, I'd have told her without your permission."

"I know you would. I was just kidding," said Stratton. "Thank you both, I had *such* a good time."

Georgia Reese said to her husband: "Watch out, Ev. You may be taking on a responsibility that you didn't ask for."

"I've thought of that," said Evan Reese. "But the poor son of a bitch."

"Yes," said Georgia Reese. "We were lucky with ours."

"It wasn't all luck."

"No, it wasn't."

"Any more than what's happened to this fellow was all bad luck. Or what's happened to his sister. That old lady with her telescope, and her fake paintings. I must find out more about her. And the father, her husband."

"Well, you'll find out more from people like Elwood Blawen and Charley Cooper. Bob and Jennie Hewitt want us to think they knew the Strattons better than they really did."

"Frank Stratton? You mean the old man?" said Charley Cooper. "I don't know's I could tell you anything about him, beyond that he loved the almighty dollar. I aint saying he was a stingy man, not by any manner or means. He got rid of it, but he knew where every penny went and he made sure he always got value received. Take for instance when we voted to get rid of the horses and buy motorized equipment down't the hose company. We went to Mr. Stratton and asked how much we could count on from him. And he said, and I remember because I was there, he said if we went about it the usual way, not a penny. He said he wasn't going to give any money for a fire truck, knowing that some slick salesman would arrange to take care of certain parties on the committee. Well, now how did Francis A. Stratton, a mul-tie-millionaire, know that that was the usual way? But he knew it, and that's the way it was going to be done, till he spoke up. Embarrassed hell out of the committee, and I was tickled pink, because I didn't figure to get a red cent out of it. So what Francis A. Stratton did, he bought the fire truck through one of the big corporations he was interested in. Through a regular purchasing agent. And then he *do*nated it to the borough. But he wouldn't let a few fellows have their little graft.

"Same thing with other opportunities for a bit of hanky-panky. Like one time he bought fifty dollars' worth of chances for some prize the Legion was auctioning off. By golly, the night they had the drawing, there was Francis A. Stratton, with all his stubs, in case one of his numbers won. That was kind of embarrassing, too. Because some of the Legion boys had it all arranged that one of their wives was going to get the prize. But when Francis A. Stratton showed up they had to quick dump a lot of his tickets in the bowl, and of course he won. A Victrola, I think it was. Yes. A Vic. And as soon as he won, he said he was donating it to the children's ward at the hospital. Made a certain friend of mine's wife sore as all hell. But that's the way he was, old Stratton. He you might say kept us honest. On the other hand, like donating land for a playground, he done that without the least hesitation. I guess you'd say, about honesty, he carried it to an extreme."

"Tell me about his appearance. What did he look like?"

"What did he look like? Oh-ho. If you was a stranger in town and you saw Francis A. Stratton, you'd know right away who was the big noise around these parts. If he wasn't riding in one of his Rolls-Royce English cars, if you happened to see him before he took sick, he was a regular country squire. Derby hat, checkered riding pants and polished-up boots, one of them there white collar-and-tie affairs only the tie and the collar are the same piece of cloth. They had a name for them."

"Stock."

"Stock is right. Stocks and bonds. I ought to be able to remember that, talking about Francis A. Stratton. Well, once in a while he'd take a notion to come down to town on horse-back. He usually rode a white horse, although he had every color of horse there was, and every kind of carriage and buggy. But he'd ride down and leave the horse at the livery stable and do his errands, carrying one of them riding whips. And if he didn't look like he owned the town, no-body did. Polite and all. But he was Francis A. Stratton and nobody knew it better than he did. The time he fell off his horse, he lay there because nobody had the nerve to touch him. They didn't. They stood around and looked at him lying there, unconscious, till somebody had sense enough to send for Doc Frelinghuysen."

"He fell off his horse? Was he drunk?"

"Well now that's where you won't get any two agreeing, on whether he was drunk or sober. If he was drunk, it was the only time any town people ever seen him in that condition, and some didn't believe he was a drinker. But for others it was a pretty well-known fact that Francis A. Stratton sometimes would come home from New York and more or less lock himself up with a bottle and stay out of sight for a week at a time. He had a stock ticker in his house. You know, one of those stock tickers? And he had a fellow worked for him as secretary, O'Neill, that they used to say knew as much about Stratton's business as Stratton did. And maybe more than business. Never liked that O'Neill. He was honest, but the people in town never trusted him. Everybody always shut up when O'Neill was around, for fear he'd carry tales back to Stratton. But he was faithful to Stratton, no doubt about that, and I always heard that O'Neill was a bitterly disappointed man when Stratton didn't leave him anything in his will. Must of been some reason, but I never knew what it was."

"So Stratton was a secret drinker?"

"Well, I don't know's you'd call him secret. The way he lived, as far as the town people knew, he was a secret eater. By that I mean, he didn't drink with town people, but he didn't eat with them neither."

"How old was he when he fell off the horse?"

"Along. Fifties. Maybe more. I understand he got some kind of a clot in the brain from it, but maybe that was just talk. It didn't stop him from working. Or riding horseback. He was out again in a couple months."

"He was quite a handsome man, wasn't he? Or was he?"

"Well, yes. Yes, he was handsome, for a man. Bald-headed, and he had a little black moustache. Not as big a moustache as most men wore in those days. I don't know whether you'd call him handsome or not. If you're thinking of a movie actor's looks, no. Had a nice set of teeth, I remember. In fact, you could have taken him for an Eye-talian, in the summer. Sunburned from being outdoors so much. She used to play tennis with him. They had two tennis courts, one inside and one outside, and they were the first ones around here to have a swimming pool. That was considered the height of luxury then, to have a swimming pool. But I considered the height of luxury having an inside tennis court. It's the ways they think of to spend their money that makes one rich man different than another. I used to think, who would want to play tennis in the winter? Who'd ever think of it? Would you? Maybe now you would, but not that long ago. Tennis wouldn't of been my game in the middle of the summer, let alone spend a wad of money to play it inside in the winter. But Francis A. Stratton wanted to play tennis, so he built himself a house for it, and a lot of famous players used to come there and practice."

"Who, for instance?"

"Oh, don't ask me. I never cared for tennis that much. My sport was cycling. Frank Kramer was my man, the *Iron* Man, they used to call him. I used to go over to Newark, to the Velodrome, just to watch him. If I could of been anybody else I'd have been Frank Kramer. The Iron Man."

"I don't think I ever heard of him."

"Well, that's the same way I was with your tennis players."

"To each his own, as they say."

"Yes, as far as I know, Francis A. Stratton never rode a wheel, so we didn't have much to talk about, him and I."

"What was he like, to talk to?"

"Well, as I said before, polite. There was men in town that he could buy and sell, that they wouldn't treat you as polite as Mr. Stratton. The help all liked him, too. I only ever heard of one quitting on their own accord, but she didn't quit on account of Mr. Stratton." Charley Cooper giggled. "That was a funny one, but it happened long after Francis A. Stratton passed on. You know Lorna Disney, works in the post office?"

"Know her to say hello to," said Evan Reese.

Cooper giggled again. "A fine hello she got one day. Lorna was Lorna Parton then, a hired girl working for Mrs. Stratton, and one day young Frank was home from school and had a friend visiting him. Lorna walks in to do her dusting and there sat Frank's friend in his bare skin, not a thing on him, and playing the piano. Must of been quite a shock to Lorna. She quit then and there. Did her some good, though. She got married soon after. Left an impression, you might say. Oh, there was always something to talk about going on up at the Strattons', but they had so many foreigners working for them and they didn't mix. Lorna could tell you a thing or two, but don't ask her about the piano player. She don't like to have that brought up. *I* can joke with her about it, but she wouldn't like *you* to."

"No, I guess not."

"Everybody has some story about the Strattons, everybody that was living here forty-fifty years ago, what you might call their heyday. Since then you don't hear so much about them. Young Frank—well, I don't know. And Bunnie, now that she's an Italian princess. But they're a different generation, gone to pot. And they moved away. Just as well they did move away. Young Frank, he liked the boys. And Bunnie, she liked the boys, too. If they'd of stayed around here there'd have been trouble, for certain. The old lady was right in kicking them out."

"She kicked them out?"

"As good as. Wouldn't let them hang around here. If they were gonna make damn fools of themselves and get into scrapes, she didn't want it to happen here. And don't forget, it wasn't as easy to buy their way out of trouble. Mrs. Stratton, the widow, didn't carry as much weight as Francis A. when he was alive. I doubt if she's worth a tenth as much as when Mister passed on."

"Where did it all go?"

"You tell me. A fellow like myself, an ordinary working man, I been making money and saving it all these years. But I don't know what happens to a big fortune. Taxes, but that don't explain it. I think she must of got hold of some bad advice in the stock market. I don't know *where* it went. But it's a shame and a disgrace to let a big fortune like that get all pissed away. They could of done a lot for this town if they'd of held on to it, but I'll bet you when she dies there won't be enough to pay the inheritance taxes, and nowadays you can't *give* away a house like that. They used to have thirty people working up there, but the last couple years she only has me there two days a week, and two women in the house, and Elwood Blawen helps out. You know, when she

married Francis A. Stratton and got him to build that house
and all, it looked like High Ridge was safe and sound. But
the last twenty-five-thirty years she's been selling land, and
school taxes went up four or five times and this town, I'm pre-
dicting, this town inside of another couple years will be so
changed nobody will recognize it. I don't want to be living
here when *that* happens, and my folks have lived here since
the 1700's. No matter what you say about Francis A. Stratton,
he was pretty fond of this town. And I guess when you come
right down to it, we were pretty fond of him."

"That's what I wanted to hear you say."

"Well, I never would of thought to say it if it wasn't for
getting started talking this way. But it's a fair statement. He
didn't suck up to nobody. He wasn't natured that way. But
he was polite to people, and he didn't infringe on anybody's
rights. He wasn't so different from any the rest of us, except
richer, and nobody minded him marching around in his riding
pants. What the hell? We wouldn't of trusted a man that rich
that went around wearing overhalls."

"All in all, you liked Mr. Stratton, then?" said Evan Reese.

"That's what I been trying to tell you, Mr. Reese. You
wanted to know some facts, and I's willing to give them to you.
You're entitled to any facts I have—"

"Why? How am I?" said Evan Reese, vaguely complimented.

"How are you entitled? Well, facts is the truth, and the
truth will out, and everybody's entitled to the truth. But there's
different ways of telling facts, so one person telling the same
facts could give a different impression. 'S far as we know,
you're a reliable man and that entitles you to the facts the
way I see them."

"What if I hadn't been a reliable man, Mr. Cooper?"

Cooper smiled. "You'd be surprised how little you'd find
out."

"Oh."

"Newspaper reporters been around here two-three times.
Once when Bunnie run away and got married. Once when
Francis A. Stratton died. And a scandal sheet when Frank

Junior got into trouble. They all went back and wrote up High
Ridge people like we was afraid to talk about the Strattons.
Afraid? Not afraid, Mr. Reese. One thing we never was was
afraid. There was Coopers buried here two hundred years before any Stratton ever set foot in High Ridge. And plenty
of Crowders in the same churchyard. She was a Crowder."

"Ah, now I see. She belongs to High Ridge, too."

"Sure does."

"So it wasn't so much that you liked Mr. Stratton that made
you protect him, as much as her being a Crowder?"

"I thought you knew that, Mr. Reese."

"Well, it's a little hard to follow, unless you bear in mind
that Mrs. Stratton was a Crowder."

"That's the whole thing. If she was just some stranger."

"But your real loyalty was to her, to Mrs. Stratton."

"To High Ridge, put it that way. Take Lorna Disney, for
instance. Lorna wouldn't have no difficulty proving kinship to
Mrs. Stratton. She might not be as close as the Coopers, but
the Partons go back, and Lorna was a Parton."

"What about the Hewitts, for instance?"

Charley Cooper shook his head. "Not High Ridge. They
come up from South Jersey, an altogether different breed of
cat, you might say. There was some Coopers and some Hewitts
got together in New York, but these weren't the same Hewitts.
These here in town came from South Jersey."

"Then I take it Mrs. Stratton is a cousin of yours?"

"Yes indeed. The Crowders and the Coopers married over
and over again. You take a walk through the churchyard
and you'll wonder if they ever married anybody else. Didn't
always draw the line at first cousins, either. Back in those days,
I guess they didn't always know for sure, when it was mostly
farms. Twenty miles away'd be a good strong young woman,
and a young farmer had to have a wife. A young fellow tried
to run a farm without a wife, he couldn't *do* it. You had to
have a wife. And not only for the work, either, if you know
what I mean. Come a certain age, and a young fellow had to
have a *woman*."

"To go to bed with?" said Evan Reese.

"To, right, go to bed with. It was that or start buggerin' the sheep. Or one another. And when that happened it wasn't long before everybody'd know it. A farmer that didn't have a woman, first he'd go to pot. Usually he'd stink so that nobody'd want to go near him. And pretty soon the farm would go to hell."

"Was this in your lifetime?"

"Sure was in my lifetime. I remember one Crowder had a piece of land he tried to farm without a woman. Him and his brother, the two of them. Jack'd never bring the brother to town with him, just come by himself. Stink? That fellow you could smell him a hundred yards off, and he grew his hair long and a beard. He couldn't read or write and to tell the truth, his vocabulary was pretty small. Just enough to ask for what he wanted in the store, like salt, molasses, shells for his gun. Children used to yell at him and he'd throw stones at them. Hit them, too. But he never run after them. He was the slowest-moving white man I ever saw."

"And what happened to *him?*"

"The brother run away one day, and Jack shot himself with the shotgun."

"And what happened to the brother?"

"They found him living in a cave, couple of miles from the farm. They put him away, he was an idiot. And he died of some sickness a couple months after they locked him up. The sheriff accidentally on purpose set fire to the shack they lived in. He told my father no self-respecting pig would live in it. Slaughtered the stock, a couple of cows, and the court awarded the land to the next of kin. That was an uncle, and the uncle was a cousin of Mrs. Stratton's father. So you see?"

"Mm-hmm." Evan Reese nodded. He was not sure whether he was supposed to see that a farm could not be run without a wife, or that Mrs. Stratton had some odd relatives.

"We had just as bad among the Coopers, I guess. They hung a Cooper when I was a young boy, and the sheriff that sprung the trap was a Cooper. How's that for family relations?"

"Well, where I come from in Pennsylvania there were over a dozen Evan Reeses in the same town, and five Reese Evanses. Originally r, h, y, s, but pronounced Reese. And Billy Williamses and Tommy Thomases and Johnny Johnses."

"Then you ought to know," said Charley Cooper. "But here it's been like that for close to three hundred years."

"I guess it was a good thing Mrs. Stratton married a stranger."

"Why?"

"New blood," said Evan Reese.

"New blood? Take a look at Frank Junior. Take a look at Bunnie. If that's all new blood can do for you, you're no better off than as if you married your first cousin. You can't go by that with people."

"You have a point," said Evan Reese. "But maybe Frank's grandchildren will be all right, or Bunnie's."

"Well, I doubt if I'll be around to see it, so I don't intend to let it worry me. I got one of my own grandchildren the brightest boy in his class at Rutgers, and another, his sister, in a mental institution. They had new blood, too. You figure it out, Mr. Reese."

"All right, Mr. Cooper, and if I do I'll call you up."

Cooper smiled. "No hurry, Mr. Reese. They're gonna make babies no matter what you tell them. That we won't be able to stop. Nobody could of stopped *me* when *I* was the right age." He jabbed a thumb in Reese's rib. "Didn't wait till it was legal, either."

"I'll bet you didn't."

"There's a few extra Coopers in addition to them that have the name. Know what I mean?"

"A few extra Coopers, eh?"

"One or two, must be. And I often think to myself, I wasn't the only one after nooky. Consequently, if I's getting mine, other parties were getting theirs, and the old saying, it's a wise child that knows his own father."

"True the world over, I suppose," said Evan Reese.

"I don't know about the world over, Mr. Reese. I only know

about High Ridge, but I sure know my High Ridge. An education in itself."

The conversation was taking place in Evan Reese's studio, to which Cooper had gone to report on some trees that had been overburdened in the snowfall. In cold weather it was never difficult to get Charley Cooper to talk, if the studio was warm. "Well, if you let me have your saw, I think I'll trim off some of them limbs," said Cooper, reluctantly.

"Hanging in the closet," said Evan Reese.

"Always used to rub a little ham fat on a saw," said Cooper. "As good as anything I know to keep the rust out. I never put a saw away without rubbing a little ham fat, but I guess oil's all right if it does the trick. How you coming along with your picture-painting?"

"Slow but sure," said Evan Reese.

"These here pictures, they look as good to me as some the Strattons paid thousands of dollars for."

"Thank you. They bought some very valuable paintings," said Evan Reese.

"So they did," said Cooper.

Evan Reese waited. He knew that Cooper was on the verge of saying something about the Stratton pictures.

"That puts me in mind of a question I wanted to ask you, Mr. Reese. What do they do when they *clean* a picture? Supposing you had an expensive picture. Would you send it away to have it cleaned?"

"I might, yes."

"Oh, you would?"

"Oh, yes. To have an expert job done."

"Put it in a crate and send it off to New York, eh?"

"Yes, that's done all the time, with valuable paintings. Why?"

"Costs a lot of money, I'll bet."

"It's not cheap, but it's worth it for a good picture."

"Mrs. Stratton used to do it. Anyway, she did it some years ago and I wondered why anybody'd want to go to all that trouble. She had me up there building crates for two or three pictures, oh, back before the war. That is, a fellow came from New York and told me how he wanted the crates built. That was carpentry, so I had to charge her extra, but she didn't complain. I made her a price of $15 a crate, labor and materials. Well, that's one of the ways the rich have of spending their money."

"In this case, protecting an investment."

"Very likely," said Cooper, unsatisfied. "Fifteen dollars apiece to me, and then whatever the cleaner charged. What *would* he charge?"

"That depends on the value of the painting."

"Say a painting by Van Dyke?"

"Oh, probably a thousand dollars. I don't know. Maybe more."

"Then I didn't overcharge her for my crates."

"I think that was a fair price."

"I wondered. 'S far as I know, she never sent any more away, and I wondered if she thought I overcharged her."

"The Van Dyke is the one that's hanging in the hall?" said Evan Reese.

Cooper nodded. "I wouldn't of remembered Van Dyke, except there's a whole family of Van Dykes living around here."

"Did they do a good cleaning job?"

"I don't know. I didn't unpack it for her, and I don't get in the hall very often. My work don't take me but to the cellar and the kitchen, generally speaking." He paused. "Supposing she wanted to sell a picture like that. What would she get for it?"

"Oh, Lord. Fifty, a hundred, a hundred and fifty thousand. Possibly more. The market changes, and some paintings are worth much more than others by the same man."

"What if, supposing a fellow come to you with a picture and wanted to sell it to you. Would you know right away if it was genuine?"

"That depends. If I knew the painter's work very well I

think I could tell. And of course you realize that some individual paintings are famous. The Mona Lisa, for instance.
Everybody knows where that is."

"I don't. I heard of it, but I don't know where it is."

"It's in the Louvre, in Paris. And to a certain extent that's
true of a great many famous paintings."

"Then if you took a look at a painting by Van Dyke, you'd
know right away if it was genuine?"

"If I had occasion to study it, probably. Why? Have you
been wondering about Mrs. Stratton's Van Dyke?"

"Oh, I wouldn't want you to say that," said Cooper. "No,
sir, I wouldn't want that at all, Mr. Reese. Don't put words
in my mouth."

"I wouldn't think of doing that, Mr. Cooper."

"Hope not," said Cooper. "Well, this aint getting my work
done, much as I enjoyed talking with you."

"I enjoyed it too. Come in any time."

"And everything I said this morning—?"

"Oh, absolutely between the two of us."

"She never liked anybody talking about her. Starting with
marrying a man twice her age."

"I imagine."

The expected call from Mrs. Stratton came later in the day.
"I'd like your advice on something, if you have five minutes,"
she said. It was an invitation that unmistakably excluded Georgia Reese. "My son's gone over to Princeton for lunch, so it'll
be just you and I."

Evan Reese was led by the maid to the study-office.

"Some coffee, Mr. Reese?" said Mrs. Stratton.

"No thanks."

"Do have some? It's here, and it's hot, and I always feel
more like a hostess if my guests take *something*. Sugar?"

"One lump, please." He accepted the demitasse and took a
chair facing hers.

"Mrs. Reese isn't going to say anything about those frauds,
is she?"

"Of course not."

"No. She's a lady. I knew that. I sold the pictures quite a long while ago. It was the only way I knew to provide for my grandchildren. Even so, I didn't get a very good price for them. The dealer took a larger commission than usual. *He* said because he wasn't getting any publicity, but what he meant was that *I* wasn't getting any publicity. In other *words,* he'd keep his mouth shut for a price. Well, I had no choice but to pay him."

"I think I ought to warn you that Charley Cooper is suspicious." He reported some of his conversation with Cooper, and she listened in silence until he finished.

"Yes," she said. "Charley Cooper would like somehow to collect a little money from me for *his* silence. But first he has to have someone to back up his suspicions. He'll try you, later, when he's decided you can be trusted. Not that that will be a very high compliment, Mr. Reese."

"No, it won't be, will it?"

"I know Charley so well because he's my cousin, or has he told you that?"

"Yes, he's told me that."

"The question on Charley's mind would be whether to risk losing the few dollars I pay him fifty-two weeks a year. When he was younger he was more trustworthy. Not more honest, but more trustworthy. He was satisfied with ten or twenty dollars a week. But he's old now, and why is it that the old like money so much? Is it because that's all there is? As a young man Charley was quite dashing. The girls in High Ridge swooned over him, if that doesn't tax your imagination. He was a handsome young man, scorching about on his bicycle. My husband used to give him a lot of his clothes, and Charley cut quite a figure. But then he married and settled down. His wife made him refuse my husband's old suits, and he became very strait-laced. Always had two or three jobs at the same time and brought up his children with an iron hand. Isn't it always that way with reformed rakes? Were you a rake when you were a younger man, Mr. Reese?"

"I did some raking, but I don't think I was a rake."

"Charley was a rake, by High Bridge standards. He's supposed to have been the father of at least two children by other men's wives. Luckily for him, though, the mothers were the kind that couldn't be sure. There was more of that here than we like to admit."

"There is, no matter where you go."

"I daresay. But I didn't ask you here to discuss my cousin Charley Cooper. I want to know what you think of my son. Is there any hope for him?"

"In what way?"

"In any way. You may not think it's fair of me to ask you such a question. You don't know me very well, and I haven't been very cordial to you and Mrs. Reese. But I'm a very old woman, and we haven't got time to get acquainted by easy stages. The nice thing about being old is that I can dispense with those easy stages, dinner twice a year for ten years, tea four times a year, and so forth. You and I can make up our minds about each other much more quickly. And I knew from the way you acted after you saw those fake pictures that I could tell you anything and ask you anything. If I had known you all my life I couldn't be surer."

"Thank you."

"You're welcome. And so—what about my son? I'd hoped that when he was divorced he'd be able to face his problem squarely. In plain language, stop torturing himself with this pretense of being like other men. He never has been. He loved the girl he married, and he loves his children. But he forced that girl to marry him by convincing her that she would be his salvation. Salvation! He very nearly ruined her life as well as his own. And he knew what a dreadful thing he was doing to her, and that was what made him take to drinking. As to the children—they're exactly like dolls, animated dolls. When he speaks of them that's the way he sounds, as though he were talking about dolls. And he loved dolls when he was a little boy. But only too well I remember that for no reason at all he would smash a doll, and I sided with his wife on the question of custody of the children."

"Well, aside from his drinking, what's the matter with him now?"

"You say *aside* from his drinking? There *is* nothing *aside* from his drinking, Mr. Reese."

"But he hasn't been drinking since's he's been here."

"He doesn't drink here because I won't have it. But in New York he drinks all day long, every day."

"What do you mean when you say you won't have it? Do you lock up the whiskey supply?"

"Nothing as easy as that. He simply knows that if he takes more than a few cocktails before meals, I'll send him away. I won't have him in my house. And he understands that."

"So he complies?"

"He has no alternative," she said.

Evan Reese stood up and went to the window.

"You seem to me to want to light your pipe," said Mrs. Stratton. "Go right ahead."

"How sensitive you are. That's exactly what I want to do," said Evan Reese.

"I like the smell of pipe tobacco. I don't like the smell of pipes, but the tobacco burning is very pleasant."

"Well, I'll light up as quickly as I can," said Evan Reese. He filled his pipe and lit it, and remained standing. "Mrs. Stratton, I agree with you that we can dispense with the early stages."

"That's good."

"But even if I'd known you, we'd known each other, all our lives, that wouldn't necessarily mean that complete candor existed between us."

"No, that's true. What are you getting at, Mr. Reese?"

"This. Whether we've known each other a couple of days, or forty or fifty years, the question is how well do we know each other? In other words, what things can we say, and what things must we not say?"

"There's nothing we can't say, when I've asked you such a terribly inside-of-me, intimate question about my son. I should think that such a question would make you feel free to answer me with complete candor. In fact, Mr. Reese, as a gentleman you *have* to reply to my question with the same candor. That's the only courteous thing you can do."

"I wonder."

"Oh, don't *wonder*. It *is*. It cost me something in pride and humility to be so frank with you."

"But I don't want to be equally frank with you. It won't cost me any humility or pride, but it might cost me your friendship. I have that, haven't I?"

"You have indeed. In fact, you may be my only friend. I can't think of any other, so I guess you are."

"Madam, I *am* your friend," said Evan Reese. "Will you believe that?"

"Yes. I promise."

"Then I'll say what I think, but I hope you'll forgive me."

"Please go on."

Evan Reese emptied his pipe in the fireplace and again seated himself, facing her. "First of all, I'm what I am, a painter, and not a psychiatrist."

"I don't want a psychiatrist."

"Your son has made a failure of his marriage. He has affection and I suppose admiration for his wife. He has a great fondness for his children, his dolls. He got out of his marriage, with its heterosexual obligations. But getting out of his marriage didn't make him happy, or give him any release. You tell me that he drinks heavily all the time."

"Morning, noon and night," she said.

"*Except!* Except when he comes here, Mrs. Stratton. Except when he's here with you. The only time he's at all happy, the only time he doesn't need to drink—"

"He knows I won't have it in my house—"

"Mrs. Stratton, he doesn't drink here because he doesn't *want* to drink here. This is where he wants to be, with you."

"Do you know what you're saying?" she said.

"Of course I do. Of course I know what I'm saying."

"Then stop saying it. You know it isn't true."

"What isn't true, Mrs. Stratton?"

"What you're thinking. It was never true, never in my life."

"I believe you."

"Then why must you say these things?"

"I believe *you,* Mrs. Stratton. *You.* But I don't disbelieve what your son feels."

"He feels nothing. He's past all feeling."

"Then let him be happy, here with you."

She shook her head. "I'm too old. I don't want him here," she said.

"My dear lady, you sent him away once before. Twice before. What happens when you send him away?"

"Oh, you know these things?"

"Yes," said Evan Reese. "And now you're old, Mrs. Stratton, but even so you'll probably outlive him."

"I'm sure I will."

"Then let him stay, the more reason."

"I *am* old, you know. But he is my son. The poor, bloated, miserable boy. I hardly know him any more. Tell me, Mr. Reese, so wise and kind you are, why does *this* last?" She held her hand to her bosom.

"Something must," he said.

The Weakness

Bob Buzzell had about seventy-five thousand dollars left out of the money he had made in the ring; seventy-five thousand dollars and his senses, he was fond of saying; seventy-five thousand dollars and a lot of memories, recognition, respect, and a clear conscience by the standards of the racket. He had thrown two fights in the beginning of his career, and he had carried one fighter whom he could have knocked out after becoming champion. At thirty-three he had all his marbles, and enough money to open a cigar store–poolroom, with the half promise of backing for a bowling alley if the cigar store–poolroom caught on. He was thirty-three years old, had a wife and two children, a house on the edge of town, fourteen suits of clothes, a four-year-old Cadillac, and all those memories of luxury-travel, association with the famous in show business and politics, two nights in bed with one of the all-time greats of the movies, and a roomful of statuettes and scrolls and belts and photographs. He would never again have to dry out to make the weight, like a goddam jockey; or stay away from women, like a goddam priest; or go through that dreary routine of bag-punching and road work and leg exercises, like a goddam college football player. And he would never again have to listen to Marty Carroll, who the boxing writers said had managed, or piloted, him into the championship but didn't have a mark on his face and did have a lot more than seventy-five thousand dollars to show for their nine years together. He would never again have to listen to Marty Carroll referring to him as "my guy" or how "we" had won twenty-two straight without a knockdown.

"One more," Marty Carroll had said, when Bob Buzzell told him he was quitting.

"No, no more," said Buzzell.

"Don't be stupid. I can get you Rubinello."

"I don't want Rubinello. I don't want nobody."

"Now listen, wise guy, I said I can get you Rubinello, and then if you ever want to come out of retirement you'll be a light heavyweight."

"You talk like I was going to lose to Rubinello."

"Rubinello right now would have a hard time making you last five rounds. Five rounds is the most he could stretch it, if you stayed away from him the first two rounds. Right now Rubinello could drop you in Round One if he took the notion."

"This is suppose to boog me, hey, Marty? Well, it don't. It shows I'm right, wanting to quit."

"All right, quit. I always knew there was some mouse in you. Just a bit of kayoodle. I seen it come out the first time when you fought the Frenchman."

"Yeah, he had me scared. So did Burns."

"Burns, you weren't scared. The Frenchman, you were. You give the Frenchman everything you had, and when he didn't go down you got the lump, but big. You butted the Frenchman and you should of lost that one. You're what I call a desperation dirty fighter. A front runner. All right, I could of got you Rubinello, insurance for the future. But you walk out on me now and you got nothin'. A big fat nothin', now or any other time. Wuddia plan to do? Get a job teaching philosophy? You got the mind for it. That's a great brain you got there, you know. Go on, get the hell out of my office."

"Rubinello must want me pretty bad. You thought you had it made, eh, Marty?"

"Oh, I got it made without the like of you. I got a little put away, don't you worry. And I had it when you were still fighting for fifty-dollar watches."

"Only now you got more."

"Yeah, I got more." Marty Carroll picked up the newspaper and opened it wide, and Buzzell walked out of the office for the last time.

At the end of the first year the cigar store–poolroom had

lost some money. The early curiosity trade had been profitable, but after six months it dwindled down to the regulars, and Bob Buzzell could tell from week to week how much they would spend. The soft drink and candy vending machines and the pool tables were profitable as were the pay telephones, but there was no money in cigars and the patrons bought their cigarettes cut-rate at the chain drug store. He had some visitors from the numbers racket and a salesman wanted to install a machine that dispensed contraceptives, but currently there was a local campaign against juvenile delinquency and he was quite aware that the numbers and contraceptive people needed him more than he needed them, and he put them off. He was also anxious to close a deal with the bowling alley people, and this more than any moral consideration influenced his stand. He was lucky. The district manager of the bowling alley concern appeared one morning and said he liked the way Buzzell was running his business. "We had to see if you'd go for the fast buck. No offense, Bob, but you could of got tied up with the numbers racket and one thing another, and then you wouldn't of been worth a dime to us. The bowling alley is the biggest thing in the U.S. today, and it got that way because the whole family bowls. The women, and the school kids. And with the automatic pin-spotter, a bowling alley is a big investment. I mean big. You start in six figures, you know. Well, you passed the test. You lost a little this year, but you're clean. No numbers. No dope pushers. No trouble with the law, so we have a proposition."

They used his name, they required his presence five nights a week, and they paid him a salary and a small percentage of the gross income. They kept the books and did the hiring and firing. The contract was for one year, with renewals annually at increases in salary so long as the grosses were maintained at the first year level, and larger salary increases if business warranted additional lanes. They encouraged his participation in community activities, but he was not allowed to run for public office. In spite of their reluctance to have him face the electorate the bowling entrepreneurs made no objection when the grand opening of the Bob Buzzell Bowling Alleys was attended by the mayor, the sheriff, the State assemblyman, the district Congressman, and the chief of police; as well as clergymen of several denominations, the president of the chamber of commerce, the commanders of the Legion and V.F.W. posts, the coaches of nearby town and consolidated high school teams, the sports editors of the local daily and the county weeklies and other such dignitaries. The radio station covered the event for half an hour, and music was provided by the high school orchestra. The mayor, bowling the first official ball, completed a split on his second try, and Mrs. Dora Ringgold, vice-president of the school board, received a canvas carrying case for bowling the first strike.

"You got time now for a little home life," said Betty, his wife, after the bowling alley had been in business a few weeks.

"How do you mean, home life? I gotta be there five nights a week."

"Yeah, but with the poolroom you were there from ten o'clock in the morning to past midnight. I mean like gardening. I don't mean you ought to take up gardening, and I'm not complaining, Bob. Don't think that. I was just thinking we have the daytime we could do things together."

"Like what, for instance?"

"Well, like little trips in the car. The kids are off to school by ha' past eight in the morning, and don't get home till near four. That would give us time to take a *lot* of trips."

"Yeah, but like where?"

"Well, take for instance, we been to Los Angeles and Montreal, Canada. But I'd like to go to Gettysburg."

"Gettysburg? You mean where they had the battle? What the hell's the attraction to Gettysburg?"

"Well, it's historical. My great-grandfather's name is on the Pennsylvania Monument."

"You want to drive over a hundred miles to see your great-grandfather's name on a monument?"

"I would. For all you know, maybe you have some ancestors that their names are on the Monument."

"I got my name on the roll of honor in front of the Legion post. I can see that any time without driving a hundred miles to see my great-grandfather's name. How do you know your great-grandfather is on a monument?"

"I seen it when I was a little girl. My parents took me."

"All right, you seen it once. Wuddia wanta see it again for?"

"Oh, you don't understand. Anyway, I don't care about Gettysburg. It's just the idea of you don't have to be at the bowling alley till six o'clock. That gives us nearly the whole day we could be doing something."

"I thought you had plenty to do, the housework."

"I do, but once in a while we could take a trip. I could arrange my housework."

"I'll take you on a trip, but Gettysburg. Jesus! I just as soon go back to Guadal. At least on Guadal I could show you where your husband knocked off a couple Japs, not some great-grandfather's name on a monument. What is this, anyway, Betty?"

"Well—you're a real businessman now. All those big wheels when they opened the bowling alley. You aren't just a retired fighter with a poolroom. You're a big man in town."

"A big man in town. What was I before? Just a bum?"

"I didn't say that. I didn't even hint at it. But you got to admit it yourself, you're better off now than fighting. You don't have to be afraid somebody's gonna put your eye out."

"I was never afraid anybody would put my eye out."

"You were so. And you didn't want to end up punchy. You told me that a hundred times."

"I was never afraid of anybody."

"You say that now, Bob, but you used to be."

"Ah, shut up. Don't tell *me* what I was."

"Wuddia wanta argue with *me* for? I'm trying to tell you you're better off. You don't have them things worr'ing you. You can sleep nights and you don't have to go around with those no-good gangsters and creeps. And *I* can go places without people thinking I'm one of those tramps."

"What tramps?"

"Oh, what tramps? Those women. I used to feel ashamed of myself to sit in a night club with those women. As if I was one of them. If you'd of thought more of me you wouldn't of made me sit with them."

"I didn't make you sit with them. You wanted to be there, and I never saw you break no cameras when the photographers came around."

"Yeah, and that time my picture was in the paper, only it said I was one of them tramps and the tramp was Mrs. Bob Buzzell."

"Oh, God, you never got over that."

"No, I never got over it, because that's what they were all thinking. I go all the way to Los Angeles and they don't know I'm your wife. Well, now it's time I got some enjoyment out of life. You're out of that racket and I wanta live respectable. I did it your way for nine years, but now it's your turn to take into consideration me and the children. I don't care if you don't take me to Gettysburg, but from now on I want to live decent for a change."

"I didn't hear no beefs all the time you were staying at them big hotels."

"No, and I didn't beef when I didn't see you for three months at a time, either. But I didn't beef when you were in the Marines, either."

"Well, that was damn nice of you."

"Well, it was. Listen, I know you. That's why I was willing to overlook certain things, because I know your weakness. But you got some things to make up for, Bob Buzzell."

"Wuddia trying to tell me, Betty?"

"All right, I'll tell you. I was a good wife and mother and everybody in town knows it. I went to church and brought up the children neat and clean, and polite. And I'm entitled to some credit."

"All right, I give you credit. I never said I didn't."

"I got more to say."

"I just bet you have."

"And you better listen. I just happen to know that before

they'd put up all that money for the bowling alley, those men investigated me, your family life."

"Oh, I get it. You're declaring yourself in."

"Not for money. Don't think I'm trying to get money out of you. But if I was one of those tramps that hang around prize-fighters, you wouldn't of had a prayer to have your name on that bowling alley. You ask Reverend Buchholtz. You ask the mayor. So don't think you got the bowling alley just because you won twenty-two straight fights. *I* had something to do with it, too. And when I ask you to show a little gratitude, I'm only asking for what I'm entitled to."

"Yeah, but what if I thought you were entitled to a poke in the nose?"

"Only once you'd have to do that, Bob. I'd never take it from you. I seen enough of that when I was little. Once a woman lets a man beat her, if she don't get out right away he'll do it again. I seen it with my aunt, and some others, too. There aint a man that's worth it."

"Well, then don't aggravate me. Because if I'm only gonna get one crack at you, believe me, kid, it'll be a good one."

"My advice to you is you better stop thinking along those lines."

"And my advice to you is just don't aggravate me," he said.

She had waited nine years, and she had learned patience. For the time being it was enough that she had stated her wishes, and she did not soon again ask him to take her anywhere. He had arrived at his decision to quit prizefighting without any discussion with her. It was what she wanted but had not dared to speak of. Now, with a little prodding, he might proceed from the bowling alley to something else, like a store, or real estate, a garage, or insurance salesman—some business in which he could stop calling himself Bob, and she would become Mrs. Robert Buzzell, or Mrs. Robert W. Buzzell. She hated the sign on the roof of the bowling alley, with the phony signature, Bob Buzzell in neon tubing. She hated their name on their mailbox. All the other mailboxes in the neighborhood were William J., John H., or F. J., or

B. F. Nobody had nicknames on their mailboxes. Bob Buzzell
on their mailbox seemed like an invitation to tramps and
strangers, and in nine years she had seen enough tramps and
strangers to do her for the rest of her life. She wanted to be
like other wives, with a husband like other husbands, and to
have people gradually forget that she was the wife of a man
who was most often photographed with his body bare from the
waist up, who had made his living by punching other half-
naked men into insensibility. He was the masculine version of
the beauty pageant girls, revealing himself as much as possible,
and with his physical measurements printed all over the world.
She had seen the letters he got from foolish women and from
men who were not really men, letters that sometimes enclosed
photographs of themselves. They had made him laugh, but they
had never struck her as funny, and she had destroyed letters
and photographs before anyone else could see them. But
she knew that he had only stopped showing her the letters.
The letters had not just suddenly stopped coming; he had
simply stopped showing them to her. And once in New York
she had seen a message asking him to call a famous movie
actress at the Savoy-Plaza.

Marty Carroll had never wanted Betty around while Bob
was training for a fight, but he was equally insistent on her being present at ringside when the fight took place; and of all
the people at the parties after Bob's fights, the only one she
had any use for was Marty. He had a mean face; cold, blue
little eyes and a thin nose that was more like a beak; almost
invisible lips; and a dead-white, closely shaved skin as white
as his brushed-down hair. She did not like Marty Carroll, but
there was something about his coldness and his extreme personal cleanliness that set him apart from the rest of Bob's paid
and unpaid hangers-on. In nine years she had never seen
him laugh, and when he smiled it was always because of
some little triumph over somebody. And yet Betty was more
comfortable with him than with any of the others. She never
called him anything but Mr. Carroll, and he never in nine
years suggested that she call him Marty; but when other

people—including Bob Buzzell—called him Marty she had the feeling that they were taking liberties and that in so doing they cheapened themselves without getting any closer to him. All sorts of people called him Marty, but he called no one by a first name or a nickname. Betty was Mrs. Buzzell; Mrs. Marty Carroll lived in New Jersey and not even Bob Buzzell had ever laid eyes on her. All Bob knew about her was that she lived in New Jersey and had a kennel where she bred Kerry Blues, and that when Mrs. Carroll spent the night in New York, she and Marty stayed at a hotel on the other side of town. No one connected with prizefighting had ever been invited to the Carrolls' farm. Sometimes Betty had envied Mrs. Carroll, but she had never been able to ask Marty about her. He plainly considered Betty one of the people who would never be invited to the farm and with whom any discussion of his wife would be a waste of time.

Two things she had come to understand about herself and the Marty Carrolls: she had wished that Bob could be like Marty, making the money that was in prizefighting, but remaining aloof from the people in it; and she had wished that she could be like Mrs. Marty Carroll, who derived all the benefits and still remained even more aloof than her husband. The sums of money that Bob was supposed to be making while fighting were exaggerated and came to fractions of the originals by the time Bob put the money in the bank; but even what was left after taxes and expenses and Marty Carroll's cut and the honest truth had reduced the size of the purses was still more than a Bob Buzzell had a right to expect. He had no education, no trade, no business ability. He happened to have been born quick and strong, naturally left-handed, and able to remember to do what he was told while receiving punches. The boxing writers refused to put him among the great, but they called him tough, aggressive, and a crowd-pleaser, who gave the fans their money's worth and never dogged it. Possibly because it was so obvious, they refrained from commenting that in the ring as well as in the negotiational stages he was master-minded by the old fox, Marty Carroll. Obvious or not, it was a fact that Betty Buzzell discovered for herself, and from the moment of her husband's retirement she was determined to emulate Marty Carroll in his guidance of Bob Buzzell. Marty Carroll knew all about prizefighting, but Betty Buzzell considered herself an authority on home life, the kind of home life she wanted for herself and her husband and children. They had the money and the first respectable job of Bob's new career, and the rest was up to her. She was not quite sure what a Kerry Blue was, but she had earned her right to have a kennelful of them just as much as the remote Mrs. Marty Carroll. She did not resent Mrs. Carroll's having Kerry Blues with money that Bob Buzzell had made. That was life. Brains did it, and the brains belonged to Marty Carroll. But Betty had had a lot of time to think, and if Bob Buzzell could be managed into a world's championship, he could be made into something more important than proprietor of a bowling alley in a third-class city in Pennsylvania. In this situation his weakness was her strength, and she had certain advantages. No matter how many women Bob may have slept with, he always came back to her. She could be as indispensable as Marty Carroll had been, and from observing Bob Buzzell's dependence on Marty Carroll she had learned that her husband had to have someone to think for him.

Betty Buzzell had never been to bed with any man but her husband, but there was a whole world of sexual knowledge in the experience of ten years with him. Not the love that he avowed or the admiration of her body that he displayed was the strength of her hold on him. It was shame. He laughed about sex, he liked to talk dirty in front of people and to make fun of peculiarities. Betty, limiting her actual experience to this one man, had come to understand the subject universally. He lied about the other women, and she never believed the lies. He wanted every pretty woman he saw, and some who were far from pretty, but none of them lasted; he always came back to her, and she knew why. He was proud of his strength, of his masculinity, and she knew he took women to bed with him. She could often guess which women; she could always

guess when. He needed women as he needed kids with autograph books and instant recognition by taxi drivers, and this
need was covered by the all-embracing term, his weakness.
Her use of the term included women without specifying them
as it included the taxi drivers' recognition without mentioning
it. The weakness was adulation and the public flexing of
muscles, showing off and being admired. But Betty always
knew when he had gone to bed with one of those easily
available women. He would come to her with his unfulfilled
desire to be hurt, his basic need to have love-making accom-
panied by the infliction of physical pain. There was his shame.
As the public symbol of masculinity he could not in private
reveal his special peculiarity, and he would quickly drop a
woman for fear that in a continued affair she would find him
out. Always there had to be pain, and he was most grateful
when Betty would surprise him with a new way of inflicting
it. "Why is that?" she once asked him.

"I don't know. I just can't help it. But don't talk about it
no more." He was ashamed of the peculiarity and doubly
ashamed of her knowledge of it, and notwithstanding his
momentary gratitude there was anger in his command for
silence. All at once she knew that some day he might kill
her, but he would never leave her, and she was not afraid of
him.

The bowling alley stayed open till two in the morning. As
though to discourage such things as excursions to Gettysburg
he formed the habit of waiting at the bowling alley until
closing time, and stopping for a hamburger at an all-night
diner, although his contract did not require his presence after
midnight and he did not have to pay for hamburgers at the
alley. He got home nearer four o'clock than three, was careful
not to wake her, and slept seven or eight hours. She would
make his breakfast and have her lunch with him. The arrangement left them with at most four hours together before the
children were let out of school, and every day, depending upon
the season of the year, he would go to a driving range and hit

golf balls, or go for a swim, or go ice-skating. When the weather was bad he would go to the Legion and play pool. He would get home at five o'clock and have early supper with Betty and the children. Thus, and almost without deviation, they passed a year. For two weeks in the summer they placed the children on her father's farm while they drove to Canada on a vacation trip.

Everywhere they went people would ask him when he was going to come out of retirement, was it true he was going to fight Rubinello as a light heavyweight, what did he think of this new Swede. It was two years since he had been away from home, and the still lively interest of filling station attendants and motel proprietors and highway patrolmen—even a Mountie asked about the punch that had knocked out a promising Canadian five years earlier—was just what he needed to enjoy the vacation. In Montreal he called up some prizefighting friends who invited him and Betty to lunch, but she told him to go without her. She did not want to see them. He did not return to the hotel until after seven that evening, and she knew immediately that he had been with a woman.

"What you do all afternoon?" she said.

"Oh, they broke out the wine and Jules made his load and we got to talking."

"You didn't have any wine, did you?"

"You know anything makes me sick. Why'd you ask me that? I aint had a drink of anything since I got out of the Marines, and you know it."

"Then you did a lot of talking. Nearly seven hours." She had no desire to make an accusation, but she wanted him to feel guilt through her unspoken suspicion.

"Well, there was a whole gang of us. Some of them I didn't see since five years ago. You want to go out and eat?"

"Sure, I been ready since six o'clock."

"All right, put your dress on and we'll go out and eat."

She removed her wrapper, and in her pantie-girdle and brassiere she took her time deciding which dress to wear. As she expected, he postponed their departure and made love to her, and she gave him pleasure. When it was over he lay on the bed, smoking a cigarette and staring at the ceiling.

"Aren't you gonna take me out and eat?" she said.

"I been thinking, maybe I ought to get a match with Rubinello."

"You go back in the ring and that's the end of you and me," she said.

"Why? I'm in good condition. You notice I take exercise every day. It'd be six months before Rubinello could fight me, maybe a year. He has a return match with Munson he gotta take care of first, so maybe it'd be a year. By then I'd be ready and I could take him."

"And he'd have it in the contract that *you* had to give *him* a return match," she said. "So it wouldn't be one fight, it'd be two."

"And all that loot. Jules would guarantee me eighty-five gees for my end. Stage the first fight here in Montreal."

"Give me a hundred dollars," she said.

"What for? I give you a hundred dollars the day before yesterday."

"I spent it. I want a hundred dollars to go home. I don't want to be in the same room with you till you get some sense into you."

"That's the way you feel about it, take a hundred dollars out of my wallet."

"I will, but don't you come home till you get some sense. Stay here with Jules *and those friends of his.*"

"I'll do that. That's exactly what I will do. And you better not start hangin' by your thumbs till I come home. In other words, Betty, don't hold your breath that long."

By plane and bus she made her way home, was there before midnight and spent the night alone in their house. To the people she saw in the next few days she explained that Bob was working on a business proposition in Montreal, and she was so elaborately secretive that her story was accepted.

She knew his weakness. The woman in Montreal would

last him two or three nights and then there would be another, and then he would come home. But she would take him back only on her terms, and for a week she planned what the terms would be. He would have to start going to church. Church was very important in her plans for him. He would have to do more at the Legion than just shoot pool. He would take an active part in Little League baseball. And she decided that his contacts could be used to best advantage in the insurance business. Inside of a year, two years at the most, he would be able to give up the bowling alley and demand a partnership, a name partnership, in one of the insurance agencies. In a way she was grateful for the week alone; it gave her time to think.

On the night of the seventh day of their separation she went to bed early. She had heard nothing from him, but she was not alarmed when she was awakened by the sound of the garage door rolling up, then rolling down; the familiar kick of his foot against the bottom of the kitchen door, his heavy tread on the way upstairs. She already had the bedroom light on when he opened the door.

He needed a shave badly. He was wearing slacks and a sport shirt and he put his suitcase down gently. "Hello," he said.

"Hello," she said.

"You're not surprise to see me?"

"No."

"You been listeninga the radio?"

"No, why? Is there something on the radio about you?"

"Could be," he said.

"Could be? You mean there is. What are you, in some kind of trouble?"

"Uh-huh. Yeah, I guess you could say that."

"What did you do?"

"Oh, I got in a jam in Montreal. I'll tell you about it tomorrow. It's too long a story."

"Not too long for me. What did you do?"

"Betty, I drove all the way from Montreal. I been thinking about you all the way."

"It's near time you thought about me. A week you didn't phone."

"That's because you walked out on me," he said. "That's what got me in the jam."

"What jam are you in, Bob? Are the police in it?"

"I wanta get in bed with you and stop asking me questions."

"No. You're in trouble with the police, aren't you?"

"If I'd of stayed in Canada. But I aint in Canada. I'm in Pennsylvania."

"Will it be on the eleven o'clock radio?"

"Maybe it will and maybe it won't."

"It's some kind of trouble over a woman. Did you kill her?"

"I didn't kill nobody. I give her a beating."

"Oh, God," she said wearily.

"Well, you walked out on me and what did you expect? A wife walks out on her husband, she got no claim on him if he gets another woman. And you walked out on me, you got to admit that. Wud you tell them in town?"

"I said you were staying there on business."

"Well, that's what I was."

"And beating up one of those tramps. You were with her the day I walked out."

"No."

"Yes you were."

"Well, all right, so I was. But I didn't start it. She started it."

"How bad did you beat her up?"

"I hit her a couple times."

"And what?"

"I broke her jaw. That's what I heard on the radio. The radio from Albany, New York. I was in the car, and I had the radio going and I heard it, that she was in the hospital and the Montreal cops were looking for me. But by that time I was over the border."

"God in heaven," she said.

"Didn't nobody phone you? The papers or nobody?"

"I was next door till ha' past nine, and then I come home and went to bed." She looked about her, at the furniture, the draperies, the pictures on the walls. "The kids are still with **Mom**."

He forced a smile. "Well, it's lucky you didn't have some guy here."

"Yeah. Judging other people by yourself."

"I was thinking of you go to the bank tomorrow and get the money out and I'd go somewhere till this blows over."

"And then what? You come back and manage the bowling alley again?"

"When this blows over."

"Are you crazy? I bet if you look tomorrow night they won't even have your name lit up."

"So what? I'll get a fight."

"Who with? Some whore?"

"Hey, now, don't *you* aggravate me. That aint what I come home for," he said.

The Man with the Broken Arm

Anna Lyman's rudeness to Charles Weston was so deliberate and thorough that hardly anyone among the passengers failed to notice it and comment on it. She was so careful and cruel that I did not expect to see Weston again during the rest of the voyage. But on the morning after the ship's concert, where the rudeness had occurred, Weston was up and about, taking his jaunty walk past the rows of steamer chairs, nodding and smiling to this one and that one, tipping his cap in semi-military salute, and seeming to spring up from each step in his rubber-soled brown suèdes. It was a courageous performance, and I felt like telling him so when we met in the smoke-room before lunch, but he had anticipated me.

I had met Weston several times through the years, but until this trip we had never sat down together for a meal or conversation. Now, two men traveling alone, we usually had a drink together before going to the dining-room. From the first day out we had started, of course, with a mutual acquaintance of a thousand men and women in the theater and films, and conversation was easy for us.

"Annie certainly gave it to me last night," he said, as he took his seat. "Were you there?"

"Yes, I was there," I said. "Why did she do it?"

"She had her reasons," he said. "And this was her chance. She wanted to show me up in front of that kind of an audience. The big wheels in television. Two English managers. The picture people. The English duke. And all these millionaires." The jauntiness faded as he recalled the audience. His clothes were perfect; a reddish tweed jacket, sleeveless sweater, tan slacks, Tattersall shirt, knitted necktie. But for the moment his costume seemed to be sitting there unoccupied by a living man, while the living man consisted of head and hands. The wrinkles and lines stood out, now that he was sitting quietly; the carefully brushed hair showed more grey. His lips moved although he was not speaking, and he had to hold his head up to maintain a chin line. In one spotted hand he held a cigarette, which he smoked busily, and in the other hand he kept turning a gold Zippo lighter. "It's just as bad to know something about somebody as it is to do them a dirty trick. In fact, it's a dirty trick to remember things. At least Annie thinks so. How long have you known her?"

"I can't say that I know her at all," I said. "About as well as I knew you, and about as long, I guess."

"That's another dirty trick. I shouldn't be around to remind her of her exact age. Fifty-six. Annie's fifty-six. There must be a lot of people on this boat that can guess at her age, but I'm the one that knows it exactly. Do you know something? Last night was the first time she spoke to me since we left New York. She saw me the first day out, even before they printed the passenger list, and she refused to speak to me. Well, I thought, if that was the way she wanted it, what the hell? But I didn't think I'd spoil her trip just by being aboard. However, I found out last night. You knew I was once married to her?"

"Yes, I knew that," I said.

"I just wanted to make sure you knew that. A lot of people *don't* know it. She'd rather forget it, but she can't. She's been married three times since she was married to me, but I'm the only one she hates. The only one that was nice to her, never gave her a bit of trouble, never took her for any money, never traded on her reputation. And probably the only one that ever really loved her. Loved her at the time, and never got over it, even though I've been happily married since Annie divorced me. I only thank God my wife and two boys weren't there last night. I have a boy at Lawrenceville and another at Princeton, and if they'd seen what happened last night I really think I'd have gone over the side. You see, Jim, the reason why I'm not more upset about last night is that years ago I took everything a man can take from that woman. She can embarrass me, as she did last night, but the only way she could ever really do me any more damage would be if she made a fool of me in front of my boys."

"What about your wife?"

"My wife knows the whole story, and she regards Anna Lyman as something cheap and evil. No, not cheap. Stupid and evil. Unintelligent and evil. No man could ever have the same contempt for Anna that my wife has. You know how we feel about some guys that women like? That's the way my wife feels about Anna Lyman. To her there's no attractiveness about Anna. Anna is the kind of mistake men make because they're men." He smiled a little. "You know how women see right through other women? It gives them a great sense of superiority over men when they see what kind of women we sometimes fall for. And of course a woman judging another woman isn't befuddled by sex, the hay department. Jonesey, my wife, isn't a bit jealous of Anna Lyman. She considers Anna as something like whooping cough. Maybe a form of whooping cough that I got when I was in my twenties, but still one of those ailments that you get and then get over. Unfortunately I never did completely recover. I did, in a way. But I still remember the illness, the way you remember an illness you actually had in childhood. Or a broken arm. When I was a boy I broke my arm, falling off an ice wagon, and I remember all the attention I got. Privileges. Presents from my grandparents and so on. Broken arm." He lifted a hand and with his forefinger pointed to our nearly empty glasses. The steward nodded.

"If you knew I was married to Anna Lyman, then you must remember about her and L. M. Zeeman. You knew she was his girl friend?"

"I heard that, yes."

"Well, you see, I didn't. I didn't know a damn thing about her and Zeeman. I was a Broadway actor, not a movie actor. I was the thitta, old boy, not feelms. I don't suppose it would have made a damn bit of difference if I had known. I was so stuck on Annie that if someone'd told me she was working in a house in Port Said, I still would have married her. Two months after we were married Zeeman sent for her to do a picture, and *I* didn't know she was going back to her old boy friend. I was in a play, and she was in a picture, and that was show business. The fact of the matter is that she only married me because Zeeman wouldn't get a divorce, and she was punishing him. Two months' punishment, and he was going crazy. That was our married life. Two months. We were married longer than that, but that was all we lived together. I was the chump of all time. When she finished her picture I expected her to come back to New York, but she stalled around and I finally got some sense in my head and my brother told me what was going on. So I called her up and issued an ultimatum—and I can still hear her laughing over the phone. I was crushed. I thought the world had come to an end. I began hitting this stuff and I finally went to George Chisolm and asked him as a friend to release me from my contract, which he did. The play was about ready to fold anyway, and so I went out to the coast and little Annie wouldn't even let me spend the night at her house. Out there she was honest enough. She told me why she'd married me and all the rest of it, but even then I wanted her back. 'You must be crazy,' she said. 'I'm Zeeman's girl.' She told me to go ahead and get a divorce. Zeeman would pay for it, or she'd pay for it. She even hinted that Zeeman might hold still for some extra money if I wanted it. Have you ever felt that way about a woman? You know she's sleeping with another guy, crazy about him, and still you want her back?"

"No, I don't think I have," I said. "I've had affairs with married women, but that's not the same thing. If I were married and my wife slept with another guy, that would end it for me."

"Then you must think I was a real chump, and I was. I said I'd go back to New York and let her think it over, and she said there was nothing *to* think over. She'd promised Zeeman never to sleep with me again and what the hell did I get out of staying married to her? Why not get a divorce? Well, back in New York I carried a torch, as we used to say, and I chased around and drank a lot, but even *I* couldn't go on like that forever and one day Zeeman's lawyer offered me $50,000 for a divorce and that was too much for me. I didn't take the money, but I played one hell of a big scene to an audience consisting of Zeeman's lawyer and my lawyer, and I must say I gave myself some very good lines. Cliché stuff, but damn good. Both lawyers said I was magnificent. Well, how often does an actor give up fifty thousand bucks to play a scene? I wouldn't have played it nearly as well if I'd been *paid* that much."

Charles Weston finished his drink and put the glass on the table with a decisively audible click. "Let's go to lunch," he said.

We were at different tables in the dining-room and our conversation was thus interrupted but, I knew, would continue. I could not believe in Weston's sudden characterization of himself as an actor playing a scene in a lawyer's office. The man who had been telling me the story of the marriage to Anna Lyman was not a wisecracking youth; he was very nearly an old man, permanently injured a long time ago, and badly wounded again in the past twenty-four hours. It had cost him an effort to circle the ship and face the witnesses to Anna Lyman's rudeness, and in so doing he had behaved admirably, with courage and grace. There was even some grace toward Anna Lyman; as though by pretending he had not been affected by her rudeness he was assuring her public that she had not really been rude, that it was intra-professional badinage, or rough kidding, as it was oftener called. But no one was deceived. She had been brutal.

The concert had consisted of two solos by an operatic baritone; some rather good feats of magic by an amateur, one of the television executives; two tap dances by the wife of another television executive, a former musical comedy star; and a dramatic reading by Anna Lyman, who was the only big star aboard the ship. Charles Weston was master of ceremonies. Anna Lyman's dramatic reading was a scene from *Perihelion,* a play in which she had made one of her biggest hits, and her first small rudeness was in asking the magician to play the tiny part of the clergyman whose questions cued her into her two long speeches. The magician literally read his lines from a play-script, and he was not good. Everyone wondered why Mr. Weston, a professional, had not been chosen instead. This snub was followed by another: when Weston moved the standing microphone out of the way, obviously implying that as a good actress she did not need mechanical help, she said, so all could hear: "Really, Mr. Weston? Don't you want them to hear me?" I had no doubt that if he had moved the microphone in front of her she would have told him to take it away. He could not win either way. Then, as she was taking her bow after playing the scene, Weston reached out his hand in courtly fashion, to lead her onstage. She ignored him and left him standing with out-stretched hand. Her final rudeness was at the end of the concert, when all the performers were taking a company bow. Anna Lyman placed herself between the baritone and the magician, linking arms with them and during the applause presenting her cheek for each of them to kiss. Weston and the tap-dancing woman stood to the right of the arm-in-arm trio, but unmistakably out of the position of prominence. It remained for Weston to thank the audience and to announce that dancing would take place in the lounge in fifteen minutes. In the middle of his announcement Anna Lyman burst into laughter at some private joke between her and the baritone, and she gathered together the baritone, the magician, and the tap-dancing woman and they marched off before Weston had quite finished. As I went to my room I saw Weston, uncomprehending, and alone for a few seconds until the purser, fully comprehending, went to him and shook his hand.

The purser was having one of his cocktail parties on the afternoon following the concert, and I was the first to arrive. "Have I got my facts all mixed up, or weren't Miss Lyman and Mr. Weston once husband and wife?" said the purser.

"They were, a long time ago," I said.

"Quite a show last night, wasn't it?"

"A show of bad manners, yes," I said.

"Well, yes it was, wasn't it?" he said. "Tell me, that is if you don't mind, was he terribly upset?"

I knew this purser, a man named Breckenridge, from voyages I had made in this and other ships of the line, and between us there was the friendliness of old acquaintance if not real friendship. He always provided those small extra courtesies that added to the pleasure of my trips, and he noticed things. He was a subtle, unobtrusive, humorous man, and I liked him. "Yes, he was upset," I said.

"I was afraid so," said Breckenridge. "I'd like to do something to—you know—restore his morale. He's leaving the ship at Cherbourg, and I won't get much chance to see him in the morning. Miss Lyman is staying aboard till Southampton. Can you think of anything I might do, that would buck him up?"

"Offhand, I can't."

"I've even looked up the date of his birth on the off chance that his birthday might be close. But it's months away, so that's out. Naturally I'll see that the French press make a fuss over him, but I'd like to do something tonight to make up for last night's disaster. The same people, you know."

"We could throw her overboard," I said.

"Oh, that occurred to me," said Breckenridge. "But that's an impulse I've learned to control after so many years in this job."

"I imagine so," I said.

"And it isn't so much that I'd like to do something *against* her as wanting to do something *for* him, although the end result may be the same. But she mustn't have cause for complaint, you know. It very definitely isn't part of my job to provide cause for complaint. Well, let's see if we can think of something between now and dinner-time. And here is Mrs. McMurray. How nice. Mrs. McMurray, may I present Mr. Malloy, Mr. James Malloy, the author?"

Mrs. McMurray and then Mr. and Mrs. Fishbein and Father Kelly and Sir John and Lady Pancoast and Professor Ropes and Charles Weston and the Countess di Palacci and Mr. Howe crowded into the purser's reception room, and I left to finish my packing before dinner, or so I said in making my departure. Actually I had finished my packing some hours earlier, and I left because Mrs. McMurray was most anxious to have me read the war letters of her son, which she did not have with her, but had apparently memorized. She was sure that in the right hands, the letters could be processed into another *Mr. Roberts*.

I wandered about and inevitably stopped at my usual table in the lounge and ordered an Americano. The room was almost deserted except for a group at a large table across the dance floor. There were about a dozen men and women at the table, and it seemed to me that I had seen precisely the same group when I had stopped in for coffee after lunch. I did not have to eavesdrop very closely to realize that they had all been drinking all afternoon. One of the men was drunk, and kept getting up from his chair to circle about, kissing the back of the women's necks. "Harry is a kissing bug," said one of the women.

"Harry is a kissing bug, Harry is a kissing bug," said Harry.

"Harry, sit down before you fall down," said his wife.

"That's what I'm trying to do, sit down before I fall down," said Harry.

"Does anybody know what time it is?" said one woman.

"Where?" said a man.

"Well, what the hell? If it's five o'clock it's five o'clock. Oh, no, that's right. We do something funny—" said the woman.

"You do something funny," said the man.

"I meant we do something funny with the clocks. Twenty minutes ahead, or forty minutes behind."

"Oh, *that's* what you meant," said the man. "You're either twenty minutes ahead or forty minutes behind."

"Oh, go to hell," said the woman. "Whatter you two whispering about? Anna Lyman, what are you whispering? Jack, what's she whispering?"

"You're too young to know," said Jack.

"I'll bet it was dirty," said the woman.

"It's ha' past six," said a man. "It's twenty-five of seven. It's the cocktail hour."

"Well then what are we waiting for?"

"Anna Lyman, I asked you a question. What were you two *whispering?*"

"When?" said Anna Lyman.

"A minute ago."

"A minute ago? I wasn't whispering—oh, when I was whispering to Jack? Oh, well I don't think I'll tell you."

"All right, then don't. But it isn't polite."

"Believe you me, it wouldn't be polite if I *didn't* whisper it," said Anna Lyman.

"What was it? We're all friends," said a man.

"We're not that good friends," said Anna Lyman. "At least not *yet.*"

"Oho, that sounds promising," said a man.

"Hey, who has some French money?" said another man.

"Every French whore," said another man.

"Hey, that's pretty good."

"No, now seriously, has anybody got any French money?" said the man. "Is the purser's office open?"

"Are you getting off at Cherbourg? I thought you were going to Southampton."

"You got me mixed up with somebody else. I'm getting off at Cherbourg."

"Let's everybody get mixed up with somebody else," said a woman.

"I think some already have," said another woman.

"Not me. I'm fancy-free," said Anna Lyman.

"You may be fancy, but I'll bet you're not free," said the woman.

"Just how did you mean that? Explain that remark," said Anna Lyman.

"I don't have to if I don't want to," said the woman.

"Well then get away from this table and take your kissing-bug with you. Go on, scram. I didn't invite you anyway, you and your kissing-bug. Kissing-bug. I'll bet." Anna Lyman whispered to Jack and Jack laughed.

"Come on, Harry. We won't stay where we aren't wanted."

"Too bad you didn't think of that hours ago," said Anna Lyman.

"I don't want to go," said Harry. "Anna, I think you're the greatest actress in the American theater."

"And I think you're the biggest pest on the Atlantic Ocean. And I wish you were at the bottom of it. So scram," said Anna Lyman.

"Huh?" said Harry.

"Come on, Harry. Come on, now."

There was a silence while Harry and wife made their departure, then Anna Lyman spoke. "Who *are* they, anyway? Does anybody here know them? I never saw them before this afternoon."

"Oh, what difference it make who they are? We'll never see them again," said Jack.

"Well, as far as that goes, I never expect to see any of you again," said Anna Lyman.

"I thought we were all having lunch in London the day after tomorrow. Quaglino's," said a man.

"I changed my mind," said Anna Lyman. "Look at Nosey over there, all by himself, taking notes for his next book. Hey, Nosey, did you get a good earful?"

"Yes, I got a pretty good earful, Anna," I said.

"Well, come on over and I'll really give you an earful," said Anna Lyman.

"No thanks," I said.

"I'll give you an earful about your friend Mr. Charles Weston," she said.

"Anna, why don't you shut up?" I said. I left some money on the table and started to go. Anna Lyman picked up a small club soda bottle and threw it at me, missing me by yards. "Close, but no cigar," I said.

"That's for you and your friend Mr. Charles Weston. I know you've been gabbing about me. Why don't you two go steady?"

I went out and walked around the promenade deck, in my first anger unable to think clearly. And then I remembered Breckenridge's eagerness to do something for Weston and I went to his room. The last of his guests, Father Kelly and Mr. Howe, were just leaving, and when they had gone I said: "I've thought of something."

"Good, let's have it," said Breckenridge.

"It's a bastard, but it'll make Weston look better than Anna Lyman."

"That's what we want," said Breckenridge.

"All right. All you have to do is get her on her feet and in front of a microphone. You won't have to do another damn thing. She'll do the rest."

At about eleven o'clock that evening the bingo game ended and Breckenridge spoke into the microphone. "That about does it, ladies and gentlemen, and now the next announcement will be made by that pre-eminent star of stage, screen and the telly, Miss Anna Lyman. Miss—Anna—Lyman, ladies and gentlemen. A *nice* hand for this great star."

Anna Lyman got up from her table, very drunk, and made her way to the microphone. "Good evening, ladies and jella-men, thizz your old friend Singing Sam," she said. "I forget what the hell I'm suppose to say. Oh, yes. There will be dancing until one o'clock. Where is the dancing gonna be?"

"The Little Lounge," said Breckenridge.

"The Little Lounge, that's right. Until one o'clock, so all you dear, lovely, stupid people—"

"Attaboy, Anna," the man named Jack shouted.

"Oh, you shut up. You bore me."

There was some laughter among the passengers, but it was nervous and unpleasant.

"What do I get for this, anyway?" said Anna Lyman. "I been playing one benefit after another, ever since I been on this God damn old tub."

Again there was laughter, tentative, as though the passengers were anticipating a big joke. Charles Weston, who was sitting at my table, said: "She'd better think of an exit line quick."

"I would like to say that I enjoyed every minute, every second of this trip, but if I did I'd be the biggest God damn liar that ever sailed the ocean blue."

Laughter again. This was more like it.

"We will now have the orchestra play 'Nearer My God to Thee' and all you jerks remember, women and children first. Personally, I like men first."

More laughter, then silence awaiting her next utterance. But her mind had stopped, and she stood unsteadily, looking slowly from right to left.

"She doesn't know how to get off," said Weston. "She's stoned." Then suddenly he rose and threaded his way among the passengers and took her by the arm. She looked at him gratefully, and without resisting she allowed him to steer her out of the room. All the way out, and for a few seconds after they had gone, the passengers applauded.

"It didn't work out quite as we'd expected," said Breckenridge, sitting at my table.

"What does?" I said.

The Lighter When Needed

The girl was having a good time. The orchestra was playing "From This Moment On," a dear old tune that dated back to dances before she had officially come out, before love, before second love and marriage and first baby, and a century-and-a-half before the besetting problems that for the moment she could forget. Dear old "From This Moment On." Dear old society bounce. Dear old Lester Lanin hat.

The young man she was dancing with was from the dinner party she had been to. He had been in the golf tournament that day and had won something and was feeling pretty good about it. "I don't often tie one on," he was saying, "but I've been trying to win one of those tournaments since I was seventeen years old."

"Goodness," said the girl.

"You mean did they have golf when I was seventeen years old? Sure. They had it when I was fifteen. We go back a long way together, golf and I. You don't play, do you?"

"Yes, I play."

"I'll bet you play pretty well, too, the way you said that. Have you ever played here? I don't think you ever made this scene before, did you, Mary? I've never seen you here."

"I've been here, but when I was very little. We came here one summer when my father was in the Navy. My mother used to come here, though."

"What do you shoot in? The low eighties, for instance?"

"I've been in the high eighties. Once I had an eighty-four, at home."

"That's good. That's not bad. If you can shoot consistently

around eighty-four you'll win most ladies' tournaments. Home. Where is home?"

"Pittsburgh."

"Oh, sure. *There's* a Pittsburgh man, a fellow townsman of yours. At least originally. I guess he doesn't live there any more."

"Who?"

"Arnold Abbott."

"Where? Where is Arnold Abbott? Point him out to me."

"Sitting at that table on the way out. Talking to Mrs. Rhodes. Or *not* talking to Mrs. Rhodes. The somewhat aging couple at that table. That's Arnold Abbott, and with him is Mrs. Llewellyn Rhodes. Why the interest in Arnold Abbott? Don't you know him?"

"No, I don't."

"Come from Pittsburgh and don't know Arnold Abbott? Mary, you must be one of the poor people. Or else you're one of those that don't approve of Arnold Abbott."

"Neither one. He's just a bit old for me. He was a bit old for my mother, as a matter of fact."

"I guess so. Boy, the stories they used to tell about him. And they must be true. You don't get a reputation for spending money like that unless you had the money. And spent it."

"I never heard about spending the money. I just heard he was the charm boy."

"Arnold Abbott? Are you sure? He and Mrs. Rhodes have been a thing ever since I can remember."

"Is there a Mr. Rhodes?"

"Would you like to touch him? You're only two people away from Lew Rhodes. The heavy man. Plaid dinner coat."

"Oh. Let's dance over toward Mr. Abbott. I want to get a closer look at him."

"Listen, I'll introduce you to the old boy if you like."

"No, I just want to see him close to."

Arnold Abbott sat straight up, watching the dancers. Once in a while Mrs. Rhodes would say something to him and he would nod, sometimes but not always adding a word or two of his own. She too sat up straight, holding her chin up, gazing at the dancers, now and then breaking her impassivity with a surprisingly bright smile of greeting to a couple dancing by, but as soon as the greeting was over a curtain seemed to come down over her face. An invisible curtain, that as it rolled down erased all animation from her expression. It was like that gesture of children, pretending to "wipe that smile off" their faces.

Mrs. Rhodes chain-smoked, and Arnold Abbott sat with his lighter in his hand, flicking it on when she needed it for a fresh cigarette, turning it over in the palm of his hand until it was needed again.

"Mary, they're going to get wise if you keep staring at them. Let's sit down with them for a minute?"

"Do you think they'd mind?"

"Mind? Nobody pays any attention to them. They'll sit that way all night."

"They seem perfectly content—but I would like to meet him, just to say hello to."

They danced over to Arnold Abbott's table, and Abbott rose. "Hello, Jack," he said.

"Hello, Jack," said Mrs. Rhodes.

"This is Mrs.—oh, Mary, what *is* your name?"

"Mrs. Elliott," she said.

"This is Mrs. Elliott, and Mary, this is Mr. Abbott. May we sit down a minute?"

"Do, please," said Mrs. Rhodes.

"Champagne, or Scotch, Mrs. Elliott?" said Arnold Abbott. "It's one or the other, I'm afraid. Or ginger ale. Somebody seems to be drinking ginger ale."

"She doesn't drink, so give her ginger ale. I'll personally have Scotch and just a little spoiler. Just a touch of plain water. You don't know each other, you two Pittsburghers?"

"Are you a Pittsburgher, Mrs. Elliott?" said Abbott.

"Well, I'm not, and Mrs. Rhodes isn't, so that more or less automatically leaves you two," said Jack. "I think it just about cancels us out, Mrs. Rhodes and I. Mrs. Rhodes, care to dance?"

"Oh, no thanks, Jack. I hardly ever."

"Are you a native Pittsburgher, or one by marriage?" said Abbott.

"Both. My maiden name was Husted."

"Oh, yes. Schenley Park district. I knew your father. He was younger, but I knew him. Doug Husted?"

"That's right."

"And your mother was a Pittsburgh girl? What was her name?"

"Jean Buckingham."

He nodded. "Mm-hmm. Knew her, too. They didn't live right in Pittsburgh, did they? The Buckinghams, I mean. Didn't they live out toward Rolling Rock?"

"*Then* they did."

"Are you down for the summer, Mrs. Elliott?" said Abbott.

"No, just for a long weekend. I'm staying at Frank and Mollie Holt's."

"Oh, yes. *They* had the big party tonight. Is your husband here?"

"No. He couldn't make it, unfortunately."

"I haven't asked you to dance, but I hope you'll forgive me. I don't like these crushes, do you? Do you remember those pictures of Eisenhower in India? And Kennedy? And those were friendly crowds. That's why I'm never late for the theatre. That last-minute pushing and shoving before the curtain goes up."

"I hate it, too," said the girl.

"Do you? You see what I mean, then? It doesn't mean that we have an aversion to people, does it? It's just that we don't like to be mauled, don't you think?"

"Really hate it," said the girl.

"Now isn't that interesting? We could have known each other for ten years and never known that we had that in common. What else do you feel that way about? How are you on, for instance—well, sudden noises? I could fall sound asleep in the very middle of that orchestra. But if I'm at home reading in the evening, and there's an unusual sudden noise, I can't concentrate again until I've found out what it was."

"I don't think that bothers me so much. We live in an apartment in town, and there are a lot of sudden, unusual noises."

"Oh, yes. But you do object to being moved along by a crowd?"

"Hate it."

His hair was almost all grey, brushed down smoothly, and she noticed that he had a habit of running his hand over it gently to keep it smooth. His eyelids were heavy, and the lower lids especially made her think that they were full of tears of sadness. When he smiled, the last muscles to move were those that controlled the area about his eyes, and the smile was over before it was quite complete.

Now, without seeming to have noticed that Mrs. Rhodes had taken a fresh cigarette from a square gold box, he held out his lighter for her. Mrs. Rhodes, in conversation with the younger man, muttered her thanks to Abbott without interrupting what she was saying to Jack. And yet, the girl noticed, the lighting of the cigarette maintained the closeness between Arnold Abbott and Mrs. Rhodes, in spite of the separate conversations in which they were taking part.

"I've heard a lot about you, Mr. Abbott," said the girl.

"You've heard a lot about me, my dear?" He smiled. "There *was* a *time,* I must admit. But I thought I'd stopped giving people anything to talk about—oh, before you were born. What on earth would people say about me in your lifetime?"

"It was nice."

"Oh? Well, that's a comfort. It wasn't always, you know. I, I, uh, supplied food for conversation. Uh, food for conversation. Those little sandwiches that they serve at tea-time. That kind of, uh, food for conversation." He was not altogether satisfied, and he went on: "That kind of food for that kind of conversation. That's what I wanted to say. But that was before you were born."

"That isn't what I meant, though."

"Not the parties I used to give? That's chiefly what I'm remembered for."

"Not by everybody. I never heard about the parties—well, till tonight. But I did hear about the charm."

His face went blank. "In connection with me? Charm? My dear, I'm afraid you've got me mixed with my brother, Stuart Abbott. He was the one that had the charm. But there again, before you were born. He was killed in World War One."

"*Arnold* Abbott. I've never *heard* of *Stuart* Abbott."

"Oh, I'm afraid there's been a mistake somewhere. Much as I'd like to appropriate some of it for myself, I'm afraid—"

"What are *you* two talking about?" said Mrs. Rhodes.

Abbott smiled faintly. "Will you tell her, Mrs. Elliott?"

"I'd love to. I was just telling Mr. Abbott that I'd always heard of his great charm."

Mrs. Rhodes gave a little laugh. "Ho! He's the most charming man I've ever known in all my life. I'm sorry, Jack, but that's a flat statement. Hope for you when you get older, but this is the most charming man I've ever known."

"Me?"

"Why, yes, of course, Arnold."

"I don't see it," said Abbott.

Mrs. Rhodes looked at the girl. "He doesn't see it," she said. "Arnold, you're a fool. Here is by all odds the most attractive young woman at this party, and she hasn't looked at another man since she sat down at this table. Was your mother in love with this man, Mrs. Elliott?"

"I think she must have been."

"You can see why she would have been," said Mrs. Rhodes.

"Oh, yes."

"But I didn't know your mother, not really. She must have been—I don't know—probably in pigtails, when I still lived in Pittsburgh."

"What difference does that make?" said Mrs. Rhodes. "If you have it, it works on females of all ages. Isn't that true, Mrs. Elliott?"

"Absolutely true."

"As long as I've known you, you've never given me the slightest hint of this," said Abbott.

"Too cagey for that, my love."

The music stopped, and Llewellyn Rhodes and a youngish woman came to the table. "Oh, now who is this? I'm Llewellyn Rhodes. What's your name? Another worshiper at the shrine of A. Abbott?"

"Yes. I'm Mary Elliott."

"Well, Mary, you're barking up the wrong tree. Hello, Jack. Hear you finally won one. What did you do? Bribe your caddy? Who was your partner?"

"Frank Holt, and I carried him all the way."

"The hell you say. Oh, Mrs. Elliott, this is Mrs. Corbin."

"We've got to get back to our party," said Jack.

"You go, and leave Mrs. Elliott. I'll see if I can't seduce her away from A. Abbott."

"I'd love to have you try, but I'm afraid we must go back," said the girl.

"Come to lunch tomorrow," said Mrs. Rhodes. "Jack, you come, too."

"Not on that kind of an invitation, I won't," said Jack.

"Well, that's the best you'll get. Mrs. Elliott, I invite you, too," said Llewellyn Rhodes. "Arnold, you'll be there, as always?"

"Yes, thank you, I'll be there," said Arnold Abbott.

"I think my hostess is having some people, but could I come after lunch?" said the girl.

"Any time. It's buffet, and starts at two," said Mrs. Rhodes. "Come for lunch if you can, and if not, drop in and have coffee with us. Bring anyone you like."

It was easy to get away from Mollie Hunt's Sunday lunch; the hung-over wanted to take naps or stay close to the bar, the athletic were off to the golf links and the tennis courts. Mary Elliott borrowed Mollie's car and drove alone to the Rhodeses' beach house, which was a fair distance from their main house.

Approaching the beach house from the parking area Mary Elliott saw with relief that only Mrs. Rhodes and Arnold Abbott were there, and sitting as they had sat the night before, with the difference that now they were in beach clothes, watching the ocean and two bathers instead of the crush of dancers. She regretted that her sponge-rubber soles gave them no warning of her approach, but she was not ungrateful for the opportunity to see them this way, so close, so quiet, so—resigned.

She had to walk around and in front of them before they were aware of her presence, and Arnold Abbott immediately got to his feet. He was wearing yellow slacks and a club blazer, with a Paisley neckerchief. He had on sun glasses. Mrs. Rhodes, likewise wearing sun glasses, had on a pajama suit that buttoned to the neck. "Oh, there you are," said Mrs. Rhodes. "How nice of you to come."

"Good morning, Mrs. Elliott. Some coffee? Large or small?"

"Good morning, Mrs. Rhodes. Mr. Abbott. Could I have a small coffee?"

"It's right here. Sugar? Cream?"

"One sugar, please, and black. Have you been in?" said Mary Elliott.

"Oh, yes. Hours ago. We were in and out before you were awake, I daresay," said Mrs. Rhodes. There was not the slightest doubt that "we" referred to Abbott and herself.

"I don't expose my shanks to the public view any more than I have to."

"You have good legs, so hush," said Mrs. Rhodes.

"Mrs. Elliott, your visit has brought on a rush of compliments. Mrs. Rhodes isn't always this kind."

"No I'm not, am I? But how else can I hope to compete with someone as pretty as this young woman. Did you stay long at the dance?"

"Forever," said Mary Elliott.

"So did Lew, my husband. I hear that there was another skinny-dipping party."

"Nude bathing," said Arnold Abbott.

"Yes, I got it."

"Oh, dear. Do you remember the first one, Arnold? At least the first one I ever went to."

"I'd be very damn ungallant if I said I didn't. Of course I remember."

"That was on a Saturday night too. Sunday afternoon I was packed off to my uncle's camp in the Adirondacks, to spend the rest of that summer in the woods. Mollie Hunt's mother was sent abroad. And at least one other girl was put in a private hospital in Westchester. Physical examinations that I assure you were totally unnecessary. The whole thing couldn't have been more innocent."

"May I correct you? Sinless. Not innocent," said Abbott.

"I stand corrected. Sinless. Forty years ago, almost. I sometimes think that we'd all have been better off if we'd been allowed to run riot that night. Let nature take its course, man and his mate. I'm the only one of those girls that hasn't been divorced at least once. And . . ." She could not have said more plainly in words: "And look at me."

"The same is true of the men, except me. All the men have been through the mill once or twice."

"Do you think that's the answer, Mrs. Rhodes?" said Mary Elliott. "Throw the girls and boys together, and let nature take its course?"

"Oh—I wouldn't say that. I wouldn't say it to you, because I don't know anything about your marital status."

"I have a husband and two children."

Mrs. Rhodes looked at her quickly, sharply, and Mary Elliott nodded. "Yes, I'm temporarily separated from my husband. We hope it's temporary—or do we? I don't know."

"Well, I guess that's not so unusual these days," said Mrs. Rhodes. "Isn't that a perfectly innocuous comment?"

"Yes, perfectly. In this case I'm the problem one. I'm the one that wants out."

"What years are you thinking about, Mrs. Elliott?" said Mrs. Rhodes.

"What years am I thinking about? Oh, you mean am I thinking about the present, or the future. Why, the present. I *have* thought about the future, of course."

"Tell her, Arnold. That's why she came. Isn't it, Mrs. Elliott? You wanted the advice of two aging lovebirds, Arnold and I."

"You embarrass her," said Abbott.

"Not really, a young woman who's had two children. I don't embarrass you, do I, my dear?"

"I guess not. Except I didn't think it was written all over me. I thought I was more subtle."

"Subtlety is much more embarrassing in the long run," said Mrs. Rhodes. "And what you want is help. It's a great compliment to us, your wanting to talk to us, but Arnold is the better talker. You talk, Arnold."

"I'll answer any questions," said Abbott.

"Mrs. Rhodes said what years was I thinking of, and my immediate response was the present. But you and Mrs. Rhodes, you must have been in love all these years. I don't know when I've seen two people of any age so much in love. And yet you never got married. *Have* you been in love all these years?"

"Well, over thirty of them," said Abbott.

"I'll help," said Mrs. Rhodes. "Why didn't we marry? Because I was married when we fell in love, and loving Arnold wasn't a good enough reason to divorce my husband. Does that shock you?"

"Yes it does, a little. It's so old-fashioned that it's almost super-modern. And coming from you."

"Call me old-fashioned. I don't mind. But I hate divorce. I hated it as much as I hated what I was doing to Arnold. You heard of the Arnold Abbott parties and Arnold Abbott the playboy. Now you know why he gave those parties, why he— all those movie actresses and English ladies of title. Those were the bad years, Mrs. Elliott. That's why I asked you what years you were thinking about. Now we have our good years. I see him every day, every day of my life. We don't happen to sleep in the same house together every night, but except for those hours we're together more than most husbands and wives. And will be, as long as we're both alive. The bad years are over for us."

"I know what the next question is going to be—or would be if Mrs. Elliott weren't so nice," said Abbott.

"Of course," said Mrs. Rhodes. "But she may ask it if she wants to."

"I do ask it, because I must. What happens when one of you dies?"

Mrs. Rhodes put her hand on Arnold Abbott's hand, the hand that continually turned his cigarette lighter over and over. "We have a solution to that, haven't we, my love?"

Arnold Abbott smiled.

The Pioneer Hep-Cat

Every time I come here you all seem to want to hear some more about Red Watson. I declare, if I ever thought there would have been such a demand for stories about Red Watson I would have sat down and written a book about him. I've told you story after story about people that I thought were much more interesting than Reds. Big people. People that made something of themselves instead of a man that nobody ever heard of outside of two or three counties in Pennsylvania, and even here the name Red Watson never meant a thing to the people generally considered worthwhile. You young people nowadays, I'd much rather tell you about a mine-boy, a young lad that worked in a breaker but was rescued from that and went away to a seminary and became a cardinal. We had one young fellow in this town that most of you don't even know he was born here, but he was. I'm talking about General Henry T. Corrigan. Lieutenant-General Corrigan was born right here in this town and sold papers here till his family moved away. I used to play ball with Henny Corrigan, out at the old Fourteenth Street schoolyard. He caught, and I played shortstop on a team we used to have, called the Athletics. I guess *some* of you would be able to guess where we got that name. Those of you that can't guess, we didn't get the name from Kansas City, if that's any hint. And I might mention that a few years ago, when I was attending the newspaper editors' convention in New York City, the principal speaker was none other than Lieutenant-General Henry T. Corrigan, all decorated with a chestful of ribbons and surrounded by famous editors and publishers from all over the country, all wanting to ask him questions about the Strategic Air Command. And there I was, not a very important person I must admit, but when it came my turn to meet the general he looked at me and then he looked at my name on the convention badge we were all wearing and he burst into a big smile. "Winky Breslin!" he said. That was my nickname when I was young. "Winky, you old son of a gun," and with that he took me by the arm and the two of us went over and sat down and you'd be surprised how many local people he remembered, some now dead and gone, but quite a few still living. Some of them the parents and grandparents of you here today. I ran a little story about it at the time, but I guess not many of you saw it. In any case, that's the kind of man I'd rather talk about, but every time I'm asked to speak at one of your Press Club suppers your representative either asks me outright or gives me a strong hint to the effect that the person you'd like me to talk about is Red Watson. I don't understand it.

I'd understand it a lot better if Reds were still alive, and some rock-and-roll idol. But he passed away before you even had swing, let alone rock-and-roll. And it isn't as if there were any of his old records floating around. Reds never made a record in his life. I don't say he wouldn't have been good, or popular. He would have been. If they'd ever heard of him outside of this section of the country, he might have been, well, not as popular as Gene Austin, or the early Crosby. He had a totally different style. As I've told you before, or your predecessors, there's nobody around today to compare him with. The styles of singing have changed so much from when Reds was around. Beginning I'd say with Rudy Vallee and then on to Russ Columbo and Bing, the crooners came in. All toned down as far as the volume was concerned and running ahead of or behind the beat. Not Reds. When Red Watson let go, he belted out a song in a way that you'd think was going to break every window in the place. And on the beat. Perfectly on the beat. And he was a tenor. The singers nowadays, if you can classify them at all, you'd have to call them baritones. But Reds was a tenor, a high tenor.

I was thinking the other evening, I happened to be watching a show on TV and one of your Tommy Sandses or Bobby Darins came on and those squealing girls, that I suspect are paid, began screeching. And I thought to myself, Red Watson hit a higher note than any of those bobby-soxers, but when he did it it was music. Yes, it was. That's the sad part about it that there aren't any records around to prove it.

When I was the age of some of you, or a little older, the name bands used to come through this region, playing the parks in the summer and the ballrooms in the winter. I notice you don't get many big bands any more. In fact, I'm told there aren't any, to speak of. But when I was a young fellow there wasn't a name band in the country that didn't play here and all around here. And over and over again. It won't mean anything to you, but I can remember one night when Paul Whiteman, with a thirty-five-piece band, was playing a one-nighter and only two miles away was Vincent Lopez, with *his* big band. How to compare it nowadays, it would be like—I don't know the names of the bands any more. Ray Conniff and Neal Hefti, I guess. But I can tell you this much, one of the singers with Whiteman was a young practically unknown singer with a trio, named Bing Crosby. And if memory serves, the famous Bix Beiderbecke was also with Whiteman around that time. Those of you that collect records will recognize the name Bix Beiderbecke. First name, Leon. Played cornet. Also piano. You have a musician today, Bushkin, he plays piano and horn, but Bushkin was never idolized the way Bix was. They even wrote a novel about him, and if I'm not mistaken, it was turned into a New York play.

Well, what I don't understand is your interest in Red Watson, because Red died around the time I've been speaking of. He was popular *before* Whiteman and Lopez started playing the parks and the ballrooms in this section. The big band then was the Sirens. The Scranton Sirens. Of course you've heard about the Sirens. Both Dorseys played with the Sirens. We had that in our paper when Tommy and Jimmy passed on there a little while ago, and I got a lot of letters from some of your mothers and fathers and I guess your grandparents, that still loved the Scranton Sirens. But with all due credit to the Dorsey boys, the real attraction was Red Watson. Mind you, it was a fine band. None better in the whole United States, because I heard them all. All the big ones of that day. Fletcher Henderson. Earl Fuller. The Barbary Coast. Art Hickman. Oh, my, just saying the names takes me back. Ted Weems. The Original Dixieland. Goldkette. Paul Biese. The Coon-Sanders Kansas City Nighthawks. Jack Chapman. I can remember more than once driving all the way to Atlantic City in a friend of mine's flivver, just to hear a band at the Steel Pier, and then *driving back the same night* so I'd be at work in the morning. That was a long trip then. It's still a long trip, but when we made it—I guess there isn't one of you here that would know how to vulcanize an inner tube. I can see you don't even know what I'm talking about. In those days you could go in any five-and-ten and buy an ignition key for your Ford, and it had a square hole cut in the key to turn on the tank for your headlights. No, you don't register. I might as well be talking about whip-sockets.

You must bear in mind, when I graduated from this school, in other words the same age as some of you within sound of my voice, jazz was such a new thing that they weren't even sure how to spell it. Some spelt it j, a, s, s, and I've seen Victrola records with Jass Band instead of Jazz Band printed on the label. But I'll tell you one thing. If you ever heard Red Watson sing "Jazz Me" you knew it was spelt with two z's. To be quite frank with you, I'm always hesitant about coming here and speaking about Red Watson, because as the I hope respectable editor of a family newspaper, I don't consider Reds a proper subject for a talk before a group of young high school students. If I weren't so convinced that you know as much about some things as I do, I'd have to decline your invitations. Or at least I'd choose another subject. But then I always say to myself, "These young people today, they know a lot more than I did when I was their age, about certain things, and maybe I can sneak over a moral lesson somehow or other."

And I can. You see, boys and girls, or young ladies and gentlemen, Red Watson was an example of great talent wasted. He had a God-given voice, completely untrained, but I was told that he was given many offers to go away and take singing lessons. He came from a little town outside of Scranton and several rich people up there wanted to pay for his vocal training, but he'd have no part of it.

The story was—and those of you that were here two years ago must excuse me for repeating it—but according to the story that I always heard, and I could never summon up the courage to ask Reds to verify it—Reds was a breaker-boy, too. Like that cardinal. But when he was about thirteen years old, working in the breaker, his arm got caught in the conveyor and was so badly mangled that they had to amputate above the elbow. Thirteen, maybe fourteen years old. You can imagine what dreadful torture he must have gone through. The accident itself, and then the amputation which left him with a stump about, well, he used to fold up his left sleeve and pin it with a safety pin just under the shoulder. He was an orphan, living with relatives, and after he got out of the hospital he tried selling papers, but that wasn't as easy as you might think. A paper route was just about impossible to get, and selling papers on street corners was just as hard. You had to fight for the busy corners, and Reds only had one arm. So he used to get a few papers and go around to the saloons and try to sell them there, but somehow or other they found out that he could sing, and he began to make as much money singing for nickels and dimes, and pennies, as he could selling papers. At the age of fourteen he was known in all the saloons, and sometimes the miners used to get him liquored up, even though he was hardly more than a child. They'd give him whiskey and get him singing, and he told me himself that by the time he was sixteen years of age, he could drink beer all night long without getting intoxicated. Whiskey was another matter, but beer he could drink till the cows came home, and it wouldn't affect him. That much of the story is true, because Reds told me himself.

This part I can't vouch for, but you can take it for whatever you think it's worth. I've never been able to make up my mind one way or the other whether it's just imagination on someone's part, or based on the truth, and I never asked Reds. But according to the story that a lot of people believed, when Reds wanted to hit his high note, he'd think back on the time he lost his arm and the pain would come back to him and he'd scream. I don't know. It wasn't the kind of question I could ever ask Reds, although I got to know him pretty well. But I remember hearing a story about Caruso, too. He was supposed to be the greatest tenor that ever lived, and they say he hit his highest note when he was in pain from an abscess in his lung. Who knows? I have a hard time believing it, but I think Caruso died of an abscessed lung, or the effects of it, so there may be some connection between the pain and the high note. I know that Red Watson's stump always bothered him, and he became a heavy drinker to take his mind off the pain. But he wouldn't see a doctor. Oh, no. He said another operation—well, not to be squeamish about it, the stump was so short that there was hardly anything left of the arm, and where would they go after that? He said to me once that he wasn't like most people, because he knew exactly how long he had to live. He said he didn't have to measure it in years, like most people, but in a few inches of bone.

People ask me what Reds was like, because when I was a young fellow, I confess that it wasn't only my duty as a reporter that took me into the various places where alcoholic beverages were for sale. And I guess I was one of the pioneer hep-cats, although they didn't use that expression, and in fact I'm told by the modern generation that you don't even say hep any more. Hip? Or is that passé, too? Well, anyway, I know that the musicians used to call us alligators, because we'd stand in front of a band with our mouths open like alligators, so if you ever heard the expression, "Greetings, 'Gate," that's where it came from. The alligators. And I was one back in the early Twenties, just after the first World War. When we wanted to hear a good jazz band, an orchestra that didn't play waltzes all night, we had to go to the public dances on Saturday nights at the Armory, and whenever I hear you young people being called juvenile delinquents, I have to remind myself that there was plenty of it when I was about your age. Those dances at the Armory, I think the admission was fifty cents for ladies and seventy-five for gents. It may have been less. Fifty for gents and twenty-five for ladies. We had a name for those dances. We called them rock fights. In fact, we didn't even bother to call them by the full name, rock fights. We used to say, "Are you going out to the rocky tonight?" And out of that grew another nickname, the quarry. We used to speak of the rock fights as the quarry. In front of our parents we could say, "I'll see you at the quarry," and our fathers and mothers would think we were talking about going for a swim in the quarry dam. Oh, we were just as wild as you think you are, or almost.

You know, I don't often get to see TV in the daytime, but last year when I was laid up with arthritis I watched you kids, or young people of your generation, dancing on an afternoon program. And one great difference between you and us, *you* don't seem to be having a good time. You hardly even smile at each other. It wasn't that way in my youth. Good Lord, everybody was laughing and jumping around, racing all over the floor when they played a one-step. Now you just glare at your partner and she spins around and you pull her towards you. You don't have any fun. Incidentally, I don't think you dance very well, either, but that's a matter of opinion. I remember a fast tune called "Taxi!" When they played that you moved fast or you got out of the way. That was good exercise, and fun. There'd always be a few fellows pretty well liquored up and they'd take a spill, but that was part of the fun. And there was always at least one fist fight at the rockies. At least one. You see, most of the girls at those dances, they were high school age, but they weren't going to school. They had working permits and a lot of them worked in the silk mill, the box factories, and some of them were servant girls. You hear the expression, going steady, and you think it's new. Well, it isn't. Girls and boys went steady then, and what that meant was that a girl would go to a rock fight and pay her own way in, dance with as many fellows as she wanted to, but she always went home with the boy she was going steady with, and if she tried to go home with somebody else, there'd be a fist fight. That's really where those dances got the name, rock fights. They didn't throw rocks, and they wouldn't have called them rocks anyway. They called them goonies. A gooney was a piece of stone that boys would throw at each other on the way home from school. In some sections of town the boys used to in the winter take a gooney and wrap it up in snow. A snowball with a gooney in it could inflict a lot of damage. See this scar here in back of my ear? That was a gooney wrapped in snow. I never knew who or what hit me at the time, but a bunch of boys from Third Street school were waiting for us boys from Fourteenth Street one afternoon, and I was one of the casualties. My poor mother when they brought me home!

Well, you're very patient with me and I don't know why it is that the mere mention of Red Watson opens up the floodgates of reminiscence, only it's more about me than about Reds. I started to answer the question, what was he like? Well, in spite of his name being Watson, he had a real Irish face, no doubt about it. He wasn't a very big fellow. In fact he was on the short side. But he looked a lot older than his real age. When I first knew him he was only about twenty years of age, but he looked easily thirty. Face was almost purple from drink and he was already starting to get bald. He was usually smiling and he was *always* smiling when he got up to sing. He'd flirt with all the girls around the bandstand that gathered around when he took his place to sing. He was a cake-eater. That was slang for fellows that dressed a certain way. They were also called sharpies. A sharpie, or a cake-eater, wore a suit that was padded at the shoulders and tight at the waist, then flared out. It had exaggerated peaked lapels that went all the way up to the shoulders, hence the name sharpie. The coat was buttoned at the waist with link buttons, sometimes three pairs of link buttons. The cuffs flared out and they were divided. The trousers were very wide at the bottom, and if you were really sharp, they were laced at the sides, like Spanish bullfighters'. The sharpies wore either tiny bow ties, on an elastic, or very narrow four-in-hands. And they wore low-cut vests so that the whole shirt-front was exposed. Tiny little collars. Hair was plastered down with vaseline, and the cake-eaters wore side-burns. And that was the way Reds dressed, with one sleeve pinned up to his shoulder. You boys and girls are even too young to remember the zoot suit of twenty years ago, which was different from the cake-eater's outfit, but if Reds had lived in a later era, he'd have worn a zoot suit. I think.

As to his personality, he had two. One when he was singing, and the other when he wasn't. When he wasn't singing he wasn't a very remarkable young fellow. Good-natured as a rule, although quick-tempered at times. He liked the girls, and they certainly liked him, not because of his looks, you can be sure of that. And not only because of his singing. He had a car, a yellow Marmon roadster it was, and I went on a couple of rides with him after we became friendly, and we'd drive to Reading and Philadelphia, places where they didn't know him at all, and we'd stop some place to get a sandwich. If they had a waitress that was halfway good-looking Reds would start to kid her a little, and always end up with a date. Sometimes he had no intention of keeping the date, but he just had to con-vince himself that he was irresistible. And he usually was. In fact, too much so. I guess I knew him two or three years before he happened to mention that he was married when he was eighteen and had a baby daughter. He supported his wife and child, but he wasn't a good husband or father by any stretch of the imagination. I could understand his not getting along with his wife, but I've never been able to understand why he didn't seem to take the slightest interest in his daughter. But that was a closed subject, and I decided it was none of my business. In my opinion Reds was one of those people that seem to have a talent for certain things, such as music, writing, art, but they're deficient in the common-ordinary, everyday things that you don't hear so much about, but they're an accomplishment nevertheless. I mean the simple, ordinary things like the sacrifices that some of your mothers and fathers make for you boys and girls, that you may not even know of unless you stop to think about it. Forty boys and girls in this room. How many of you girls had a new dress this year? Don't raise your hands, because my next question is, how many of you girls got a new dress this year because your mother got one for you instead of for herself? And you boys. How many of you have cars—and don't *you* raise your hands, either. Because some of you must know, if you stop to think, that you wouldn't have a car if your fathers didn't decide to spend that money on you instead of on themselves. This isn't a lecture. I'm not at all sure what it is except an informal talk by a newspaper editor to some young people that are interested in the field of journalism. And you don't especially want me to talk about the newspaper business. But in fairness to you, if I'm invited to talk about a colorful character whose example I wouldn't want you to follow, in fairness to you I have to call your attention to the fact that you all have fathers and mothers that do set a good example in love and kindness, and patience and understanding. My conscience won't let me talk about Red Watson, and glamorize him, unless I point out to you that Reds only lived to be twenty-five years of age, and as far as I know—and I knew him pretty well—he never did anything for anybody but himself. With that understanding, I'll continue talking about him. But I had to make that clear. He never did anything for anybody but himself, and he died—well, I'll save that till later, inasmuch as half the members of your Press Club probably are hearing about Reds for the first time. The seniors and juniors were here when I spoke two years ago, but the sophomores and freshmen weren't.

So to continue about his two personalities. The one, he was fun to be with, but I only saw him on his visits to town, maybe four times a year. I don't know how he'd have been as a steady diet. Selfish, and no respect for girls whatsoever, and as I said before, he seemed good-natured, but he had a quick temper, too. I guess if I had to be completely frank about it, I was flattered because he wanted me for a friend. I was just a young fellow starting out in the newspaper business, and I used to enjoy it when some of our local prizefighters and celebrities would call me by my nickname. And in that little world, Red Watson was as big a celebrity as Kid Lefty Williams or Young Packy Corbett, two fighters we had at the time, both since passed on. Made me feel big, even though I had some misgivings about Reds.

But I'll tell you this, you always forgot what he was like when he got up to sing. I mean the things about him that I didn't go along with. It'd come his turn to sing a number and he'd go behind the piano and take a swig out of a pint bottle of whiskey, and a couple of fast drags on his cigarette, and then he'd go to the middle of the bandstand and stand there grinning at the people gathering around while the orchestra played a full chorus. And then he'd close his eyes and put his head back and start singing. It didn't make any difference what the number was. It might be a sort of a risqué song like "Jazz Me" or it might be a ballad. But the dancing would stop and everybody would stand still, as close to the bandstand as they could get, and you'd look at their faces and they were hypnotized. They'd be moving in time to the rhythm, but not dancing, and it was almost as though he were singing for them. Not only to them, but for them. I can remember thinking of him as a misplaced choir boy, and the crowd around him some of the toughest characters in the county. The girls just as tough as the young fellows. They'd all stop chewing gum while he was singing, and even when he happened to be singing a dirty song, they'd smile, but they didn't laugh. And if it was a ballad, he could make them cry. There's a high note in "Poor Butterfly"—"but if he don't come *back*"—that *always* made them cry. Then he'd finish his song and open his eyes and smile at them while they yelled and applauded, and he'd wink at them, and they'd start dancing again. One chorus. No encores, one song every half an hour. That was his agreement. He was paid fifty dollars a night with the band. But then after the dance was over we'd all meet at some saloon and after he had enough to drink you couldn't stop him. He'd get up on the bar and sing whatever you asked him, till the joint closed. The next night it'd be the same thing in some other town, six nights a week.

How he kept it up as long as he did, I don't know. He slept all day, but when he had his breakfast, at seven o'clock in the evening, that was often the only meal he ate all day. By eight o'clock he was hitting the bottle, and usually at half past eight, sometimes nine, he'd be with the band, ready to sing his first number. Naturally he couldn't keep that up, and he began failing to show up with the band. The first few times that happened, he got away with it, but then the crowds were disappointed and the managers of the dance-halls were afraid to advertise that he was coming. Then the band broke up and for about a year I didn't see Reds at all. I heard he was forming his own band, Red Watson's Syncopators. And he was leading the band, himself. But that didn't last long. Two or three months of that was all he could stand. And all the musicians could stand. He'd order special arrangements, but then he wouldn't pay for them, and he got in trouble with the union about paying his musicians, and the first thing he knew he was put on the unfair list. After that he just disappeared, and whenever I'd ask about him from people around Wilkes-Barre and Scranton they had conflicting reports, probably all true. I heard he'd opened a speakeasy in Wilkes-Barre and someone else told me he was in prison for non-support of his wife and child. The last time I saw him I was in Scranton, covering a United Mine Workers meeting, and I asked around and finally tracked him down. I asked him how things were, and not knowing I knew anything about him, he put on a great show. He said he'd got rid of the yellow Marmon and was buying a Wills Sainte-Clare. That was an expensive car. He had offers to go in vaudeville, et cetera, et cetera. And he wouldn't let me pay the check. We were in a speakeasy where his credit must have been good, because he told the bartender to put it on his tab and the bartender made a face, but said okay, Reds. I had a feeling that the bartender would have much preferred my cash. So I said to Reds, approaching the subject in a roundabout way, I said I was glad things were better. And he asked me what I meant by better, and I said I'd heard he'd a little trouble. Well, such vituperation! Such invective! And all directed at me. I was a cheap newspaper reporter that never made more than thirty dollars a week in my life, which was true, but I was also a snooping so-and-so, probably sent there by his wife's lawyer to find out all I could. He took a beer bottle off the bar and smashed the neck off it. That was a weapon known as a Glasgie Slasher, and he held it up to my face and said I deserved to have my eyes gouged out, snooping around and asking questions. I didn't dare move, for fear I'd get that thing in my face. And then I guess because I hadn't made any move he dropped the broken bottle in the gutter in front of the bar, and ran out.

I was given a drink by the bartender, and I needed it after that experience. "He'll murder somebody yet," the bartender said. "He's suspicious of everybody." I asked the bartender how Reds lived, and the man told me. I don't have to go into that here, but Reds was about as low as a man can get to make a living. Any real man would rather dig ditches, but Reds only had one arm and all he ever did was sing. Anyway, he had a place to live and a little cash. And then the bartender, a nice fellow, asked me how well I'd known Reds. Had Reds ever told me that he didn't measure his life by years, but inches of bone? And I said yes, he'd said that to me some years back. And the bartender said, "Well, he's heard the bad news. No more inches, and no more years. Months, and more likely weeks." Then he said he just hoped Reds got through the next couple of months without killing somebody.

Well, he did, boys and girls. The next I heard of Reds was a few weeks later at the office, the city editor handed me a little squib that came in over the U.P. wire. Patrick Watson, known throughout the coal region as Red Watson, the popular tenor, was found dead on the bandstand of the Alhambra dance-hall in Scranton. It was summer, the wrong time of the year for a dance at the Alhambra. So I got Scranton on the phone and checked. Yes, they found Reds at the Alhambra. Nobody else in the place, which was closed for the summer, and the watchman had no idea what Reds had gone there for. There was nothing worth stealing.

But you and I know why he went there, don't we? Yes, I think as I look at you, you know.

Thank you.

The Sharks

Mr. Plastic Rain Cover for His Hat was taking his daily constitutional. "There he goes, Mr. Plastic Rain Cover," said Betty Denning from her position at the window.

"Let him," said her husband.

"But come here and look at him," said Betty Denning.

"I've seen him."

"No, come here. You've only seen him once."

"Oh—" her husband growled, but he got up, took off his reading glasses and went to the window, still holding his newspaper.

"He's looking up here," said Betty Denning.

"Why don't you wave to him?"

"Shall I?" she said. "I wonder what he'd do."

"Well, you can easily find out."

"No, then we'd have him all the time."

"How do you know?"

"He's the type. I wonder which house he has?"

"How do you know he has a house?"

"Because he's on his way back. Yesterday and the day before, he walked toward the west, then fifteen minutes later he walked toward the east and then I didn't see him again. He's going eastward now, which means he's on the way home. That's how I know he has somebody's house. Also, there are no hotels toward the east of us and there are four toward the west."

"Well, you could ask in the village."

"I think I will."

"And then when you have that information safely tucked

away? . . . All you have to do is take the field glasses and see where he leaves the beach. We could easily figure out whose house he has."

"I don't want to stand out in the rain just for that," she said. "And that wouldn't tell me his name."

"Why do you want to know his name? I thought you just wanted to know whose house he has."

"I always like to know people's names when they arouse my curiosity."

"I must say I have damn little curiosity about a man that would wear one of those things. God, they're awful. And the worst of it is, people that wear them never wear good hats."

"You're a sartorial snob," said Betty Denning.

"Indeed I am, and that's hardly news."

"But you don't get anything out of it."

"Of course I do. I get a lot out of it. For instance, a man that wears one of those things isn't likely to be in my circle of friends or any of my friends' circle of friends."

"I know," she said. "I know all that. Therefore you've put your finger on it, why I'm curious about Mr. Plastic Rain Cover."

"How? Or why?"

"Should be obvious," she said. "Who among our circle of friends has rented their house to Mr. Plastic? He's been there now at least three days. Whose house is for rent this summer?"

"Nobody's, up in that direction. All the beach houses are occupied."

"Then who is he visiting?" she said.

"I think you'd better get on the horn and ask around. You could start by calling Fred at the police station."

"Oh, I wouldn't want to do that."

"Fred would know."

"No, I'll ask around more casually when I do the marketing."

"You really don't want to have your mystery spoiled."

"Perhaps," she said.

He began to sing. " 'Perhaps—she's putting on her wraps—

perhaps—she's putting on her wraps perhaps.' Now may I finish Mr. Joseph Alsop?"

"Do," she said.

The three-day nor'easter came to an end in the middle of the afternoon, and they went for a swim. "God, the beach is positively filthy," he said.

"You could pick up some driftwood," she said.

"And put it all in a neat pile, and then some kids would come along for a beach picnic and steal it all. I'm through breaking my back for the little bastards."

"It's good exercise if you remember to bend your knees. Uh-oh. We're going to have company. Mr. Plastic Cover."

"I forgot to ask you. Did you find out anything about him?"

"Tell you later."

Mr. Plastic Cover, now not wearing a hat, came toward them. He had on bathing trunks and a Madras jacket. He was walking eastward, and now there could be no doubt that he would stop. "Good afternoon," he said.

"Good afternoon," they said.

"I was admiring your house earlier. That's your house, isn't it?"

"Yes it is," said Betty Denning.

"I was wondering, is it on the market?"

"No, not really," said Betty Denning.

"Not at *all*," said Denning. "We rented it last summer, but to friends."

"But you don't want to sell. Well, I don't blame you. Nice to see the sun out again."

"Very nice," said Denning.

"Well—pleasure talking to you," said Mr. Plastic Cover.

He moved on and when he was out of earshot Denning said, "What'd you find out?"

"He has the Warings' house for the rest of the season, but he's not renting it."

"Who is he?"

"He's supposed to be some relation of Mona Waring's. He

seems to have plenty of money. He's from out west and he brought a car with a chauffeur and two of his own servants besides, a cook and a maid."

"You wouldn't think to look at him that he had that kind of money. Aren't the Warings coming down?"

"They were, but now they're going abroad instead. A sudden change of plans."

"A sudden deal with Mr. Hat Cover."

"We don't have to call him Mr. Hat Cover any more. His name is Joshua B. Simmons."

"Well, Joshua's going to be in the hospital with second degree burns if he doesn't stay out of the sun. Did you notice his legs, and his nose and forehead? Wow!"

"I don't think that was the sun. I think that's just Mr. Joshua B. Simmons. He put in a big order for liquor. I found that out. And he buys only the most expensive cuts at the meat market. He gets all the New York and Chicago papers and the air mail edition of the London *Times*. He's having five people down this weekend. And he rented one of the large boxes at the post office, the kind that they usually rent to stores."

"You did quite a job on him. Is he married?"

"I had no trouble at all. The natives were more than willing to talk about him. Naturally they all speak well of him. He's spending money. This is his first summer on Long Island. I haven't answered your question about his marital status because I didn't do so well there. Nobody seems to know. The cook does the marketing by telephone. I guess Mona gave her the names of all the clerks."

"Why would he be interested in buying our house?"

"I think that was just to make conversation."

"More than likely. Well, he's exhausted that topic, and now maybe he won't bother us any more."

"Oh, don't be too hopeful. Tomorrow I'm going to the library and look him up in *Who's Who*. I've become fascinated by him."

Betty Denning was not the only one who was fascinated by

Joshua B. Simmons. It soon transpired that he was asking owners of all the most desirable summer houses if their places were for sale, invariably getting no for an answer, and always commenting that he did not blame them. "I don't think he wants to buy," said Betty Denning. "I think it's just a conversational gambit he thought up."

The Warings apparently had made some arrangement for Mr. Simmons to be, in Betty Denning's word, whisked into the golf club and the beach club. It had not been difficult; as soon as his name came up some of the governors recognized it; he was on the board of one of the big Chicago banks and of other imposing corporations. "He was graduated from the University of Chicago," Betty Denning told her husband. "I've never known anyone that graduated from the University of Chicago, have you?"

"Walter Eckersall. Eckie. Great football player before my time, but then he used to officiate. He let me stay in a game once when he could have put me out. There was a Princeton guard named Marlow that was holding me on every play, and I finally smacked him one. Eckie saw me do it and he said to me, 'All right, he had it coming to him, but don't do that again.' And I didn't."

"Was that Tubby Marlow?"

"Yes."

"You didn't hit him hard enough. Anyway, Mr. Joshua B. Simmons is sixty-four years old and not married. Do you want to know what he belongs to?"

"Sure."

"Well, a whole list of clubs in Chicago, and Phi Beta Kappa, and something called Sigma Nu. Unfortunately the *Who's Who* in the village library isn't very up-to-date. In fact, 1940. Nothing about the war, and of course he could have got married since 1940, but I doubt it."

"So do I."

"Do you think the same thing I do?"

"Yes. I think he's a fag."

"You mean his walk?" said Betty Denning.

"Everything about him, not only his walk. I think he's an old queen."

"Well, you're right. I told you he was having five guests last weekend. He did. All men."

"Well, I hope that's not any criterion. I've had five men here during the duck-shooting."

"Huh. That's not what I worry about when you have five men here. Quite the opposite."

"I've never had any women here when you weren't here, and so stop your innuendoes. What about Mr. Simmons and his house party?"

"I'll get to it. Three of the men were young, two of them were about the same age as Simmons."

"Well, that's handy. They could square-dance."

"They would have been better off if they had. Saturday night they all got very tight and went for a moonlight dip without any clothes on. Old Mrs. Howard was kept awake all night and she reported them to Fred. You can imagine her, looking out and seeing six naked men and looking around for six naked women. Fred and one of the other policemen went up to investigate, but by that time they'd all got in cars and gone some place else. But Mr. Simmons has been given his first warning."

"Fred tell you all this?"

"He didn't tell me but he told Jim Carter and Peg relayed it to me. Jim is boiling mad at the Warings, especially Mona."

"Maybe she didn't know about her uncle, or whatever he is."

"Uncle is right. Her mother's brother. No, I can't go along with that. Mona's never liked it here much, and I think she and Billy just took off for Europe and let Uncle Joshua run riot. You can't tell me *Billy* doesn't know about Uncle Joshua."

"No, I guess not. But Billy will overlook anything if he can make a buck out of it, and I imagine Uncle Joshua sends a few bucks his way. He's probably Simmons's New York broker, and if there's thirty-five cents in it, Billy wouldn't care what the old guy did."

"He's having another houseful this weekend, Mr. Simmons."

"I wonder why we haven't seen him on the beach?" said Denning.

"Oh, I've seen him, when you were taking your nap. He prances by, always looks up, but he doesn't see me. Maybe he has his eye on you, dear."

"Maybe. I've always been popular with both sexes. Next time he walks by, wave to him."

"I will not. I don't find the situation very funny. I love this old place, and when an old pansy and his pansy friends start coming here, things aren't the same."

"Things aren't the same anyway, old girl, as you well know. No, it isn't a funny situation. I'm glad our boys are grown up and married."

"Well, Jim and Peg wish theirs were. The thing is that this nasty old man has been inquiring about properties, and the first thing you know we'll have a colony of them. That'll be the end of this place."

"You thought Simmons was just making conversation."

"I was wrong. He made a firm offer to the Ludlows. Forty-five thousand, and they may take him up."

"They wouldn't! Well, maybe they would. They're not getting any younger and their children don't come here any more. Good God, that would bring Simmons that much closer to our house."

"Why don't you and Jim Carter buy the Ludlows', as an investment?"

"I'm afraid that isn't the solution. We might be able to beat him to it on the Ludlow property, but Jim and I can't go on buying every property Simmons bids on."

"What is the solution?"

"There is none. With the best of good will in the world, people like the Ludlows can't afford to let sentiment, nostalgia, interfere."

"You mean that pansy's going to win? He's going to take over and ruin this lovely old place, where we've had such good times? I can't bear it."

"I've often said to you, the Lord doesn't care much about money. Look who He allows to have it."

"That's no comfort, I must say."

"I didn't offer it as comfort, Betty. We're not young ourselves, so let's try to enjoy this summer and next. After that? Well . . ."

"You wouldn't *sell?*"

"I wouldn't *not* sell if the Simmons types get a toehold."

"Oh, no! Can't we *do* something?"

"Suggest something."

"Let's just kill Mr. Simmons."

"In some ways, the only sensible solution." He squeezed her hand. "You wouldn't even kill a shark."

"What good does it do? Kill the shark, and it only attracts a lot of other sharks."

"Well, we've had a lot of good years here. Between us close to eighty."

"The sixty together were the best. I mean thirty."

On the next Sunday night Mr. Joshua B. Simmons, of Chicago, was murdered. He was stabbed in the chest and neck repeatedly by a young man named Charles W. Randolph. It was all on the radio and in the papers, in time, in fact, for the Monday morning papers.

"Do you know who that is?" said Betty Denning. "That's the boy they call Dipstick Charley, he's always so polite when we get gas. Do you know which one I mean?"

"Sure." Denning was reading the newspaper account of the murder, which differed very little from accounts of similar murders in similar circumstances. The millionaire Chicagoan had taken friends to the station to put them on the Sunday evening train to New York. He had then, according to police, gone to a "cocktail lounge" and there encountered Randolph, whom he invited to his fashionable beach residence for a drink. He made overtures to Randolph, who claimed to have repulsed him, and a scuffle occurred, during which Randolph stabbed him, using a dagger-like letter opener. Randolph then fled in the murdered man's Cadillac sedan and was arrested by state police who suspected him of driving a stolen car. Randolph was brought back to the Simmons beach house, reenacted the crime, and signed a full confession. He was being held without bail in the county prison. There were photographs of Randolph in his army uniform and of Simmons in a business suit, of the dagger-like letter opener and of the beach house and Simmons's Cadillac, and of Randolph in custody between Fred and a state policeman.

Even the tabloids could not keep the story built up for more than the fourth day. "Poor old Mrs. Howard's had a heart attack," said Betty Denning. "She's over at the clinic. Reporters and photographers and you have no idea how many morbid people, mistaking her house for the Warings'."

"They've started to come here."

"What on earth for?"

"The sharks. Do you remember what you said about killing a shark—it only attracts other sharks?"

"Oh, don't remind me."

"It was a very astute remark. While you were doing the marketing I had a caller. He wanted to know if this house was for sale. I said no, and he said he'd been given to understand by a certain friend of his that maybe we might sell. I asked him who the friend was, and he said, 'Well if you must know, it was Josh—Josh Simmons, poor boy.' Poor boy."

"What did you say?"

"I said, 'You get your ass out of here before I kick you out.' He said, 'Oh, you wouldn't do that, would you?' So I showed him I would."

"You kicked him?"

"Of course I kicked him. He won't be back, but others like him will be. You were certainly right about the sharks."

"Oh, dear. Oh, dear," she said.

The Girl from California

The limousine stopped and the driver paid the toll and waited
for his change. The attendant in the toll booth looked at the
couple in the back of the car and smiled. "Hyuh, Vince. Hello,
Barbara," he said.

"Hyuh, fella," said Vincent Merino.

"Hello," said Barbara Wade Merino.

"Going to Trenton, Vince?" said the attendant.

"That's right."

"I knew you was from Trenton. Good luck, Vince. So long,
Barbara," said the attendant.

"Thanks, fella," said Vincent Merino. The car moved along.
"He knew I was from Trenton."

"Jesus, I'm glad to get out of that tunnel," said his wife. "I
get the worst claustrophobia in a tunnel."

"Well, with me it's the opposite. I hate to ride in an airplane."

"I know," said Barbara. "Jack Spratt could eat no fat, his
wife could eat no lean."

"We're gonna both of us eat plenty of fat where we're
headed for. Today you forget about the calories. *And don't be
nervous.* Take it easy. My fathernmother are no more different
than your fathernmother. My mother aint even Italian."

"I know. You told me."

He tried to distract her. "You see them broken-down shacks
and all? That used to be a pig farm, and you know something?
The guy that owned it ran for President of the United States."

"Who cares?"

"Well, your mothernfather are always talking about America, the land of opportunity. Now you can tell them you seen a pig farm on the Jersey meadows, and the owner run for President the United States. I never heard of that in California."

"Thanks for trying to take my mind off it, but I wish today was over. What else will we do besides eat?"

"I don't know. Maybe the old man will make the load. If he's as nervous as you are, he could easily make the load. He could be starting right now. I hope not, though. He starts hitting the grappa, by the time we get there he could be passed out."

"How long does it take for us to get there?"

"About an hour and a half, I guess."

"Maybe I could go to sleep."

"You mean now?"

"Yes. You got any objections?"

"No, no objections if it'll calm you down."

"You sound disappointed."

"Not exactly, but if you go to sleep you're not gonna see New Jersey. I just thought, I know a hell of a lot about California, but you never saw New Jersey except from ten thousand feet up."

"On the train from Washington last year, when I was making those personal appearances."

"Yeah. The only reason why you took the train was because the whole East was fogged in. A hell of a lot you saw that time. All right, go to sleep if it'll relax you."

She put her hand on his cheek. "You can show me New Jersey on the way back."

"Sure. That's when *I'll* want to sleep."

"I wish we were both in bed right now," she said.

"Cut that out, Barbara. You're taking an unfair advantage."

"Oh, go to hell," she said, and turned her back and pulled the robe over her shoulder.

In a little while she fell asleep. She was always able to fall asleep. On the set, when she was making a picture, she could finish a take and go to her portable dressing-room and sack right out. Or if they were home and had had a fight, she would slam the bedroom door and in five minutes' time she would be sound asleep. "With Bobbie it's a form of escape," her sister said. "She's very fortunate in that respect."

"I'm built like a cow, so it's only natural," Barbara would say.

"Don't knock the build," Vincent had said. "It gets you two hundred gees a picture. And me. It got you me. You'd of been one of them boy types I wouldn't of looked at you. I wouldn't of *looked* at you."

The smell of a cigarette or the sound of the radio would wake her up, so he postponed a smoke and sat in silence as the car sped along the Turnpike . . . Then he realized that he had been asleep, too. He looked out on both sides but failed to recognize his surroundings. From his watch he made a quick calculation; they were ten, fifteen—more or less—minutes from the Trenton exit. He put his hand on his wife's hip and shook gently.

"Bobbie. Barbara. Get with it, kid."

"Huh? Huh? What? Where are we? Oh. Hello. Are we there yet?"

"I figured we're not far from it."

"Ask him. The driver," she said.

Vincent pressed the switch that lowered the division. "How much longer we got, driver?"

"We'll be in Trenton in five minutes, Mr. Merino. Then it's up to you."

"Thanks," said Vincent. "How about a little coffee?"

"All right," she said. "I'll do it." She poured coffee from a vacuum bottle. She put a lump of sugar in his cup and drank hers black and unsweetened. He gave her a lighted cigarette.

"Well, we're almost there," he said.

"Is the fellow from *Life* going to be there?"

"I don't know for sure. I doubt it. As soon as I told them it wasn't gonna be every Italian in Mercer County they lost interest."

She looked at herself in her vanity mirror. "Thank God for that, at least. Anyway they make a habit of sending a photographer and bossing everybody around, and that's the last you ever hear of it."

"I know. I don't even know for sure if my brother's coming from Hazleton. Both of my sisters will be there, that's for sure. But I bet their husbands have to work. My other brother Pat, him and another fella from Villanova. You couldn't *keep* them away."

"I hope I get them all straight."

"Pat's the college boy and he looks something like me. My eldest sister is France. Frances. My younger sister is Kitty. She's about the same age as you."

"Frances is the older one and Kitty's the younger one. And Pat's the college boy, and resembles you. What about your brothers-in-law? What are their names?"

"Take my advice and don't find out their names. That way my sisters won't get jealous, if you don't know their husbands' names. Anyway, I bet they won't be there."

"Who else?"

"The priest. Father Burke. And maybe Walter Appolino and his wife. He's a senator. State senator. If he wants us to pose for a picture, why, we better."

"What's the priest gonna be there for?"

"Well, maybe he won't come, being's we got married by a justice of the peace."

"Are they all going to make a stink about that? Because if they do, I'm going to turn right around and go back to New York. I don't have to take anything from them."

"You won't have to. Kitty's husband aint a Catholic and her kids aren't being raised Catholic. I aint worried about that, so don't you be. The only trouble I predict is if my old man makes the load, and Pat starts trying to make a pass at you. I'll give the son of a bitch a punch in the mouth if he does."

"Listen to who's talking."

"Right. Exactly. Listen to who's talking is right. He patterns himself after me because just because he happens to be Vince Merino's brother. Well, hands off Vince Merino's wife, Pasquale Merino, if you don't want to go back to Villanova minus a couple teeth. And don't you encourage him. Don't stand too close to him. He don't need any encouragement in that direction."

"Is there any of your old girl friends going to be there?"

"Not unless my brother Ed comes from Hazleton. I used to date her before Ed did."

"Did you score with her? I don't have to ask, I guess."

"Well, if you don't have to ask, why ask? What's the use of asking a question that you know the answer beforehand? Sure I scored, but not after she started dating Ed. Only Ed don't believe that. I don't think Ed'll be there."

"She probably throws it up to him that she could have married you."

"Hey, you're pretty smart. That's what she does do. And is she ever wrong? I wouldn't of married her even if I'd of kept on living in Trenton."

"Why not?"

"Because she thought she owned me, and she didn't."

"*I* own you, don't I?"

"Well, I guess so, but that was my own free will. I wanted to own you, so I let you own me. But I never wanted to own her. What the hell? I did own her and I never even wanted to. She was all right for then, but I never intended to be stuck in Trenton all my life. I hope they don't come. I hope there's only my two parents, and my sisters without their stupid husbands, and my kid brother if he behaves himself. Oh, Walter Appolino. Walter is more used to meeting celebrities, like he goes to New York all the time and every time he goes to the Stork Club. Walter was the first guy I ever knew that went to the Stork Club, when I was sixteen or seventeen years of age."

"Large deal."

"Come off it, Bobbie. When you were sixteen who did *you* know that went to the Stork Club?"

"When I was sixteen—well, *seven*teen—I was going there myself."

"Yeah, I guess so." Vincent now gave his full attention to the task of directing the driver through the streets of Trenton. In time they stopped at a detached white frame house which had a front porch, a front and back yard, and a one-car garage in the rear. "This is it," he said. "Is it worse or better than you expected?"

"Frankly, better."

He smiled. "My old man's a bricklayer at Roebling's. I bet he makes better than your old man."

"I didn't say he didn't. That's your mother in the doorway?"

"Yeah, that's Mom. Hey, Mom, wuddia say?" He got out of the car and embraced his mother. Barbara followed him. "Three guesses who this is."

"How do you do, Mrs. Merino?" said Barbara.

"I'm pleased to meet you, Barbara." Mrs. Merino shook hands with her daughter-in-law. "Come on in and be introduced to the others."

"Who all's here, Mom?" said Vincent. "Did Pop make his load?"

"What kind of talk is that? No, he didn't make any load. Is that the way you talk about your father?"

"Forget it. Who else is inside?"

"The Appolinos. Walter and Gertrude Appolino. He's the state senator. Senator Appolino, but a great friend of ours. And his wife. And my two daughters. Vince's two sisters, Frances and Catherine. Both married. Barbara, do you want to go upstairs and freshen up first, or will I introduce you to the others?"

There was no need to reply; all the others came out on the porch and Mrs. Merino made the introductions. As soon as all the names were mentioned there was a sudden, blank silence.

"All right, everybody stand here like a bunch of dummies," said Vincent. "Let's go inside or we'll have the whole neighborhood standing around." Two girls and a boy in their early teens came forward with autograph books and held them out to Barbara and Vincent.

"Put 'To my old friend Johnny DiScalso,' " said the boy.

"The hell I will," said Vincent. "Who are you? Pete Di-Scalso's kid?"

"Yeah."

"Your old man arrested me for driving without a license. You're lucky I sign my name for you. Who are you, girl?"

"Mary Murphy."

"Which Murphy? Your old man sell washing machines?"

"He used to but not any more."

"Is this your sister?"

"Yeah, I'm her sister. Monica Murphy. Our father used to sell washing machines but now he don't any more."

"Leo Murphy, Vince," said Senator Appolino. "I got him fixed up as an attendant over in the State House. Very good man, Vince, you know what I mean."

"Oh, sure. Leo's all right. Give my regards to your father, girls."

"Thanks, Vince," said the senator. "All right, girls, run along now. And, Vince?"

"What?"

"Forgive and forget. Put 'To my old friend Johnny DiScalso.' I'd appreciate it, you know?"

"Votes?" said Vincent.

"Sixteen guaranteed, sometimes more," said the senator. "And, Barbara, you, if you don't mind? Just something personal for Johnny? 'To my friend,' or something like that? Appreciate it. Appreciate it very much, Barbara."

"All right," said Barbara.

"Fine. Fine," said the senator. "Vince, I'm sorry Gert and I have to go to a colored funeral, but we'll be back later and your parents said it'd be all right if I brought a few friends back with us. Okay?"

"I don't know how long we'll *be* here, Walt."

"Yeah, but I'd appreciate it very *much*, Vince. I kind of promised these people, you know what I mean?"

"How many, Walt?"

"Under forty or fifty. They just want to say hello and like

shake hands with you and Barbara. Ten minutes of your time, that's all, and a couple pictures for the papers. Ten minutes, fifteen minutes."

"If we're still here, Walt," said Vincent.

"Yeah. Well, I'd appreciate it, Vince. I really would. I more or less promised them, and I sure would hate to disappoint them. It'd look funny, you know, you coming back to the old home town and didn't see anybody. You know what some people would say, and I wouldn't want them saying that about Vince Merino and his lovely bride Barbara. I'm not gonna say goodbye, folks. We'll be back before you know it."

The senator and his wife departed, and the group on the front porch went inside to the parlor. "Pop, wud you tell Walt?" said Vincent after the women went upstairs.

"Huh. I didn't tell him, he told me. Right away he seen it in the paper you and Barbara was in New York, would you be coming to Trenton? Your mother told him yes. Here he is."

"You need him?"

"Well, I don't *need* him. Maybe he needs me as much as I need him, but you got that crazy brother Pat, you never know what he's gonna do, so it's no use antagonizing Walt."

"Yeah. Where is Pat?"

"He'll be here, him and his roommate with his second-hand, third-hand Jag. The roommate keeps the car in Philly. They'll end up with a broken neck, the two of them. Well, it won't be long till the army gets him. He won't be staying at Villanova much longer."

"Why don't you knock a little sense into him?"

"Wait'll you see him and you'll know why. You didn't see him since he filled out. He could take you or me or maybe the two of us."

"Huh. How's Ed?"

"Ed? Oh, him and Karen are like cats and dogs. She was here in Trenton a couple weeks ago but she never came near us. She was here for two weeks last summer and never came around. They're all washed up. Ed was here in March or April, sometime, and he stayed drunk for two days. Your mother and I couldn't get anything out of him, but you can put two and two together."

"Well, give me some *good* news. Are France and Kitty all right?"

"Oh, I guess they're all right. Kitty was fooling around with some married man till your mother and France, and Father Burke got into it. Harry was responsible for that, but that don't give Kitty grounds to fool around with a married man."

"But France is all right?"

"Yeah. Well, you'd never know it now that France was a pretty girl when she was around sixteen."

"No."

"You got a good-looking girl for a wife. She even looks better in real life. You gonna have kids?"

"Well, not for a while."

"Yeah, I see what you mean. She put on weight you might have a hard time getting it off again. I don't blame you. Save your money and then have the kids. What is she? Twenty-three or four?"

"She's twenty-four."

"Well, maybe she could have one the year after next and then wait a while."

"How are *you*, Pop?"

"Oh, hell, I'm all right, I guess. Why? Do I look as if I wasn't?"

"You look all right. How old are you now?"

"I'm a day older than I was this time yesterday. How old do you think I am?"

"I don't know. Around fifty?"

"Well, close. I'm forty-eight. I was bothered with this hernia last year, you remember when I was operated? I was made foreman, so I don't have as much heavy work."

"You still like your booze?"

"Huh. You wouldn't of had the nerve to ask me that five years ago. I don't drink no more. A little beer and a little wine, but no hard stuff. I cut out the hard stuff. Monday mornings I used to start getting dizzy up on the scaffolding, so I quit everything but a little wine and beer. But Ed's making up for it, and so's Pat. They'll scrape him up off the road one of these days. He's a wise guy, you can't tell him anything that he don't know all the answers. Is that your Chrysler outside?"

"Hired."

"What are you driving now?"

"I got an Austin-Healey, but I had it for two years and I'm thinking of getting something else. I only put about fourteen thousand miles on it, being away so much making pictures overseas."

"What happens with Barbara when you go away like that?"

"Well, the only time since we were married, she was in the same picture."

"Yeah, but I see where you're going to Portugal and she won't be there. What do you do then?"

"I don't know. It never happened since we were married."

Vince's father pointed a finger at him. "Start a baby. Take my advice and start a baby right away. Maybe it'll keep you straight. I don't know her, but I know you. The only thing that'll keep you straight is maybe if you have a baby started. Maybe. Forget the money, Vince. Forget it."

"Pop?"

"What?"

"How are you and Mom getting along?"

"What kind of a question is that to ask me? Who the hell do you think you are?"

"Oh-ho-ho. I touched a sore spot. Accidentally I touched a sore spot. Are you fooling around with somebody, Pop?"

"Did she say something to you?"

"When would she have a chance to say something to me?"

"Over the phone she could have."

"No, she didn't say nothing. But you took it so big, as soon as I asked you how you were getting along. I knew if it wasn't the booze it's either a woman or money. And you were never stingy. I'll give you that."

Andrew Merino's blue Tyrolean eyes showed trouble. He put his hand on his son's knee. "You're a man now, Vince, but some things you're still not old enough. I don't want to talk about it."

"Who is she? She older, younger? Married?"

"When I tell you this, it's the God's honest truth. I was never in bed with her."

"Oh, Pop. Come off it. You're a pretty good-looking guy."

"Oh, hell, I was as bad as you or Pat back in my twenties."

"Does Mom know the woman?"

"Don't say it that way, Vince. That sounds as if there was something, and there aint. I have a cup of coffee with her."

"At her house?"

"I never been inside her house."

"Does she feel for you?"

Andrew Merino hesitated, then nodded. "But she won't see me after work. She's in the office."

"Then what's Mom's beef?"

"Huh. Wait till you're married that long. We were twenty years of age when we got married. You'll find out."

"I come here to show my wife a typical Italian family, my folks. My Italian father and my Irish mother by the name of Merino. Mr. and Mrs. Andrew Merino, Trenton, New Jersey. And you wanta know something? The old lady give me a look when I got out of the car, and right away, *right away* I got the whole picture. You hung back and didn't hardly say anything. Then I thought to myself, Pop had this operation a year ago."

"No, it aint the operation, Vince."

"Oh, you don't have to tell me now, but that's what I thought. Five years ago you wouldn't of let Walt Appolino be the take-charge guy, not in your house. You sure you don't have a guilty conscience, Pop?"

"I got a guilty conscience for my thoughts. But what do you want, Vince? Do you want me to tell my own son that I don't love his mother? That's my guilty conscience, but I don't have to tell that in confession."

"You go to confession?"

"No."

"You don't, hey?"

"No, and that's why your mother thinks there's something going on. I been two years without making my Easter duty. She says to me, next Sunday's the last chance to make your Easter duty. I tell her to mind her own business. Then she's positive I'm going to bed with Violet Constantino."

"Oh, Violet Constantino. Johnny's wife. That's who it is? She used to be a good-looking woman."

"She didn't only used to be. But Violet don't have to make her Easter duty. She's a Methodist, so your mother can't keep tabs on her that way."

"Pop, you gotta get this thing straightened out."

"I know. I know, Vince. To tell you the truth, I was hoping I could talk to you about it. I can't talk to nobody else."

"What does Johnny Constantino think of the whole thing?"

"Johnny Constantino," said Andrew Merino. He shook his head. "Him and I go bowling every Wednesday night."

"That don't answer my question, Pop."

"It wasn't suppose to. I was just thinking, him and I go bowling every Wednesday night, plus I give him a ride home from lodge meeting once a month. And I wonder. We been friends all our life, from boyhood, then I reach the age of forty-six and all of a sudden I fall in love with Violet, his wife for twenty years. I don't get anywhere with her, a cup of coffee in the morning, and 'How are you?' "

"Wuddia mean you never been inside her house?"

"I never been inside of their house. The two women don't get along. When do you remember me or your mother being inside the Constantinos'? Never."

"Well, they always lived the other side of town somewhere."

"If they lived over there next door it would be the same."

"Why don't Mom like her?"

"Well, the last couple years you can figure it out why. But before that your mother didn't like any woman that had a job. Violet had a diploma from commercial school and she could always get a job in an office. The best your mother could ever get was waitress or extra saleslady at Christmas. It wasn't her fault. She didn't have the education. But she used to say Violet was high-hatting her. But if it wasn't that she'd of found some other excuse. She don't like Johnny, either. Your mother don't like many people outside of her own family. The Appolinos and Father Burke. But she don't like ordinary people. I'm surprised those Murphy kids and Johnny DiScalso had the nerve to come here today. She chases any kids that run across our lawn."

"Not when I was a kid."

"Oh, not when you was a kid. You know why. She wanted all the kids playing in our yard. That way she'd know where you were. And France. And Kitty. And Ed. But the minute they all grew up, no more kids playing on the front lawn. No more kids in the back yard. It's a wonder France or Kitty ever got a husband. 'Go down and tell them it's time to go home,' she used to say, when one of the girls had a boy friend. Eleven o'clock! Those girls were brought up strict. They might as well of had Father Burke living in the house. You didn't see any of that, but I saw plenty. And what could I do? Give her any opposition and she'd say, all right, if I wanted to be responsible. You remember young Audrey Detmer?"

"On Bergen Street?"

"Got knocked up when she was fifteen and they had five boys that she didn't know which one was the father. 'You want another Audrey Detmer in your own family?' she used to say. Your mother. Well, we almost did, with Kitty. Kitty's first was six months after she got married."

"Listen, Pop, I could of told you a few things about Kitty."

"I wouldn't of been surprised. Well, here they come down. You want a shot of something, or a cocktail? What kind of a cocktail does Barbara drink?"

"She can't handle it. She'll drink a little vino, and that's all I want."

Andrew Merino grinned. "You still got the weak stomach?"

"For liquor."

"Well, you can get drunk on wine, but you don't get Irish-drunk like Ed and Pat."

"Yeah? What about you and your grappa?"

"I never drank it because I liked it, Vince. I only drank it for the effect."

"To forget about Mom, huh?"

"Now, now, you don't have to say that," said Andrew Merino.

"What don't he have to say?" said his wife.

"I was talking to *him,* Kate. I wasn't talking to you," said Andrew Merino.

"All right, have your secrets," said Kate Merino. "I guess we're gonna have to start eating without Pat and his friend. Barbara, you sit anywhere you want to."

"She's suppose to sit next to me," said Andrew Merino.

"Well, she don't have to if she don't want to."

"The place of honor is on my right."

"I was gonna have her sit next to Walt, but he had to go to some funeral," said Kate Merino.

"Yeah. I wish it was his," said Andrew Merino. "Sit here, Barbara. You like Italian food?"

"I love it."

"You got any real Italian restaurants out in Hollywood?"

"Oh, sure. Lots of them."

"Well, my wife is Irish but she knows how to cook Italian food, so dig in. You know what that is, don't you? Thatsa leetla beeta Eyetalian prawn? You like da prawn?"

"Oh, cut the dialect, Pop," said Kitty.

"I no talka the dialect. Me speaka da perfect English, yes-no, Barbara?"

"Sure. Perfect."

"Lay off, Pop," said Vince.

The meal proceeded, and since they were all good eaters, the conversation was incidental to the enjoyment of the food. "I want to help you with the dishes, Mrs. Merino," said Barbara.

"No, we'll leave them till later, but thanks for making the offer," said Kate Merino.

"Would you smoke a cigar, Vince? I got some cigars," said Andrew Merino.

"No thanks, Pop. Maybe Barbara would like one."

"Don't give them that kind of an impression," said Barbara. "But I'll have a cigarette if you'll give me one."

"I ate so much I don't want to get up from the table. I don't want to move," said Vince, lighting his wife's cigarette. He passed his case along to the others, and they lit their own.

"Boy, solid gold," said France. "Can I read what it says inside?"

"From the studio. I know it by heart. 'To Vincent Merino for the Oscar he earned and will some day get. 1958.' That's when everybody said I was gonna get the Oscar."

"It shows what the studio thought of you, and that's what counts," said his mother.

"You're so *right* it's what counts," said Vince.

"We all sat here that night watching the TV," said France. "We were just as nervous as you were, if not more so. They put the TV camera on you, and you sure were nervous."

"Who did you go to that with, sweetie?" said Barbara.

"Renee Remy, who else? Who did you?"

"I don't remember."

"Brad Hicks," said France. "The TV director."

"Figures," said Vince.

"Well, I didn't know you then."

"Was that the front door?" said Kate Merino. "That'll be Pat, just when we're all finished eating."

Kitty Merino got up and went to the hall door. They all watched her, and she held her hand to her mouth and whispered to them: "It's *Karen*."

"Oh, Christ," said Andrew Merino.

"Anybody home?" Karen's voice called out.

"We're all back here, Karen," said Kitty. "Come on back."

"Is that you, Karen?" called Kate Merino. "We're in the dining-room." Then, to the others: "Now don't anybody say anything, then maybe she won't stay. Just be polite."

Karen appeared in the hall doorway. "Hello, everybody. A regular family gathering, eh? Hello, Mrs. Merino. Pop. Kitty. France. Oh, hello, Vince."

"Hello, Karen," said Vince. "Ed with you?"

"No, he had to work but he sends everybody regards."

"Introduce you to my wife. Barbara, this is Karen, my brother Ed's wife."

"Hello, Karen," said Barbara, extending a hand.

"Well, naturally I recognize you, but I'm pleased to meet you personally."

"Did you have your lunch, Karen?" said Kate Merino. "We're keeping stuff warm for Pat and a friend of his, but the way it looks I don't think they're gonna be here."

"Oh, I ate over an hour ago, thanks. At my family's."

"How's your mother?" said Kate Merino.

"She seems better."

"Karen's mother had a serious operation for cancer," said Kate.

"They think they got it all," said Karen.

"We called up when she was in the hospital," said France.

"She told me, yes. She appreciated it."

"How's Ed?" said Vince.

"Oh, just the same."

"I wish he would of come with you. I didn't see Ed since you moved to Hazleton."

"Is it that long? Well, you'd still recognize him."

"Will you have a drink of something, Karen?" said Andrew Merino.

"No thanks. Ed takes care of that department," said Karen.

"Is Ed lushing it up?" said Vince.

"Now, Vincent!" said his mother.

"Yes, speak to him, even if he is the big movie star," said Karen. "Ed's your own brother."

"I just asked a simple question."

"Yeah. Simple," said Karen. "You ever been to Trenton before, Barbara?"

"No, only passed through it on the train."

"Yeah, that's what they say about Trenton," said Karen. "What part of the country did you originate?"

"Well, I was born in Montana, but my parents moved to L. A. when I was two years old."

"I had an uncle worked in Montana. Did you ever hear of Missoula, Montana? It sounds like you ought to use it cooking, but there is such a place."

"I heard of it, but I left there when I was two years old."

"Azusa. You got some funny names in California, too. Is there such a place as Azusa, or did they just make that up for a gag?"

"It's real," said Barbara.

"They got just as funny names around Hazleton, where I live. Did you ever hear of Wilkes-Barre? And they used to have a place called Maw Chunk. M, a, u, c, h, c, h, u, n, k. I don't pronounce it right but then they changed it to Jim Thorpe. From Maw Chunk to Jim Thorpe."

"Let's go sit in the front parlor," said Kate Merino. "It's nicer in there."

"What's wrong with here? I like sitting around the table," said Vince.

"The dirty dishes. Come on, everybody. Andy, bring two chairs for the Appolinos."

"Oh, is Walt coming?" said Karen.

"Walt and Gert. They were here early and then they had to go to a funeral," said Andrew Merino.

"What did you think of Walt, Barbara? Quite the big shot around here, so he thinks."

"He seemed all right."

"Who else was here? Father Burke?" said Karen. "He's usually here, too."

"Is that suppose to be some kind of a crack, Karen?" said Vince.

"You haven't changed."

"No, neither have you," said Vince. "You always came in this house with a chip on your shoulder."

"Take it easy, everybody," said Andrew Merino.

"Goodbye, everybody," said Karen.

"Goodbye? You just got here," said Kate Merino.

"I know where I'm not wanted," said Karen. She looked at everyone in the room, individually, except Vince, then went back in the hall and out the front door.

"Huh," said Vince.

"I wonder when she came down from Hazleton," said Kitty. "I bet she's been here a week or more."

"What possessed her to come over here today, if that's as long as she was going to stay," said Kate Merino. "To see Vince and Barbara, I know, but common politeness she should have stayed longer."

"Well, common politeness or whatever you want to call it, Bobbie and I gotta be going," said Vince.

"So soon?" said Kate Merino.

"Mom, I didn't give any time how long we'd stay. I got an interview at five o'clock at the hotel, and Bobbie has to do a TV tape."

"Well, this wasn't much of a visit, but I guess it's better than none. I don't know what we'll tell Walt," said Kate Merino.

"Vince didn't make Walt any promises," said Andrew Merino.

"I didn't make anybody any promises. I wasn't sure we could get here at all," said Vince.

"I wish I would of thought to bring my camera," said Kitty.

The chauffeur was asleep in the car, and a dozen women and children were standing quietly on the sidewalk when Vincent and Barbara left the house. As though by some tacit agreement the family all stood on the porch to wave farewell.

"Back to New York, Mr. Merino?" said the chauffeur.

"But fast," said Vince. "Go to the end of this street and turn right, then the first left and that'll put us on U.S. 1. After that you look for Turnpike signs." He pressed the button that raised the division.

"If you got anything to say, save it till later," said Vince. "I don't want to talk about them."

"Well, now you know something."

"What?"

"You used to say to me, why didn't we go visit my folks. It was only thirty miles."

"You knew it was gonna be like this?"

"It could have been a lot worse," said Barbara. "You showed good sense leaving. They hate us, they all hate us. Either way, they hate us. If we're nice, they hate us just as much as if we treat them like dirt."

"All but Pop."

"Yeah, I guess he was all right, but he didn't fit in with the rest of them."

"Pop didn't? How didn't he fit in?"

"Don't ask me how. I just felt sorry for him," said Barbara. She took his hand. "What are you smiling at?"

"That Pat. Wait till he gets there and we're halfway to New York."

"Families," she said. "They're just like everybody else. They don't like us. Well, I didn't use to like Ava Gardner before I was in pictures. Or Lana Turner. Who did they think they are?"

"And now they're you, huh?"

"Sure."

"You want to go to sleep?"

"Wait till we get out of the built-up section. They're liable to think I'm drunk."

"I'd like to see the look on Walt's face, with his fifty politicians."

"Erase them from your mind, honey, It's the best way," she said.

A Cold Calculating Thing

For Ada Trimball it was a rush of mail, considering; considering, that is, how seldom she got two personal letters in the same delivery. Sometimes it seemed hardly worth the trouble to memorize the combination of her mailbox, and sometimes it was not worth the trouble to raise that heavy garage door and back the Volkswagen out of the garage and drive it to the post office. But then there were times, too, when nothing seemed worth the trouble; and yet she went on, taking the trouble to make a home for herself and her ungrateful mother, going to the trouble of looking nice, of *being* nice to the people in the post office and the village shops, of watching her money and getting the most out of it, of keeping up with her reading, and voting and attending church and going to the dentist and taking vitamins and getting a permanent and not giving in to that nagging doubt that anything was worth the trouble.

She stopped at the window and laid down the crumpled old card that informed her that there was a parcel too large for her mailbox. "Good morning, Mrs. Dombrowski. You've got something for me?"

"Morning, Miss Trimball. Yes, I think it's a book. Uh-huh. A book." Mrs. Dombrowski pushed the parcel toward Miss Trimball and picked up the crumpled old notice and leaned with her fat forearms on the counter.

"Thank you, and I'd like, let me see—twenty postcards is sixty. Twenty postcards, and ten four-cent stamps, please. A dollar even." Ada Trimball had an adequate supply of postcards and stamps at home, but she wanted to show Mrs. Dombrowski that she was in no hurry to read the two personal letters in this morning's mail, and also to compliment Mrs. Dombrowski by a purchase. She had heard somewhere that the government kept tabs on the sales of stamps in individual post offices, and where sales fell off, the staff was reduced. Mrs. Dombrowski licked her thumb, flipped twenty postcards from a stack, recounted them for Miss Trimball's benefit, and then efficiently tore ten stamps from a page.

"Dollar even," said Mrs. Dombrowski, smiling, again resting her fat forearms on the counter and crushing her comfortable breasts against her arms. "How's your mother?"

"About the same, thank you."

"Well, when they stay the same that's a good sign. I hear Mrs. Diehl took a turn for the worst last night."

"Oh, really?"

"Uh-huh. I was surprised, too, because Monday the report was she'd be home from the clinic by the end of the week. Well, I guess she'll be home, but not the way they expected. But she's more up in years than your mother, Mrs. Diehl. She'd be eighty-five in April. Eighty-five. I never want to be no eighty-five."

Ada Trimball smiled. "Maybe you'll change your mind when you're eighty-four."

"Not me. I'll lose interest as soon as my grandchildren get married. The good Lord willing, I'll stay around to see that, but there isn't much in it for a woman after that. At least that's the way I look at it."

"Oh, I'm not so sure. I'll just bet you'll want to be there to see your first great-grandchild."

"Nup. Not me. What's a lady like Mrs. Diehl had out of the last five-ten years? Crippled with the arthritis and all? And what it costs to be sick nowadays. I guess she has a little put away, but George Diehl told me himself, the week he's had her at the clinic ran him over three hundred dollars. I don't want them spending that kind of money on me at that age."

"Well, it's a long way off, for you." Ada Trimball smiled and departed, knowing that Mrs. Dombrowski would be standing at the counter and smiling at her and thinking what a nice woman she was.

At the drug store and at the dry cleaner's she heard again that old Mrs. Diehl was poorly, and at her last stop, the meat market, she was told that the word was just in: Mrs. Diehl had died shortly after nine o'clock that morning. George Diehl's wife had ordered extra food for the relatives who would be arriving for the funeral.

"What took you so long?" said Ada Trimball's mother.

"I had to hear all about Mrs. Diehl. She passed away this morning."

"Had to hear all about her? What was there you didn't know? I could tell you all about her. She ran around with young men half her age."

"Oh, Mother. She couldn't have. She's been crippled for years."

"I'm talking about when she was in her forties and fifties, before you knew what it was all about. Her husband was no good, either. Karl Diehl. Forty years ago Karl Diehl was a rum-runner. Every night he and his crowd would be off Montauk, bringing in the liquor. And she'd be entertaining some young man, as brazen a performance as you could ever hope to see."

"Well, it doesn't seem to have shortened her life."

"Ada! What a thing to *say*."

"I know. Aren't I just *terrible,* Mother?"

"Sometimes you say terrible things."

"But fortunately I never *do* anything terrible. It's just talk," said Ada Trimball.

"It may be just talk, but you have to think a thing before you say it."

"Well, you *will* let me have my thoughts, won't you?"

"I could never do anything about that, no matter *how* hard I tried," said Mrs. Trimball. "What's the book?"

"I haven't opened it yet."

"I can see *that,*" said Mrs. Trimball.

"Probably the bird book I ordered for you."

"It took long enough to get here," said Mrs. Trimball. "Any interesting mail? Not that you'd tell me."

"Just an invitation to have dinner at the White House, and a cheque for ten thousand dollars. The usual."

"I can't fathom you, you're so flip this morning. A body might think you enjoyed hearing about Mrs. Diehl. If that's what's responsible, let me remind you that human life is sacred. She wasn't a good woman. She was a bad woman. But that doesn't entitle you to gloat over her passing on."

"But I wasn't gloating. I always rather liked Mrs. Diehl."

"I didn't say you had to like her, Ada. All I said was that it isn't right to ignore the fact that human life is sacred. God puts us on this earth for a purpose, and life is a precious heritage. We must do all we can to preserve life, human or otherwise, our own and everybody else's."

"Cora Dombrowski doesn't think so."

"Cora Dombrowski? At the post office? Are you getting your ideas from her nowadays?"

"I'm not getting *my* ideas from her, but I do listen to *hers.*"

"Well, all I can say to that is, don't try to convert *me* to Cora Dombrowski's ideas."

"The two of you see alike in some things."

"Not many. Not very many. It just happens that the Polish Catholics have it in for the Communists, but don't tell me Cora Dombrowski is against the preservation of human life."

"She's done her share, with five children," said Ada Trimball. "No, she isn't against the preservation of human life. But—"

"But what?"

Ada Trimball could not bring herself to tell her mother what Mrs. Dombrowski had said about old age. "Oh, why talk about Cora Dombrowski?" said Ada Trimball.

"You brought her into the conversation, I didn't," said Mrs. Trimball. She put on her glasses and unfolded her newspaper, and Ada retired to her room.

There was something absurdly exciting in the thought that a letter from Walter Hughes and a letter from Alice Wells had been together in her pocket for almost an hour. Ada Trimball took the letters out of her pocket and she saw that they had been crushed together, very much as though in an embrace, wrinkles fitting into wrinkles and the warmth from her own body penetrating through the letters.

She opened first the letter from Walter: he was going to be duck-shooting in the neighborhood, and could he come by for a drink and a chat with her and her mother. He would be at the Mill Pond Inn. The letter from Alice Wells was ridiculous. "Imagine being ten miles away all these months and not knowing it? This was our first summer on Long Island and Gerald is completely won over. We have an option to buy and I am positive we will, we love it so. I have kept the house open through the fall so that we can come down for long weekends. Gerald has a new hobby, painting. Has taken it up with the same thoroughness he does everything. Really quite good too. Do you still play golf? Maybe we could have a game, but I would just as soon just sit and talk. So much to tell you after—oh, dear? Is it fifteen years? Yes. Fifteen. Please do 'phone me. Mill Pond 3-4832 any Thursday, Friday, Saturday, or Sunday. I usually fly down Thursday after lunch and Gerald flies down the next afternoon. By the way, any time you care to fly back to N.Y. with us on Monday morning there is usually room in the Beech for one or two more passengers."

The coincidence could have been nothing more. If Alice and Walter had taken up with each other again, the very last person in the world they would want to know about it would be Ada Trimball. Plainly, Alice was bored in Mill Pond on her long weekends, so bored that she sought relief in the company of a woman to whom she could display her Gerald, with his thoroughness and his option and his painting and his Beechcraft, as well as his unmentioned oil company (or was it companies?) and box at the opera and fairly recent membership in the Links Club.

"Did you take my glasses by mistake?" Mrs. Trimball never bothered to knock on her daughter's door, not even on her bathroom door.

"Mother, you startled me," said Ada.

"I'm sorry, but I have the wrong glasses. Who's your letter from?"

"Do you remember Alice Ryder?"

"I should say I do. Pushy little thing from Englewood, New Jersey. I should say I do remember her. And her mother. They used me to get her in all the dances, then conveniently forgot us when Alice married that Wells man."

"I was a bridesmaid."

"*That* didn't hurt Alice. What's she writing about now, after all these years?"

"She and her husband have a house down here."

"That's no news, surely. They're in the papers every chance they get. That dance they had last summer. Is she apologizing for not inviting you?"

"Why would anybody invite me to a dance for the Jet Set? No, she wants me to telephone her. They come down weekends."

"Of course. Now that there's nothing to do. I remember how hard she tried to get Walter Hughes, right under your nose, and pretending to be your dearest friend. I hope you remember *that* before you jump at her command."

"Walter Hughes. Walter Hughes. Mother, that was all in your imagination. There was never anything between Walter and I."

"That depends on what you mean by anything. He was too much of a gentleman for some things, but what went on between Walter and Alice Ryder is another matter."

"And no concern of ours, is it?"

Her mother looked at her steadily. "No, not now," said Mrs. Trimball. "But there was a time when it should have concerned you."

"Then I was blissfully ignorant, and if you want your other glasses, I think they're on the sideboard, where you usually leave them."

She could not remember when she had won against her

mother, nor could she think of anything her mother had passed down to her, beginning with her looks. At sixty-six and with a bad heart Constance Trimball was a handsome woman, stout but not fat, and vain of her legs and her complexion. Her hair was not as white naturally as for some preceding years it had been when dyed. She wore light blue cashmere pullovers and always a pearl necklace, which was a combination to comple-ment her blue eyes and her teeth. All her life men had been attentive to her and she had had proposals after the death of her husband, but she had been unwilling to better her financial status in exchange for the companionship of the aging men who were her suitors. "We have enough, you'll have enough, and I won't marry a man that wants to be taken care of," she told her daughter. "I took care of your father gladly, but we had thirty-five good years before that." It was a form of de-feat for Ada Trimball that her mother was still getting pro-posals of marriage at the same time that proposals to Ada were for anything and everything but marriage.

A man would study her—sometimes it would be an old friend, sometimes the husband of an old friend—and she had come to know just when he would suggest a week somewhere, a *cinq à sept* in New York, a flight to Paris, a couple of nights on a cruiser. She had a woman's body, she did not get drunk, and as a lady she could be counted on not to make a fuss. And always, when she came home, her mother would refuse to play the game of lies about her absence. The beginnings and endings of her trips were always the same. "I think I'll run over to Philadelphia to see Peggy's new baby," she would say. And her mother would say, "Of course. You're free to go wherever you please." But her mother would not ask her a single question about the Peggys or their babies or Philadel-phia. Mrs. Trimball could not more plainly have shown her disbelief and disapproval, and on occasion she had made small effort to hide her disgust. On such occasions Mrs. Trimball would take her text from the newspapers, decrying and de-nouncing the immorality of the young and the famous for so

long as it took her disgust to wear off, by which time she had
effectually destroyed Ada's lingering pleasure in the recent
rendezvous.

Now her trips were less frequent and of shorter duration,
seldom longer than overnight in New York, and the rendezvous would originate with her and her need. She would go to
the booth at the village railway station and telephone one of
the men—there were three possibilities. "Would you like to
see me sometime this week?" she would say. Rarely would all
three men have other plans, but it had happened; and when it
did she worked a little harder at home, gave herself extra chores
so that her mother would not notice her pain. On such occasions she was glad that she had her reading, her volunteer
work with the League of Women Voters, her church activities,
the things that she called her busy-busy boondoggling. In a
peculiar, self-contradictory way she was glad she had her
mother. They could come close, but they had never actually
lost control during their flare-ups, never said the terrible things,
the unforgivable truths and accusations and counter-accusa-
tions, and for Ada Trimball the exercise in self-controlled
sarcasm was the nearest to triumph that she ever came; for
her mother was a rather stupid woman, not really quick, and
Ada was sure that she could inflict hurt, even though it might
take some time before her mother, retiring to her room, could
think back on what had been said and realize that Ada had
been cleverly cruel. There was not enough money for them to
live apart from each other in the genteel circumstances they
required. As year-round residents of the village where once
they had passed only the summers, they were able, first of all,
to live in a *house*. They were not, as they said, cooped up in a
New York apartment. They had three acres of ground behind a
tall hedge. They were in residence. They wore their good country clothes and had their economical German car, and they
could refer to themselves as having gone native, which pointed
up the difference between the true natives and themselves, so
that it was hardly necessary to mention that the true natives
were never invited to the Trimball house. Likewise, in June,

when the summer people began to arrive, Mrs. Trimball and Ada assumed the position of the established, people who had been there all the time, and the more recent summer people were as much strangers to the Trimball house as the natives. Ten miles away was Mill Pond, with its rich and its Jet Set and their children with their T-Birds and Bikinis, and their noise, vulgarity, and publicity. Ada and her mother were unified in their attitude toward natives, summer people, and Mill Pond. Mill Pond was the perfect place for Alice Wells and her husband, and they were perfect for Mill Pond. Walter Hughes would find few of his old friends still there.

Walter Hughes. Alice Ryder.

Ada Trimball wrote him a note. "Do come. Mother and I would love to see you. I am not going to tell her you are coming but will save your visit for a surprise. So please pretend that you have just dropped in." Her complimentary closing was "Cordially."

The note from Alice Wells required no written answer, which suited Ada Trimball's plans. She wanted to have a look at Walter before doing anything else.

On the afternoon of Walter's visit Ada could not resist telling her mother he was coming. It was a small, but complete triumph. "He wrote me and asked if he could come, and I said of course."

"Why didn't you tell me? What was behind *that?*" Mrs. Trimball's anger was barely controlled. "How do you know I want to see him?"

"You can always be upstairs with a headache."

"Ridiculous! I wish when you're having people to my house you'd tell me."

"I am telling you. Now. But why this sudden animosity towards Walter? I've never heard you say a word against him before. Stay upstairs, if you don't want to see him."

"Oh, you miserable fool!" said Mrs. Trimball.

She recovered her composure before Walter's arrival. She wore her blue bouclé dress, her little pearls, and no other jewelry, not even her wedding ring. When he entered the sitting-room she gave him her hand, but he said: "Don't I rate a kiss?" She put up her cheek and he kissed her.

"Would you like tea, or would you really prefer a drink?" said Ada Trimball.

"If there's tea, I'd rather have that. I limit myself to two drinks before dinner," he said. "Well, this is like old times."

"Where is it you live now? Colorado?" said Constance Trimball.

"Denver. Been there ever since the war, and I guess I'm really settled there."

"I'll get the tea things," said Ada Trimball.

"Can I help?" said Walter Hughes.

"Not a bit. You entertain each other for a minute." Ada left them.

"I've always heard that you have to get used to the altitude in Denver. Is that true?"

"It's true. How *are* you?"

"I'm very well, thanks."

"You look well," he said. "Aren't you surprised to see me?"

"Not at all. Alice Ryder's in Mill Pond, so you were bound to turn up there sooner or later."

"Alice Ryder? I didn't know that. I haven't seen her in nearly twenty years."

"Well, you're both in Mill Pond. She and her husband came there this summer, and they're down every weekend."

"Have you been seeing her?"

"Alice Ryder? Hardly."

"You still don't forgive me my one mistake."

"I was the one that made the mistake, Walter. There was nothing to forgive you."

"I never considered what you did a mistake. What we did. I thought it was beautiful, and I still think so. That's why I wanted to see you again. I'm not a boy any more, and as you get older you look back and remember the few beautiful things that happen in a lifetime. Our—whatever you want to call it —romance—love affair—was beautiful."

"No, I'm afraid it wasn't."

"You never told Mr. Trimball about it, did you?"

"I never told anybody. But it wasn't beautiful, Walter. It was a cold, calculating thing on my part."

"That's simply not true."

"Then I must tell you it was. I wanted you to marry Ada, but Alice Ryder had her cap set for you, and I wanted to take you away from her."

"Well, that didn't work very well. I had an affair with Alice anyway."

"Of course you did. And you always thought I didn't forgive you for that. It wasn't a question of forgiving you, Walter."

"Oh. You mean you just gave me up as a bad job."

"A bad job on my part. I failed. What I tried to do didn't work, and there's Ada today, fighting off being an old maid."

"I never *was* in love with Ada."

"I know that, but she'd have been a good wife for you. She was desperately in love with you. There's never been anybody but you."

"Oh, come."

"You know about Ada?"

"No, but she hasn't stayed a virgin all these years."

"No, but as far as love is concerned she has. So be nice to her."

"Hell, I like Ada. I'd even—"

"But don't. She has men friends. She pulls the wool over my eyes, or so she thinks. But it's never been love."

"And you never loved me at all? Did you ever sleep with anyone else?"

"No."

"Just me and your husband?"

"Yes."

"You slept with me to get me away from Alice."

"I thought I could. I was an attractive woman, Alice was nothing but a little chippy."

"You took an awfully big chance."

"Well, when your children are involved, you do. You have children. You must know that. You fight with the weapons at your disposal."

"I suppose so," he said. "What would Mr. Trimball have said?"

She shook her head. "I don't think he would have believed me."

"Would he have believed me?"

"He might have believed you, Walter. And killed you. He would have thought you were, as they used to say, forcing your attentions on me."

"And the cause of it all is over in Mill Pond."

"The cause of it all is in the kitchen," said Mrs. Trimball.

"Yes, if you look at it that way," he said.

"There's no other way to look at it. And not be ashamed."

Walter Hughes stood up and went to her and took her hand. He raised it to his lips.

She touched the top of his head. "Thank you, Walter," she said, and smiled.

You Can Always Tell Newark

Not many people ever see the game and not all those who see it can follow the scoring, and among those who can score it fewer still can play it, and, finally, in the entire world there are probably fewer than fifty men who play it well. It is a beautiful game to watch, requiring a quick eye, a strong wrist, and a dancer's agility of its players; but as is the case with another exciting game, high goal polo, it can become a bore. Too much skill, too much beauty, too much excitement, too much excellence, and the spectator's attention will wander, in polo, at a symphony concert, in court tennis, as in life itself.

The girl had been applauding good shots during the first set, and applauding them in a way that indicated she had some knowledge of the game. She was sitting in the first row of spectators, and from time to time one of the players, when it was his turn to serve, would address some remark to her, apparently not seeing her, but speaking her name. "How'd you like that one, Nance? Who you betting on, Nance?" he would mutter, and she would smile, and the young people sitting near her would turn and smile at her, with what they deliberately intended to be a knowing smile. There was some small joke between her and them, some special knowledge.

There were three rows of benches for the spectators, benches without backs, but the men and women in the third row could rest their backs against the wall. It was cold on the court, and not warm where the spectators sat, and at the end of the second set, when the two players stopped to sip iced soft drinks, all the spectators rose to stretch. It was then that Williams saw that the girl was pregnant, probably in her seventh month.

When play resumed the girl sat down, but now she knew how tired she was, and she sat with her back against the second-row seats, and the young couple behind her, in the second row, made room for her, but it was an uncomfortable position. Williams watched her; she was tired, and once she hunched her shoulders in an involuntary reaction to the cold. Williams, from his seat in the third row, tapped her arm, and she turned and looked up at him, a stranger and an elderly stranger at that.

"Wouldn't you like to sit up here? Support your back? We can make room for you," said Williams.

"Oh, no thanks. I'm all right, thank you." She smiled with her mouth only. Now she sat up straight and lit a cigarette, and there was exasperation in the forceful blowing out of smoke and in her stiff manner of sitting. Plainly she was annoyed that a stranger had noticed her pregnancy and tiredness, and she did not look at Williams again. She wanted no help from anyone. When the match was over and the winner and loser were photographed receiving their silver bowls she did not applaud.

"What's the matter, Nance?" said one of her young companions. "Just because your man lost?"

"Oh, shut up," she said. "And stop *saying* that. Let's get out of here."

"There's free booze," said one of the young men.

"Oh, all right," said the girl. "But let's not stay forever? I'm cold."

"Have a couple of scoops and it'll warm you up," said the young man.

The picture-taking over, the player who had been speaking *sotto voce* to Nancy crossed the court to the place where she had been sitting. "Hey, Joe, where's Nancy?" he said. "Isn't she staying? She go?"

"She's staying. Hard luck, by the way."

"No, he beat me. Listen, tell her to be sure and wait, will you? I have to take a shower, I stink. But I won't be more than ten or fifteen minutes. Will you tell her?"

"Okay, Rex. See you," said Joe.

"Be sure and tell her, Joe. Now don't let her go home without my seeing her. I'll be fifteen minutes at the most," he said, then, in a lower voice: "Is Bud here?"

Joe laughed. "Bud come to see you, especially when you had a chance of winning? Get *with* it, boy."

"Well, I wanted to be sure. I have to go back to New York on the seven o'clock train."

They were all young enough so that what was overheard by someone as old as Williams did not matter. He was fifty, and they were their own world.

"Well, Ned, shall we go have some of that free booze?" said Williams's host and companion.

"Sure," said Williams. The two men smiled.

"Aren't you glad we have all that behind us?" said Smith.

"Sometimes I am," said Williams. "Who is she?"

"I'm all prepared," said Smith. "Her name is Nancy Phillips, married to Bud Phillips. They live in Chestnut Hill. Her name *was* Nancy Standish. That ought to help you."

"*Oh*. That *does* help. The daughter of Bob Standish and Evie Jeffcott."

"Uh-huh."

"No wonder I was drawn to her, so to speak."

"I was terribly amused, you know," said Smith. "I thought God damn it, here is history repeating itself right before my very eyes."

"Is that what you thought?"

"That's what I thought. Don't you think she looks a lot like Evie?"

"Well now I do, but it never occurred to me before," said Williams. "And it isn't actually that she looks so much like Evie."

"No, not terribly much, but at least you're consistent."

"Yes, I guess you could say that. So is the girl, for that matter. Her mother didn't like me the first time she saw me, either."

"She made up for it," said Smith. "We go down this way."

"Why didn't she say hello to you? Where are her manners?"

"What manners? None of them have any manners any more. No manners, no style, no ambition. They're a bunch of self-centered little pigs."

"I wonder what we were?" said Williams.

"Self-centered little pigs, no doubt, but we damn well had our manners drilled into us. These little bastards blame our generation for the state of the world. I think they're taught that in school and college. So they hate us. Really hate us, Ned. I don't think there's a God damn one of them that ever stops to think that we weren't responsible for 1929. We were the victims of it. And World War Two, we get blamed for that. What the hell did we have to do with it? We went, that's all. We had to go, so we went. But these little pricks blame us for the whole damn shooting-match. They don't even know their history. Or Social Studies, as they call it. Jesus Christ! You're lucky you have no children."

"You make me think I am."

"Well, as you know, I have four, and after they're ten years old they start taking pot-shots, and by the time they're fifteen— oh, brother. 'Daddy, you just don't *know*.' That's their stock answer for everything. I just don't know about segregation, or about war. I have one snot-nose about to go in the Army and *he*'s telling *me* how awful war is. And if I *told* him about Guadal he'd accuse me of wallowing in it, so I've never told him. I've learned to keep my mouth shut, the only way to avoid having a scene. 'Daddy, you just don't *know*.' If I'd said that to my father I'd have been clouted over the head. And if one of my sisters had said it to my father, my mother would have taken good care of her. Actually they loved my father, in a way that my daughters have never loved me. They still think he was a great and wonderful man, and all he was was an honest, decent, strict father. The whole purpose of my existence is when I get through paying for their education, to come through with an Austin-Healey for graduation. As a matter of fact I couldn't have paid for their education without help from their various grandparents. Betty and I just get by, and you know how much

I make. This booze is free, so drink it up, boy. Would you like to meet Nancy?"

"Is she like the others?"

"I think so, but you can find out for yourself. She pretended not to see me before, but we'll just go right up to her. Come on. Be brave."

The men pushed through to where Nancy Phillips was leaning against a table. "Hello there, Nancy."

"Oh, hello, Mr. Smith. Have you been here all the time?" She had a drink in her hand and she smiled agreeably enough.

"Sitting right behind you. I want you to meet a friend of your mother's. *And* father's. This is Mr. Williams, Mr. Ned Williams."

"Oh, hello, Mr. Williams. *You* were there, I saw *you*. At least—weren't you the one that . . . ?"

"I'm the one that."

"Did you ever sit on anything as uncomfortable as those benches? Mr. Smith, *can't* this club afford something more *comfortable?*"

"You better take that up with your father. He's on the board. Where was he today, by the way?"

"Oh, hunting, I guess. Saturday, this time of year. Are you over from New York, Mr. Williams?"

"Just for the day."

"Just to see the match?"

"More or less. Partly business with Mr. Smith. How's your mother?"

"Mummy's fine, or I guess she is. I haven't seen her for a couple of weeks. We live in Chestnut Hill, and Mummy and Daddy are still in Ardmore. Do you know Philadelphia, Mr. Williams?"

"I used to."

"Before your mother married your father, he means," said Smith.

"Oh, you were a *beau* of Mummy's? What was she like then?"

"I don't know that she was any different then from now. I

saw her about a year ago. Nowadays I seem to see her and your father at weddings, for the most part."

"I meant as a—what did they call them—flapper? Was she a flapper, my mother?"

"I wouldn't think so, would you?" Williams asked Smith.

"Definitely not. But definitely," said Smith.

"Well, you, Mr. Williams. Were you a—playboy? I guess that would be the opposite of flapper."

"George? Was I?"

"I don't know why you say 'Was I?' As far as I know, you still are."

"Oh, are you, Mr. Williams?"

"You sound incredulous. No, I was never one of the outstanding playboys. As we used to say, I got around."

"Then how did you and Mummy get together, if Mr. Smith is right." She did not wait for an answer but said, largely to herself, "Still—Bud and I."

"Well of course we *didn't* get together or you'd be my daughter instead of Bob Standish's."

"I didn't necessarily mean that close together, Mr. Williams."

"Well, now the conversation is taking a decided turn for the better," said Smith.

"It's taken a turn, all right," said the girl. "So let's turn back."

"Any direction you say," said Williams.

Now, before any more could be said, they were joined by the tennis player, whose hair was wet. "Hello, Nance," he said.

"Hello, Rex. I'd like you to know Mr. Smith, and Mr. Williams. This is Rex Ivers, who played such spec*ta*cular tennis this afternoon. Spec*ta*cular."

"Mr. Smith. Mr. Williams. Oh, hello, Mr. Williams. I've met Mr. Williams."

"I thought you played extremely well," said Williams. "Your only trouble was that you missed the easy ones."

"Four straight. But he beat me. He played better."

"Oh, you're such a good, good sport, Rex," said Nancy.

"Well, what's wrong with that? Anyway, I'm not such a good, good sport. I wish I were."

"Yes you are, that's why you missed the easy ones, as Mr. Williams said. You were playing like a good sport instead of to win, and I consider that insulting to my opponent."

"*He* doesn't feel insulted. He got the hardware, and some of my cash."

"Oh, you actually bet on yourself?" said Nancy. "You had money going on this match?"

"Yes. We bet a hundred dollars apiece. I think you put the whammy on me. Every one of those easy shots I missed, I just happened to be facing in your direction."

"Oh, of course. And I waved my handkerchief to distract you."

"I didn't say that. I meant it as a compliment, what I did say. Where's Bud?"

"He sent his regrets," said the girl.

"I think we'll leave you two," said Smith.

"Say hello to your mother, and your father," said Williams.

"I will, thank you. Nice to've seen you," said the girl.

Smith and Williams rode the elevator in silence and went to the bar, seated themselves, ordered drinks. "Well, that was a happy thought," said Smith.

"Oh, I wanted to meet her."

"I didn't mean that. I was thinking about how she could have been your daughter."

"Oh, I see. Well, is this her first child?"

"It's no excuse. At this moment she's probably raking him over the coals, and he's so much in love with her that it's coming out of his eyes."

"That's very poetic."

"Entirely accidental. Tell me about Ivers. I didn't know you knew him."

"I don't. I just see him at the club and I guess I've met him there a few times. I was surprised he remembered me. Now *he* has good manners."

"Yes, but where does it get him in his own crowd? They not only don't appreciate good manners. Did you happen to notice during the match, he'd say something to her. Nice. And those others with her, they'd all look wise, as if they knew the whole story."

"I did notice that, yes. What's her husband like?"

"He's still in medical school, out at the University. I think he has another year to go."

"Bob Standish has plenty of money."

"Oh, the Phillipses are loaded too. No money problem there. The problem is going to be when she finds out what it's like to be the wife of a doctor. It's tough enough now, of course, while Bud's in medical school, but just wait till she finds out what the first few years are going to be like."

"She seems to be having a very hard time of it."

"For God's sake, why?"

"Oh, well there you've got me."

"Hell of an attractive mother, father's a nice guy, husband working his ass off trying to be something. Plenty of money. A nice young guy in love with her, obviously. And she's having a baby. I don't know what else a young girl could want."

"Is there any chance that this baby belongs to Ivers?"

"Oh, there's always that chance, but she didn't greet him like the father of her child. Is Ivers married, do you happen to know?"

"I happen to know he's not."

"And she's a good-looking little bitch, too. Add that to the rest of her complaints. Quite a shape, when her belly's flat."

"I could see that it would be."

"Ned?"

"What?"

"She *isn't* your daughter, by any chance?"

"Well, you know, George. She could be. Evie never said so, and I was hoping you wouldn't ask, but I was just figuring it out. She could be, mathematically."

"I sort of thought so. At least as a possibility."

"As you said, there was always that chance, but you'd think Evie would have told me."

"I wouldn't think anything of the kind."

"No, I guess not. Evie was a hard one to figure sometimes."

"Why didn't you and Evie get married?"

"Before she married Bob?"

"Yes."

"Because she wasn't in love with me."

"Oh, come."

"She wasn't. She said so."

"She gave you enough proof to the contrary."

"She didn't consider that proof of anything, except of course that she considered me safe to go to bed with. But her family were against it, and God knows I wasn't very reliable in those days, and Bob had been hanging around for years."

"But then after she married Bob?"

"Well—then she discovered she was in love with me. All right, I'll give it to you straight. She wanted to divorce Bob and I was the one that prevented it. Plus the fact that I was leaving for Quantico. It was just before Pearl. Maybe I was running away from marriage, I don't know. But that's why we didn't get married. Mathematically, this girl could be the result of the summer of '41. My daughter. George, I think she is."

"I think so too."

"Something. Even before I knew her name, who she was. I felt protective. You know, when I offered her a seat with us?"

"Sure, sure."

"And it was more than her resemblance to Evie. Maybe not more. Different from. Apart from. She didn't feel anything, though."

"Yes she did."

"Yes, I guess she did."

"Something bothered her. She looked at you, and maybe she saw something without any idea of what it was. Some resemblance to herself, maybe. Not only the color of your eyes, but the shape of them."

"Maybe that's what *I* saw."

"And maybe she did too. That can be very baffling, to see resemblances to yourself in your children. Elusive. And if you didn't know of the relationship, God knows how disturbing it might be. I imagine it must be especially true for girls, who spend a lot more time looking at themselves than we do. You didn't get any feeling that she resented you because you were on the make, did you?"

"No."

"Neither did I. She was annoyed, but that wasn't what annoyed her. Well, we've got it all figured out." Smith raised his glass. "Congratulations, Papa."

"Thank you."

"Now you're one of us. The rejected generation."

"Are we rejected, George? I'd hate to think that."

"Two hours ago you didn't give a damn."

"Two hours ago I certainly didn't. But I'll never be the same as I was two hours ago."

"No, you won't. Are you going to say anything to Evie?"

"I don't know. I don't know whether she'd tell me the truth."

"Do you need to have her tell you?"

"A little bit. Yes."

"Why don't you depend on your instinct, and to hell with what Evie says or doesn't say? Don't even ask her."

"Maybe I won't. I wish I could talk to the girl again."

"That can be arranged. My daughter sees her fairly frequently. That's comparatively easy."

"Before she has her baby?"

"Ned, nobody dies in childbirth any more, if that's worrying you."

"No, but it was cold up there today."

"Nobody dies of pneumonia, either."

"Well then what the hell *do* all these people die of?"

"Worry, so stop it," said Smith. "I don't want to rush you, Ned, but if you're counting on making the seven o'clock train . . ."

The seven o'clock to New York was a train that originated in Washington and it was late, with the result that the train crew wanted no time wasted at the Thirtieth Street station. Passengers were hurried off, passengers were hurried on, and the confusion was worse than usual. An Air Force second lieutenant with a flight kit and a guitar was blocked by passengers trying to board the train, and he in turn refused to budge for them. In the disorder the train was held up for six minutes, and the delay was fortunate for Rex Ivers, who came running down the steps, taking them two or three at a leap. He had a small suitcase and an old pigskin tennis bag of a vintage that had not been manufactured in more than twenty years. He stowed the luggage on the shelf at the end of the car, and considered where to sit. There were vacant seats, but most of them had coats or hats that belonged to passengers who were in the dining-car. "Taken? Taken? Taken?" said Ivers, walking down the aisle. "Hello, Mr. Williams? Is this taken?"

"Probably, but so's the one I'm sitting in," said Williams. "They can eat or they can sit, but they can't do both."

"There'll be a row," said Ivers.

"What if there is? I'm not budging. Have a seat till they come —and I'll bet they stay in the diner till Newark."

"All right. I'm with you," said Ivers. He seemed to be a little bit tight. His hair, now dry, fell down over his forehead. His club tie was crooked, the knot somewhere under the collar. And there was lipstick on his chin.

"I see someone saw you off, affectionately," said Williams.

"Why? Oh, have I got telltale traces?"

"On your chin."

Ivers moistened his handkerchief and rubbed the lipstick off. "All gone?"

"All gone," said Williams.

"Listen, go ahead and read your paper, sir. I don't want to bother you."

"Oh, that's all right. Light's not very good. But I may doze off."

"Yes, I might too."

"I should think you would."

"I had a couple of scoops. If I'd won I'd be high, but I lost, so the only effect is to make me sleepy."

"Have you got your ticket? Give it to me and I'll give it to the conductor."

"Sir, but you want to take a nap."

"After North Philadelphia. Push that gadget and the seat goes back. Get yourself a nap."

"Well—thanks very much. Just a nap's all I want." He handed his ticket to Williams, altered the angle of the seat, stretched out and was asleep in three minutes, heavily, deeply, helplessly, rather sadly asleep.

"Teeks for North Philadelphia. North Philadelphia teeks please," said the trainman.

Williams read his *Evening Bulletin,* saw that the sleeping young man at his right—according to this edition of the newspaper—was one of the finalists in the court tennis tournament. It was strange to come upon this item after the outcome had been decided, like having a look into the future with the certainty that what one saw would take place. Williams read the item again, then turned to the Evening Chat column, which contained society news. At this moment some people he knew in Wynnewood were getting ready to receive guests for dinner: Mr. and Mrs. John Arthur Kersley will entertain at dinner this evening in honor of their daughter Willela Kersley, whose engagement, etc. What if he knew the score of that dinner party, as he now knew the score of Ivers's tennis match? What if he could call up Jack Kersley and tell him for God's sake not to let John Jones sit next to Mary Brown, that before the night was over John Jones would say something to Mary Brown that would wreck their lives? What if he could call Mary Brown and tell her not to listen to anything John Jones said? And what if he had been able to speak to Rex Ivers and persuade him to default, so that he would not have gone to Philadelphia and seen Nancy. "My daughter."

"I beg your pardon?"

"Oh—I must have dozed off," said Williams.

Young Ivers grinned. "Like somebody hit you with a croquet mallet."

"Where are we?" said Williams. He looked out the window but could not identify landmarks.

"We just passed through New Brunswick," said Ivers.

"New Brunswick? How long have you been awake?"

"Oh, I guess I only slept about ten minutes. I woke up just after North Philadelphia. Here's your paper, sir, I borrowed it. Gave me a funny feeling to read about my match before it happened. You know, when this was printed, I was on equal terms with my worthy opponent. Now I'm second banana."

"Do you know Jack Kersley?" said Williams.

"Kersley? No, I don't think so. Should I?"

"No, I just happened to think of him. Lives in Philadelphia."

"I might have met him this week. I met a lot of guys during the tournament. Oh, I did meet an older man named Kersley. Has he got a daughter, Wilhelmina or something like that?"

"Yes he has."

"Then I did meet him. What made you mention him?"

"I don't really know," said Williams. "I guess I'm still in a bit of a fog."

"Why don't you go back to sleep?"

"No, no. A nap was all I wanted."

"You know, when you said Jack Kersley, that didn't register. But the daughter is a friend of a friend of mine. In fact, my girl. My girl is going to a dinner party at the Kersleys' tonight. The girl that saw me off at the station."

"Oh, you have a girl in Philadelphia?"

"Yes. Not the way that sounds, though. A girl in Philadelphia. A girl in Boston. A girl in Chicago."

"This is the real thing? The one and only, we used to say."

"Yes. Married, though."

"Have to watch out for that," said Williams.

"Telling *me*. Do you remember my father? Was killed in World War Two?"

"Sure, I knew him. A fine man."

"That's what everybody says, without fail. But I never knew him. I was three years old when he joined the Navy, and honestly I have no recollection of him except what I hear from my mother and his friends. And I couldn't possibly live up to his reputation. Not possibly. God, at school they had his name on a tablet and every time I got into trouble, sure as hell some master would take me for a walk and steer me in the direction of the memorial. You know. Illustrating the lecture. What I'm getting at is I guess I have some kind of a guilt complex because my father was this idol, and here I am, the original mixed-up kid. It's not something you go to the head-shrinker for, and yet I don't know any minister I'd feel like talking to. That's what it is, too. More of a religious problem."

"Ethical."

"Ethical, right. This girl would marry me. She wants to divorce her husband and marry me."

"Well, if you love her. And you say she's your girl."

"It isn't all that easy. The husband hates me, and he has good reason to. He knows I was there first, she told him. But he's—he's doing something constructive. He's doing something, a line of work, that takes up all his time and energy, and it's worthwhile work. If she left him, it wouldn't only be their marriage. Well, I don't think you know the people, so I'll tell you. The husband is studying to be a doctor and they say he's brilliant. Brilliant. But I know he's dependent on her. Not financially, but for moral support. She's dependent on me—for immoral support. Or was. I hadn't seen her till today, she turned up at the tennis match with her crowd. And she came with me to the station. God, she wants me to get a job in Philadelphia, and she'll get a divorce, and we'll get married, and the hell with her husband. There's a certain reason why she wants me to be in Philadelphia now. Sort of a crisis going on."

"Well, as I see it, Rex, the thing that's holding you back is this ethical problem. Your girl's husband and his career. But where does that leave her and the child?"

"The child? Do you know who it is?"

"I think I sat two rows behind your girl at the match. The crisis is she's having a baby, isn't it?"

"Jesus, yes. Then you know who the girl is."

"Yes, I know who the girl is."

"I know you were talking to her afterward but I didn't figure you'd guess anything. Well, sir, what would you do? As an unprejudiced observer."

"Well, I have an ethical problem, too. My ethical problem is whether to advise you one way or the other. As a matter of fact, Rex, my problem is really more difficult than yours."

"Yes, I suppose it is," said Ivers. "Why should you get into the act, eh? It isn't your responsibility." The young man chewed his lip thoughtfully. "Mr. Williams, I hope you don't think I go around blabbing stuff this way all the time."

"Of course I don't, Rex."

"Well, I *don't*. If you knew me better you'd know that. I don't know whether it was because I had a couple of drinks or what. I wish I could convince you of that."

"Don't let it bother you."

"The thing is, it does bother me. I hope everything I told you is in the strictest confidence."

"It will be."

"Have I got your word on that?"

"You have my word. I promise you I won't repeat any of this conversation to anybody."

"I wish you could forget everything I told you."

"That I can't promise."

The young man was still very uneasy. "You see, Mr. Williams, this girl's had everything she ever wanted."

"Except marriage to you."

"Yes, but it wouldn't work out now. It never will work out. She thinks she wants to be married to me, but it wouldn't last a year before she was discontented. And meanwhile she'd have broken up her marriage and possibly ruined her husband's career, and the kid wouldn't have a father. In other words, this is the time for somebody to make sense, and it's up to me to be the one."

"Probably."

"So—what I'm getting at, the importance of keeping this confidential. Nancy will get over this and stay with her husband, and in two years it'll all be a thing of the past."

"And you don't think you're being tough on her."

"No tougher on her than I am on myself. She's my girl, Mr. Williams. Make no mistake about that."

"Rex, I'm going to ask you a question you may not like."

"You're entitled to ask anything you please."

"What if this baby she's having is yours?"

"If it was, I think she would have told me."

"Would that have made a difference, to you?"

The boy—for now he looked about seventeen—shook his head. "No. It would make things tougher for me, but as long as she didn't tell Bud, her husband, she and the baby are better off."

"Thank you."

"Why do you say that?"

"Oh—thank you for trusting me with your confidences."

"Hell, I ought to be thanking you. And I do. You know, her father and mother, they're your generation, but they don't seem to know what it's all about. I could never talk to them the way I've talked to you. Of course that may be Philadelphia."

"It may be Philadelphia."

"Nancy does a big production of laughing at the whole thing, but you'd never get her out of Philadelphia."

"I guess not. Well, here's Newark. I can always tell Newark, can't you?"

"Yes, you can always tell Newark."

The High Point

One day late in the fifth decade of the century Ruth Styles went to the mailbox, which was in a cluster of mailboxes for the convenience of the rural route man. She extracted the little bundle of mail and took it back with her to her kitchen. Ruth Styles played a daily game of suspense; she always waited until the mail was on the kitchen table, until she had poured herself a cup of coffee and lighted a cigarette, before putting on her reading glasses and examining the items in the post. She would discard the junk—the items addressed to Patron and Boxholder, and the shopping center publications and the more uninteresting catalogs—and she would make little piles of her bills, her husband's letters and bills, the mail for the children, and the mail that was personally for her. In this way she got as much enjoyment out of her letters and out of the daily-except-Sunday ritual as it was possible to get. It was the high point of the morning; sometimes the high point of the day; and on this morning one letter should have been the high point—of years.

The letter was from Ray Kemmerer. The handwriting was instantly recognized; as long as she lived she would always recognize that handwriting, the carefully made letters like precisely enunciated speech; the uniform height of the small letters and of the capitals above the line; the slant; the overlarge part of the small letters and capitals below the line; the flow of ink from the same stub pen—probably the same Parker fountain pen—he had preferred since freshman year in college. She smiled and said aloud: "Now what does Ray Kemmerer, Tonawanda Manufacturing Company, Erie, Pennsylvania, want from Mrs. Edwin

D. Styles, Oak Road, Knollcrest, New Jersey? And how did he get my address?"

The letter was written entirely by hand on a good grade of business paper: "Dear Ruth:—I am sorry to have to tell you that Mother passed away on the 5th of last month. She has been in ill health for over a year & the doctors gave up hope for her several months before the end. Everything was done to make her comfortable, but she must have suffered a great deal in the final months. We welcomed the end to her suffering although she did not complain. She was always very fond of you, as I know you were of her, hence this brief note. I got your address through Sally Moffat when she and Ken stopped by a few weeks ago. Hope all goes well with you and your family. Sincerely, Ray Kemmerer."

She reread the letter twice and put it back in the envelope. Sincerely, Ray Kemmerer. Sincerely, Nobody. Sincerely, Nothing. Sincerely, the man whose presence on the face of the earth had once meant the difference between life with love and life unlived. Sincerely, the object of twenty years of scorn and jest and mockery.

Ted Styles had been thorough, and the arrival of this letter made her realize how completely successful his thoroughness had been. She had smiled in recognition of the handwriting; but the letter itself was the letter of a dullard, a clod, a semi-literate, presumptuous, oversentimental mediocrity. Ray Kemmerer was none of these things, but he might as well have been; it was the way Ted had made her see him. The letter that was supposed to announce the death of a woman who had been nice to her son's friends was in truth a confirmation of the slow murder of Ruth Styles' first love. "Oh, Ted, you really did a job on him," she said. The letter was an embarrassment; she could guess at her husband's every comment, from the handwriting to the vulgar ampersand, to the cautious wording. "Nothing here that couldn't be read in open court," Ted Styles would say. "How do you suppose they welcomed the end of the old lady's suffering? Did they beat on pots and pans? Or with firecrackers, like the Chinese?" She would not show him the letter, but only because she was already certain of his comments, which embarrassed her without being spoken.

She hid the letter in a book that Ted would never take down from the shelf, a collection of pieces by a passé humorist. It was the safest place in the house, and she had used it on other occasions. Ted regarded her continuing enjoyment of the collection as an indication of taste not far above the level of a child's ragbook of animal pictures. The hiding place thus became especially appropriate for Ray Kemmerer's letter. She did not ask herself why she was saving the letter, but in the following weeks she liked knowing that it was there. After a deliberate delay she wrote a reply: "Dear Ray—Thank you for letting me know about your mother. As you say, I was always very fond of her. Since I learned about her too late to send flowers, I have made a small donation to the Presbyterian Missions in her memory. Sincerely, Ruth." Another letter that could be read in open court, and cold enough to discourage further correspondence.

Ruth Styles wanted no correspondence with Ray Kemmerer, and did not wish to see him again. Assuming that his looks had not been damaged or had even been improved upon by the passage of twenty years, he would now be, at best, a handsome man in his late forties, with tight curly hair cut short and parted in the middle, probably deeply tanned in the summer to make darker his dark complexion. Without a doubt he would be a golfer and bridge-player, since he had played golf and bridge as a young man. He had also been a football player at his obscure Ohio college, and golf, bridge, football and the obscure Ohio college had been subjects for Ted's campaign of ridicule. She was not sure what the Tonawanda Manufacturing Company manufactured, but he was vice-president and general manager of it, according to the letterhead. It was easy enough to imagine him, without seeing him, in a white dinner jacket at a country club dance, and if he was not president of the club, he probably had been. Whatever he was now, she was aware that the picture she was creating was strongly influenced by the twenty years' comments by Ted Styles, and the

contemporary Ray Kemmerer was not her Ray Kemmerer, real
or in fancy. In fancy he was the result of the prejudices
introduced by Ted Styles; in the real he was a man whom she
had not seen in twenty years, who was married to another
woman, and who seemed to have recovered from the disaster
to his love affair with Ruth Cooper.

But as months passed after the arrival of Ray Kemmerer's
letter she found that now and then she would go to her book-
shelf and take down the volume of humorous pieces and hold
the letter in her hand. She seldom put on her glasses to read it;
there was nothing of interest or warmth or comfort in the
words. And yet there was warmth and comfort in the physical
letter and in the shape of the blurred words, so little different
from the shape of the passionate words he had written in other
times. Between the "Ruth" at the beginning of the letter and
the "Ray" at the end she could fill in other words of letters she
had long since destroyed: "I love you even when I am not
thinking about you," he had once written. "I start thinking
about you and I realize that I have been loving you all the
time." So long as she had the letter in her hand she could substitute, by recollection, the contents of letters she had not saved.
And in so doing she would be, for ten minutes, the girl he had
written to when he was writing her every night.

She was alone a large part of the day; the children were
away at school, and Ted was in New York. It made not much
difference to anyone how she passed her time between taking
Ted to the train in the morning and meeting him in the late
afternoon. It actually made very little difference to anyone
how she spent her time *any* time. The children at their expensive schools (paid for by their two grandfathers) spent less
and less of their vacations at home, more and more of their
holidays visiting friends. Ted had his work, which was more
than a job; he designed textiles, and in the firm's interest he
frequently lectured at art schools and trade conventions. He
was good, he had a reputation, and he had achieved a nice
duality in the worlds of art and industry. In either field he par-
took of the prestigious benefits of the other. "What I am is

simply an artistic whore in a Wetzel suit," he would say. "A clean-shaven, solvent beatnik." He was very disarming; his utter frankness was especially effective among new acquaintances, who would immediately credit him with astuteness behind the candor. Most men did not like him, most women did not trust him, but men respected his success and women from time to time had to satisfy their curiosity about him in brief interludes that seldom endured as affairs. His children "adored" him. Ruth said they adored him because he had the gift of treating them as equals, of seeing things their way while subtly making them see things his way. He was bad for her kind of discipline; he gave them sips of wine when they were very young, gave them money when they had exhausted their allowances, taught them naughty limericks, encouraged them to question the authority of their teachers. But he was also quick and sometimes cruel with punishment when they did not instantly obey him, and when she protested that he was being unfair to them his reply was that children did not expect a parent to be fair: "Children are little beasts. They'd knife us in our beds if they could get away with it. Neddy strangled a kitten when he was five years old, don't forget. And I give you Jocelyn Styles and the way she used to beat up on her brother. Fairness? They don't know the meaning of the word."

"But I'm trying to teach them," said Ruth.

"Don't. It's a waste of time, and it's no preparation for life anyway. That baseball fellow, I agree with him. Nice guys don't win."

"Your father is a nice guy," she said. "So is mine."

"My father was afraid of his own shadow, and luckily I found that out when I was three years old. As to your father, Ruth, I don't see any difference between a Philadelphia lawyer and a Pittsburgh lawyer. The whole idea of the practice of law is to learn all the rules so that you can get around them. While we're on the subject of fairness, if there really were any such thing, lawyers would be the worst offenders. Because they're supposed to *know* what's fair. It's all written out for them. And yet they get rich by trickery and distortion of what they've been taught. The only thing that's fair about the law is that there's always another son of a bitch trying to trick *your* son of a bitch. And there's a super-son of a bitch in a black robe to judge the whole disgraceful exhibition. Very amusing."

She had no resources against such arguments. In the very beginning he had seduced her with words before going on to the physical seduction. "You never had an affair with Tarzan?" he had said, in one of his first destructive references to Ray Kemmerer.

"We never went all the way."

"Well, for God's sake, you weren't fascinated by that fine mind. What did you ever talk about?"

They had talked about love and the life they would have together, but she was ashamed to say so to this Ted Styles person. "I don't know, just talk."

"Me Tarzan, you Ruthie?"

"Please don't say any more," she said, and it was as close as she ever came to a defense of Ray Kemmerer or loyalty to their love. She married Ted Styles and allowed Ray Kemmerer to become a tiresome joke. As the wife of Ted Styles she even agreed with his aspersions on Ray's manhood.

"You could always get him to stop?"

"I told you a thousand times," she said.

"But *you* didn't want to stop."

"Yes I did. I didn't with you, but I did with him."

"Something wrong there, somewhere. He looked like a skiing instructor, but he was just too nice."

"Maybe that was it, I don't know. Why talk about him? I never even think about him."

"Maybe you ought to think about him. Think what I rescued you from. He didn't know the first thing about you."

"No, I guess not. I didn't know myself very well, either."

"That's for sure. If you'd married him you'd have been all over the place in six months. Divorced in two years, at the most."

"Probably. I don't know."

"Sure you would. Some son of a bitch like me would have come along and you'd have been the talk of Sewickley."

"We wouldn't have lived in Sewickley. His family came from Erie."

"God, that would have been worse, although I've never been to Erie."

He had compelled her to tell him in detail all there was to tell about her romance with Ray Kemmerer, and since there had been so little to tell, he had allowed his curiosity to subside; but for that very reason it had been easy for him to use Kemmerer as a symbol of the dullness of her life before he entered it. In their marriage, in their conversations, a Kemmerer was a private word as representative in its way as Babbitt to the general public; and until the arrival of Ray's note she had had no sense of loss, no feeling of regret that her first love had been taken away from her, no twinge of conscience for having permitted the denigration of a man who had failed only in ruthlessness. Once there had been a time when his kisses were exciting enough to make her pregnant, if excitement alone had had the secret of potency; there had been a time when death was understandable because it was a form of separation from Ray; the moon and music had once been meaningful because they enjoyed them with each other. And her present habit of saving the best letter for the last had begun in the days when he wrote every night, when she would turn the key in her bedroom door so that no one would interrupt that first reading. One day she had folded a letter and tucked it in the pocket of a tennis dress, and when she had finished playing and at last could read it, it was gone. In terror and in tears she had gone back to the court, searched the clubhouse, questioned the club servants, all without success. It was gone, lost, and gone and lost forever. Nothing could ever replace it, nothing ever did. Ray repeated in another letter as much as he could recall of the original, but it was not the same and there was a hole in her life.

They had two couples for dinner and Ted had a captive audience. "It isn't so much the fear of the bomb," he was saying.

"You hear people spouting forth that the decline of humor is because of the bomb, the times we live in. Hell, we've always lived in *times*. The real reason for the decline of humor is that it's all been said. There were so damn many humorists that they covered everything there was to write about. Ruth has the right idea. *She* still reads Ransford."

"Ransford? God, that dates you," said Emily Choate.

"Not the only thing that dates me," said Ruth.

"Remember *you* said that, not *I*," said Ted.

"All right, I'll remember," said Ruth. "Ransford was terribly funny."

"He probably appealed to a certain kind of background. I mean people with a good, solid, middle-class American background," said Ted.

"That's me," said Ruth.

"It's all of us in this room," said Ted.

"Not you, for heaven's sake, Ted," said Emily Choate.

"Sure me, why not me? You too, and Tom and Alicia and Bud. We all have the same background. I *didn't* say I haven't tried to rise *above* it. I did. And I never was amused by Mr. Ransford." Suddenly he left the room and came back with the Ransford collection. He opened the book, took out Ray Kemmerer's letter, frowned at it and tossed it in Ruth's lap. "I'll read you a sample of Ransford. I think this was in the old *Life*. It's a piece about spending a weekend in the country, and *God*, how many humorists have had a whack at that." He read the piece in a voice pitched slightly higher than his normal speaking voice, and when one of the men chuckled he looked over his reading glasses and stared sternly. "That's funny? I must read it again." He finished the piece, closed the book and tossed it to Ruth. "Ransford got rich on that kind of stuff. He used to get two or three thousand dollars for one of those little adventures, so I was told. And the mothers of the John Mason Brown ladies just doted on him."

At midnight the guests departed, and Ted said: "Who's the letter from?"

"Ray Kemmerer."

"Let me see it," he said.

"No."

"Why not?"

"Because it's my letter," she said.

"Well, we won't have any of that," he said. He snatched the book out of her hands, tossed it back at her and opened the letter.

"I warn you not to read that letter," she said.

" 'Tonawanda Manufacturing Company, Erie, Pennsylvania, September 20th, 1959. Dear Ruth.' " He read the letter aloud, put it back in the envelope and threw it to her. "So poor dear Mummy passed on. What the hell was the objection to my reading that? Is it in some kind of code? Let me see it again."

"No."

"Oh, all right. I don't want to struggle with you." He sat across the coffee table and lit a cigarette. "What interests me is why you'd save a letter like that. And of course it isn't the letter, it's because it came from that All-Time All-American dullard. Do you mean to say that after all these years you've discovered that you're in love with him?"

"I don't mean to say anything."

"Why don't you say something about Emily Choate?" he said. "Isn't that sort of on your mind?"

"Not very much. Not any more."

"Oh."

"Not as much as she was on yours."

"Are you implying that I had an affair with Emily?"

"No, I'm implying that you didn't but wanted to."

"It's there any time I want it," he said.

"I don't think so. A year ago, maybe, but not now."

"You're quite right about that. If she hadn't been so eager."

"And you hadn't been so busy elsewhere. I'm going to bed."

"Sit up and talk a while. I want to find out more about that letter. Why did you keep it?'

"I don't know, but it's really none of your business."

"Take it out of its hiding place from time to time? Sigh over young love? What might have been?"

"Something like that," she said.

"Are you planning to see him? First of all, *have* you seen him?"

"No."

"But naturally you answered the letter."

"Naturally," she said.

"Did you, uh, leave the latchstring out, so to speak?"

"I don't know that I'd say that," she said.

"Well, *would* you say that you raised the drawbridge?"

"No, I wouldn't say that, either."

"You answered him in kind, then, I suppose. In other words, the next move is up to him. Well, you know what that will be, of course. He didn't write you just to tell you about his old lady. So what do you plan to do when he tries to see you, a quiet lunch at the Hotel Astor?"

"If I decide to see him it won't be for a quiet lunch at the Astor."

"Buckity-buckity, eh?"

"Why not?"

" 'Why not'? That's the most cynical remark you've ever made to me."

"Well, why not?"

"You'd better watch out for this kind of thing, Ruth. I'll divorce you, and the Tonawanda Manufacturing Company might not want that."

"Oh, I've thought of that."

"And you wouldn't do it just to get even with me, would you? Maybe a divorce is just what I want."

"I've decided that what you want is of no consequence to me."

"My, we're full of surprises tonight. And if you knew what I thought of this Kemmerer."

"I do know. You've made that clear."

"He's such a dull bastard."

"How do you know?"

"His letter. He hadn't changed."

"I hope not, not too much."

"You sound pretty determined," he said. "I warn you, Ruth. I'm not going to let you get away with anything."

"All right."

"Or him, either. All at once I find myself loathing this slob, much as I hate to admit it. I don't like anyone or anything I don't understand."

"Well, you'd never understand this, Ted. It's too simple for you."

"Explain it."

"You won't get it. It's just that I like having been in love with Ray."

"No, there's a lot more to it than that. He had something else that you never told me. He must have, to make it stick for twenty years. Some dumb, uncomplicated thing that I haven't got. Maybe you don't know what it is. Let me see his letter again."

This time she handed him the letter, and he read it slowly to himself. He shook his head, put the letter back in the envelope, handed it to her. "No. It tells me nothing. It's in him. It's some quality that entirely eludes me. Ruth?"

"What?"

"Have you ever slept with anyone else since we've been married?"

"Yes."

"I thought maybe you had, and I hate it. But that makes this so much worse. It makes Kemmerer so much more formidable." He rose. "Well, I have to go to Atlanta tomorrow. Will you drive me to the airport?"

"Sure. What time?"

"Ten o'clock. I'm only going to be gone for the day—if that makes any difference to you."

"I'll meet you when you come back."

"Oh, I can get a taxi, thanks. Goodnight."

"Goodnight," she said.

"I'll sleep in Neddy's room."

"All right," she said. "You want breakfast at seven-thirty?"

"Yes, that ought to give me plenty of time. Ruth?"

"What?"

"Nothing. Goodnight."

Call Me, Call Me

Her short steps, that had always called attention to her small stature, now served to conceal the fact that her walk was slower. Now, finally, there was nothing left of the youth that had lasted so long, so well into her middle age. Her hat was small and black, a cut-down modified turban that made only the difference between being hatted and hatless but called no attention to the wearer, did not with spirit of defiance or gaiety proclaim the wearer to be Joan Hamford. Her Persian lamb, a good one bought in prosperous days, was now a serviceable, sensible garment that kept her warm and nothing more. She wore shoes that she called—echoing her mother's designation —"ties." They were very comfortable and they gave her good support.

The greeting by the doorman was precisely accorded. No "good morning," but "You'll have a taxi, Miss Hamford?" If she wanted a taxi, he was there to get her a taxi; that was one of the things he was paid for; but he could expect no tip now and she gave him little enough at Christmas. She was one of the permanent guests of the hotel, those whom he classified as salary people because he was paid a salary for providing certain services. Salary people. Bread-and-butter people. Not tip people, not big-gravy, expense-account people. Salary people. Budget people. Instant-coffee-and-half-a-pint-of-cream-from-the-delicatessen people. Five-dollars-in-an-envelope-with-his-name-on-it-at-Christmas people. The hotel was coming down in another year, and the hotel that was going up in its place would have no room for salary people. Only expense-account people.

"Taxi? Yes, please, Roy. Or I'd make just as good time walking, wouldn't I?"

"I don't know, Miss Hamford. I don't know where you're going."

"It is a little far," said Joan Hamford. "Yes, a taxi. *There's one!*"

She always did that. She always spotted a taxi, so that it would seem that she had really found it herself, unaided, and really owed him nothing. He was wise to that one. He was wise to all her little tricks and dodges, her ways of saving quarters, her half pints of cream from the delicatessen. She must be on her way to a manager's office today. Most days she would not take a taxi. "Such a nice day, I think a stroll," she would say, and then stroll exactly one block to the bus stop. But today it was a taxi, because she didn't want to be worn out when she applied for a job. Yes, today was a job day; she was wearing her diamond earrings and her pearls, which were usually kept in the hotel safe.

"Six-thirty Fifth Avenue, will you tell him, please, Roy?"

"Six-thirty Fifth," he said to the taxi driver. She could have given the address herself, but this was a cheap way of queening it. He closed the door behind her and stepped back to the curb.

"Number Six Hundred and Thirty, Avenue Five," said the driver, starting the meter. "Well, you got anything to read, lady, because the traffic on Madison and Fifth, I can't promise you nothing speed-wise. You wanta try Park, we'll make better time going down Park, but I won't guarantee you going west."

"How long will it take us if we go down Fifth?"

"Fifth? You wanta go down Fifth? I give you an honest estimate of between twenty and twenty-five minutes. Them buses, you know. You ever go to the circus and take notice to the elephants, the one holds on to the-one-in-front-of-him's tail with his trunk. That's the way the buses operate. Never no less than four together at the one time, and what they do to congest up the traffic! You see they could straighten that out in two hours if they just handed out a bunch of summonses, but then the union would pull the men off the buses and the merchants would holler to the powers-that-be, City Hall. I'm getting out of this city . . . We'll try Fifth . . . It's Miss Joan Hamford, isn't it?"

"Why, yes. How nice of you."

"Oh, I rode you before. You remember when you used to live over near the River? Four-what-is-it? Four-fifty East Fifty-second?"

"Oh, heavens, that long ago?"

"Yeah, I had one of them big Paramounts, twice the size of this little crate. You don't remember Louis?"

"Louis?"

"Me. Louis Jaffee. I used to ride you four-five times a week regular, your apartment to the Henry Miller on Forty-third, east of Broadway. Fifteen-and-five in those days, but you were good for a buck every night. Well, I'm still hacking, but you been in movies and TV and now I guess you're on your way to make another big deal for TV."

"No, as a matter of fact, a play. On Broadway. I'm afraid I can't tell you just what play, but it isn't television. Still a secret, you know."

"Oh, sure. Then you was out in Hollywood all that time I remember."

"Yes, and I did a few plays in London."

"That I didn't know about. I just remember you rode out the bonnom of the depression in Hollywood. The bonnom of the depression for me, but not for you. You must of made a killing out there. What does it feel like to see some of them pictures now, on TV? You don't get any royalties on them pictures, do you?"

"No."

"Now they all go in for percentages I understand. Be nice to have a percentage of some of them oldies. Is Charles J. Hall still alive?"

"No, poor Charles passed on several years ago."

"You always heard how he was suppose to be a terrific boozer, but I seen him the other night on TV. You were his wife, where you were trying to urge him to give up the Navy and head up this big shipbuilding company."

"*Glory in Blue.*"

"*Glory in Blue,* that's the one. How old was Charles J. Hall when you made that picture, do you remember?"

"How old? I should think Charles was in his early forties then."

"Christ! He'd be in his seventies."

"Yes, he would."

"I'm over the sixty mark myself, but I can't picture Charles J. Hall in his seventies."

"Well, he never quite reached them, poor dear."

"Booze, was it?"

"Oh, I don't like to say that."

"There's a lot worse you could say about some of those jerks they got out there now. Male *and* female. What they need out there is another Fatty Arbuckle case, only the trouble is the public is got so used to scandal."

"Yes, I suppose so."

"You know I was just thinking, I wonder how I missed it when Charles J. Hall passed away. Was it during the summer? I go away in the summer and I don't see a paper for two weeks."

"Yes, I think it was."

"They would have had something in."

"They didn't have very much, not as much as he deserved, considering what a really big star he was."

"But there was a long time when he wasn't in anything. That's when I understood he was hitting the booze so bad. Where was he living during that time?"

"In Hollywood. He stayed right there."

"Wouldn't take anything but big parts, I guess. That's where you were smart, Miss Hamford."

"How do you mean?"

"Well, they forgot all about Charles J. Hall. Like my daughter didn't know who the hell he was last week. But she'd know you. She'd know you right away, because from TV, when you were that lady doctor two years ago, that serial."

"Unfortunately only lasted twenty-six weeks."

"I don't care. Your face is still familiar to the new generation. I don't know what any actress fools around with Broadway for."

"Some of us love the theater."

"Sure, there's that, but I'm speaking as a member of the public. You could be in *My Fair Lady* and there wouldn't be as many people see you as if you went in one big spectacular. When I see my daughter tomorrow night, when she comes for supper, I'm gunna tell her I rode Joan Hamford. And right away she's gunna say 'Doctor McAllister? Doctor Virginia McAllister?' So they took it off after twenty-six weeks, but just think of how many million people saw you *before* they took it off. Up there in the millions. The so-called Broadway theater, that's gettin' to be for amateurs and those that, let's face it, can't get a job in TV."

"Oh, you mustn't say that."

"Well, I'm only telling you what the public thinks, basing it on my own conclusions. Here you are, Six-three-oh. Eighty-five on the clock."

"Here, Louis. I want you to have this."

"The five?"

"For old times' sake."

"Well, thanks. Thanks a lot, Miss Hamford. The best to you, but TV is where you ought to be."

She hoarded her strength during the walk to the elevator, and she smiled brightly at the receptionist in the office of Ralph Sanderson–Otto B. Kolber. "Mr. Sanderson is expecting you, Miss Hamford. Go right in."

"Good morning, Ralph," said Joan Hamford.

Sanderson rose. "Good morning, Joan. Nice of you to come down at this hour, but unfortunately it was the only absolutely only time I had. You know anything about this play?"

"Only what I've read about it."

"Well, then you probably don't know anything about the part."

"No, not really. I read the book, the novel, but I understand that's been changed."

"Oh, hell, the novel. We only kept the boy and his uncle, from the novel."

"The boy's aunt? She's not in the play? Then what is there for me, Ralph? Or would you rather have me read the play instead of you telling me?"

"No, I'd just as soon tell you. Do you remember the schoolteacher?"

"The schoolteacher? Let me think. There *was* a schoolteacher in one of the early chapters, but I don't think she had a name."

"In the novel she didn't. But she has in the play."

"You really must have changed the novel. How does the part develop?"

"Well, frankly it doesn't. We only keep the teacher for one scene in the first act."

"Oh, well, Ralph, you didn't bring me down here for that. That isn't like you. Good heavens, even if I'd never done anything else, I was Dr. Virginia McAllister to God knows how many million people, and I got twenty-two-fifty for that."

"Three years ago, Joan, and you haven't had much to do since. That's why I thought of you for the teacher. I'd rather give it to you than someone I don't know. I'll pay three-fifty."

"What for? You can't bill me over the others, the part isn't big enough to do that."

"I couldn't anyway. The boy gets top billing, and Michael Ware is co-star. Tom Ruffo in *Illinois Sonata with* Michael Ware. But I admit you'd lead the list of featured players."

"You know how these things are, Ralph. Not a manager in town but will know I'm working for three-fifty."

"But working, and I'll take care of you publicity-wise. The theater doesn't pay movie or TV salaries, you know that."

"I understand Jackie Gleason got six thousand."

"He may have got more, but Virginia McAllister wasn't Ralph Kramden. I wish you'd think about this, Joan. It's not physically very demanding. You don't have to stand around or do any acrobatics."

"Or act, either, I suppose. No, I'm afraid not, Ralph, and I really think you were rather naughty to bring me down here."

"Joan, this is a fine play and with this boy Ruffo we're going to run ten months, and maybe a lot longer. For you it would be like a vacation with pay, and you'd be back in the theater. Stop being a stubborn bitch, and think back to times when I paid you sixty dollars a week for more work."

"In that respect you haven't changed, Ralph."

"Four hundred."

"Take-home that's still only a little over three hundred. No, I'm going right on being a stubborn bitch."

"I'll give you four hundred, and I'll release you any time after the first six months that you find a better part."

"Can you write me into the second and third acts?"

"Impossible. The locale changes, and anyway, I know the author wouldn't do it. And frankly I wouldn't ask him to. No more tinkering with this play till we open in Boston."

"Well—still friends, Ralph. You tried."

"Yes, I certainly tried."

She reached out her hand. "Give me five dollars for the taxi."

"Joan, are you that broke?"

"No, I'm not broke, but that's what it cost me to come here."

Sanderson pulled a bill from a money-clip. "If it cost you five to get here it'll cost you another five to get home. Here's a sawbuck."

"I only wanted five, but of course I'll take the ten. In the old days you would have spent more than that on taking me to lunch."

"Considering where we usually ended up after lunch, the price wasn't high."

"I guess that's a compliment."

"You know, you have delusions of Laurette Taylor in *Menagerie*. All you senior girls have that."

"Senior girls. That sounds so Camp Fire-y."

"You're going to be sore as hell when you see who gets this part. I don't know who it'll be, but I'm going to pick somebody you hate."

"Good. Don't pick anybody I like, because I'll hate her if the play runs."

"And yourself."

"Oh—well, I hate myself already. Do you think I like going back to that hotel, feeling sure you have a hit, *hoping* you have a hit, and stuck with my own stubborn pride? But you know I can't take this job, Ralph."

"Yes, I guess I do."

"You wouldn't stretch a point and take me to lunch, would you?"

"No, I can't, Joan."

"Then—will you give me a kiss?"

"Any time." He came around from behind his desk and put his arms around her.

"On the lips," she said.

He bent down, she stood on tiptoe, and his mouth pressed on hers. "Thank you, dear," she said. "Call me, call me."

"I hope so," he said, as she went out.

It's Mental Work

It was nearly half-past four and the last customer had been let out the side door. The barroom was dark except for the weak night light over the cash register. For early risers it was Tuesday morning, but here it was still Monday night. Rich Hickman, the bartender, had his street clothes on, very dapper, and seeming not at all tired as he came in the back room.

"You all through, Rich?" said Wigman, the owner.

"All through *here*," said Rich, with a smile.

"Yeah, you look as if you had some place to go," said Wigman. "One for the road, as they say?" Wigman pointed to the bottle of bourbon on the table.

"I don't know. Sure," said Rich. He looked at his wristwatch, a hexagonal shape with square hollow links of stainless steel. "You want company a little while?"

"Get yourself a glass and sit down," said Wigman. "I don't know whether I got a date or not. It all depends."

"Yeah, I know," said Rich, speaking while he fetched a shot glass from the bar. "Those all-depends dates. I give that up for a coupla years, but now I'm back playing the field. All depends, all depends. They give you that all-depends chowder, but it's still better than being tied down."

"I don't know," said Wigman. "I don't know which is better, to tell you the truth. I'm forty-four years of age and twice in my life I thought I was settled down. *Settled* down. But it got to be *tied* down, and I was too young for that. I still feel pretty young, but I know what I am. I'm forty-four going on forty-five, and if I'm gonna be ninety years old, I'm halfway there. Halfway to ninety. Cheers, Rich."

"Cheers," said Rich. They raised glasses and drank.

"What did we do tonight?" said Wigman.

"Around three and a quarter."

"Yeah, quiet. Well, a Monday," said Wigman.

"You don't even figure to break even on a Monday," said Rich.

"That reminds me. How is it you never owned a joint of your own?"

"Oh, I don't know. I got offered the chance to, to go partners with a guy in Fort Lauderdale, but I didn't. I didn't like the fellow. And I had a rich dame in Miami Beach used to give me the big talk, but for two years straight as soon as it was April she went back to New York, and I was still on the duck-boards. I guess she didn't have the money. The cash, I mean. She had a forty-dollar-a-day room all season, and she had a coupla rings there that shoulda been good for fifteen, twenty thousand apiece. But I know for a fact she was a two-dollar bettor at the track. Her husband wouldn't let her have any cash."

"Were you in?"

"Oh, sure, I was in. I had the use of a big Chrysler and she give me like all my slacks and sport shirts she used to put on the tab at the hotel. They had a woman's shop there that carried men's shirts and slacks and a couple times special orders for an Italian silk suit, sports jackets. And you know, that husband never got wise, because it was a woman's shop. It all went on the tab at the hotel. But cash, no. She was a two-dollar bettor. Didn't cash ten bets all season, all long shots. Every race she had the long shot. That many long shots don't come in."

"That many favorites don't come in either," said Wigman.

"No. Not when I have them at least. So anyway, I stop going steady with her and ever since I been playing the field."

"How old are you, Rich?"

"How old am I? I'm thirty-seven. I'm not so much younger than you."

"You look it, though. I got too much weight on me."

"Well, you think about it and it's very seldom you see a bartender overweight. If he's just a working stiff. An owner that tends bar, he'll put on the weight. But just an ordinary bartender, he's on his feet, moving around. Like a cashier in a bank. A paying teller. How many of them do you see fat? I figured it out why. You're on your feet all day and the lard don't get a chance to grow on you. Furthermore, you don't think of a bartender as using up mental energy, but we do. You carry on these conversations with the customers, you got maybe twenty-thirty customers at one time, and they all say, 'Hey, Rich, will you do this again, please?' and you're supposed to know what every one of them wants. Then the cash register, the prices. And the guys that want the bottle on the bar, you gotta keep an eye on them. It's mental work, and that uses up energy. We're not very different than a paying teller. Except the respectability."

"And the wages, Rich. You get better wages."

"That we do."

"And you're not stuck in the one place all your life."

"No. Oh, I'm not complaining. How long would a teller in a bank last if they found out he was driving some broad's Chrysler and living it up in a forty-dollar-a-day room? I had a room over in Miami, a fleabag over there, but most of the time I was in Miami Beach."

"A good tan goes well with your white hair."

"Oh, I used to pass for ten years younger. This broad thought I was around twenty-six, twenty-seven. Gave her a little priority over the other broads. Priority? You know what I mean. Not priority."

"Superiority."

"That's it."

There was a metallic rap on the window. "I guess I got a date after all," said Wigman.

"I'll get it," said Rich, going to the door. "Howdy do?"

The woman said: "Hello. Is Ernie here?"

"Come on in," called Wigman. "That's Rich Hickman, my bartender. Come on in, June."

"Hello," said June to Rich, acknowledging the introduction.

"Nice to meet you," said Rich. "I'll be going."

"Stick around, don't go," said Wigman.

"I better go," said Rich, looking at his watch.

"Time you meeting your date?" said Wigman.

"Well, I don't know. She was gonna be here or give me a buzz."

"Well, stick around a while," said Wigman. "So she's a little late. They're always late. Hello, Junie."

"*I* wasn't so very late," said the woman. "I told you between four and five, so I'm early."

"What'll you drink?" said Wigman.

"Oh—I don't know," said June. She looked at the bottle on the table. "Not bourbon."

"Well, you can have anything you want, and if you want a mixed drink, this is the guy to do it for you. This guy is only the best. Take my word for it."

"You know what I think I'll have is a Rob Roy. I had a Scotch earlier."

"That's easy," said Rich.

"Live up to your reputation now, Rich. Give her the best Rob Roy she ever hung a lip over."

"What an expression!" said June. She lit a cigarette and Rich went to the barroom. "What happened to the other fellow you used to have?"

"He quit, and I got this fellow. This fellow's twice as good. No spillage. No getting out of hand with the customers. And pretty, too, isn't he?"

"He's almost too pretty. He dyes his hair. Is he queer?"

"If he is, I should be as queer. The women go big for this guy."

"Does he go big for them is the question," said June.

"I got an idea that it's mutual. How was your business tonight?"

"Off. Way off. They're talking about closing Monday nights entirely. I heard they're trying to make a deal with the unions. It may pick up though, towards the end of the week. They moan and groan every Monday, but as soon as it begins to pick up towards the end of the week, you don't hear any more about it."

"I know," said Wigman. "We were way off tonight."

"It starda rain out," said June. "I just got a few drops on me, getting out of the cab."

"I owe you for the cab," said Wigman. He took a bill out of a money clip. She looked at the bill and then at Wigman. She shook her head.

"This five has an *O* behind it," she said.

"I don't need glasses," said Wigman.

"You want to give me fifty dollars?"

"Why are you acting surprised? It isn't the first time I gave you fifty dollars."

"You don't have to give me fifty dollars," she said. "I don't mind when business is good, but you said you were way off tonight."

"We were very good Saturday and Sunday."

"Ernie, you don't *have* to do this," she said.

"But I'd rather," he said. "Here's your Rob Roy. A good way to unload the cheap Scotch."

"I didn't use the cheap Scotch," said Rich. "That's as good as we have in the house."

"Well, that's all right, considering," said Wigman.

Hickman looked at the rain-streaked window. "Hey, you know it's starting to come down."

"You might as well wait here till it stops."

The fifty-dollar bill disappeared into June's purse and she sipped the cocktail, moving her eyes from right to left, left to right as she judged the taste. "Good," she said. "Just right."

"Thanks," said Rich.

"I told you, this guy is only the best," said Wigman. "You better stick around in case she wants another one."

"Well, if it's all right with all concerned," said Rich. "My friend should be along any minute, or phone."

"There's the bottle," said Wigman. "Help yourself. You know the combination."

"Do you mind if I ask you something?" said June.

"Go ahead," said Rich.

"Did you used to be in Miami Beach, driving a big kind of a Cadillac or one of those?"

"A Chrysler, yeah," said Rich.

"Last season. You know you almost knocked me down?"

"Me? I don't remember even coming close. Seriously, are you sure it was me? I don't remember no accident."

"You wouldn't remember me, but I remember you. Corner of Thirty-first and Lincoln. You were so busy talking to your lady friend you never even saw me. Or heard me. I really gave it to you, but it was all wasted. I think you were having a little fight with the lady friend. A blonde with those big sun glasses?"

"That could fit forty-five thousand dames in Miami Beach, but I guess it all adds up. I apologize."

"I knew I seen you some place before. That hair gives you away."

"Next question. Do I dye it? No, I don't. I stard getting gray hair when I was twenty-three years of age."

"I didn't ask you. That's none of my business."

"Well, then you're the exception because they all ask me," said Rich.

"That's funny, because I wasn't," she said. "It's too bad you don't have that big car tonight. You could ride Ernie and I home."

"What is this, the needle? You know damn well it was never my car or I wouldn't be tending bar for a living."

"Ernie, I thought you said this man never got out of hand with the customers."

"You're not a customer, and let's face it, you got the needle in there pretty deep. But enjoy yourself, the both of you," said Wigman.

"Yeah, how much do I have to take when I'm not getting paid for it?" said Rich. "You know what I mean? I got the apron off now, a first-class citizen after four A.M. What do *you* do, June? Are you a hatcheck chick?"

"What if I am?"

"Well, then, relax," said Rich. "You know what I mean? So you take it all night for a lousy buck, so do I. But here it is close on to five o'clock in the morning and we're people now. Not only you, but me. What'd somebody give you the big pitch tonight? Is that what's bugging you?"

"Nothing is bugging me, and nobody gave me any big pitch."

"Maybe that's what's bugging you, nobody give you the pitch. Did I strike oil there, June?"

"Easy does it there, Rich," said Wigman. "Don't get personal."

"You mean I shouldn't call her June? How's the cocktail, ma'am?"

"I must say you're a sarcastic son of a bitch," said Wigman. "I never realized that before."

"Oh, I hold it in when I got my apron on, but this is after hours, Ernie."

"Ernie, huh?" said Wigman.

"All right. *Mr. Wigman,* if that's the way you like it. But I coulda been Mr. Hickman in Fort Lauderdale, and then maybe you'da been one of my customers. Mr. Hickman and Mr. Wigman."

"You coulda been Mr. Hickman in Miami Beach if the broad had the cash, only her husband wouldn't let her get her hooks on any cash," said Wigman.

"Now who's sarcastic?" said Rich.

"I think you're making a fast load," said Wigman. "You only had three sitting here—"

"And one when I was mixing her drink, making four."

"Well, that's a half a pint in about fifteen minutes," said Wigman.

"Do you do everything fast?" said June.

"That depends on how you mean that. Some things I take it slow and easy."

"All right, Rich. Down, boy," said Wigman.

"The lady asked me a question. I thought she wanted to know. Some things I can take it slow and easy, whereas I know some women don't like it if you take it slow and easy. Speaking of shaking up a Dackery, for instance."

"Yeah. Sure. Well, I tell you, Rich," said Wigman. "I think you better take a slow and easy powder out of here while we're all still friends. I see you tomorrow night."

"Okay, Ernie. Okay. Goodnight, Ernie, and good night, June. Watch out for reckless drivers." He got up and went out the side door.

"The idea asking him does he do everything fast?" said Wigman. "You couldn't have but only the one meaning to a question like that."

"So?"

"You mean you go for that guy?"

"I don't go for anybody. I'm so sick of men. I wouldn't care if I never saw another man for the rest of my life, the way I feel now."

"Well, that won't last."

"But you're so *right* it won't last. I didn't say it would last. I was only telling you how I feel now, tonight."

"Well, you want to go home with me or don't you? Either way."

"Put me in a cab and I'll see you tomorrow night. Here," she said, and handed him the fifty-dollar bill.

"Forget it, forget it. It's only human nature. I'm kind of beat too, myself. Let me stash this bottle and I'll get you a cab."

They went out together and he hailed a cruising cab. "That's all I am, Ernie. I'm kind of beat, too. I'll see you tomorrow night, yeah?"

"Sure. Goodnight, kid."

"Kid. Thirty-six years old. Goodnight, Ernie."

Wigman hailed another cab, got in, had the driver stop for the morning papers, and proceeded to his hotel. During the night, his night, he had a heart attack and died. His body was found by the waiter who had a standing order to bring his breakfast at one o'clock in the afternoon. Ernie Wigman's lawyer, Sanford Conn, was out of town and could not be reached, and the place ran itself that night, as it always did when Ernie did not show up. But a policeman had been around, asking questions, and the news of Ernie's death was known to the bartenders and waiters and kitchen help, and to the regular customers. Rich Hickman took charge. "I'll close up," he told the others. They were agreeable; they did not want to have to account for the money in the till.

Rich got the last customer out a few minutes after four in the morning. In the back room was a cop named Edwards, the man on post whom Rich had asked to be there. "I just want you here when I tot up what's in the till," said Rich.

"I'm not suppose to do that," said Edwards.

"Well, do it anyway as a favor."

"Who to?"

"To Ernie. I think he has a kid somewhere, and Ernie was always all right with you guys. That I happen to know. I just want you to witness that I'm not stealing off a dead man."

"I won't sign anything."

"Who asked you to sign, Edwards? I'll count it up in front of you, and lock it up in the register and give you the key. Is there anything in the book against that?"

"Nothing in the book against it, but—well, what the hell? All right. But I don't take any responsibility."

"You don't take any responsibility, but this way no son of a bitch is going to say I robbed a dead man."

"You could of been robbing him all night long, that's the way I gotta look at it, Hickman."

"I couldn't of been robbing him much. All you gotta do is compare tonight with last Tuesday or any Tuesday. If I was robbing him all night long I didn't get rich on it."

"I guess that makes sense," said Edwards. "Go ahead and count it up."

The cop sat bored on a bar stool while Rich made his count. "Cash on hand, five hundred and twenty-eight dollars and eighty-seven cents. Okay?"

"That's what it looks like to me," said Edwards.

"You wouldn't do me a favor and initial this slip before I lock it up?"

"I guess I can do that," said Edwards. "There's somebody at the back door."

"Let him in, will you? No, you keep your eye on the money. I'll let him in. I hope it's his lawyer, a fellow named Conn."

"Conn is a good name for a lawyer," said Edwards.

Rich went to the back door, opened it, and admitted June. "Ernie here?" she said.

"No. Come on in," said Rich.

"What's with the cop?" said June.

"I'll tell you later."

"Trouble? I don't go for cops."

"Then wait here."

"I don't like this. Where's Ernie?"

"Ernie is dead."

"A stick-up?"

"Nothing like that. He had a heart attack. If you'll sit down I'll take care of the cop and then I'll tell you all about it."

Rich returned to Edwards, put the money in the cash register, and gave Edwards the key. "All right, Edwards?"

"I guess so."

"Thanks a lot."

"All right. See you." Edwards left, and Rich mixed a Rob Roy, put it on a tray and took it to the back room. In his other hand he carried a bottle of bourbon with a shot glass inverted and resting on the cap.

"Ernie had a heart attack at the hotel. They found him around one o'clock yesterday."

"That's when he usually had breakfast," she said. "Are they having a service for him?"

"I don't have any idea. He had a kid, didn't he?"

"He had two kids around eighteen and twenty years of age, but I don't know where they are or any of that. I guess they'll show up. He was divorced, that I know."

"I closed up tonight and I had the cop come in to see that I didn't steal anything out of the till. Do you know Ernie's lawyer?"

"Sanford Conn, his name is. He had a piece of the joint. I know him from him going out with Ernie and I a couple times."

"This joint could do a lot better, a *lot* better. Ernie was a nice guy, but I could of told him ways to save a little here and make a little there. You know Conn, eh?"

"That well. Been out with him and his wife, with Ernie. A young fellow about thirty-five. He's the lawyer for four or five joints like this, and I think he's in for a piece of all of them."

"Then he's a guy I could go to with a proposition?"

"If there was a buck in it, he'd listen . . . So Ernie cooled. You know I was almost with him last night."

"How do you mean, almost?"

"Almost is what I said, almost is what I mean. I didn't go home with him. He put me in a cab outside here. I wouldn't of liked that, waking up with a dead man."

"What stopped you from going home with him?"

"Didn't feel like it. I guess I got so burned up with you that I was sick and tired of men. Now I think of it, Ernie said he was tired, too. I wonder if he knew anything beforehand. He *said* he was *tired*."

"He often said he was tired. I used to say to him, not come right out with it, but he'd sit and put away a quart of bourbon and eat a steak and a whole meal and sometimes he was here for ten-twelve hours, eating and drinking and never get up and walk around. I said to him about a month ago, I said —well, I didn't say anything, if you want the straight of it. But I thought, this guy he never moves out of his chair, and all that booze and rich food. Ten-twelve hours he'd sit here. They get that way, some of them. I worked for guys that did the very same thing. And they kid themselves that they're working, just because they're sitting in their own joint. Work? What work? Why, one of the day men was stealing from him right in front of his very eyes, that's how much work he was doing."

"Stealing how?"

"Oh, there's ways of working with a waiter. There's plenty of ways you can steal. *You* steal a little, don't you? The concession don't get it all."

"Most of it. You know, I'd like to have the concession here."

"Yeah, but would Conn give it to you?"

"Maybe not Conn, but maybe a new owner would. Or a new partner."

"You mean like if I got to be partners with Conn?"

"You must of attended a mind-reading school," said June.

"Graduated," said Rich. "You wouldn't mind working for me? I got the impression last night you wouldn't spit in my eye."

"I wouldn't be working for you, exactly. I'd have the concession, so I'd be working for myself."

Rich thought a moment. "Usually the syndicate owns the concession, and they pay so much for it. You know that."

"I ought to know it after—I been in this business. But here they never had a checkroom. Ernie didn't want one."

"I know. But you were softening him up."

"It's a lot of money going to waste," said June. "I could do a hundred and fifty a week here."

"You could do two hundred, two and a quarter."

"So?"

"Well, that's what I think it's worth, not a hundred and fifty. So if you got it it wouldn't be on a basis of a hundred and fifty. Don't play games with me, June."

"I want to make a little for myself. It's not all clear profit. All right, so you're big-hearted and you give me a concession worth maybe two hundred a week. But first you gotta convince Sanford Conn, and who knows Sanford Conn? I do."

"Yeah, we were coming to that," said Rich.

"One word from me, either way."

"Honey, I'm with you. How much money you got, and how much can you raise?"

"Ha ha ha. Would I tell you? How much do *you* have, and how much can *you* raise?"

"This is serious. If you could get your hands on fi-thousand dollars, I think I could raise twenty-five. With thirty gees I could talk to Conn. Conn don't have to know you got the checkroom till him and I make a deal."

"You want me to put up five thousand dollars for the concession?"

"The way you say that I know you got it."

"Where is your end coming from?"

"What do you care, or what does Conn care, as long as I get it? I don't have that kind of money myself, but I can come pretty close to raising it."

"That dame that you almost killed me with in her car."

"Good for a little, but not much. She don't have any cash, only some jewelry."

"No heist. I don't want any part of a heist. Don't even talk about it. I got no record downtown and I want to keep it that way."

"If I had a record I couldn't work either. And I'm not talking about a heist. But her and a couple others I know, and a couple liquor salesmen. Plus your five, I could go to Conn with a proposition. This is a very good chance for the both of us, June. And me and you could save rent."

"Yeah, that was coming, too. You move in with me or I move in with you. Which?"

"You got an apartment, I'd move in with you. I only got a room way the hell up on West Eighty-fourth Street."

"Where do you think I live? In the Waldorf Towers? I got an apartment but it's only one room."

"By the month?"

"What else?"

"We could save money on a lease. Wuddia say?"

"I don't know. I'd have to think it over. How would I get rid of you if I didn't like you around?"

"How would you get rid of me? Start leaving your stuff on the floor, your hair curlers all over the can."

"I'm tidy."

"I noticed that, or I wouldn't broach the proposition."

"I take a bath twice a day, sometimes more," she said. She snickered.

"What?"

"This way I'd know for sure if you dyed your hair."

"You wanta know something, I touch it. It's near all gray, but I touch it."

"I like it."

"Thanks."

"Well, we didn't talk much about Ernie," she said.

"No, but we didn't say anything against him," said Rich.

"That's true. We didn't say anything against him. I guess he was that kind of a guy, Ernie. He checks out and you start forgetting him right away, but at least you don't say anything against him."

"Well, he done us a favor," said Rich.

"You mean you and I getting together? Yeah, if that's a favor. It's too soon to tell."

"I think we'll work out all right, June."

"Maybe we will. And if we don't—"

"You can start leaving hair curlers around."

She smiled. "Yes," she said. "If they all would of been that easy to get rid of."

"What are you, divorced?"

"Twice. What about you? Are you divorced?"

"No, I never got married. I came close a couple times, but something always happened, so I never had it legal. You know, I go south in the winter, and when the season's over I come north or I been to the coast a couple times, working."

"This'd be the first time you ever settled down? I mean with a place. I don't know, Rich."

"You worried about your five gees?"

"Wouldn't you be?"

"Don't worry about it. I like you. I knew that right away last night. I would of gone after you, Ernie or no Ernie."

"Yeah, and I wouldn't of run away from you. I didn't have anything permanent with Ernie."

There was a banging on the side door and Rich went to the door and peered out at two men. "I don't know these guys," he said. There was a roller shade on the door and similar shades on the windows of the back room. "We're closed," he shouted, and let the shade fall back in place. The banging was resumed.

"Maybe you better see what they want," said June.

"I think I heard one of them say Hickman," said Rich. "Will I take a chance?"

"Talk to them through the door," said June.

Rich opened the door a few inches, and immediately it was pushed against him and he was driven out of the way. "What's the idea?" said Rich.

"What's the idea? What's your idea?" said one of the men. Then he saw June at the table. "Hello, June."

"Hello, Sandy. It's all right, Rich. This is Sandy Conn."

"You're kinda rough, Mr. Conn," said Rich.

"Maybe, and you're kind of stupid. Close the door, Jack," Conn commanded his companion. Jack was obviously a hoodlum, a muscle man.

"I heard you were out of town," said Rich.

"You're Hickman, the bartender?" said Conn.

"Yes. I heard you were out of town and I decided to take care of everything till you got back."

"Yeah, yeah. All right, what's in the till?"

"Five hundred and twenty-eight dollars and some cents," said Rich. "In the register."

"A good thing it isn't in your pocket. Give me the key," said Conn, extending his hand.

"I don't have it. I gave it to Edwards, the cop on the beat."

"You what?"

"I can vouch for that," said June.

"You? I wouldn't ask you to vouch. You're in with this fellow now. Give me the key or do I get Jack here to take it away from you? Whichever one of you has the key, hand it over. I don't care which one Jack has to take it away from. Do you, Jack? You have any objection to wrestling with a woman?"

Jack laughed.

"I guess not," said Conn.

"Call the precinct, if you don't believe me," said Rich. "But if this goon gets any closer to me *or* her, I break this bottle over his head. Then I take care of you, Mr. Conn. You I could handle easily."

"I could almost handle you myself, Sandy," said June. "This man is telling the truth, you silly son of a bitch. He was protecting your interest."

"I aint worried about the bottle, Mr. Conn," said Jack.

"I'm thinking," said Conn. "What'd you say the name of this cop was?"

"Edwards. He's a patrolman."

"You don't have to tell me. If he was a sergeant I'd know him." Conn went to the telephone booth and was gone about five minutes. "I guess I owe you an apology," he said, when he returned. "Edwards has the key." He turned to Jack. "Okay, Jack. Thanks."

"That's all?" said Jack.

"Come around the office tomorrow and I'll give you a check."

"You wouldn't have five or ten on you?" said Jack.

"Here," said Conn, handing him a bill. "Goodnight, Jack."

"Thanks, Mr. Conn. Goodnight all," said Jack, leaving.

Conn sat down, across the table from June. "Too bad about Ernie, but the amount of liquor he consumed. Where you from, Hickman?"

"Why?"

"Well, I liked the way you took charge tonight. I like a take-charge guy. Bill Dickey, you remember used to catch for the Yanks? A real take-charge guy. You ever owned a joint, or managed one?"

"No."

"I know you got no police record, but give me the names of some places where you worked before."

"Why?"

"Well, June here will tell you, I got an interest in five other saloons. I kind of specialize in cafés."

"That's what you specialize in?" said Rich.

"I got other clients, naturally, but I been building up a café-owner practice."

"I thought there for a minute you specialized in something else."

"Like what? Explain."

"Like hiring some goon to beat up a woman," said Rich.

Conn tapped his fingernails on the table and watched Rich in silence. "Don't start anything, Hickman," he said presently.

"Jack ought to be a long way off by this time," said Rich.

"You lay a hand on me and it goes on your record downtown."

"Then I better make it good, huh?" said Rich.

Conn pointed to June. "She don't work, either."

"I'd of been in great shape after Jack got through with me, too," said June.

"What'll we do with him, June?" said Rich.

"If it was me, I'd kill him."

"What'd be the best way?" said Rich.

"Knock him out and dump him in the river. You got a car," said June.

"I told you the car don't belong to me, June."

"Oh, yeah, that's right. You got any other suggestions?"

"They got a walk-in icebox back in the kitchen. We could leave him there."

"I know you're kidding, you two," said Conn. "I tell you—"

"Shut up," said Rich, and slapped him hard on both cheeks. "I got a better idea." He got a hammer lock on Conn's left arm and forced him to his feet. He pushed him forward and kept pushing him through the cellar door, down the steps, and into a closet that was lined on both walls with wine bins and case goods. He closed the door and locked it.

"Will he suffocate?" said June.

"No. But I'll bet he has a headache by the time they find him. He can holler his head off and nobody'll hear him."

"How long'll he be there?"

"Oh, the day man comes on around ten o'clock. That gives him around five hours. In the dark. It's gonna seem longer."

"I hope," said June.

They went upstairs, and in the back room he said: "Well, have a good look at the joint. You won't be seeing it again."

"No," she said.

They went out the side door, and as they headed west she took his arm. "You," she said.

"That's right," he said. "Me."

In the Silence

The two friends were having coffee together after one of their Saturday lunches. As happens in friendships, they could be silent without awkwardness, and during one such silence Charles Ellis casually picked up a small book that was lying on the coffee table. It was a club roster, bound in two colors and with the club insigne stamped on the front cover, and below the symbol a slip of paper was glued on, which in typescript read: "Not to be removed from Lounge." Ellis leafed through the book and was about to put it down when a name caught his eye. "Know anybody named Holderman?"

"No, I don't think so," said James Malloy.

"Joseph W. Holderman 2d, Eagle Summit, P-A. Joined here in 1916. I've seen that name for years and I was always going to ask you about it. If anybody'd know that name, you would."

"I do know it."

"Thought you said you didn't," said Ellis.

"Holderman alone didn't mean anything, but when you gave it the full treatment, I not only know the name. I know the man. Not only know the man, I've been to his house at Eagle Summit. What would you like to know about him?"

"Well, the only reason I'm curious about him is I've seen his name in this book all these years, and I wondered about him. I've never seen him, I've never heard anyone speak of him, and why does a man that lives in a place called Eagle Summit, Pennsylvania, keep up his membership in this club? He's been a member for forty-five years, so he isn't any chicken. Nowadays you hear men like that say they're over-clubbed. Oh, wait a second, he's a life member. Doesn't have to pay dues any more."

"I think Holderman would pay dues anyway."

"What for? So that he can wear the club tie?"

"You may think you're kidding, but that's one of the reasons."

"Sounds pretty stuffy to me," said Ellis.

"He's anything but," said Malloy. "He's no chicken, as you say. He must be in his middle seventies, but I'd like to see him again before he dies. Or *I* do. Have I aroused any more curiosity about Joseph W. Holderman 2d, of Eagle Summit, Pennsylvania?"

"Some. Give."

"I'd love to," said Malloy. . . .

First I must tell you a little about Eagle Summit (said Malloy), where it is and what kind of country it's in. There's almost no such place as Eagle Summit, it's so small. It is, or was, a post office, which was also the general store. A Protestant church, very likely Presbyterian in that part of the country. A garage that was once a blacksmith shop. Mind you, I'm talking about the way it was when I saw it in 1927. There were some private houses, a doctor lived in one and had his office there. There was a little building that was a sort of township hall, with a couple of cells in the back. The village wasn't big enough to have a bank or a movie theater. It wasn't even on the railroad, not even a branch or a spur. It was in the mountains in North Central Pennsylvania, and the nearest town of any considerable size was Williamsport. Eagle Summit was hardly more than a clearing in the woods, and the people that lived there dreaded a forest fire more than anything else in the world. The village could have been completely wiped out without anyone outside's knowing the difference, at least for a week or so. There were only three telephones in the village itself. The town hall's, the general store's, and the doctor's, and one other about two miles away, at the Holdermans' house, but I don't want to get ahead of myself. I want to give you some more geography, et cetera.

The state highway didn't run through Eagle Summit. The

village was on a county road, which was originally, I imagine, scratched out by prison labor, if they could get that many prisoners, or more likely the road was built by the loggers. Timber was the only industry in that part of the State. Thousands and thousands of acres of virgin timber, but so hard to get to it and to move it away that a great deal of it was left unspoiled. It was wild country. Two hundred yards away from Eagle Summit and you were a thousand years in the past, back before Columbus discovered the country. It's doubtful if there were even Indians until the Seventeenth Century, and in two minutes by car you could be transported to a time when there was only bear and elk and deer, panther, eagles, wildcats. And I assure you that if you had to spend the night on the road, if your car broke down, you'd know they were still there. If you stopped to take a leak and turned off your motor the thing that struck you most forcibly was the silence, the enormous silence. If there was no wind—that is, if you were between Eagle Summit and the actual top of the mountain— the silence would be so absolute, such a new experience, that it became spooky, and it would be actually reassuring to hear some animal cry, some bird. And then your reassurance would vanish, because almost immediately you'd get the feeling that you were being watched. And no doubt you were. I'm told that that happens when you're in the jungle. It happened to me during the war, in the Admiralties, but then there was a reason because we'd been told that there were Japs hiding out, sniping at the Seabees. At Eagle Summit it was different. It was a civilized man, me, in a place where I didn't belong. A trespasser. And I knew I was a trespasser and felt guilty about it. This place belonged to the animals and they were sending me thought waves, warnings to get the hell out of there or take the consequences. Boy, the back of my neck was awfully cold. Anyway, I guess that's enough geography. Now for the human element.

As you know, I didn't go to Groton. I went to a school in Niagara Falls that was older than Groton but considerably less fashionable. I probably never would have heard of the school if my father hadn't gone there. It's no longer in existence. But I went there for a year. It was an all-day train ride, or a sleeper jump, and I preferred the day train because I was young and fascinated by any travel. I got a kick out of taking the train to Reading, thirty-five miles away, and any trip longer than that was sheer delight, not to be wasted in sleep. In those days I never took a nap on a train. Too much to see. Well, in 1924, I was on my way back to school after Easter vacation. I was rich, must have had twenty or thirty dollars in my kick, either from bridge or a crap game, and when I changed trains and got on the Buffalo Day Express, as it was called, I bought a Pullman chair. Two of my classmates from Baltimore were on the train, but riding day coach. The hell with them, I said. I'll ride the plush. Splurge. I can see my classmates any time.

So I sat in the Pullman, really luxurious they were then, too. Beautiful woodwork. Mother-of-pearl in the paneling. Big chairs. A brass spitoon. A polite porter who knew his job and had plenty of self-respect, instead of these characters that hate their jobs and hate you. Comfort and ease, and always the *people* that got on and off along the way. Some of them knew each other, some of them didn't.

At a place called Carter City, a station just beyond Williamsport, I looked out the car window to see who was getting on, and I noticed three people. Obviously a man and his wife saying goodbye to a third man. I'll come back to the third man in a minute, but first the man and his wife. This man was about six feet tall. He was in his middle thirties, and wearing a Norfolk suit with knickerbockers, thick-soled shoes with fringed tongues, and a cap made of the same material as the suit. A few years earlier it was collegiate to wear a Norfolk suit, but this wasn't a collegiate-type suit. This was English Country. It had four buttons, like ours, but the top button was left unbuttoned, which we never did. His wife was wearing a tweed suit, too, and a brown felt hat. She was quite short, and she and her husband were laughing very heartily at something their friend was saying. I naturally couldn't hear them through the double

windows of the Pullman. Then the conductor spoke to them—
they obviously knew him and he them—and the third man
kissed the woman and shook hands with the man, picked up
his bag, which was a beautifully banged-up but saddle-soaped
kit bag, and another piece of luggage that I thought contained
fishing tackle. He got on the Pullman-car platform as the train
started to move, and I heard him calling out a final remark in
French. I couldn't understand what he said, but there was no
mistaking it for anything but French. He was holding the door
open, and I heard the woman call out something in French,
and then she and her husband turned and headed for their car.
The car was a grey Pierce-Arrow, a Series 30, or about a 1921
or '22 model. It was a chummy roadster. That is, it seated four,
with divided front seats. Also called a clover-leaf, if you recall.
But it was a hell of an automobile. It had no trouble going
eighty or eighty-five, and this particular job had Westinghouse
shock absorbers. That model was a favorite with people who
wanted a sports car but wanted the weight and size of the
Pierce. There were two of them in my home town, and oddly
enough one of them was painted grey, too.

The whole picture fascinated me, of course. The people, the
car, and the *place*. You wouldn't have given them a second look
on Long Island or the Philadelphia Main Line, but this was in
the woods of North Central Pennsylvania. There were plenty of
rich people in Williamsport, but this wasn't Williamsport. This
was Carter City. Well, as it happened, not entirely by accident,
I had lunch with the third man. He was a really big fellow. Six-
four, two-thirty, and he had a beard. Also he needed a haircut,
and I noticed paint stains on his back hair. I'll tell you about
him some other time, but he turned out to be Rollo Fenner, the
painter. The name struck a vague gong, not that I knew anything about painters, but as we made conversation in the
dining-car he got on the subject of football and then I remembered. He'd been All-American at Harvard. Was with the
Morgan-Harjes Unit during the war, and lived in Paris. I just
didn't have the nerve to ask him what he was doing in Pennsyl-

vania. We got along fine and he gave me his card, told me to look him up in Paris, and he was such delightful company that he really made my trip.

We now perforce skip a year or two. Or three. I got out of school and went to work on a newspaper, working my tail off, loving it, and practically unaware that I was doing grown men's work for twelve dollars a week. The cheap son of a bitch that I worked for—oh, well. Anyway, I had a car, a little four-cylinder Buick roadster, and because of it I got some assignments that you could only cover if you had a car, and on a staff of two women and five men, I was the only one that could drive. So one day the editor called me to his private office, which of course he called a sanctum sanctorum, without knowing a God damn word of Latin, and he said, "James, I have a strange hunch. Read this." He showed me a piece of U. P. copy that had come in over the Morse wire. A flyer had tried to make an emergency landing on a country road near a place called Eagle Summit. Plane caught fire, and the pilot was burned to death, before he'd had a chance to get out of the plane. "Do you know who that might be? It might be Lindbergh! The Lone Eagle!" I thought he was crazy, but he'd convinced himself that Lindbergh, who *was* flying all over the country, getting receptions, was the man that was killed. I think Lindbergh was overdue some place, too. "How long would it take you to drive up there in your car?" Well, four or five hours, I told him. So he gave me some money, swore me to secrecy, and off I went, in quest of the biggest story of the century. Naturally I was to go have a look at the dead pilot, then telephone back if I thought it was Lucky Lindy, and Gibbsville would scoop the world. Or Bob Hooker would have a scoop, not I.

But I was young, so off I went. I knew the roads for the first hundred and fifty miles, and I was convinced that all I had to do was keep the throttle down on the floor-board and I'd have a Pulitzer prize. But after I got off the state highways I began to run into trouble, and the closer I got to Eagle Summit, the more trouble I had. The Buick was developing a tappet knock, or what I hoped was a tappet knock. I much preferred a tappet knock to what I really knew it was—a loose connecting rod. I knew it would be getting dark soon, and I'd seen enough of the territory to know I didn't want to spend the night on the road. Not that road.

But the little Buick made it to Eagle Summit and I went to the town hall and introduced myself to a man there, the township supervisor. I said I was from one of the Williamsport papers and asked him if I could have a look at the pilot. "What's left of him," he said. "I got him back there in a cell." So he took me back and one look convinced me that I wasn't going to win the Pulitzer prize. Whoever he was, the poor guy, he wasn't Slim Lindbergh or Slim Anybody. His face was all burnt away, but the legs and torso belonged to a short stout man. Incidentally, the town supervisor was sore as hell at the dead man. Apparently they all hated airplanes and pilots. "He could of started a fire that would destroy this town," he said. Well, I didn't argue with him. I thanked him and got in my car, but it wouldn't start. I pushed it to the garage and asked the proprietor what he thought. He had a look and confirmed my suspicions. Connecting rod. Could he fix it? He'd have to call up and see where he could get one. It wasn't loose. It was broken. So he called up a Buick dealer in Williamsport and they had a spare, but he couldn't leave right away. I asked him where I could spend the night, and he said I could drive to Williamsport with him and go to a hotel, or I could ask the supervisor to let me sleep in a cell. There were no hotel accommodations in Eagle Summit, obviously, and obviously he didn't give a damn where I slept. While I was thinking it over I heard a Klaxon outside, and I looked and saw a grey Pierce-Arrow, pulled up at the gas tank. At first it was just another grey Pierce, but then the driver got out and it was the man I'd seen at the Carter City station three years earlier. He was even wearing the same Norfolk jacket, but instead of knickers, slacks. He came in and said hello to the garage man, and nodded to me. "Fill it up, will you please, Ed? And fix the puncture in the rear wheel spare." Ed said he wouldn't be able to fix the puncture because he had to drive to Williamsport. And so forth and so on. Leave the spare, he'd fix it the next day. Joe. He called the man Joe.

Well, I was a fresh kid. Twenty-two, and the whole scene at the railroad station came back to me, so I said to Joe, "How is Rollo Fenner?" And of course that baffled him. He tried to pretend that he really recognized me, but all the time racking his brains. Where had he met this kid? Finally it was too much for him and he said so. "I'm sorry," he said, "but I can't remember where I met you." So then I told him the whole story, and he was fascinated that I'd remember. Then I told him why I was in Eagle Summit, and he talked about the newspaper business, about which he knew absolutely nothing, and then about my car. And I told him the truth, by the way. That I was from Gibbsville, not Williamsport. The only reason I'd lied to the supervisor was that I'd learned from experience that if there's anything people dislike more than a newspaper reporter, it's a newspaper reporter from some far-off place. So Mr. Joe Holderman asked me if I knew some friends of his in Gibbsville, and I did, and gave him some details that proved that I knew them pretty well. This conversation took place while Ed was filling Holderman's gas tank, and taking off the spare tire from the carrier in the rear. He didn't have side mounts on that car, unlike most Pierces of that vintage. Anyway, he said it was ridiculous for me to go to a hotel in Williamsport or sleep in the lock-up when he had plenty of room at his house, and after a polite but not very firm protest I accepted his kind invitation. I could tell that Ed, the garage man, thought Holderman was out of his mind. But I could also see that what Ed thought made not the slightest bit of difference to Holderman, and off we went.

He lived about two miles away, in the woods, and the roads were frightful, but when you got there—what a house! It was a sort of super-shooting lodge, is the only way I can describe it. It was in a clearing, but not so much of a clearing that it wasn't protected by the trees when the wind was strong, or in a blizzard. It was a log cabin, luxury style. Two stories and a garage in the cellar, and a porch that went around three sides, and after we put the car away he showed me the view from the porch. From one side of the porch you could see, oh, probably twenty miles that looked like solid timber-land. And from all three sides you saw nothing but acres of forest. It took my breath away, literally, because I just stood and looked without saying a word. It was still daylight, and a wisp of smoke in the distance he said was Williamsport, about twenty miles away as the crow flies, but longer by road. He had a big telescope on the porch, and he gave me a look through it and I could see the fire wardens' towers on the tops of the other mountains. "I'm a sort of honorary fire warden," he said. "Let me show you something." He went to an instrument on a tripod that turned out to be a heliograph. He began working it. "My wife and I have learned the Morse Code. She's faster than I am. I'm signaling to that tower down there to the southeast. He hasn't seen me yet. There! Now he's answering. I'm telling him I just got home. I always tell him when I leave, just so that he can keep an eye on our house. It gives him something to do to break the monotony. He has field glasses but they're not as powerful as my telescope. When I get a new one I'm going to give him this one."

"Have you got a telephone here?"

"Yes, we have, and so has he. But there are times when you can't depend on it. We get some pretty terrific electrical storms in the mountains, and in the winter—you can imagine the snow."

"And at night, I suppose you can communicate with a flashlight?" I said.

"Correct. I have a little flashlight in the shape of a 25-automatic, and that's all I need. Pull the trigger for dots and dashes."

"He can see that that far away?"

"Oh, my yes. When there's no moon I can see him light his pipe. Just the light from his match. He's only about five-and-a-half miles away. Of course I can't always get him right away. He doesn't sit in the dark all night. He'd go out of his mind.

And unfortunately for us, he's only there during the fire season. I mean unfortunately because he varies our routine, too.
We like to talk to him."

"Do you know him?"

"Yes, we've had him here for dinner several times. Him and
his wife. But frankly he's better company at this distance, and
so is she. He talks better by heliograph. In fact, when he's been
here he's been very economical with his words, and she's not a
very stimulating conversationalist."

"Who, me?"

We turned, and there was Holderman's wife, pretty and
short as I remembered her, although not quite so short, with
no gigantic Rollo Fenner to make a contrast. Holderman introduced me and explained that I was spending the night and
so forth, and she volunteered to show me around the house.

It was what you might imagine. Three rooms and kitchen on
the first floor. The middle room was two stories high, with
exposed rafters and an open stairway. A magnificent big open
fireplace, and on the floor were bear rugs with heads and teeth.
All around on the walls were mounted elk and deer and wild-
cat heads and some stuffed trout and pike. The trophies you'd
expect from that part of the world, and a tiger head and a water
buffalo and some others from I guess India and Africa. Big
tables. Navajo rugs. Big chairs and sofas. In a room on one side
of the center room Holderman had a desk and filing case and
typewriter and small adding machine, obviously his office.
Then on the *other* side of the big room, suddenly you're in an
elegant drawing-room. Gilt furniture, light blue carpet. Small
paintings, including two by Rollo Fenner. In other words, a
completely feminine room. Jade ash trays, for instance. A
Chippendale closet filled with bits of china. You couldn't imagine a quicker or more complete escape from the rustic, masculine atmosphere of the center room. But you didn't have to
imagine it, because on the second floor, one of the bedrooms
was just as feminine, with a canopied bed and a chaise-longue.
I almost had to laugh, but I'm glad I didn't. There were three
other bedrooms, and they were the rustic type that you'd ex-

pect, heavy furniture, sporting prints, trophies. The feminine bedroom was next door to a bedroom that you could easily tell was where they slept most of the time, but there was no connecting door between those two rooms. In her room there was one bed, not quite a double bed. In the other room, twin beds. On the other side of the second story, connected by a balcony, or a gallery, were two guest rooms, and I was given one of those. Between those two rooms there was a connecting bath, but the bathroom on the other side of the house was in the rear. It seemed like an odd arrangement to me. Her personal bedroom had the best view, south and east. It was in the front of the house, whereas their joint bedroom had only a one-elevation view. Her room was an escape from an escape, but there again I'm getting ahead of myself.

All in all, it seemed to me to be the most comfortable house I'd ever been in. Comfort, informality, and easy luxury. Because the luxury was there, too, don't think it wasn't. The center room downstairs, for instance. Polished hardwood floor. You wouldn't walk across *it* in hob-nailed boots. And the furniture didn't come from the army-and-navy store. When I said super-hunting lodge, that's what I meant, and I'm telling you so much about the house because I spent two nights there and nearly two days, and all I learned about the Holdermans was during that time.

They had a couple. I have to invent names for the couple, because I don't remember their right names. Let's say Jack and Carolyn. They had their own cabin, back of the main house and in a different clearing. They were older than the Holdermans. Jack was about fifty. Carolyn, probably in her late forties. Natives, but Joe Holderman and his wife, Violet, had taught them the little niceties. Jack was a woodsman, but he functioned as a butler, at least in some things. He wore a lumberjack shirt and no coat, but for instance he unpacked my small bag and put my things away, and he mixed and served the cocktails before dinner. But he didn't serve dinner. His wife did the cooking—or maybe he did. I don't know. But she waited on table. Not in maid's uniform, but she knew how to serve. I have to jump around a little bit. For instance, Jack ran my tub before dinner, and while I was taking my bath he pressed my suit, brushed my shoes. And later in the evening, my bed was turned down and one of Holderman's bathrobes was lying on the bed and a pair of bedroom slippers. All done by Jack and Carolyn. Dinner, by the way, was served in the big center room. There was no dining-room as such.

I was pooped. I called up my boss and told him there was no story and that I had engine trouble and wouldn't be back till late the next day. All he said was that I'd have to make it up by working some Sunday. Hell, I worked nearly every Sunday anyway. So after dinner—oh, about nine-thirty or so—Holderman suggested that I go to bed. Had a hard time keeping my eyes open. The long trip, the mountain air, cocktails and a big meal. So I went to bed and slept like an innocent child for about four hours. Then I awoke completely refreshed, turned on the light, and looked around for something to read. I could hear a big grandfather's clock strike the half hours, and I decided to go downstairs and get a magazine. They had everything. *Vanity Fair, The New Yorker, Collier's, Life, Scribner's, Spur, The Field, Country Life, Punch.* And the latest issues, at that. So I put on Holderman's bathrobe and slippers and had no trouble finding my way, because there was a light burning in the big room. Then I noticed that a light was coming from Holderman's office, although the door was closed, and on the way downstairs I heard his typewriter. I felt rather sneaky, so when I'd chosen a magazine I knocked on his door, the office door. He opened it. He was wearing pajamas and a bathrobe, and he had a pipe in his hand. I said I didn't want him to think he was imagining things, and showed him the magazine. "Oh, I heard every sound you made," he said. "Come in and have a chat, if you like." He had a Thermos of coffee and a couple of sandwiches wrapped in waxed paper. He offered me coffee, but I didn't want to get too wide awake, but I sat down and had a cigarette. "This is when I do my writing," he said. "I'm writing a history of the Holderman family, because I'm the last of my line and when I die, we disappear. We weren't very distinguished," he said, "but we did open up a lot of the country around here. I've been at it ever since my wife and I were told we couldn't have children." Naturally he didn't dwell on that, and in fact I was a little surprised that he even mentioned their inability to produce. But he gave me a few more facts, family stuff that I don't remember, but I remember what he told me about himself. He'd gone to school at Andover and that was where he'd met Rollo Fenner, and on a visit to Fenner's house in Maine he'd met Violet Fenner, Rollo's sister. He went to Cornell, but quit college to join the Morgan-Harjes Unit when Fenner did. Then he joined the American army, came home after the war, and married Violet Fenner.

Well, I began to wonder why he was lying to me, and such stupid, insane lying. He was then at least forty years old. And if he'd quit college in 1916, say at the age of twenty, he'd still only be thirty-one. But he was every bit of forty and possibly a year or two older. And yet he was telling me all this with a straight face, to no purpose as far as I could see except that he was off his rocker. And yet he seemed normal, rational, certainly well behaved. He was a polite and considerate host, and at dinner he and his wife had been conventional to the point of dullness. The only out-of-the-ordinary thing I'd noticed at all was her extra-feminine drawing-room and bedroom. And that wasn't too extraordinary. An attractive woman like that, buried in the Northern Pennsylvania woods, it would have been more remarkable if she hadn't wanted some feminine touches, some refuge from this shooting-lodge atmosphere. But I began to wonder what I'd got myself into, and frankly wished that I could get the hell out. But I was stuck, at least till morning, till I could get a ride to Williamsport.

Now this was no wild man. Everything he said was told in the belief that it would be accepted as unquestioned fact. No striving to convince me. And after about a half an hour he very politely suggested that I go back to bed and apologized for boring me with family reminiscence, et cetera. And he never had the least suspicion that I was questioning any of his statements. Nevertheless he had told me some absolutely incredible lies, and to tell you the truth, when I went up to my room, I locked the door.

Naturally I didn't go to sleep for several hours. I put out my light, and then I could look out the window and see that the light was still on in his office, and it stayed on for a couple of hours. I guess I got back to sleep sometime between four and five o'clock, and once I thought I heard people talking, but I couldn't be sure. I slept till about seven-thirty and was awakened by the grey Pierce leaving the property, with Holderman at the wheel. No more sleep for me, so I went downstairs and Carolyn was around, dusting furniture or whatever, and I ordered my breakfast. Then Mrs. Holderman, Violet, showed up. Asked me how I'd slept and so on, and said she was afraid she had bad news for me, although not for her and her husband. She said Ed had called, the garage owner, and he hadn't been able to go pick up the spare part for my car, but would do so that morning. He guessed my car might be ready late that day. So I was stuck with the Holdermans, one of them at least a congenital liar, and the other, Violet, I wasn't sure what. She had a cup of coffee and a cigarette with me, and in the most offhand way she said, "Did you and Joe have a nice chat last night?"

"Yes," I said. "He told me about the family history he's working on."

"Yes, he's been at that a long time," she said. "Sometimes I wish he wouldn't work so hard on it. But he wants to get it all down on paper. When he was in the war he saw so many men die that he developed a fatalistic attitude. The impermanence, you know. Impermanence of life. Don't count on any tomorrow."

"I guess that affected a lot of men's thinking," I said.

"Yes, and especially those that were wounded. My husband was very badly wounded at Belleau Wood," she said.

"In the Marine Corps?" I said.

"Yes. His being alive at all is a miracle, and he's had two operations since the war and is facing another. For two years after the war he was stone deaf," she said. "He hears perfectly well," she said, "but they want to operate again to correct a constant ringing noise. He has a hard time sleeping."

I said, "I hadn't realized he was in the Marines."

"Yes," she said. "He was so pleased to get in. My brother, Rollo, was quite a well-known football player at Harvard, and then he went to live in Paris to study painting, and when the war came Rollo joined the ambulance corps. Came through the war unscathed. Joe had tried out for football at Cornell, but was too light or anyway didn't do very well, and Rollo used to tease him about it. So Joe had something to crow about when he got the Distinguished Service Cross—but at what a price! I don't mean to imply that there's any hostility between them," she said. "If they were real brothers they couldn't be closer than they are." She said her brother visited them whenever he came back to the States, and the two boys, she called them, practically ignored her when Rollo was here. They'd roomed together all through Andover and had gone on a big-game hunting expedition in India the year before she married Joe. She pointed to a tiger head and skin and said that Rollo had shot it. Given it to them as a wedding present, and then gave up hunting. Joe hadn't done any hunting either, since the war. She said I might have noticed something missing in a house like theirs, and I said I couldn't think of a thing that was missing, and she said, "Well, wouldn't you expect to see a gun closet?" And it was true, there were no firearms of any kind visible. "Joe won't have them around," she said. Jack had a rifle and shotguns, but he kept them back in his own cabin.

I relaxed a bit after my conversation with Violet and I got curious about how they spent their days. Also, to be completely honest about it, although she was about forty, which was a very advanced age for me at the time, she looked very inviting in a sweater and skirt and a little pearl necklace. And as the kids say nowadays, she was sending me a message, or so I believed. Let's say the air was heavy with sex, and I wasn't sure whether she knew it or not. I would have been embarrassed to admit to any of my contemporaries that a woman of forty could make me horny, but she did. But the fact that she

was forty kept me from making a pass at her, although I had
several opportunities during the day. I had just enough doubt
about what I was feeling, or suspecting, so that I was still a
little afraid that if I did make an actual pass, she'd be horrified
—or amused. So for the rest of the day I was in a very confused
state, hoping for an opportunity to be alone with her, and then
when I was alone with her, several times, I couldn't quite
carry out my evil intentions. The first move had to come from
her.

Well, Holderman came back from Eagle Summit, with the
mail and some parcel post, and a report on my car. As to
the car, he'd simply *ordered* the garage man to close up and
drive to Williamsport. And he could *do* that. He didn't say so,
but I inferred that he had money in the garage. But the stuff
he brought back from the Eagle Summit post office was interesting. I didn't get to see any of the letters, of course, but he and
Violet opened the packages in my presence. For her, some
special kind of expensive soap that I forget the name of but I'd
heard my aunt speak of it. It was made in France. In his
package, two pipes. He'd sent them away to have new bits
put in the bowls. I could see that Holderman and his wife got
real pleasure out of their parcel post. Like kids. And he explained it. He said, "We live up here in the backwoods, but we
don't lose touch with the world. We get all the latest magazines,
and we're always sending away for things, little things." And
he told me that he kept up his membership in a New York club
—this one, without a doubt—although he hadn't been inside
the place more than twice since the war, and didn't know when
he'd use it again. And every four or five years he'd order a new
suit, give an old one to Jack, although the old one hadn't been
worn very much, and Jack would give the suit to his son, who
was in college somewhere, probably the only boy in the
school wearing a hundred-and-fifty-dollar suit. Holderman was
getting very close to raising the question why he or they chose
to live in the woods, and she was quick enough to anticipate it
and she changed the subject. I should mention the fact that
nothing he said or did would have aroused the least suspicion

as to his being a healthy, normal middle-aged man. Having been alerted to it by her, I could see that he let his hair grow in a strange way around his ear, to cover a bald spot that I assumed was where he'd been operated on. But as far as his conversation and behavior were concerned, he was perfectly all right.

They had two people coming for lunch, a state senator and his wife, who arrived in a big Cunningham phaeton driven by a chauffeur. The wife was related to Holderman, and the senator was just a dull politician who didn't contribute anything and didn't try to hide the fact that he considered the visit a waste of his valuable time. He knew my boss. All those guys knew each other, the subsidized newspaper editors and the politicians that were stooging for big industries in the legislature. They were all grafters in one form or another. They'd all sold out years ago, and they all had big cars and houses in the country or Atlantic City, and I never knew a one of them that didn't overestimate his influence. As long as they voted right they were in, but without the money from the big industries they couldn't have run for dogcatcher. Holderman was rich, but I don't believe he was the big stockholder in any single company of any size. When the senator and his wife left, Holderman was rather apologetic to me. He said his cousin was good company, but she always insisted on bringing her husband. Actually the senator's wife was a rather ordinary woman but at least she'd prattled away during lunch, and she seemed to amuse Violet Holderman. Violet said, "We do our entertaining, such as it is, between Easter and Thanksgiving. After that we can always expect snow, and people are afraid of being marooned up here." So once or twice a week they'd have friends for lunch, but very seldom for dinner.

In the afternoon, after the statesman and wife departed, Holderman and I went for a hike up to the top of the mountain. I was in pretty good shape from tennis and golf, and I lived in a hilly town, but I couldn't keep up with him. On the very top of the mountain he'd put up a sort of shelter. It was open on all four sides, but offered protection from the rain

if the rain came straight down. He explained that it was actually a shelter from the rain and the sun. I hadn't thought of
the sun. There were no chairs. Only benches, and I sat down
to get my breath, and he was quite pleased that a young squirt
half his age was winded and he was not. "You see, I'm used to
the altitude and you're not," he said. "We're almost three thousand feet above sea level here." Not a great height, but enough
to make a difference if you weren't used to it, he said. The view
there was of course better than from his house, and he enter-
tained me with a geographical and historical lecture. It was
mostly all new to me, and he told it well.

We went back to the house and Violet was waiting for us.
That is, she had tea for us and she liked breaking out the best
stuff. Holderman commented on it. He said I ought to be complimented, and I was, although I had no way of knowing that
she didn't use the silver tea service every afternoon. It would
have been in character for her, or them, to use the silver set
regardless of guests or no guests. There was a great deal of
elegance to the way they lived, notwithstanding the tweeds
and lumberjack shirts and the atmosphere of roughing it in
the woods. They *weren't* roughing it in the woods. I caught on
to the fact that what they were doing was living like the rich on
the North Shore, or maybe more like Aiken, although I've never
been to Aiken. But with the difference that they didn't belong
to any colony, like Aiken people or Westbury people. Then I
realized, of course, that the big difference was really the isola-
tion from people. They had people in for meals, but they
didn't say anything about going out. No mention was made of
going to other people's houses. And then I began to see, with
what I'd already found out, that they lived the way they wanted
to live because it was the way they *had* to live.

I wasn't finding out much about how they spent their days,
what they did with their time, and then within two or three
minutes I got some enlightenment on that subject. Holderman
finished his tea and said he thought he'd have a nap, and he
left us. She said to me, "I'm so glad when he does that. Sleep
is *so* important." Then she told me, just as though I'd asked her

a direct question, that they never planned anything far ahead, and never had people in more than twice a week. In that way, with such an open schedule, he could go take a nap whenever he felt like it. So that was how they spent their days, waiting for sleep to overtake him. I asked her, "What do you do, Mrs. Holderman?" "What do I do?" she said. "Well, I sew. I do needlepoint." She was teaching Carolyn needlepoint. She'd tried painting, but had given it up because she'd felt that all the talent in that direction had gone to her brother. Very discouraging to look at some of the things her brother had dashed off when he visited them, and she had to work so hard to no avail. She took me to the drawing-room and had me take another look at her brother's paintings, and I dutifully admired them, although actually I was more interested in nature's handiwork —her figure. And ready for the first sign of an invitation from her. But no sign was given. However, the cosmic urge, as we used to call it, was somewhere in her thoughts, in the back of her mind. We went back to the big room and she asked me all about my marital status or engagement status. Did I have a girl? Did I have a lot of girls? Were the girls as wild as older people said they were, or was that exaggerated? Girls had so much more freedom these days, et cetera. The people who'd been there for lunch that day had a daughter that was causing them all sorts of trouble. Sent home from Wellesley, et cetera. Violet said she was glad she didn't have to bring up a daughter in 1927, and that, of course, brought us right back to the house in the woods.

A young newspaper reporter sees so much in the first few years that he begins to think he's seen it all. That makes for a very unattractive wise-guy attitude, what I call unearned cynicism. After you've lived a good many years I don't see how you can be anything but cynical, since all any of us have a right to expect is an even break, and not many get that. But I thought I knew it all, and I didn't. It took me many more years to realize that a reporter covering general news lives an abnormal life, in that he sees people every day at the highest or lowest point of their lives. Day after day after day, people in trouble with the law, having accidents, losing control of themselves—or experiencing great successes. In one month's time a district man would see enough crime and horror and selfishness to last most people the rest of their lives. I can remember a young reporter telling me, when I first went to New York, that when you've seen one electrocution you've seen them all. Well, at that stage of my career I probably would have said the same thing, if I'd thought of it and had seen any electrocutions. God knows I'd seen plenty of nasty things. But I was much too young and comparatively inexperienced to be so omniscient about the Holdermans. At about five-thirty that afternoon, after Violet and I had had our little chat, I was ready to be on my way, quite convinced that I had them ticketed. They'd been interesting enough. Unusual. A war casualty and his reasonably attractive wife, holed up in the woods in an atmosphere of quiet luxury. But they'd become what they call in the newspaper business a one-day story, and I was ready to move on.

From this distance I can be perfectly honest and admit that I was still a little bit hoping she'd make a play for me. I'd never necked or laid a woman quite as old as forty, but there was one in her thirties that used to call me up when her husband was out of town. I don't know why she counted on my keeping my mouth shut. Twenty-two-year-old boys do a lot of boasting. But anyway, Violet was *there,* and *I* was there, and we had a whole evening ahead of us, possibly just the two of us. And she was radiating sex.

Well, she went and had a bath before dinner and so did I, and when I came downstairs she said Holderman was still asleep and we'd eat without him. We did, and after dinner we listened to the radio. They had a special high-powered set, marvelous reception up there in the mountains, and I asked her if she wanted to dance. I'll never forget how she looked at me. She smiled and shook her head, and for the first time I realized that she'd been reading my mind. She didn't say a word. Just smiled and shook her head. She was nice enough not to put it into words. You know—she could have said we didn't dare. Worse yet, she could have danced with me and *then* made a big thing about loyalty to her husband. In any event, I knew right away that she was never going to make a play for me, and that I'd better not make one for her. And with that out of the way, definitely, I relaxed and had a better time. I turned off the radio and we talked. About books and authors. All along the balcony above us the walls were lined with books, and she'd read them. I read a lot then, much more than I do now, and we'd both read a lot of the same things. It wasn't often that I got a chance to pour out what I felt about writing, especially to an attractive woman, and pour it out I did. Then along about nine-thirty Holderman appeared, very apologetic about missing dinner and yet not very refreshed from his long nap. He was in a fog.

She got him something to eat but she wouldn't let him drink any coffee. She wanted him to go back to bed, but he argued with her and as a matter of fact got a little nasty. Nasty for him, that is. "I don't really need you to decide when I should sleep," he said.

"Not deciding anything, just suggesting," she said.

Well, I hung around for a little while, then I said goodnight to them and went to my room. I went to sleep and I don't know how long I slept. Past midnight. And I was awakened by a sound that I thought was some animal. A roaring sound. Not so much noisy as deep, as though the animal were saying the word roar over and over again. Roar, roar, roar, roar. I got fully awake and got up, and by this time I realized that it was not an animal but Holderman, having a nightmare in his office. I was going to go downstairs and actually had my door open, and then I saw her. She was in her nightgown, hurrying across the big room to Holderman's office, and in a minute or so they came out of the office. They had their arms around each other's waists and she was talking to him. I couldn't tell what she was saying because he was talking too. Then they went up the stairs to her room, the fancy bedroom, and she closed the door, and I closed mine.

Try and go back to sleep under those circumstances, but I did, eventually. In the morning I went down to breakfast and

Holderman was there, I remember he was wearing the same old Norfolk jacket and smoking a pipe. "Your car is ready," he said. "I'll take you down to Eagle Summit as soon as you've had breakfast." He was rested and relaxed, and affable. Violet waited on me herself, and she was happy too. I was finishing breakfast and Holderman said he'd go down and get the Pierce started and I could come down when I was ready, no hurry. Soon as I finished my packing.

She lit my cigarette while I was having my second cup of coffee. "Now you understand us a little better," she said.

"A little," I said.

"Oh, you will a lot when you think about us," she said. "I saw your door open last night."

"Oh," I said, which was all I could think of to say.

Then she said, "You're going to be a nice man, you have feelings."

And I said, "Well, you're a nice woman. You have feelings."

"People aren't nice without them. *He* has them." Then she said, "Do you see anything here you'd like to take home with you? As a memento?" I looked around and God knows there were a lot of things, an embarrassment of riches, so to speak, and she obviously wanted me to take something, so I picked up an old-fashioned silver match-safe. "How about this?" I said. "It's yours," she said. "And this," and she kissed me. "Just a token," she said. And she knew what I was thinking—wondering why all the generosity. "Why?" she said. "Because I've watched your young eyes taking in everything, and your curiosity's been very complimentary," she said. "Give me your address, where I can write to you. I think you'll want to know how he comes out of this next operation, and I'd like to be able to tell you. I hardly need tell you that it won't be on his ear," she said.

Well, she never did write to me, never a line. And while I'm on the subject, I haven't the faintest idea what happened to the match box. It was very good-looking. On one side was a picture of a pack of hounds baiting a bear. I think the other side was blank.

First Day in Town

At twenty-five past one Nick Orlando, alone, got out of a taxi, punched the doorman playfully in the ribs, and entered the restaurant. In the foyer there was a crowd, mostly women, who wanted to sit downstairs but who, as matinee time got nearer, were about to decide to go upstairs. Nick Orlando firmly pushed his way forward among these women. At his touch they would turn angrily and say, "I *beg* yaw podden—*oh, Nick Orlando!* It's Nick Orlando!"

The captain of waiters raised his hand high. He had not immediately seen Nick Orlando, whose height only flatteringly could be called average, but the repetition of the Orlando name reached the captain. "I have your table, Mr. Orlando," he said. Then, when Nick Orlando had pushed his way to the rope, the captain whispered, "I don't have a table, but maybe you see somebody." Nick Orlando, who had not said a word since getting out of the taxi, squeezed the captain's arm. He nodded; he saw somebody.

He made his way to a banquette where two women were seated side by side; the one a girl of twenty or so, with a scarf knotted about her neck; the other a woman in her late thirties, who had a ballpoint pen in her right hand and was writing something in a stenographer's dictation tablet. Nick Orlando, heading for this table, picked up a chair without asking permission of a threesome at an island table. He set the chair down so that he faced the two women on the banquette. The girl squinted. "Go away. You're lousing up my interview," she said, laughing.

"Oh, say, this is a treat," said the interviewer. "Nick Orlando. You know where I met you? At Harry Browning's."

"Who is Harry Browning?" said Nick Orlando.

"Get him! Pretending you don't know who Harry Browning is," said the girl. "Five years ago you *didn't* know who Harry Browning is, you'd be telling the truth then, you big faker. When did you get *in,* you dog?"

"What's the interview for?" said Nick Orlando.

"My syndicate. My name is Camilla Strong."

"Your syndicate? I bet it aint the syndicate I got friends in. Syndicate. A syndicate is a man that knows the price of everything and the value of nothing. Who said that, Camilla?"

"Oscar Wilde."

"You *know,* hey? Wud you, go to college, Camilla?"

"I sure did," said Camilla Strong.

"This jerk just stard reading books three years ago, and now the whole field of literature is all his. All his. Nobody ever read anything before him, hey, jerk?"

"Where did you two know each other? Is this a thing with you two?" said Camilla Strong. "Should I have known about this?"

"Her? This tramp?"

"Don't make it too emphatic, jerk, or otherwise she'll think we did have a thing," said the girl. "No, we didn't have a thing, but not for want of him trying."

"That's where everybody makes a mistake with this tramp, is trying. Nobody has to try with this one."

"Oh, I wish I could write this the way it really comes out," said Camilla. "If they'd ever print it."

"Go ahead write it," said Nick Orlando. "You're not gonna destroy any illusions. You seen her that night on the Paar show."

"Aah, shut up with the Paar show," said the girl. "Why'd you have to remind her of that? We been here since one o'clock and not a word about the Paar show till *you* crashed the party."

"Two nominations for Tonys, and one Academy Award, and what are you famous for?" said Nick Orlando.

"You know what really happened, Camilla, was I never

drink. I don't have any tolerance for it. And this jerk made me take two drinks before I was to go on. Two, and one is all I need to get looping. Write that in your article. The inside story of Mary Coolidge getting cut off the air. I think he did it on purpose, too."

"What else? I told you I did it on purpose. You were getting too big for your britches. Your *head* was getting too big for your britches."

"You know, Nick, I really hate you. I hate you with a cold, consuming, venomous hatred."

"I know you do, but I can't get you to admit it."

"You kids, do you talk this way all the time?" said Camilla.

"When we're talking. Sometimes we aren't on conversational terms," said Nick Orlando.

"I wish that was now," said Mary Coolidge. "How did you know I was here?"

"Stop with the kidding. Camilla knows I was with you till an hour ago," said Nick Orlando.

"Oh, now you said too much, Nick," said Camilla. "Unfortunately I've been with Mary since ten o'clock this morning."

"She said you were here since one o'clock," said Nick Orlando.

"Interviewing. But all morning I was with her picking out the dresses for the new play. If you're going to ruin a girl's reputation you've got to do better than that, Nick. What about *you*, by the way? I know you're in town for the opening of *Mad River*."

"You seen it yet?"

"No, I missed two screenings, but I hear you're only great in it. If I call Irving Rudson maybe we could set up an interview. Are you booked pretty solid?"

"Irving don't know I'm in town. I come in a day early."

"To louse up my interview," said Mary Coolidge. "And you succeeded, so go away."

"Oh, he didn't louse it up, Mary. I can have sort of fun with this. It'll read better than just an ordinary interview."

"I don't give ordinary interviews," said Mary Coolidge.

"Ooh, I think this one is burning," said Nick Orlando. "I don't know if it's me or you she's sore at."

"Mary isn't sore at anybody. Where are you staying?"

"Sixteen Twenty-four Pitkin Avenue."

"That's Brooklyn. You're from The Bronx."

"Kidding. I got an uncle living on Pitkin Avenue. I'm at the Sherry. You set it up with Irving."

"And I'll come along and louse it up," said Mary Coolidge.

Camilla Strong pressed the button of her ballpoint, and closed the notebook. "I don't know what your act is, you two. I can't fathom whether you're a thing or not a thing. Come on, level with Camilla before I go."

"I'm mad for him, but religion keeps us apart," said Mary Coolidge.

"Religion? You're both Italian extraction, aren't you?"

"Yeah, but I want to be a nun and he wants to be a priest. So religion keeps us apart," said Mary Coolidge.

"This is a very fast little girl, Nicky," said Camilla.

"Talking, but not running," said Nick Orlando. "She can outtalk anybody but I never heard of her outrunning anybody. Never."

"I kind of think she outran you," said Camilla Strong. "But I'll find that out when I interview you. 'Bye now, kids." She left.

Nick Orlando moved to the vacated seat. "That'll be the day. When that broad interviews me."

"You son of a bitch. I had her in the palm of my hand till you came along. I'm doing the sweetness-and-light bit. The new Mary Coolidge. You know what's in that notebook? All about how I want to do Joan of Arc, for God's sake."

"They all want to do Joan of Arc."

"They all *do* do Joan of Arc, but I'm right for it. I'd hit them with a Joan of Arc that they could smell burning flesh."

"I'd pay to see that. Where did you go last night?"

"None of your God damn business."

"I heard Harry Browning was giving a party. I damn near went," said Nick Orlando.

"Who is Harry Browning?"

"That's *my* line. When did you get my wire?"

"I got your wire Sunday, in plenty of time if I'd of wanted to have a date with you, but I don't. You're a Hollywood hambo."

"Oh, that again. If you were prettier and more photogenic there wouldn't be any knocks on Hollywood."

"You got it mixed up. I said *you* were a Hollywood *hambo.*"

"Is that worse than a Broadway hambo?"

"Infinitely. A Hollywood hambo is chicken, sells out for security. At least a Broadway hambo fights for parts, parts he wants. But you Hollywood hamboes take anything the studio says."

"Not me. I don't have to, it's in my contract."

"Mad River. I hear you play a cowboy. You a cowboy?"

"So you're right for Joan of Arc. What the hell are we talking in circles? Why won't you have a date with me? And don't give me that Hollywood hambo answer."

"I could ask you, why do you keep pestering after me? From the first time I ever met you you thought all you had to do was ask, and I'd give you a date. That *paisana* stuff."

"Answer the question. Why didn't you? Why don't you now?"

"Because nobody gets a date with me that I don't want to go out with. You tell me I'm not pretty. All right, then why do you want a date with me? You know why? Because from the first I'd never go out with you and it's no different now with you a star and me a star. You know what the trouble is? You're jealous of me, and if you get me in bed with you you think you don't have to be jealous any more. The kind of a fellow you are, I go to bed with you and it doesn't make any difference if I'm a better actor than you. You can go around and tell everybody you slept with Mary Coolidge. I know bellboys that slept with famous actresses, but does that make them a better actor? You want to get in bed with me, Nick, I'll be proud to —when you're a good enough actor so I can brag about sleeping with you. But not before. So give up. You know who I get phone calls from? From Paris and London and all over? A really big star. Not like you or I, but a *big* star. And you know why I won't have a date with him? Because as an actor he stinks. And you know what his trouble is? He's jealous of me. He's like you. Last season he came to see me every night for a week and two matinees, torturing himself. 'If I could be as good as that little bitch up there, that homely little bitch.' So he wants to take it out in going to bed with me. Like you."

"What the hell is acting?"

"Right! It's a phoney business, but you don't have to be a phoney *in* it. If you're gonna be an actor, don't be a phoney actor. If you're gonna be in a phoney business that's all the more reason why you shouldn't be a phoney in it."

"You're a phoney."

"No. If I was a dishwasher I'd want to be a good one. You know what I'm gonna give this waiter for a tip? Ten dollars. Because he's a good waiter. That waiter over there, I give him ten percent if it comes to forty-eight cents. I count out the three pennies."

"They pool their tips, so what's the difference?"

"Because this waiter I hand him the ten bucks and say thank-you, and the other waiter I just put the money on the dish and say nothing. That's the difference, and they both know the difference. My applause. Don't tell me applause doesn't mean anything to you?"

"You want to know something? I get a hand in *Mad River*. I got two scenes in there where I get a hand."

"How many takes?"

"What?"

"How many takes before you got the scenes right?"

"Ah, nuts," said Nick Orlando. He got up and pushed his way through the matinee-bound crowd. *"Nick! Nick! It's Nick Orlando! Could I have your autograph please? On this menu? On this package?"* He did not stop until he reached the curb.

"Get me a hack, quick," he said to the doorman.

"Right away," said the doorman. He stood in the street, a few feet from the curb, waving for a taxi. "I hear very good reports on *Mad River*," he said.

"Yeah, I'm spreading them all over," said Nick Orlando.

The doorman laughed. "Well, I'll say this for you, Nick. You didn't change. You're just the same. Some of them go out there. . . ." He shook his head.

2

At the next restaurant Nick Orlando was not so well known. He was recognized by the doorman and by the hatcheck boys, but this was not a theatrical crowd, and Nick Orlando could not count on a headwaiter to fake a reservation. "Good afternoon, Mr. Nick Orlando," said one of the proprietors. "You meeting someone?"

"Well, sort of," said Nick Orlando. "I have a sort of a half date."

"Well, if they're here I can tell you. Who is your party?"

The first name that came to Nick Orlando's mind was Harry Browning's. "Sort of looking for Harry Browning."

"Mr. Harry Browning is here, lunching with the eminent playwright Mr. Asa Unger. You know Asa, I'm sure. I'll take you right to them myself. Just follow me, sir."

The proprietor led Nick Orlando to a remote table, in a section usually referred to as left field. Nick Orlando hated every step of the way, which took him farther from the choicest tables, and his only consolation was that Harry Browning, a steady customer, and Asa Unger, a writer of hits, had done no better. Browning and Unger were sitting with their backs to the wall and could see everything that was going on, including Nick Orlando's approach. They both showed some surprise when it became unmistakable that Nick Orlando was joining them.

"Nick-ee, Nicky boy!" said Harry Browning.

"Your party," said the proprietor, leaving them. Nick Orlando did not speak until the proprietor was out of earshot and unable to guess that he had not been expected.

Harry Browning held out both hands and closed them over Nick Orlando's hand. "You know Asa, Asa Unger."

"Sure. Hi, Asa," said Nick Orlando.

"Hello, Nick. Long time."

"Long time is right."

"Cohasset, four years ago," said Asa Unger.

"That's right, you played Spike in *Dangerous Illusion*. Right?" said Harry Browning. "Nicky, why don't you stir up a little enthusiasm for a picture buy? Asa don't need the money, but I'd like to see *Illusion* a picture. I *always* said it was a natural for any studio that had the right man for Spike. Well, you're it, Nicky, and they'll listen to you now. They *gotta* listen to you now. *Mad River*—a blockbuster. I was talking to Irving Rudson before, and he read me the *Time* and *Newsweek* notices over the phone. You see them yet, Nicky?"

"No."

"Irving read them to me over the phone. They echo what the trade reviews said. Nicky, what did they bring *River* in for, do you happen to know?"

"Two million four was the last figure I heard."

"It'll do seven and a half. It'll do eight. You eat yet or you meeting someone?"

"I ate before, but I'll have a cup of coffee with you," said Nick Orlando.

"Listen, fellows, I got a train to catch," said Asa Unger.

"Asa opened in Philly the night before last," said Harry Browning.

"I know," said Nick Orlando, lying. "How'd it go, Asa?"

"Don't read the Philadelphia notices," said Asa Unger. "I'm getting into another line of work."

"They weren't that bad, Asa. Honestly they weren't. You read them over again and the *Bulletin* fellow, he only said what we were saying all along. I'll be over tonight on the six o'clock train. See you, Asa."

"Hang in there, boy," said Nick Orlando.

"Thanks," said Asa Unger. He left.

"Take his seat, Nicky. Sit here," said Harry Browning. "Asa

got a real dog for himself this time. They murdered him in
Philly. Sheer murder. He didn't want to show his face in the
theater. You know, a sensitive guy like Asa. He wrote a kind of
an open letter to the cast, that he wanted to put up on the bulletin board, but I persuaded him. I said id be a mistake. But
he's taking it to heart, Asa. Nicky, get the studio to offer him
forty thousand for *Illusion,* and I'll let it go for fifty."

"They don't want it for five. They don't want it for free."

"I don't know, Nicky. You may be making a mistake," said
Harry Browning. "He may have other properties later on, something you like. This guy's an in-and-outer, and maybe the next
one could be very big. Take *Illusion* for fifty now, and I
promise you first refusal on his next hit. That's a firm promise."

"I can't do it. *Illusion* stinks."

"All right, well I tried. Now what's with you? Got in when,
yesterday? I had a big bash and I looked for you, but I guess
you had something lined up."

"Something, yeah," said Nick Orlando.

"There's a lot around. I don't know where it all comes from,
but suddenly there's seventy-five new faces. It happens that
way every year. Suddenly you look around and while you been
busy the new stuff's been catching up on you. At my party
there was four or five I never saw before."

"You been busy?"

"As busy as an agent at option-time—and who else should
that happen to? Yeah, I been busy. A little thing called Mary
Coolidge that I don't doubt for a minute that you know her, but
who would ever figure me going for her? Talent and all that,
but a mutt. A homely mutt. And egotistical? That's all right if
she was doing the intellectual bit with Asa. But I'm not Asa. I
like a dumb, pretty broad that looks good without any clothes
on and never knew from Ibsen. Nevertheless, I found myself
calling her up two-three times a day and couldn't wait, *couldn't
wait* till I got her in the kip. And it's nothin' there, believe me.
Oh, you know, it's all right, but can you explain to me what I
want to bother with her for, when you know yourself, Nicky,

like you see that broad just getting up over there? The tan suit? I get a call from her about every two-three months, notwithstanding although she was kept by two millionaires and married one of them." The handsome girl in the tan suit turned and waved to Harry Browning, just a tiny little wave with her fingers to which he responded in kind, an exchange which passed unnoticed by others in the restaurant. "The Ivy League type with her is the husband. I can have that any time I want to, but the last six months I been concentrating on Mary Coolidge."

"Does Coolidge go for you?"

"I gotta be truthful with you there. In three words, I don't know. Here's the situation, Nicky, and you figure it out. This egotistical, homely little mutt, she got two pet names for me. Not dearie or sweetheart. She calls me rascal and scoundrel. Hello, Rascal. Hello, Scoundrel. She says I'm the only pure, unmitigated scoundrel she ever knew. Well, I get called all kinds of names and epithets, but who is she to call me anything? Five years ago she was lucky to get a walk-on in that play of Asa's, *Mainliner*. About the junkies. What was *I* doing five years ago? Well, I had my elder son graduating from Deerfield and I give him a T-Bird for graduation. I had a little piece of property, six acres in Mount Kisco. I had twelve people on my payroll in New York, and I was spending more money in this place alone than Mary Coolidge could earn in two years. Then. She's big now, I grant you. Money-wise and billing-wise, she's big. But I saw bigger ones come and go before she knew if rascal was spelt with a *k*. She's what I call a ten-dollar thinker."

"Yeah? How, Harry?"

"Well, I tell you. She'll give a waiter a ten-dollar tip for a meal that only runs her three or four dollars. Or else she'll give the waiter thirty-five cents, depending on if she likes the waiter."

"I get it, yeah."

"No, I didn't finish. The point is, she has a ten-dollar psychology. Ten dollars is still a lot of money to her. The big gesture. That's the difference between her and some of the dames I used to know. A lousy sawbuck? I used to go out with dames that gave a sawbuck to the woman in the little girls' room. This one, this Mary Coolidge, she'd be good for a quarter, a half a dollar at the most. You know, I wish I'd of known somebody like Anna Held. *There* was no ten-dollar psychology. Or even Bernhardt. Bernhardt was slow with a dollar, but you know what she used to do on tour? She got twenty-five hundred dollars a night, and every night before she'd go on, it had to be all there in gold. In gold. Before she'd go on. Ten dollars for a tip. Big deal. Nicky boy, where can I take you? You want to use my car and shofer for the afternoon?"

"What are you riding in these days?"

"The same. I got the Rolls. You know me, Nicky. I gotta hear that clock ticking. Very soothing. You sure you don't want to help Asa? I gotta go over to Philly tonight, and I wish I had something to tell him on the positive side."

"Well, I know the studio is looking for something."

"You're my boy, Nicky. Offer forty and we'll take fifty, and then you can burn the God damn play. Asa will come up with something one of these days, and he listens to me."

"You're a scoundrel, Harry."

"I know. And a rascal. Thank God I don't have to listen to that tonight. Gettin' weary, Nick. If you want to make a move in that direction, she's all yours."

"Why would I?"

"Well, we did a lot of talking about her. That's what I call buyer-interest. We wouldn't of done that much talking if you didn't show some buyer-interest, Nicky. Hey?"

"A little. I know her, but I never thought of her that way."

"Well, as far as I'm concerned, I've had it. You take it from the top, boy."

"Maybe I'll do that, once around," said Nick Orlando.

3

"Take me over to 414 East Fifty-second. I'm sure you know the way," said Nick Orlando.

"I been there a couple times," said Harry Browning's chauffeur.

"How long did Harry have this rig?"

"This is our fourth year for it."

"You buy it new?"

"Imported it brand new. Mr. Browning has a corporation."

"Oh, yeah. That gag."

"The garage we use, there's eight other Rolls and there's only the one owned private. The government'll slap down one of these days, but we'll still have a good car. We only got less than seventy thousand miles on this."

"Just driving around New York City?"

"Oh, no. I go to Boston for when the boss has a play opening there. Like tomorrow I go to Philly."

"Why doesn't Harry go with you?"

"He gets car-sick on a long ride. Over twenty miles he goes by train or flies. And like some of the clients have the use of the car as a favor. Where you're going now the young lady had me and the car for a week in Boston and a week in Philly, a year ago, during tryouts."

"She a good tipper?"

The chauffeur shrugged his shoulders. "I get a good salary."

"In other words, she's a stiff?"

"I don't want to talk about a client."

"Come on, give. What the hell?"

"Well, you don't have to tell *her* this, but if you're gonna ride around in a Rolls, you don't have to give out with a lot of communist propaganda. I'm not ashamed to wear a uniform. A uniform goes with the job. She wouldn't insult a subway guard, but he has to wear more of a uniform than I do. If it wasn't for the cap you wouldn't know this *was* a uniform.

And the cap ain't so bad. It's just a cap that matches the suit. I wear this suit to Mass on Sunday, with a regular hat."

"What's the most tip she ever gave you?"

"Oh, I don't want to talk about that."

"For a week in Boston? Ten bucks?"

"On the nose."

"And in Philly?"

"In Philly, nothing. I give her an argument in Philly. I told her, I said she had to wear costumes in her line of work, and I wear a uniform in mine, and I didn't see no difference. I don't, either. I'm not a downtrodden servant. I'd just as soon punch you in the nose if I had cause to. Or anybody. But I bet you she wouldn't punch Mr. George Abbott in the nose, or Eli Kazan. Would you punch Spyros Skouras in the nose?"

"I'd think twice about it."

"Well, there you are. Any of those people I'd punch them in the nose if I was driven to it. I'm not show business, see? Oh, where you're going, she don't like me. I seen her for a phoney right away." The back of his neck had begun to redden. *"And you can tell her, go ahead!"*

"What made you so sore all of a sudden?"

"That's the way she affects me. As soon as I begin thinking about her I boil up."

"She's your boss's girl friend."

"Oh, he knows how I feel about her. It's impossible to keep a thing like that from Harry Browning. He's too smart. In some ways. In other ways—but he's learning about this one."

"You think he is, eh?"

"I know he is. Nine years with a man, I can tell when he's getting fed up sometimes before he knows it himself. You're from The Bronx, aren't you? What parish are you in?"

"I used to go to St. Nicholas of Tollentine."

"Yeah? Our Lady of Mercy, not very far away. The same section."

"Our Lady of Mercy, sure. We used to call it Old Lady Murphy."

"This creature you're on your way to, she attended O.L.M., but you wouldn't know it today, to hear the propaganda. Her and the boss have arguments, and there's a man that made a couple million dollars at least. Maybe he don't have it all, but he made it. And *she* tells *him* about the economic system. Why, a day that he don't net a thousand dollars he considers it a waste. He told me that, himself. A funny man. He'll spend forty dollars for lunch any time it'll net him five thousand. That's what he says to me. I could listen to him by the hour. Orlando. Did you've a cousin living on Marion Avenue worked for Con Edison?"

"No, Orlando isn't my real name. I took the name Orlando because my own name was too long. Too many *c*'s in it."

"Pete Orlando. He lived on Marion Avenue near 196th Street. He had a job with the Consolidated Edison, and I used to bowl with him. You know what her name was before she took Coolidge?"

"Cuccinello. Mary Cuccinello. That had a lot of *c*'s in it too."

"Fred Allen would have been just as funny with the name Sullivan."

"Fred Allen? Oh, Fred Allen."

"Don't tell me you're forgetting the great Fred Allen."

"Oh, no, I used to listen to his program when I was a kid. That was on radio."

"Senator Claghorn and Mrs. Nussbaum? Don't you remember them? And the feud with Benny? Jack Benny? That was great entertainment. Who have they got like that today, I ask you? Well, maybe Bob Hope, if he was on oftener. But what do they consider funny nowadays? This young woman you're on your way to, accidentally on purpose saying something dirty."

"You think she did it on purpose?"

"Sure I do. I said to my wife, 'You watch her. Before the night's over she'll say something dirty,' and by God it wasn't two minutes later she come out with the remark and they cut her off the air. They ought to have some way to fine them when they do that, a good big fine, five thousand dollars, and they'd soon put a stop to it. If they knew there was a fine hanging over them, there wouldn't be them slips, so-called."

"How did you know she was going to say something?"

"Because I had enough experience with her, driving her here and Boston and Philly. I know her ways."

"What if I said I was in love with her?"

"Huh. Then I'd say God help you."

"Your boss has been stuck on her for a long time."

"Huh. You don't know the first thing about it. Harry I. Browning knows what he's doing, every minute of the time, whether it's a girl friend or a client or who it is. Well, here we are. I'll be parked along here somewhere."

"You don't have to wait."

"The boss said you could use the car all afternoon and tonight, if you wanted to. I don't mind waiting. I'll be up talking to the other drivers up at River House, in case you don't see me when you come out."

"I don't know when I'll be out."

"Well, you suit yourself about that, Mister. If you don't want me to wait."

"I don't. Here. Thanks." Nick Orlando gave the driver a ten-dollar bill.

4

"What made you so sure I'd let you in? What made you so sure I'd even be here?" said Mary Coolidge.

"I wasn't sure, but I had a hunch you'd be here reading the new play. I know that much about you," said Nick Orlando.

"Smart."

"What is the play? What kind of a part have you got?"

"You don't read the New York papers any more? You got to that stage, hey?"

"I been on location in Idaho. You know where Idaho is?"

"Yeah. Lana Turner comes from Idaho."

"On location, living in a trailer. You weren't in pictures long enough to spend much time on location."

"The name of the play is *A Pride of Lions*," she said, waving a script. "Nobody in Idaho will ever see it because there's no picture in it."

"Maybe that's a good reason for going back to Idaho. Who wrote it?"

"You never heard of him. But you will. He's a young Pakistani, or he was. He hung himself two years ago at Cambridge University, in England."

"Well, that way you're not gonna have any author-trouble at rehearsal. Who's directing?"

"A brilliant, brilliant boy I discovered in an off-Broadway theater last winter. A brilliant, brilliant, brilliant boy."

"Is he grateful, grateful, grateful?"

"Huh?"

"This brilliant, brilliant boy. You know what I like in a director is a director that will take direction, but they're pretty hard to find."

"This boy is creative."

"Oh, then him and you are rewriting the play."

"Wud you come here for, Nick? To rape me or just upset me?"

"I don't know. What do you want me to do?"

"Go back to Hollywood is what I want you to do. You know what I see when I look at you? A dead man. Dead. You started out with something and then you sold out for a Hollywood Cadillac."

"A Maserati. I got a special Maserati. Cadillacs are for Squaresville."

"Then you oughta have one, because you're cubic, man. That's square to the nth degree. Cubic."

"I read you, Maria. Loud and clear. What are you doing tonight?"

"Working, on this. We start rehearsals in two weeks."

"Don't *tell* me you're not up in your part. I thought you were a perfectionist."

"My part? You know how many lines I got in the first act? Four. The second act, ten. The third act, ten or eleven. The fourth act, two."

"What happened to the fifth act? Were you running over? Who has the speaking parts in this play?"

"This play is almost pure pantomime."

"Jevver see a picture, *The Thief,* with Ray Milland?"

"No, but I heard about it. Propaganda."

"No dialog, though."

"Don't mention it in the same breath."

"Then three or four years from now, after you finish your run in this play, you want to do Joan of Arc, you said."

"I don't know if we'll be finished with it in three years."

"We? You mean you and some writer are collaborating on a new one?"

"Not *some writer.* A. R. Lev."

"Who?"

"A. R. Lev, my director in *A Pride of Lions.*"

"Oh, *that* A. R. Lev. I thought you were talking about A. R. Lev that works for J. P. Morgan and Company."

"What's with this dichotomy of yours all of a sudden? Ha' past one you were like a high school teen-ager that I wouldn't give a date. Now you sit here and all you are is destructive. What happened in the meanwhile?"

"I don't know. I guess I finally figured out what a real jerk you are."

"Then why are you sitting here in my apartment?"

"Yeah, but I'm not." He got up. "I just wanted to have the pleasure of telling you. So long, Cuccinello."

"*Nicky!* Don't leave me?"

Exactly Eight Thousand
Dollars Exactly

What had once been a pleasant country club, its members consisting largely of young couples on the way up, was now an "industrial park"; and on the old site of the tennis courts was a long, low, windowless building, a laboratory for research in synthetics. The clubhouse was still recognizable beneath the renovations that had converted it into executive offices, but the first and eighteenth fairways were leveled off and covered with blacktop, a parking area for the plant employees. At approximately the location of the second tee there was a roped-off space, with a sign that warned against getting too close to the helicopter which transported plant officials to the municipal airport. One reminder of the former character of the place remained: a golf cart carried officials from the helicopters to the executive offices. A ten-foot-high fence surrounded the entire property and above the fence was strung barbed wire. The fence proper was painted white, but there is no way to make barbed wire look like anything but barbed wire.

The man in the small Renault stopped his car at the gate, and a man in uniform, with a badge that said "Security Officer" and a revolver holster, bent over to speak to the driver of the car. "Good afternoon, sir. May I help you?" The *may* sounded false and sissy, as though it seemed false and sissy to the officer himself.

"Yes, thanks. I'm here to see Mr. D'Avlon."

"Yes sir. Name please?"

"Mr. Charles D'Avlon," said the driver of the car.

"Oh, right. You're expected, Mr. D'Avlon." The guard

could not refrain from a surprised look at the small car. "Will you just pin this badge on your lapel and return it to the officer on duty on your way out?" Charles D'Avlon accepted a plastic square which had a safety pin attached to the reverse side; on the obverse side was printed "VISITOR—D'Avlon Industries—355—This badge must be worn at all times while visitor is on Company property. Please return to Security Officer, Main Gate, on completion of visit."

"Where do I park?"

"A space reserved for you, Number 355, executive parking. That'll be that third row. One, two, three. Please leave your key in the car."

"Oh? Why?"

"That's regulations, sir. All cars."

"My brother's, too?"

"Yes sir. Mr. Henry D'Avlon leaves his key in the car just the same as I do."

"A somewhat different car from mine, though, I imagine."

"Well, you see that black and gray Rolls? That's your brother's. But the key's in it just the same. That's in case we have to move the cars in a hurry."

"In an emergency?"

"Correct."

"Such as an explosion?"

"Any emergency that comes up," said the guard. He did not like the word explosion or the slightly frivolous tone of D'Avlon's remark. "By the time you got your car parked the escort will be there to escort you to Executives' Reception." The guard went back into his glass sentry box and picked up a telephone. D'Avlon drove to the parking space.

The escort was a younger man in a uniform similar to the guard's but without the revolver. "Your first visit, I understand," said the escort.

"My first visit to the plant. I've been here before, but when it was a golf club."

"Oh, yes. That was quite some time ago."

"I would think before you were born."

"I guess *so*," said the young man.

"Are we waiting for someone else?"

"Just waiting for you to pin your badge on."

"Even if I'm with you?"

"Everybody has to wear his badge. You wouldn't get ten feet without it."

"What would happen to me?"

"Be detained. If you didn't have a satisfactory explanation you'd be arrested for trespassing. You saw all those signs on the fence. This is a pretty efficient operation."

"Is that since the explosion?"

"We've always taken security precautions here," said the young man, evasively.

"Why don't *you* carry a gun?"

"What makes you think I don't?" The young man reached in his pocket and brought out a .25 automatic. "It's no .38, but a lot of women have got rid of a lot of husbands with one of these. They aren't bulky, slip into your pants pocket, and some visitors don't feel right walking with a man with a holster. But if you hit a man in the throat with one of these slugs, he wouldn't be much use."

"Can you hit a man in the throat?"

"In the eye, with a little time and the right distance. Some cops call it a jealousy gun. And we practice firing it. The women don't even practice, and look what they do with it. It's a mean little fellow. This way, sir."

The handsome young woman in Executives' Reception bowed and smiled at Charles D'Avlon and apparently pushed a button that released the lock on the door into a corridor. At any rate she did not speak to D'Avlon or to the young security officer. "This way, sir," said the young man. They rode one flight up in an automatic elevator, then proceeded to the end of the second-story corridor, to a door marked President. The young man held that door open for Charles D'Avlon, and a man rose to greet the stranger.

"Okay, Mr. Lester?" said the security officer.

"Okay, Van," said the man addressed. He was about forty-five, wore half-shell glasses and a blue four-in-hand that was embroidered with what appeared to be a long exclamation point. His dark blue suit had narrow lapels and his pocket handkerchief, neatly folded, showed enough to reveal, in the very center, the initials D.W.L. "Have a seat, Mr. D'Avlon. Your brother will be right with you. You have a nice trip out?"

"Out from town, or out from Connecticut?"

"Well—from Connecticut."

"Oh, it was all right. Gave me a chance to see a lot of the country."

"Didn't you use to live here?"

"Oh, sure. We were born here, but it's all changed. I used to play golf here when I was a young man. Do you know where you're sitting?"

"How do you mean?"

"You're sitting in the ladies' can. That's what this was. The ladies' locker-room."

"I wasn't with the company then."

"There wasn't any company then."

"No, I guess not," said Mr. Lester. He sat with his hands folded on his desk.

"Go ahead with your work, if you want to. Don't let me hold you up," said Charles D'Avlon.

"I'm waiting for—there he is," said Mr. Lester. He rose as the door at his right was opened.

"Hello, Chiz," said the man in the doorway. "Come on in."

"Hello, Henry," said Charles D'Avlon. The brothers shook hands and Charles entered the president's office.

It was a corner room with a magnificent view of the rolling countryside and a distant mountain. "I was just telling your man Lester, his office is in the ladies' can."

"Well, that proves one thing," said Henry. "You haven't changed much. You always liked to throw people a little off balance."

"Don't be disagreeable, Henry. It's tough enough to be here under the circumstances. Don't make it tougher."

"Chiz, you're the one that always makes things tougher for yourself."

"I didn't say you made things tougher. I just said they were tough enough. I swore I'd never ask you for a nickel, but here I am."

"Yes," said Henry. "Well, we got right to the point. How much do you want?"

"A lot."

"Oh, I guessed that. If it was a little you wouldn't feel you had to make such a long trip. How much, Chiz?"

"Eight thousand dollars."

"All right. But why eight? Why not five, or why not ten? I'm curious to know how you arrived at the figure eight thousand."

"I thought it would sound businesslike."

"As though you'd figured it out very carefully. Okay, it does," said Henry. He spoke into the inter-com on his desk. "Dale, will you make out a cheque, my personal account, eight thousand dollars, payable to Charles W. D'Avlon, and bring it in for my signature as soon as it's made out? Thank you."

"Aren't you interested in what I want it for?" said Charles.

"Not very much. You have some story, and it comes to eight thousand dollars. You probably need five, but you thought you might as well get three extra."

"That's right," said Charles. "But I hate to waste the story. I had a good one."

"Write it and sell it to a magazine."

"I can't write. If I could write I'd have plenty of material, but first you said you were interested in why I said eight thousand, and in the next breath you don't want to hear my story."

"I wanted to see if you'd admit it was a story. If you hadn't admitted it I'd have had the cheque made out for four thousand. But you were frank, and that's as close as you ever come to being honest. So you get your eight thousand."

"If I'd known it was going to be this easy—"

"No. You might have got ten, but no more."

"Then give me ten."

"Not a chance," said Henry. There were two light taps on the door, Lester came in and laid the cheque on Henry's desk and departed. Henry signed and pushed the cheque toward his brother.

"Cheque protector and everything. Exactly eight thousand exactly," said Charles. "Now I'm interested to know why you gave me any money at all. You didn't have to. Does it give you a sense of power? Does it go with that Rolls-Royce you have down there, and all this high-powered security stuff?"

"To a certain extent I guess it does. But there's more to it than that, Chiz."

"Of course."

"You see, I've always wondered when you'd finally put the touch on me. Not that I lay awake nights, but I knew you would some day. And now you have, for eight thousand dollars. I'm getting off light. Because you must know damn well that this is all you'll ever get from me."

"That occurred to me."

"When we were boys and you used to knock me around I used to feel sort of sorry for you. You'd beat the hell out of me and walk away with something of mine. A fielder's glove, or a necktie. But what you didn't know was that I was dying to *give* you the God damn glove or tie. Anything you asked for of mine, you could have had. But you preferred violence and theft, and naturally I could take only so much and then I began to hate you."

"And still do."

"Does that surprise you? Yes. Because as you grew older that was the way you were with everybody, all through your life. If you look out that window you'll see a research laboratory where the tennis courts used to be. One night after a dance I was getting in that little Oakland I had, that Grandmother gave me for my twenty-first birthday. You ought to remember it, you smashed it up, you son of a bitch. Anyway, I didn't have a date and I was by myself and I heard a girl crying. It was Mary Radley, sitting on the bench between the first and second courts. She was ashamed to go back to the clubhouse with her dress all torn. You. You didn't have to be brutal with Mary Radley. Nobody did, but especially you. But that was your way, and that was when I first realized that it wasn't just a question of being a bully to your kid brother. You were a bully, net."

"Okay," said Charles. "Well, it's your turn to be the bully. Thanks for the money."

"Wait a minute. I haven't finished. I want you to hear a few things, and you'll damn well listen or I'll stop payment on that cheque."

"Captive audience. All right," said Charles.

"You've never changed. Both your wives took all they could stand, your children don't want to be anywhere near you. Have you ever wondered why?"

"Not very much. The children were brought up by their mothers, and their mothers saw to it that I didn't get any of the best of it. I wrote them off very early."

"Not your daughter. You showed up at her graduation and made her leave her mother and stepfather to go on some excursion with you. Whimsical cruelty, that was. Because you then sent her back to her mother and never did any more about her. Not a thing, financially or otherwise."

"Her mother has plenty of glue. One thing I did for my children was make sure they had rich mothers."

"Yes. Who also could afford *you* before there were any children, and after."

"The fact of the matter is that both my wives proposed to me, Henry."

"I have no doubt of it. You were very skillful. I understand your first wife forced you to accept a wedding present of two hundred thousand dollars."

"Two-fifty. A quarter of a million. All long since gone, I regret to say."

"But your second wife—"

"An iron-bound trust. I couldn't get my hooks on any of that. Where did you find out so much about my affairs?"

"When I was around trying to raise the money to get this business started, I encountered a certain amount of resistance because of the name. Even when they found out I wasn't you, people were still very dubious, especially New York and Philadelphia people. Don't ever go back to Philadelphia, Chiz. They really don't like you there."

"I'm desolated."

"You're not, but you ought to be."

"I really am. There are a couple of rich widows in Philadelphia that could make me entirely independent of people like you. But the Girard Trust Company and that other one, they probably take a dim view of me. It's too bad, too, because both of these women, or I should say either one of them could make me comfortable in my old age. I'm crowding sixty, you know."

"Oh, I know."

"The next fifteen years, I don't look forward to them the way things are at present. You may have to take me on as a night watchman."

"Fat chance. And that brings me to another point I was going to make. Or my earlier point about your being a bully. Do you realize that before you came in this room I already knew that you'd been shooting off your mouth about the explosion we had here three years ago? Our Security people couldn't believe their ears. The first man you talked to lost a brother in that explosion. The second man, the young fellow, was very badly burned and had to have skin-grafting operations that took over a year. But your feeble jokes, aside from any question of taste, were your way of bullying people, the way you used to be to caddies and waiters when this was the club. Five men were killed in that explosion, and it's no joke around here. It's no joke anywhere. For your information, both Security officers were convinced that you were an impostor, that you weren't my brother at all. For your additional information, Chiz, I wish they'd been right."

Charles D'Avlon rose. "Well, that sounds pretty final," he said. He went over to the window and looked out at the laboratory. "Mary Radley," he said. "She was certainly a little tramp."

Mary and Norma

There was a pie, a deep-dish apple pie, sitting on top of the light blue bread box, and though a wax-paper sheet covered the pie, Mary Kneely could see that a good-sized wedge had been cut out of it, a slab not quite a quarter of the whole pie. In the sink was a coffee cup and saucer, rinsed out but not washed, and she knew without looking that there would be a dozen cigarette butts in the garbage can. He had waited up for her, smoking, drinking coffee, and finally getting at the pie instead of the whiskey. She wished he had got at the whiskey instead. He had never been able to drink much whiskey; it made him sick or put him to sleep, sometimes both. But now he would be lying awake from the coffee, probably smoking in bed in violation of his own strict rule, and thinking up some sarcastic remark to greet her with.

She covered the pie more securely and put the cup and saucer and knife and fork and spoon on the right side of the sink, where they would be joined in the morning by the breakfast dishes. He had forgotten to clean the percolator, and she dumped out the coffee grounds and cleaned it herself and made it ready for the morning. She ran the cold water over her own cigarette and dropped it in the garbage can with his butts. Then she switched off the kitchen light and made her way to their room.

He was lying in bed, pretending to be reading an old *Field & Stream,* an issue that featured the firearms and fishing tackle that he would never buy. Every year he bought that special issue, if not of *Field & Stream,* of its competitors, and all winter long he would look at the pictures and read the descrip-

tions of the guns and rods and reels and lines; just as in the
spring of the year he would pay a dollar for a magazine that
contained pictures of boats: big cruisers, yachts for charter, the
newest in outboards, and the latest thing in houseboats for the
rivers of Florida. Once he had sent away for the plans for
building one of those boats, paid around fifteen dollars for
the plans; but he did not know the first thing about carpentry,
and the boat that had seemed so attractive in the photographs
became less so in blueprints. One day he just threw the blueprints away, when she was out of the house.

He looked up at her, then back at his magazine. "You're
home early," he said.

"Am I?"

"Yeah, it'll be two-three hours before daylight."

"Oh," she said.

"Who brought you home? I didn't hear any car."

"Came home in a taxi," she said.

"Frank Whalen's?"

"No. The Italian fellow, Joe's."

"Why didn't you call Frank?"

"I did, but he was busy."

"Yeah, and he knows me better than the Italian fellow. He
ask you a lot of questions, the Italian fellow?"

"Didn't ask me *any* questions. I didn't have any conversation with him at all. Just told him the address."

"Why did you have to tell him the address? He knows who
you are by this time."

"Maybe he does, but I told him the address anyway."

"Did you sit up front with him?"

"I sat in his lap!"

"It wouldn't surprise me."

"Oh, *nothing'd* surprise *you*, Ed. You know all the answers
to everything."

She hung up her dress and stood behind the opened closet
door to finish her undressing and get into her nightgown and
bathrobe. She took a long time in the bathroom, but he was

still looking at the magazine when she came out. "Is it all right if I put the light out?" she said.

"Go ahead," he said.

She pressed the button in the base of the lamp. "Goodnight," she said.

"Goodnight, hell," he said, and in the darkness got into her bed. When he returned to his own bed he quickly fell asleep, making the whistling sound that was almost as bad as snoring. She got up and went to the living-room and smoked a cigarette in the dark, unwilling to let the neighbors see a light on. When she began to feel sleepy she went back to bed.

"Where are you going today?" she said, as she gave him his breakfast.

"This morning I gotta go over to Huntington," he said. "Al Proser. I get finished up with Al and then I gotta go see a new fellow in Riverhead. A new fellow just starting out. And if I have time I was thinking while I was over that direction I'd drop in on some of the guys in Southampton."

"And home by way of Center Moriches?"

"Yeah. Why?"

"A few beers with the Kneely family. I won't start dinner till seven o'clock."

"There won't be any beers with the Kneely family. Buddy's in New York for a convention, and Vince and I had an argument."

"Oh, how could anybody ever have an argument with dear sweet Vince? Why he has the disposition of a saint."

"You and your sarcastic remarks."

"That's what your mother says. Vince has the disposition of a saint. She must know some different saints than the ones I ever heard of."

"You can say that again. Any saints *you* know about, my mother wouldn't know them. What are *you* gonna do today?"

"The same thing I did yesterday. Help your sister with the moving."

"Where you were till two o'clock this morning?"

"Why didn't you call her up if you thought I was some place else?"

"Because the two of you are both alike, birds of a feather. I wouldn't believe Norma any more than I'd believe you."

"You're afraid to be right and afraid to be wrong, that's your trouble," she said.

"You're birds of a feather, you and Norma. It's a terrible thing to have to be ashamed of your own sister, but believe me, when the time comes I'm not gonna stand by her."

"When what time comes?"

"The time. When Harry walks in on her some night. Her and one of her boy friends. My own sister. And you stay out of it, too. If Harry starts shooting, and I wouldn't blame him,' maybe you'll stop a slug yourself."

"I thought cops were supposed to be able to shoot."

"Harry can shoot all right."

"Well then he won't hit me."

"You just stay out of it."

"All right, I'll stay out of it. If I see Harry coming in with a gun in his hand I'll ask to be excused."

"You know what I mean. You know damn well."

"Maybe it would solve your problems if he did hit me."

"I don't need Harry to solve my problems."

"Well, maybe it would solve *my* problems."

"Aw, go to hell. If I didn't have any more problems than you have I'd consider myself lucky."

"You don't have any problems. The only problems you have are is dinner ready on time, and what's on TV."

"Sure. You never heard of competition in business, I suppose."

"All you do is go to a contractor and ask him how many cubic yards he needs. Or tons. Or truckloads."

"That shows how much you know about sand and gravel. Nine years, and you think all I am is an order-taker. Huh. If that's all I was you'd starve to death."

"I wouldn't mind starving as much as you would."

"Cracks about my appetite don't have the slightest effect, not the slightest. When I lived home, before I was married, the only one of six children that didn't have a good appetite was Norma, your pal."

"Your sister."

"Don't remind me of it. She had to be made to eat her meals, and look at her. A skinny, temperamental, neurotic pushover. My own sister."

"She has two children, and they're healthy. And that stupid cop she's married to, he's not underweight."

"She's a neurotic pushover. I don't know what any guy would see in her. And they wouldn't if she wasn't a pushover. Harry's the one I feel sorry for, but he'll get wise to himself."

"And when he does, bang-bang, huh?"

"It'll be her own fault. Her own damn fault. I won't stand by her. I told her plenty of times."

"Oh, I know you did."

"Well, she can't say I didn't warn her. That much I did, and if she don't wanta take my advice, I did all I could."

"Yeah. You and Buddy and Vince."

"*And Paul.* Even her brother a priest didn't have any effect on her."

"He wouldn't have any effect on me, either."

"Oh, hell, you're a Protestant."

"Whatever I am, Paul Kneely wouldn't have any influence over me, Protestant, Catholic, Jew, Holy Roller."

"You let him marry us."

"As a favor to you, that's all. I didn't pick him."

"You be careful what you say about Paul. He isn't only my brother. He's an ordained priest."

"I'm always careful what I say about him. The only one's not afraid of him is Norma. All the rest of you're afraid of him."

"It isn't fear. It's respect."

"Well don't ask me to respect him."

"Not asking you. I'm *telling* you."

"For the one thousandth time," she said. "If you see any place selling beach plum jelly, stop and get some. It goes good at breakfast."

"I'll see you when I see you," he said, and departed.

She did her morning chores until Norma came to fetch her to Norma's house. "It's as much trouble to move from one end of town to the other as if we were moving to California," said Norma. "More. Nowadays the movers pack everything in barrels, all labeled. The woman I'm moving next door to came all the way from Seattle, Washington, and she says they take care of everything. If you tell them what room to put the stuff in, they'll do that. She and her husband came by car and had a three weeks' vacation driving all over and stopping at places, and the movers got here the day after *they* did."

"That's not my idea of a vacation, three weeks in a car with your husband."

"You'd have different ideas if you saw the husband. He looks like William Holden. They say that about a lot of men, but this one really does."

"Be careful, Norma," said Mary.

"Oh, I only said hello to him a couple of times. But I saw him first, so don't *you* get ideas. Duane Jensen. Nice name."

"Duane Jensen. It's all right."

"He's a major in the Air Force, and he has something to do at Grumman. They have three children. I think she was ready to get snooty when I told her Harry was a cop, but she acted different when I told her Harry was a major fifteen years ago."

"*Was* he?"

"In the Military Police. He sure was. So you could see her doing a little mental arithmetic and figuring if Harry was a major fifteen years ago, he'd be a lot higher than major now. So she stopped acting snooty."

"I know you, Norma, and you better be careful. You get to be friends with the wife first. Then the next thing is it's you and the husband."

"Not always," said Norma.

"Well, pretty often. Don't you ever get afraid of Harry?"

"Harry's a lunkhead or I'd of been dead by now," said Norma. "It isn't Harry I'm afraid of. He's a lunkhead. But those brothers of mine. Especially Ed. He's liable to say something sometime in front of Harry, and that's what I'm afraid of. A lunkhead like Harry, they aren't the ones that make the trouble, but it's when they hear it from a third party. If I ever get in any trouble it'll be Ed that caused it."

"You're so right."

"Oh, sure. I know that. You know what Ed's trouble is— or maybe you don't. No, maybe you don't."

"He eats too much."

"That, and something else."

"He'll eat a whole chocolate cake. I've seen him do it when he gets upset about something, where another man would get drunk."

"Oh, he did that from a kid. Encouraged by my mother. Any time anything happened to one of us, but Ed in particular, Mom would stuff us full of something to eat. But that isn't Ed's basic trouble."

"What is?"

"Well, if you want to know, Ed wanted to be a priest. He was the one that *wanted* to be the priest in the family, but Mom decided that Paul had the true vocation. Therefore, Ed was the one that they always made jokes about girls. Mom used to say 'Our Ed, the girls won't leave him alone,' till he got to believing it himself. But I guess you know plenty about Ed in that department."

"Yeah."

"Vince and Bud, out every night raising hell but Ed was the one Mom called the ladies' man."

"Why didn't she want Ed to be a priest?"

"The only reason I can think of is because Paul was the youngest and that way she could hold on to him longer. She didn't really care what happened to the other brothers, just as long as she could have her Paul. Well, it's a good thing in a way, because God help any girl that would of married Paul after Mom got through with him."

"Did he ever fall for any girl?"

"What chance did he have? She would never of let Ed marry a Protestant if she cared what happened to him. You must of been surprised when she didn't put up more objections. I know Ed was in fear and trembling because you weren't a Catholic, but he didn't have anything to worry about." Norma chuckled. "She almost outsmarted herself, though."

"How?"

"Paul. From the time he was ten years old he got a brain-washing, that the only life for him was the priesthood. And he believed it, absolutely. He was an altar boy and served Mass practically every morning, weekdays and Sundays, and he had holy pictures in his room and all that. Then one day he dropped a bombshell, a real blockbuster. He told Mom he wanted to be a missionary. He wanted to go to China or some place and be a missionary. Oh, was that a catastrophe! I don't know how she talked him out of that, but she did. But believe me, that had her worried. So now he's just a parish priest and doesn't even get to go overseas and travel. His vacation he comes home to Center Moriches and tries to sermonize me. What the hell does he know about me? I think Ed puts him up to it. That's what Vince thinks. Vince had an argument with Ed over me. Did Ed say anything to you?"

"I knew they had some kind of an argument. I didn't know what about," said Mary.

"It was over me. Vince told Ed that what I did was Harry's business, not Ed's business or Paul's business or anybody else's. Vince, you know Vince, he's a holy terror. He'd have an argument with the Pope if he felt like it. You ought to hear him on the subject of Harry. 'That lunkhead,' he calls him. He hates cops, and *I* think he hates *priests*. He'll say anything in front of Paul, just to shock him. He goes too far sometimes. Vince doesn't realize that Paul never had a chance."

"I never thought of it that way, but I guess it's true. To me Paul is just a big fat nothing."

"They all are. And if we lived in Center Moriches, Mom would have Harry, because don't think Vince is all that independent, because he's not. Mom still holds on to the purse-strings, and Vince isn't a very good businessman. He owes Mom over four thousand dollars. And if we lived there she'd figure some way to have Harry obligated to her. And he'd go for it. Sometimes I think Harry's more like one of my own brothers."

They got out of the car and entered Norma's house, their footsteps starting small echoes on the now bare floors. Norma offered her sister-in-law a cigarette, lit it and lit her own. She rested one arm across her waist, giving support to the elbow of the other arm, and holding her cigarette high in the air. She contemplated her next move. "I could do the rest of it myself," she said. "But I'm glad to have your company. I was just thinking, I lived in this house over fifteen years, the only house I ever lived in since I was married. You'd think I'd have some pangs about moving, but I don't. The children don't, either. Harry's the only one that tried to get sentimental about it. God! It's a good thing these walls can't talk."

"I'll say," said Mary.

"I didn't mean you, Mary. I was just thinking about myself."

"Oh, I know."

"The closest I ever came to getting caught, it wasn't Harry. It was my brother Vince. This friend of mine just left by the kitchen door, and two minutes later Vince barged in the front way. He had made quite a load on his way home from the harness races, and suddenly decided to pay a call on his sister."

"Why do you take such chances?"

"Why do you?"

"Yeah, I guess you're right, but I don't have any children, and Ed isn't liable to kill me. Harry would kill you, Norma."

"Maybe, if he caught me. But did you ever stop to think of how many times I thought of killing him? He comes home at five or six o'clock in the morning when he's on night duty. He takes off his uniform and hangs up his gun belt in the closet, and gets into bed with me. The usual thing, then rolls over and goes to sleep, and it's time for me to get up and get the kids' breakfast. How many times, I wonder, have I looked at that gun and thought, 'You lunkhead, what do you think I am? Some kind of a cow?' No consideration, nothing nice about it. Wakes me up out of a sound sleep just so I can be some kind of a cow. If that's all there is to it for him, it isn't enough for me. Oh, I'd never shoot him, but if he knew how many times I thought about it, he wouldn't bring his gun home."

"Ed is always looking at pictures of guns."

"Oh, I know. He always did. He even asked Harry—maybe I shouldn't tell you this. But I will. He asked Harry one time last winter how to go about buying a gun. It's against the law in this State. A revolver. Harry told him it was practically impossible in New York. Possession is illegal without a license, and you had to go through a lot of red tape to get a license."

"I'm not afraid of Ed."

"No, I wouldn't think you would be. But I'll bet there'd be times when you'd be afraid of yourself if you had a gun in the house."

Mary stood in the middle of the emptiness, not thinking of what Norma was saying. "You lived here fifteen years," she said. "I remember when you papered this room. I guess the people that bought the house, the first thing she'll want to do is re-paper it."

"I wouldn't blame her. I was beginning to get sick of it," said Norma.

"And then there won't be anything left of fifteen years you lived here."

"Yes there will. She bought the icebox and the washer and the dryer."

"But nothing personal. Wallpaper I consider personal. Like appliances, I don't."

"Oh, yes. I see. No, I guess there won't be much of that left. It could have been anybody lived here."

"Nine years I've been married to Ed, but we lived in four different places. You lived here fifteen years."

"Mom's in the same house over thirty-five. They put additions on it, but it's the same house. Now it's too big for her, but she won't let go of it. She could save money if she did, but then she couldn't have the whole tribe around at Christmas, queening it over everybody. Making everybody eat too much. You've been there, you've seen her."

"Sure have. I sure have. 'Mary's lucky. She won't have to get up and go to early Mass.' Every Christmas Eve for nine Christmases. 'Mary can sleep late.' "

"I know."

"The funny thing is, I went and got myself mixed up with another Catholic."

"You don't have to tell me unless you feel like it."

"Joe Angelo."

"That has the new taxi business?"

"Yes."

"He's married, Mary. You know that."

"Sure, I know it."

"I guess he's all right. It takes money to get started in the taxi business, and he doesn't have a criminal record. Harry seems to think he's all right, and he'd know if anybody did. But don't let Harry find out about this, or he'll make it tough for Joe."

"That's what Joe's afraid of. He's more afraid of Harry finding out than Ed."

"I was wondering who it was," said Norma. "I knew you had somebody, but I didn't want to say anything till you told me yourself."

"Yes, since last spring."

"Well, all I can say is good luck and be careful."

"If it isn't me telling you to be careful, it's you telling me."

"Yes, but I had more experiences in that line, Mary. I'm married to a real lunkhead, but Ed Kneely's no lunkhead. He's shrewd, mean and shrewd. And one of these days he's going to be a rich man."

"Ed?"

"He's like my father. My father didn't start making any money till he was well up in his thirties, and Ed's branching out. He's getting known over in Suffolk. You know, five years ago Ed wouldn't have had an argument with Vince. Vince was always kind of the big shot, the one that made the most noise.

But like now Vince owes Mom over four thousand dollars, and she doesn't figure to get that back. It'll be taken out of Vince's share when she dies. Ed'll get his full share, and if she hangs on another five years he'll come into it just about when he needs it in the business. Ed Kneely's going to be a rich man, so don't spoil it for yourself. You're entitled to reap the benefit."

"The benefit of what?"

"Sticking with the son of a bitch all these years. The only thing that'll stop Ed is if he eats himself to death. Which he'll do if you worry him too much. Keep him off the pies and cakes till he makes his fortune."

Mary smiled. "Then what?"

"Then let him enjoy himself. Give him waffles for breakfast and pie à la mode every night. He'll eat it, and you'll be a rich widow when you're still in your forties. I wish it was as easy as that with Harry, but Harry didn't gain ten pounds since he got out of the Army."

"I wonder if they hate us as much," said Mary.

"If they didn't, we wouldn't be talking this way."

"I guess not."

"I got the look from Duane Jensen. He knows. But I'm 'way ahead of him. I'm thinking of when he begins to wish he never saw me, when he wishes he was back in Seattle."

"Yes. Joe said last night I ought to use Frank Whalen once in a while, just to throw people off."

"That's one of the first signs," said Norma. "He wouldn't have told you that last spring. *I* hate *them*. It isn't only them hating us. But what are you gonna do?"

The Cellar Domain

Not just anyone and everyone got their hair cut and their faces shaved at Peter Durant's shop. Peter had a system to discourage new customers who in his opinion had not earned the right to join his clientele. Peter had, of course, the first chair, but he kept his eye on the other six chairs in his shop and on the order in which his customers arrived and should be attended to. A barber would finish with a customer, and Peter, almost without missing a snip at his own customer's hair, would call out: "You're next, Judge. Bobby, take Judge Buckhouse." Customers and barbers alike accepted Peter's decisions without argument, and an unwelcome newcomer would sometimes find that he had been passed over in favor of five or six men who had not been in the shop when he arrived. Once in a while there would be one who would say: "I think I was next."

"Can't help that," Peter would say, and that settled it. If the customer didn't like it, he was free to go elsewhere, which was exactly what Peter Durant intended. A young businessman, a young lawyer or doctor making a first appearance at Durant's, would know better than to risk a scene in the presence of Peter's established customers, who were the county's most prominent professional and financial men and some others who had received Peter's approval. In those long-gone days it was an important occasion when Peter Durant would say to a customer: "I'm ordering you a mug. Do you want your name on it or just your initials?" No one had ever declined the honor of a mug at Peter Durant's or hesitated to pay the two dollars for the mug and its gilt lettering. It was a diploma, the acceptance of a man's racing colors, membership in a club like the Philadelphia Union League, a rating in Bradstreet's, a commission on the Governor's military staff. It was all these things, because there were men in the county who had achieved one or another of these things but had not been invited to pay two dollars for a mug at Peter Durant's.

Although the shop was in the cellar of the hotel, it was not a convenience for hotel guests. Traveling salesmen were accommodated at Durant's only in the less busy hours of mid-afternoon, and even though some of his barbers might be shaving themselves, or sitting on the customers' bench and reading the Philadelphia *North American* or the London *Illustrated News,* Peter sometimes would take a quick look at a stranger and say: "Be an hour's wait."

"What about those men?" the stranger would say, nodding toward the idle barbers.

"That's my business. Better go down the street. You got a good barber down towards the railroad station."

The stranger would glare at Peter, but depart, and Peter would say: "That's the kind of a son of a bitch would ask for a manicure." Peter's barbers would laugh. They liked Peter; he paid them well, he did their thinking for them, and he backed them up in any dispute with a customer. There were only two rules they had to obey: a barber was not supposed to work if he had liquor on his breath; if he wanted to go on a drunk he could take the day off; and the other rule was that no barber, no customer for that matter, was permitted to address him as Pete. He was not deceived by the obsequious newcomer who called him Mr. Durant; but no judge, no doctor, no clergyman, no bank cashier, no retired millionaire got an answer when he said Pete instead of Peter. But then they never made that mistake; they knew better. Casual use of the diminutive had kept some men from getting a mug.

The shop sold nothing but shaves, haircuts, and facial and scalp massages. No tonics, no combs or brushes, no cigars or cigarettes, and only one special service: some men who shaved themselves would bring their razors to Peter for honing. A great deal of betting went on among the customers, especially during political campaigns, but Peter Durant participated only to the extent that bets made in his shop were recorded in a notebook he kept in his cash register. Both parties to a bet would see what he wrote in the notebook, sign their initials, and Peter would say: "Now nobody has to ask me do I remember who bet what." But Peter thus became the repository of valuable information that he kept confidential, and inevitably his customers' trust in his discretion got him in on some good things. He went on shaving men whom he could buy and sell, even though they might not know it.

Generally Peter Durant discouraged the favorite-barber custom, and among the newer customers it was not permitted. "One's as good as another in this shop," he would say. "Harry's as good a barber as me, and Elmer's as good as Harry." But Peter had his own favorite customers, and he would linger over a haircut, or speed it up, so that one of his favorites would get in his chair. Peter's chair, the first, was nearest the street windows, and certain customers would stand on the sidewalk and look down into the shop until they had attracted his attention. If he nodded, they knew he would fit them into the order so that he would cut their hair; if he shook his head and made a face, they knew it to mean that they would have to take another barber. The other barbers, who were not fools, made every cooperative effort to see that Peter's favorites got to his chair, but it was a different matter altogether for them to understand why Peter Durant preferred some customers to others. They could understand why Edwin E. Patterson was entitled to the first chair, but most of the barbers could not understand why Andy Keever got in the shop at all.

Ned Patterson was in town a lot because he had business at the court house; not a large amount of business, and obviously not highly profitable, what there was. He usually got off the trolley-car from Swedish Haven at the corner across the street from the barber shop on mornings when he was to be in court. On court days he liked to be shaved by Peter Durant, and it did not escape the notice of the barbers that Peter often trimmed

Ned's hair—"neatened it up," he called it—without charging him for a regular cut. "Now I guess you look all right," Peter would say.

"Thank you, Peter. Thank you very much," Ned would say, and lay down the same quarter and nickel—twenty cents for the shave, and ten-cent tip—and be off to the court house. At this time, shortly after the First World War, Ned Patterson was in his sixties, a good ten years older than Peter Durant, but nearly everyone still called him Ned. On court days he wore a black suit, black necktie and shoes, and starched collar and cuffs and shirt-bosom. Walter, the bootblack-porter at Durant's shop, could not have improved on the shine Ned had already given his shoes. Ned Patterson seldom encountered other lawyers in the shop; he was there too early in the day. But Judge Buckhouse sometimes arrived for a shave as Ned was leaving, and Ned would say: "Good morning to you, sir."

"Good morning, Ned. If you're not in too much of a hurry I can give you a lift."

"Very kind of you, Judge, but I've got a man waiting." He was fifteen years older than Judge Buckhouse, and the last two blocks to the court house were a steep climb, but he never accepted the judge's offer. Always, when the offers were made, Ned would explain that he had a man waiting, presumably a client, but Buckhouse knew that Ned Patterson sometimes came to the court house, wandered up and down the corridors, listened to trials, mingled with colleagues in the lawyers' room, and represented no client. Just by being there at every session of every term, Ned sometimes would be appointed by the court to defend a case and receive a fee that he would not get by staying in Swedish Haven. Sometimes a colleague would put something his way—a dreary job of searching in the prothonotary's records—that would be worth twenty-five dollars. Ned Patterson rarely went home empty-handed at the end of a term of court, but the juicy receiverships went to other lawyers, more aggressive or younger or more learned in the law. "In a jury trial," a lawyer once said, "it ought to be worth a few dollars to have Ned sitting with you at counsel table. That white hair and smooth skin, and that undertaker outfit he wears. He's the next thing to having a bishop on your side. But I don't know how often it would work. The jury might start wondering why God didn't examine the witnesses, or why He didn't make the closing address. Some juries would begin to think that maybe Ned didn't—quite—go along with you, and they'd smell a rat. And as for letting him examine a witness, you'd be taking a chance of ruining your case then and there. I like old Ned, but to tell you the truth he doesn't even copy things right. He knows his law, and loves it, and in some respects he'd have made a good judge. But not for the County. He'd never send anybody to prison." And so, in his late-middle sixties, Edwin E. Patterson, Esq., attorney-at-law, sole surviving member of the firm of Patterson & Patterson, was still waiting for the success that had seemed to come so easily to his father many years ago, the success without which Ned could not have continued his own unprofitable practice of law. For the truth was that Ned and his wife subsisted on the small income from his father's estate, and his professional fees provided him with the luxury of being a lawyer. He was a gentleman-at-law, an amateur of the law, who went to the court house as some men, old friends in Philadelphia, went to the opera. Some of *them* could not sing a note, but they loved Verdi. In much the same way, on court days, Ned Patterson would come to town, humming, as it were, the Rule in Shelley's Case.

In a sense, then, Ned Patterson's visits to Peter Durant's barber shop were time spent in the dressing-room, before the performances at the court house in which he might or might not take active part. The quiet dignity he maintained while covered with lather was genuine enough, lifelong and natural, but Peter Durant had no way of knowing that Ned at such times was especially content because he was already enjoying the promise of the day's later developments. "Never seen that man when he wasn't at peace with the world," Peter Durant would say. "Shaving him's a good way to start the day." The more remarkable, then, that Peter Durant's other favorite customer should be Andy Keever.

Andy Keever's membership in the Durant clientele was of-
fensive to more than one of the regulars. He knew everyone by
name, and as he made an entrance in the shop he would walk
past the waiting customers on the bench, speaking to each—
"Mr. Hofman . . . Dr. English . . . Mr. Chapin . . ."—and
shedding his outer clothing, removing collar and tie, and apparently not noticing that there would be a closing of ranks so
that the men of substance would not have to make a place for
him. He would stand at the far end of the shop, hanging his
clothing on the rack, and call to the owner: "Hey, Peter, you
coming to the hose company picnic?"

"Oh, sure," Peter Durant would say, smiling because everyone knew that he never went to hose company picnics. "I'll be
there with bells on."

"Never mind the bells, we'll bring them." Andy would stand
at the clothes rack, surveying the room and waiting for the exactly right moment, and then he would move quietly forward
until he reached Elmer Bitzer's chair, without being seen by
Elmer. He would goose Bitzer and simultaneously whistle
through his teeth, a loud, piercing whistle, and Bitzer would
jump. Everybody would laugh, but the hardest laugher was
Peter Durant, who would drop his hands to his sides and bend
over, weak with giggles. "That fellow, he kills me," he would
say to the customer in the chair. "I can't help it, he makes me
laugh." Even Bitzer, the perennial victim, would grin.

Andy Keever would find a place on the bench, look about
him, stand up and say: "Any reverends here?"

"No," one of the barbers would say.

"Who's that under the hot towel? Not a reverend, sure?"

"Mr. Miller."

"Then I got a good one for you. Hey, Peter, I got a good one
for you. There was this railroader come home and found his
wife in bed with a Chinaman. You know, a Chinaman . . ."

Andy Keever never laughed at his own stories. When he
finished one he would look around at all the men, and if one
of the men had not been listening, was reading a newspaper,

Andy would make a face at him and raise his voice and tell a dirtier story. Sometimes he would have French postcards and phallic toys that he would hold out to a barber, and then as the barber reached out his hand, Andy would quickly pull away. "Naughtee, naugh-tee. You're too eager," he would say. "I'm saving this for Walter. Hey, Walter, I bought you something in Philly."

Andy Keever was new in town, had come there after being mustered out of the Army early in 1919. One of the breweries, resigned to what was about to happen, was making the change from beer to ice cream, and Andy Keever was put in charge of a crew that canvassed candy stores and poolrooms and the like, signing up customers for the new product. Andy Keever was a live wire, a hard worker, and in a few short months it was understood that the brewery family were so pleased with him that it was only a question of time before he would be made general manager of the ice cream plant. He was a charter member of the Legion post, a sports fan, a founder of the Lions Club, a forward on one of the businessmen's basketball teams at the Y.M.C.A., and, within a year, one of the leaders of the small group who got things done. They were virtually a standing committee of Rotarians, Merchants Association members and Masons who ran the drives and campaigns that represented community activity, and Andy Keever was the first new face in that group in five years. Some of these men were patrons of Peter Durant's shop, which was the only place where they would frequently encounter those other men, men who were known as the Lantenengo Street crowd, the Gibbsville Club crowd, the plutocrats and "our would-be aristocrats." As individuals, in man-to-man relations, the members of the two leading groups got along nicely; but as group members they kept to themselves, recognizably different in clothes and manners. At Peter Durant's shop, there never was any doubt as to the proprietor's preference, and after waiting in vain to be sold a mug, some of the Rotarians would take their business elsewhere, invariably complaining of the service at Peter Durant's and omitting mention of the fact that a Ned Patterson got more cordial treatment than a director of the Building & Loan Society.

"I think Mr. Keever goes a bit too far," said one of Peter Durant's favorites one day.

"Fresh as paint, but he puts me in stitches," said Peter. "I don't know what there is about that fellow."

"Well, if *you* can put up with him," said the customer. "But I wouldn't like to be in Elmer Bitzer's chair, with Elmer holding a razor at my throat."

"Oh, you take notice sometime. Keever don't do that to Elmer when Elmer's shaving. Keever has more sense than that."

"Good. Glad to hear that, anyway."

"Oh, sure. That's something I never *would* put up with. In this business you learn to have an awful lot of respect for a razor."

"I should think so," said the customer.

"When I was learning the barber trade, if I nicked a customer my old man would fine me a week's pay, even if it wasn't my fault."

The customer closed his eyes, the signal to end conversation that was always respected by Peter Durant. There were other men who in other conversations revealed a distaste for the presence of Andy Keever, and Peter thought about the matter; but Keever's jokes and little pranks went on, and Keever remained a customer. Peter began to feel that criticism of Keever was by way of being criticism of himself, and he had had little experience of that. He ran his shop to suit himself, a first-class shop with first-class barbers, where the best men in the county sat with their collars and ties off, and one man—Peter Durant—was the only boss.

"You don't know a fellow named Andy Keever, do you, Ned?"

"Andy Keever. Keever? That's a new name to me," said Ned Patterson. "What does he do?"

"He's up there at the new ice cream plant. They got him in charge of the salesmen," said Peter Durant. "He's a customer, but never this early in the morning. Ha' past ten or eleven he usually comes in."

"Don't know him, but why do you ask?"

"Well, he rubs some people the wrong way. Other customers, and I kind of wondered did you ever hear them say anything."

"No, but you've always been able to get rid of men like him. True, you have to serve him, legally, but you have your methods."

"I don't want to get rid of him."

"Then by all means, don't. I've seen men in this shop that despise each other, but they behave themselves here. You have a gentlemen's institution here, Peter, and you've made it that and kept it that."

"Keever isn't what you'd call a gentleman."

"Well, I didn't mean that they're all the cream of the crop, but they behave like gentlemen."

"Not Keever."

"*Not* Keever? Then I don't see what your problem is, Peter. Very few places that men gather together and conduct themselves as well as they do here, but this is one of them. If this Keever man—what sort of thing does he do that annoys the other patrons?"

"Oh, jokes, and stuff like that."

"Well, if you mean dirty jokes, I've never heard you tell one, or enjoy one. I don't mind them myself, if they're really funny and well told. Abraham Lincoln. Mark Twain. John Kendrick Bangs. Arthur Twining Hadley. An off-color story didn't bother them, and I certainly wouldn't condemn your man Keever on *that* evidence. Unless, of course, you're referring to the reverend clergy. I know you have two ministers and I believe Monsignor What's His Name comes in here."

"He don't tell them in front of them."

"Then what's troubling you, Peter?"

"I don't know whose side I'm on, that's my trouble. Andy

Keever makes me laugh till I'm weak, but a lot of my best customers—you can tell by the way they look at him. But on the other hand, is it my shop or does it belong to the customers?"

"I begin to see your problem, yes," said Ned Patterson.

"*You* see my problem."

"I do. One: does the proprietor claim the right to select his customers? Two: having selected his customers, have they in turn any inherent rights? Three: do those inherent rights include that of rejecting a new customer?"

"I follow you."

"I'm trying to see it as a lawyer might when he prepares a case for a judge's opinion. But now I have to follow a different procedure. The question really comes down to a matter that isn't governed by set rules. In other words, it becomes a matter of personal preference, Peter. Taste, on the one hand, and business expediency. Do you want this man around, and do you want him around enough to jeopardize your business? From what you've told me, and from what I know of your clientele, you may be running a real risk."

"That's what I've been thinking about."

"And now that you've told me as much as you have, you've suddenly shed some light on something else."

"What's that, Ned?"

"Well, you and I've been friends for a long time."

"Close on to thirty years," said Peter Durant.

"When court's in session I make it a habit to have my lunch at the club."

"The Gibbsville Club."

"Yes. Otherwise I never go near the place, and I hardly ever know what's going on up there, although I've been a member since my twenty-fifth birthday. But I *have* heard some talk, let me see, during the present term and during the May term— of putting in a barber chair. Putting in a chair and hiring a barber. I paid very little attention, but it's just possible, Peter, that some of your customers may be deciding to act."

"Oh, they are, eh?"

"It's a possibility. It's a probability. Most of the men at the club are customers of yours, and it may be more than a coincidence that there's been this talk of hiring a barber."

"You didn't hear who they were thinking of hiring, did you?"

"No, but there I'd draw the line at confiding in you. You understand that, of course."

"You wouldn't tell me if it was one of my men they were hiring?"

"No, I wouldn't. I don't mind passing this information on to you, since it may help you to decide your problem. But it would be quite another matter, Peter, to reveal any names. Either names of customers or the name of the barber, if I knew it. So, this conversation may only have added to your dilemma, but you've been warned."

"Well, I wouldn't expect you to name names, Ned. Just to tell me if it was one of my men."

"No, I wouldn't tell you that, either. Out of six men that you've had with you for a long time, you wouldn't have much trouble narrowing it down."

"You bet I wouldn't," said Peter Durant. "And I got a pretty good idea already."

"A word of caution. Better think about Mr. Keever and how much you like to have him as a customer. Don't spend your time wondering if one of your men has been offered another job. I don't think *I'd* like Mr. Keever, but I'm just throwing that in, free gratis."

Two days later Peter Durant fired Bobby Little, the second-chair barber who had been in the shop for more than twenty years. Bobby denied having had business conversations with Gibbsville Club men, but Peter Durant called him a liar. The firing took place in the evening, after the last customer had gone and the shades were drawn. "You think I'm stupid, you think I don't know what's going on behind my back?" said Peter to Bobby and to the other five barbers.

"You're gonna find out you were wrong, Peter," said Bobby Little. "But don't ask me to come back. I don't work for no man calls me a liar." He went to his post, wrapped his razors and scissors in the black leather case that he used on visits to sick customers, and held out his hand. "Give me me time."

"I'm giving you two weeks' pay."

"Give me me time, up till tonight. I don't want no favors from you. Two weeks' pay after twenty-one years. Calling me a liar. Pay me up till tonight and that's all. But believe me, Peter Durant, you got some things to learn."

Peter Durant handed Bobby three five-dollar bills and Bobby turned to the others. "Goodnight, fellows." The others said goodnight to him and stared at the curtained door after he left.

"I hope you're sure, Peter," said Harry Slazenger. "As far as I'm concerned, Bobby never said nothin' to me about no Gibbsville Club offer."

"That's a bright one," said Peter Durant. "Why the hell would he want to tell you? He'd be afraid you'd tell me."

"Well then he'd of been wrong, because I wouldn't of told you," said Harry Slazenger.

"No? Maybe you're in it, too. Maybe they're gonna have *two* chairs up there."

"I don't know. This is the first I heard about it that they were gonna have *one,* but if you don't believe me, Peter, why don't you come out and say it?"

"All right, I will say it," said Peter Durant. "I think you knew about this. Bobby's your brother-in-law."

"Are you calling me a liar?"

"Yes, I'm calling you a liar," said Peter Durant.

"Give me me time."

"With pleasure," said Peter Durant. "You want to be proud, like your brother-in-law, or will you take the full two weeks?"

"I'll take the two weeks. I'll take all I can get. If you want to give me two months I'll take it." Slazenger turned to the other barbers. "How many you fellows gonna show up for work tomorrow?"

"Leave me out of it, Harry," said Elmer Bitzer. "You and

Bobby have your fight, but that don't say we gotta go without work."

"You trying to call a strike?" said Peter Durant. "This aint a union shop."

"Too bad it isn't," said Slazenger.

"You'll get three days and not another nickel," said Peter Durant. He opened the cash register, took out the money and slapped it on the shelf in front of Harry Slazenger's chair. Slazenger packed his equipment in a case similar to Bobby Little's.

"Something got into you, Peter. We all been noticing it. *They* won't admit it, but you got something festering inside of you."

"Take your God damn stuff and get out of here," said Peter Durant.

"You want me to tell you something?" said Slazenger. "Pretty soon you won't need six barbers. You'll be able to do it all yourself. Ned Patterson and that fellow Keever, that's who you'll have for customers."

"You worried about if I'm gonna have enough to eat?" said Peter.

"Oh, you got money, Peter. We know that. But you lose Bobby and now me, and even so you didn't find out who's going to the Gibbsville Club. One of those four, maybe. But which one, eh, Peter? Which one?"

"I got the right ones," said Peter Durant.

"No. But it's one of these four," said Slazenger. He laughed and departed.

Peter Durant looked at the remaining four barbers, but decided against making a speech. "Whose turn is it to open up tomorrow?"

"Bobby's," said one of the barbers.

"Well, I'll take his turn tomorrow," said Peter Durant. He locked the cash register and went about pulling the cords of the ceiling lamps, and the men said goodnight and departed.

The news that Peter Durant had fired two of his oldest em-

ployees got about very quickly, but during the first few days
most of the regular customers were too tactful to inquire for
details. On the Friday morning, however, Judge Buckhouse,
who was president of the Gibbsville Club, asked Peter to join
him in a corner of the hotel lobby upstairs.

"You made a mistake, Peter. You shouldn't have discharged
those men. There *was* some talk about putting in a chair at the
club, but I don't think it's going to come to anything."

"You'd say that now."

"I beg your pardon?"

"Maybe you decided you wouldn't put a chair in, but how
do I know you didn't dicker with Bobby Little?"

"You don't know, but you can take my word for it," said
the judge. "We never got to that stage."

"You didn't talk to any of my men?"

"The whole idea never got beyond the discussion stage."

"I don't know," said Peter Durant. "He acted very suspicious.
And that Harry Slazenger! That son of a bitch."

"*What* don't you know? I said that the idea never got beyond the discussion stage, and you said 'I don't know.' Are you
doubting my word?"

"I doubt everybody's word."

"Then there's nothing more to be said. That's all, Peter.
Good day."

"Good day? What do you mean by that?"

"Goodbye, is what I mean."

"You're not coming in any more?"

"Certainly not. I wouldn't think of it."

"Well, I guess I'll have to get along without you, then. Where
do you want me to send your mug? You paid two dollars for
it, so it belongs to you."

"Oh, I don't care what you do with it, Peter."

"Your mug?"

"Throw it in the wastebasket. Now I have to be getting
along." The judge crossed the lobby to the revolving door and
entered his waiting limousine. Peter Durant slowly walked
through the door marked Barber Shop—Gentlemen and down

the steps to his shop. He removed his suit coat and put on his white jacket and took his place at his chair.

"All right. Who's next?" he called.

"Hey, Peter, you didn't say hello to me. Am I fired, too?" Andy Keever, from his place on the bench, was pleased with the big laugh he got.

"Oh, go to hell," said Peter Durant.

The Properties of Love

Mrs. Henry D'Avlon thanked the pilot and copilot of the airplane. They were employees of her husband's company, but they were not his servants, and they required a special courtesy due their professional expertness. At the same time they were not executives; they wore a uniform that went with their job. It was a dual purpose uniform: a grey double-breasted suit when the pilots were off duty. It became a uniform when they pinned on their pilots' badges, silver wings with the company's trademark tastefully cut into the shield. The badge, in a miniature version, also appeared as a cap device for the Air Force type caps that matched the grey cloth of the suit. Mrs. Henry D'Avlon had chosen that material and had designed the badge.

Joe Barton, assistant to the vice-president in charge of public relations, was waiting on the landing strip, smiling up at Mrs. D'Avlon as she descended from the airplane. "Good morning, Joe," she said.

"Good morning, Mrs. D'Avlon," he said. "Good flight?"

"Very good. A few bumps over western Pennsylvania, but otherwise serene. As a matter of fact, Pete and Ernie got me here ten minutes ahead of our E.T.A."

"I know," said Joe Barton. "I just got here."

The company Cadillac was standing in the reserved parking section, and Matthews, the company chauffeur, seemed genuinely glad to see Mrs. D'Avlon again. "Hello, Bert," she said. "My, you make this car glisten."

"Thank you. Nice to have you notice it," said Matthews.

She thought she detected an implication directed at Joe Barton, who probably never complimented Matthews on the appearance of the car, but it was not her wish or her place to take sides. Matthews put her luggage in the rear deck and they left La Guardia and headed for the hotel.

"Sorry the boss couldn't make the trip with you," said Joe Barton.

"Yes, it's too bad, but he hates to fly when he has a cold."

"I don't blame him. So do I," said Joe Barton. He was a very Christian young man, a thought that she had had on first meeting him five years earlier and which she did not quite understand until one day she realized that with his blue eyes, clean-cut features, perfect teeth, blond hair and gold-rimmed spectacles he had instantly made her think of Y.M.C.A. And there it was. Association. Young Man. Christian. Y.M.C.A. He was thoroughly male, and completely sexless. At thirty-seven he was as far as he would ever go in the company. He would be paid more money, and he would get a better title, but he would never achieve the policy level. He had a wife and two children and he commuted from Rye, and there was no reason to suppose that he was not saving his money. Fredericka D'Avlon had never met Barton's wife and was not likely to, but she knew that Mrs. Barton would not be a bit jealous during the next two days, when Barton would be her escort at dinner and the theater in place of Henry D'Avlon. Mrs. Barton—any woman who would be the wife of Joe Barton—would know that that was part of his job, and that Fredericka D'Avlon was fifty-two years old. Mrs. Barton, in Rye, would probably make little jokes about Joe's being out with the boss's wife; but they would be prideful little jokes, too. "Joe's at the theater with the big boss's wife," she would say. "How about coming over, you two, and watching TV?" And when Joe got home after the theater, Susie, or whatever her name was, would make *safe* little jokes, as though there were no need to be jealous of a woman in her fifties. And Joe Barton, being a Joe Barton, would *expect* his wife to make the safe little jokes. Well, it was only fair; Henry D'Avlon would make safe little jokes about Joe Barton when *she* got home.

They were on the approach to the Triboro Bridge, and as

always in clear weather, the view of the skyline gave her a
single, brief thump in the stomach. It always happened, and
it always took her by surprise in spite of her knowing the
cause of the dull, quick pain. That first look at New York
from the ground had the same impact as the time in a restaurant when she heard a man at the next table saying, "George
Reed is downstairs." It was all she heard, but it was enough,
as the first look at the skyline was always enough. George Reed
was downstairs all over New York for those two seconds in
which she had a new glimpse of the tall buildings that were not
Chicago or Detroit or Cleveland.

"I'm very lucky," she said. "I almost never get colds."

"I wish I could say that. I'm good for one cold every winter,
usually when I'm taking my two weeks in Florida. And another
one in August, around Labor Day weekend."

"You ought to be able to guard against that. Whenever I
feel a suspicion of a cold I take some ascorbic acid tablets.
You ought to try them. I forget who recommended them. I
think I read about them somewhere. Dr. George Reed."

"Oh, *well,* if *George Reed* recommended them they must
be the best. I'll get some."

She was mystified by her lie. George Reed had never recommended anything in any publication that she was likely to
read. George Reed was a surgeon, who avoided personal publicity as though it were that staph-something infection that terrified hospitals. Nevertheless she had deliberately and wrong-
fully attributed to him a cure-all for the common cold, and
that was not justifiable or excusable by her simple impulse to
say his name. Yes, she admitted to herself, she took pleasure in
saying his name.

"Do you *know* Dr. Reed?" she said.

"I don't, but he operated on my wife's uncle. A seven-hour
operation for cancer of the lung. I don't understand the tech-
nicalities, but they say he's an absolute genius. No question
about it."

"Yes, you hear a lot about George Reed. I don't think he

was the one that recommended ascorbic acid tablets. It was somebody else."

"Well, frankly, it didn't sound much like him."

"No, it *didn't* sound much like Dr. Reed. I realized that as soon as I said it. Have you ever met him?"

"Yes, once, in the hospital. And I must say he *looks* like a great surgeon."

"Oh, why do you say that?"

"Well, he gives you the impression of strength. Confidence. He's quite tall. Over six feet. And he has this iron-grey hair cut very short. Actually, when I think of it, he could also be taken for a general. A four-star general. I guess that's responsibility and being accustomed to giving orders. Giving orders and expecting them to be obeyed. A lot of people can *give* orders. I almost studied medicine. I sort of wanted to when I was in high school, but my family couldn't afford that long expensive education. God, they're in school for at least seven years and they're two more years before they start making any money at all. I guess it must cost close to thirty-five thousand dollars minimum to get an M.D., and my family didn't have that kind of money. I imagine it was a lot different when George Reed was starting out."

"It was, but—well, I don't know why I say that. I just take for granted that it was," said Fredericka D'Avlon.

"But if my son wants to study medicine, I'll find the money somehow. He hasn't said anything yet, but he likes biology and gets very good marks. English, he can't write a two-page letter. But I'll be interested to see if he's any good in chemistry, and if he is, I'm going to encourage him to study medicine."

"Heaven knows we need doctors," she said.

"And where are they going to come from? How many men can swing thirty- thirty-five thousand dollars for a son's education? You know much more about the company than most executives' wives do, so you must know approximately what I make. And I'll be able to put Buddy through. By the skin of my teeth, but I could make it. But how about—well, Bert Matthews up there. What if he had a son that wanted to study medicine? This darn income tax hurts him every bit as much as it hurts people like me, in higher brackets. I'm sure Bert's the kind that saved his money, but a man in his job probably never earned more than six thousand dollars a year top. Top. And if he was able to save a thousand a year, every year for thirty years, he was darn lucky. In fact, I don't believe he could save that much. I'm a little better off because the company gives us those stock options and the bonus plan. Oh, I'm all right as long as D'Avlon Industries is all right, and you might as well say as long as the country is all right."

Fredericka D'Avlon let him prattle on, with his mixture of frankness and loyalty to the company. For a moment he had been a person, an individual, but he was competing for her attention with her thoughts of George Reed, now made more delicious by her having spoken his name for the first time in so many, many years.

So now he was giving the impression of strength and confidence. A four-star general. She knew that he had operated on a king, that he had saved the life of an opera singer, that among his patients had been a first-rate movie star and a prime minister and at least two men who were the opposite numbers in their corporations of Henry D'Avlon in D'Avlon Industries. She had read his brief bulletins on the condition of his famous patients, and the newspaper articles in which it was reported that Dr. Reed declined further comment. The Queen had given him the O.B.E., and Harvard, an honorary degree; but Fredericka D'Avlon had seen no photographs of him, had not heard his voice, did not know, for instance, where he spent his summers or what kind of cigarettes he smoked or whom he was having dinner with that night in 21. This little man, Joe Barton, had seen him and talked with him and had described him as he was today. What chaos there would be in the back of the limousine if she were to say: "George Reed is the love of my life." But she was not strongly tempted to confuse and embarrass Joe Barton. His astonishment and incredulity and fears were so predictable. He was such a *Christian* young man. But if she would not shock him, she still could use him, and before she had had time to plan with her customary thoroughness she was uttering the words: "Joe, I wonder if you could keep a great secret? It's something you can't even tell your wife."

"Why, yes, of course, Mrs. D'Avlon."

"Could you arrange to get me an appointment with Dr. Reed?"

"I'm almost sure I could," he said. "Are you—worried about something, Mrs. D'Avlon?"

"I haven't told my husband, or anybody. But I think I'd like to have more than just a routine check-up."

"You are worried, aren't you? Listen, Mrs. D'Avlon, I'll get to work on it right away. You're going to find out that D'Avlon Industries carries a lot of weight in unexpected places. I will have to mention your name, but it will be top-secret."

"How will you go about it?"

"There are several ways, but first we want to guard against any rumors that would affect D'Avlon Industries itself, don't we?"

"Oh, good heavens yes."

"That rules out a friend of mine at the bank who's on the hospital board. Ordinarily that would be the obvious way. But I can call Dr. Reed's secretary because she knows who I am on account of my having paid the bill for my wife's uncle. You see? Then I ask to speak to Dr. Reed, and he won't be there, but I'll say it's Mr. Barton of D'Avlon Industries, and he'll call me back. Not because of my uncle, but because of D'Avlon. And D'Avlon is the magic word not because Dr. Reed needs money, but because we distribute about two million a year on research projects, and I'm sure he'd like to get some of that for the hospital. I'll explain that you don't want any publicity, and believe me that's something he'll respect. You want an office appointment first, don't you?"

"I hope it's all I'll need," said Fredericka D'Avlon.

"So do I, and it probably will be. But you're wise to play it safe. I'll be back to you on the phone within an hour."

She had a bath and changed her clothes, and the telephone

rang. "You have an appointment at his office, two o'clock this afternoon. I spoke to him myself on my first call, and I didn't have to do any skulduggery. He remembered meeting me, and when I told him who the appointment was for he said he'd change his other appointments to accommodate you. Now don't you worry, Mrs. D'Avlon. You're in good hands, the best in the world."

The receptionist at George Reed's office said: "Go right in, madam. The doctor is expecting you." It was ten minutes of two, and Fredericka D'Avlon noticed that there were no other patients in the waiting-room.

She knocked twice on his door and heard him say "Come in, please."

He rose and stood behind his desk with his hand outstretched. "Hello, Fritzie," he said.

"Hello, George."

"I've just been having a sandwich. Have you had your lunch?"

"What did you have? Chicken with mayonnaise, and no lettuce?"

"Exactly," he said. "Do you want half?"

"No, you finish it."

"Would you like some coffee? I'd feel better about eating my sandwich if you'd have some coffee with me," he said.

"All right, yes. I'd like some coffee, if it's made."

"This place is like the Navy. There's always some coffee," he said. He spoke into the inter-com. "Some more coffee, please, Miss Ryan. And another cup and saucer."

"Is that all you have for lunch? After twenty-five years haven't you learned to eat more sensibly?"

"That's the kind of question I'm supposed to ask," he said. "I vary it sometimes with a hamburger. Tuna fish. But chicken is my favorite."

"Well, you've kept your waistline. But what have you done with your hair?"

"It's more comfortable this way when I'm operating. Ah,

here we are. Thank you, Miss Ryan." The receptionist served the coffee and went out.

"May I smoke?" she said.

"Sure."

"How about you? Will you have one?"

"All right, I'll have one thanks."

"You say that as if you didn't usually."

"I don't carry them, and I don't keep any in the office. That's my way of cutting down. I haven't given it up entirely." He lit his cigarette.

"Finish your sandwich, George."

"Well—all right."

"There's nothing wrong with me. I'm here under false pretenses."

"I see. You want to ask me about your husband?"

"No. I don't want to ask you about anybody. I just came to see you."

"What prompted your curiosity?"

"I don't know exactly, but this morning I had occasion to speak your name, the first time in all these years, and I had to see you. Our friends are beginning to die, and I'm going to, sometime, and so will you. And I wanted to see you. Do I have to say any more than that?"

"No. But if you do, I won't hold it against you. Shall I say it first? I love you, and I've never stopped."

"And I've never stopped."

"No, we could never stop, could we?"

"Well, of course we did stop," she said.

"Seeing each other. But we had to do that," he said.

"*I* had to. Or I thought I had to."

"You did have to, Fritzie. You did the right thing. I couldn't have gotten married for another five years, and I didn't. For another seven or eight, I guess it was."

"Has your marriage worked out well?"

"Very well, at least for me. I've never been sure that Polly's as happy as she deserves to be. She knows about you, of course."

"That was a mistake. Henry D'Avlon *doesn't* know about you."

"How did you manage that? You weren't supposed to be a virgin, were you?"

"No, but I didn't have to tell him about you. There was somebody else after you."

"Who?"

"What difference does it make?"

He laughed. "You're quite right. But I'm jealous, all the same."

"You have a nerve," she said, smiling.

"I know," he said. "Isn't it odd, we two sitting here like this, studying each other, more or less like strangers, when we should be just about getting ready to have our twenty-fifth anniversary? You've had two children, I've had three. But little by little we're going back to what we used to be."

"Yes. I love you as if none of it had happened."

"It's nice, isn't it?"

"I guess it is. As long as we *don't* think about five children and a husband and wife."

"We don't have to think about them, not for the present. I'm glad you came to see me, and I wonder why you did. I mean, why just now?"

"I don't know. It could have been any time. Well—no, not the first five or ten years I was married. I was still very busy getting you out of my life, and I couldn't possibly have seen you. But then my life began to be regulated by my husband, my children, home, taking an interest in my husband's business. And I was safe. Then I could admit to myself that I was in love with one man. You. But that took about ten years."

"Very much the same thing happened to me, too. I remember reading an article about your husband. I guess it was in *Fortune*. It said that you were one of the modern corporation wives, very active. Very helpful to your husband. Have you got a keen business sense, Fritzie?"

"It didn't say that."

"No, but something like it. Oh, I don't know. I'm more interested in finding out what brought you here today. I'm glad you came."

"Are you, George?"

"Yes, I'm glad you didn't put it off much longer."

"Why? Is there something the matter with you?"

He nodded. "Yep."

"You mean you're going to die?"

"Yes, I think so. I'm going to have what's called exploratory surgery, but I'm fairly sure I know what they'll find."

"Why didn't you have the operation before?"

"Oh, hell, I was so busy, and a few months wouldn't have made much difference. The interesting thing is, Fritzie, you knew I was going to die, didn't you?"

"I guess I did."

"*I* think you did. I think our loving each other is the explanation. We never stopped. And we never will, will we?"

"No."

"You see, in my business, you never know it all. Things I was taught twenty-five years ago are now no longer true. Some young guy in Pasadena, California, may be holding up a test tube at this very minute and shaking his head and saying he doesn't understand it. But he will understand it, maybe two years from now, and out goes everything we believe today. And good luck to him. But no guy in Pasadena or Paris or Moscow or anywhere else is going to be able to tell why you came to see me today. They thought they had it when Freud began publishing, and lately they've been doing things in the extra-sensory line. But I think they're a long way off. The poets are closer. They do a lot of research and make their reports, but they're very careful not to commit themselves to a definition. They go right on describing the properties of love, but by avoiding a definition they keep an open, scientific mind. But if anyone wants the proof of it, here we are. You and I."

"Oh, my dear, I'm too much of a materialist."

"You always were, but what of it? It didn't stop me from loving you, or you from loving me. You have everything a woman is supposed to want, and you're a successful materialist.

Just as I'm a successful alleviator of suffering and a non-materialist. But this morning you discovered that the man you love is going to die, and the only person in the world that also knows it is me. And how did you know? The only way you could know. The poet's way. The scientific way. And not the dull, unimaginative way of some near-sighted son of a bitch in Pasadena."

She smiled. "This is like our talks on the top of the Fifth Avenue bus. Do you remember when I used to ride up to the hospital on the bus, and have to come home alone? Goodness, we used to talk."

"Remember? Do I remember?"

"I wonder what ever happened to Mr. Cletus Connaughton."

"Who?"

"Mr. Cletus Connaughton. Our favorite bus conductor."

"You're making that up," he said.

"I am not. He had a badge that said Mr. Cletus Connaughton. He was a red-faced Irishman that used to hold the bus for me while we said goodnight. Mr. Cletus Connaughton."

"The one with the advanced case of acne rosacea. Was that his name?"

"Mr. Cletus Connaughton. He was sweet," she said.

Reassurance

Henry and Olive Rainsford stood on their porch, observing that moment of silence between the saying of goodbyes and the starting of their departing guests' car. Olive Rainsford, in sweater and skirt, had her arms folded close against her bosom; the air was chilly. Henry Rainsford, in tweed jacket and moleskin slacks, had his pipe in one hand and a kitchen match in the other, and he was smiling. Mary Roberts lowered the window on her side of the car, and said in a quiet voice: "It was such fun." Her remark was a kind of afterthought; it did not belong with the already spoken farewells.

"It was, wasn't it?" said Olive Rainsford. Her remark was immediately lost in the roar of the engine turning over.

"Okay, Keith?" said Henry Rainsford. Keith Roberts did not hear him; he put the car in gear and turned it toward the gate. By the time the Robertses' car was halfway down the driveway, Henry and Olive Rainsford were inside the house. "You're shivering. Let's have a cup of coffee?"

"All right," said Olive Rainsford. Elsie, the maid, was coming down the front stairs. "Elsie, would you bring us some coffee, in Mr. Rainsford's den?"

"Yes ma'am," said Elsie. "Mrs. Roberts forgot this."

"What is it?" said Olive Rainsford.

Elsie handed her a small blue leather case. "Cosmetics," said Elsie. "Facial tonic, and cold cream and stuff."

"Well, we'll have to mail them to her."

"Maybe she'll be back for them," said Henry Rainsford.

"No, she won't miss them till tonight, and by then they

ought to be in Savannah. They're planning to spend the night in Savannah. All right, thank you, Elsie. And the coffee."

Henry Rainsford lit his pipe and seated himself in the tufted leather chair. "I love them dearly, but one night is about as much as I can take," he said.

"I don't see why you don't go right ahead and smoke your pipe while she's here. It's your house."

"Mary knows that I know she can't stand my pipes. So if I lit up, she'd know I was doing it deliberately," he said. "Once a year. It's all we ever see them."

"Why do they insist on *driving* to Florida? That must take it out of Keith, and he's no young boy."

"He's sixty. Just my age."

"Well, I wouldn't let *you* drive those long distances. I can think of nothing more exhausting. It must take them a week to recover, even her, just sitting there. She's fifty-five."

"She's fifty-six. Well, they want to have the car while they're there. And I think driving gives them an excuse to visit us."

"To have an annual look. To see if we're still speaking to each other."

"I suppose so. It isn't as if Keith didn't have all the money in the world. He could ship the car, or rent one while he's there."

"And it isn't exactly a car for a man sixty years old."

"Oh, I don't mind that. As long as he lives Keith will be driving the latest thing, and I wouldn't take that away from him."

"No, I guess I wouldn't either, if he has to go on living with her."

Elsie brought the coffee and departed.

"I don't think that's the way it is, exactly," said Henry Rainsford.

"The way what is?" said Olive Rainsford.

"It isn't that Keith has to go on living with her, unquote. She has a lot to put up with, too."

"Your great love," said Olive Rainsford.

"Yes. Till I was twenty-two. You say that every year, and I guess I always have the same answer."

"You have."

"But the woman who stops here every year on her way to Florida isn't eighteen-year-old Mary Vondermuhl. And I'm not twenty-two-year-old Henry Rainsford."

"How very true, but while she's in this house you're both back at Princeton."

"Yes, we are, in a sense."

"Innocent?"

"No, I said, in a *sense*. Oh, innocent, sure. Good Lord. Innocent to the point of stupidity. Then."

"When she lost her innocence it's too bad she didn't lose her stupidity."

"Well, she had sense enough to latch on to Keith, and God knows he wasn't a very bright prospect when she married him. She gave up a pretty good thing when she divorced Miles Larkin. Financially, at least."

"I wonder what they're saying about us, right this minute," said Olive Rainsford. " 'I never thought it would last this long.' "

"Oh, hell, Mary'd be saying a lot worse than that. She doesn't spare anybody else while she's here, so I'm sure she doesn't spare us when she leaves."

"All right. What *would* she say?"

"Well, considering that she doesn't really like you—"

"Putting it mildly."

"And on a basis of her remarks about other people, she probably does a lot of speculating about our sex life."

"Which wouldn't interest Keith."

"Which would interest Keith more than almost anyone I know."

"Really? Keith?"

"Clinically, yes. You see, he's only known you for ten years, and that's about as many times as he's seen you, ten, so he wouldn't open up in conversation with you. But he'd be interested, don't think he wouldn't. All his life."

"So that when I thought he was falling off to sleep, he was actually studying you and me."

"Sure. All the time."

"Horrid thought."

"Oh, well."

"Horrid thought, because it's like being told later that someone watched you taking a bath. Being told by the person that watched you."

"Except that Keith would never admit to you that he'd been studying you."

"Then after he's been studying you all evening, I suppose he tells her what he's found out, or thinks he's found out."

"More than likely."

Olive Rainsford nodded. "That's what she meant by that remark. 'It's been such fun.' "

"No, I don't think she meant anything by it. I don't think she's all that subtle, Mary. But I'm sure she listens to all of Keith's analyses of people. He does it scientifically, clinically, and she listens because underneath it all, Mary's a twenty-four-karat bitch."

"That's surprising, coming from you."

"Well, you never really inquired as to what I really thought of Mary."

"I can almost feel them listening to this conversation, can't you?"

"They're probably talking about us." He looked at his wristwatch. "At five minutes of ten, fifteenth of January, 1961, we were talking about them and they were talking about us. It would be amusing if we could check up on that, but of course we never can. What are you going to do this morning?"

"I'm going over to Betty's to pick up some things she bought for me in Washington. She'll want me to stay for lunch, but I won't, unless you're going to be out for lunch. What are your plans?"

"I'll be right here, working on my speech."

"What speech?"

"Oh, my speech. You know, next month. The dinner for Tom Whalen. New York."

"Why do you have to make a speech for Tom Whalen?

Aren't you doing enough, just by going to New York? Three days shot."

"Not really. I'll get some things done in New York. It's a good idea to show your face at the Trust Company every once in a while. I go see Snyder and he tells me what he thinks I ought to get rid of and what to hold on to—things he can do by letter or telephone. But then at lunch he tells me about his son at Columbia Law School, and his new grandchild, if he has one. He always has. And he always ends up by telling me how smart I was to get out of the rat-race."

"Do you have to be told?"

"Well, it helps. Fifty was pretty young to retire."

"You didn't retire. You changed from being a banker to a farmer. You had the money, so you did what you always wanted to do. Do you need reassurance, Henry?"

"Sometimes. Not often, but sometimes."

"When? For instance?"

"Oh, when Gene Black asked me to go to India with him that time. And when Eisenhower used to have those small dinner parties, most of the fellows were friends of mine. I'd have enjoyed having dinner with the President of the United States in the White House. My daughters would have been proud of me. So would you."

"I'm just as proud—well, not proud, but pleased, when I compare your blood pressure now with ten years ago. If you want to give this up—"

"Don't even think of it! This *is* the way I want to live. The only thing that ever causes me doubt is once in a while I wonder about you. Are *you* happy, stashed away in Virginia, away from your friends and New York?"

"I wouldn't go back to that life no matter what happened."

"Not even if I died?"

"I'd stay right here. I'd get a job teaching school, or something."

"It's settled, then."

"It was settled when we came here. I knew what I wanted,

too, Henry. And it wasn't a question of geography. It was *you*."

"Thank you," he said. "It wasn't a question of geography with me, either. Or switching occupations. I never would have made the move with anyone else."

"Some more coffee?" she said.

He smiled. "Why of course some more coffee. *Please*."

She was back a few minutes before one o'clock, and he was sitting at his desk in his shirtsleeves, his tweed jacket lying on the seat of the tufted chair. "How's Betty?" The room was full of smoke.

"Limping. A horse stomped on her toe."

"Painful, especially at our age. Broken?"

"No. The skin's broken, but not the bones. She had X-rays. She's probably going to lose the toenail. Did you finish your speech?"

"No. I wasn't satisfied with the way it was going, so I started all over again. I think I have it this time. The first draft I tried to be funny, and I'm not a humorist."

"And they'll all try to be funny."

"Exactly. So I began all over again, starting with the question, why are we giving Tom Whalen a dinner?"

"Thirty-five years with the bank, isn't that why?"

"That's the official, public reason."

"Oh? What's the real reason?"

"Tom's been given the bad news. He has about a year to live, if that. Cancer."

"Is he going to know that you all know it?"

"No, and only three of us do. Me, Brownie Johnson, and Jack Stegall. Mollie told Brownie and he told Jack and me, swore us to secrecy. Then *Tom* told Brownie, because he thought somebody ought to know at the bank. So Tom will know that Brownie knows, but he won't know that anyone else knows."

"Does Tom want a party?"

"Yes. Very much. The day after the party they're going to announce his retirement from the board, and he wants to see the whole crowd before the announcement. He's not going back. I mean, he's not going to go to his office again. He wants to see the whole crowd, but he doesn't want a lot of individual farewells. So most of the fellows are going to the party in a jovial mood, for a festive occasion, and that's what Tom wants."

"This makes me like Tom, and I never have. That big, gruff Princeton football player having such sensitivity. I think of how he used to bore me when Princeton would lose."

"He bored everybody, but that happened to be one of the things he cared about. Princeton football got Tom Whalen a lot of things he never would have got without it. He made good on his own at the bank, but first he had to make the original connection, and football did it for him."

"How serious are you going to be in your speech?"

"I'm going to make the point that a man has to care about something besides his work, and that in Tom's case it was Princeton football. It isn't very profound, but Tom will like it. In recent years he's had to take a lot of kidding on that score, and some of it wasn't very nice kidding. Some of it wasn't kidding at all, although it was put in an ostensibly kidding way. And Tom knew it. He didn't talk quite so much about Princeton football in recent years, and I know why. He told me that he shut up about football because he was afraid his enthusiasm was beginning to hurt the bank. Well, he was right, there. To quite a lot of people he symbolized the bank, the only name they knew on the board. And there was a certain amount of criticism on that score, having a perennial undergraduate as the bank's representative. I don't know why it was any worse to have a football nut on our board than some other banks that wanted nothing but Skull & Bones types, but football is supposed to be juvenile, and Skull & Bones is supposed to be mature. I *guess*. I always failed to see the difference, but then I'm a Princeton man."

"I never appreciated Skull & Bones *or* Princeton football," said Olive Rainsford. "Is it true that they wrestle in the nude at Skull & Bones?"

"Search me. I always heard they had a swimming pool down in the cellar. Or maybe that was the other one, Keys."

"Lunch, ma'am," said Elsie.

"Thank you." They said no more until they had had their tomato juice. "I meant to ask you, what reason are you giving for this dinner for Tom, in your speech?"

Henry Rainsford touched the napkin to his lips and cleared his throat. "I'm trying to more than say something nice about Tom. I'd like a lot of the fellows there to realize that they're not wasting their lives. More and more they confide in me that they wish they'd done what I did. But what if they all had quit? Consider the fantastic notion that all the fellows from our bank and all the other fellows that will be at Tom's dinner—that they had all followed my example ten years ago. There'll be seventy-five men at that dinner, practically all of them between the ages of fifty and seventy-five. I don't imagine that a single one of them hasn't at some time or other thought of chucking the whole thing. So let's consider the mathematically unlikely possibility that they all had quit, ten years ago, when I did."

"All right, let's consider it."

"In my honest opinion, if that had happened the effect on the country would have been as bad as the loss of a major battle. I've been tempted to compare it with the dropping of an atomic bomb on one of our big cities. But we don't know anything about that, so I say the loss of a major battle. The men that will be at that dinner carry around in their brains the financial-economic, long-range and day-to-day plans of the nation. There'll be fifteen or twenty men at that dinner who have the experience and information that enable them to make decisions that affect every man, woman and child in this country for at least the next twenty-five years. Not one of those men is indispensable, of course. But any five of them are, and fifteen or twenty of them disappearing all at once—it's frightening to contemplate."

"Well, it didn't happen, and it won't happen."

"No, it didn't happen and it never will. That would be carrying coincidence too far. But the fact—and this *is* a fact, even if it's conjectural—that if you concede the fantastic possibility, you have automatic chaos, and I say it's frightening to contemplate. And I'm going to say all this in my speech, because in a way I represent an outsider's opinion, and these guys get an awful lot of abuse from outsiders. It's time someone said something that will make them feel good. Important. Responsible. They aren't all in it for the money. All of them could quit. I did, and they all have more money than I have. I'm not going to say it's patriotism that makes them stay on the job, because that wouldn't be true. And yet it is a kind of peacetime patriotism. Take Tom Whalen, for instance. The bank has eighteen hundred employees, and he's thinking of them when he quits. That's what the bank is to Tom. But then take Charlie Bennington, who'll be at the dinner. His company employs over two hundred thousand, and I know that Charlie never makes a decision without considering them as a factor. The effect on them, and the secondary effect on the entire public. Charlie's grandfather was a master mechanic in Quincy, Illinois."

"Charlie Bennington?"

Henry Rainsford nodded. "A master mechanic, in the railroad roundhouse."

"I thought Charlie Bennington was from a long line of Harvard Benningtons."

"A long line of two. Charlie, and his father. I guess with a name like Bennington if Charlie wanted to go back far enough he'd find some Harvard men in his background, two hundred years ago, but the family fortune as he knows it dates from the master mechanic in Quincy, Illinois. And he's never forgotten it. Nor should he. A master mechanic puts in as many years learning his trade as a Harvard A.B. In fact, more."

"Are you going to say all *this* in your speech?"

"No. But it's going to be in my mind as I prepare the speech. I'm going to get up there and tell those fellows how good they are. Something I never would have thought of doing while I was still in their midst, so to speak. I would have been embarrassed. But this way I say my say, and the next morning I'm on the train for home."

"Your good deed done."

"My good deed done. I won't have to slobber over Tom, but what I say about all of them will apply to Tom, and he'll sense it. Even if he doesn't get it right away, he'll get the underlying meaning when he has time to think it over."

"Very good. I approve of that. I was afraid this was going to be—"

"Sloppy sentimental, induced by too many Martinis. I know."

"Yes, and 'Rah, Tiger, Sis-boom-bah.' "

"There'll be some of that, but we'll keep it to a minimum."

Elsie entered. "Ma'am, you're wanted on the phone. It's Mrs. Roberts."

"Did you tell her you found her case?"

"Yes ma'am, but she wanted to talk about something else. I'll take your plate and keep it warm."

"Thank you," said Olive Rainsford. She made a face and her husband laughed. "Well, she must *know* we're in the middle of *lunch*." She took the call in Henry's den. "Hello, dear. We found your case. At least Elsie did. I'll mail it to you this afternoon."

"That isn't why I called," said Mary Roberts.

There was silence. "Mary? Mary? Are you still connected? Hello."

"I'm here. Olive, I'm calling from the hospital in Blake Falls, North Carolina. It's Keith."

"Oh, dear. What, Mary?"

"It's all over."

"You mean he's dead?"

"He collapsed at the wheel and we ran off the road."

"Are you all right? I mean were you hurt?"

"I'm all right. We weren't going very fast. We'd just stopped for a traffic light and were starting up again. And it happened. He just fell forward, slumped over the wheel. He didn't say a word, Olive. Just slumped over the wheel."

"How awful for you, dear. Do you want us to come and get you, or anything?"

"I'm all alone, Olive. They're all so nice. The doctors and

the police, but I don't *know* anybody. I don't know what to do. I didn't know which way to turn."

"Well now you just take a room at the hospital, and Henry and I'll be on our way in ten minutes. How far is it?"

"I don't know."

"Never mind. I can look it up on the map. If you can't get a room at the hospital, go to the hotel, if there is one. But anyway be sure and leave word where you'll be. We'll go straight to the hospital. And you tell the doctor that Henry and I will be there as soon as we can. Two hours, would you think?"

"Yes, I think it's about two hours from your house."

"You get some rest, dear, and don't worry. Henry and I will take care of everything."

She hung up and then saw that her husband was standing in the doorway. "Keith die?" he said.

"I gather he had a heart attack. They're in Blake Falls, North Carolina. He died immediately, at the wheel. Car went off the road, but she's not hurt."

"Well, at least it was quick."

"I was just thinking. I'll have to pack a bag for New York She's all alone, and I'll have to go back with her."

"She could call her sister, lives in Englewood."

"She could, but she didn't. She called us. She *really* called *you.*"

"No she didn't, Olive."

"She doesn't know it, but she did. Oh, I don't mind. She talked to me, but she was appealing to you."

"Well, maybe, poor thing. Keith's brother's in New York. And as far as that goes, Mary has children of her own."

"I know all that, Henry. But she didn't call them, she called us. Her own age, and an old love, you. That was instinct, and we have to respect that."

"Okay. We'll both pack for New York, but I hope we don't have to go."

The car was heated; the citizens of the Virginia and North Carolina villages were staying inside, and the nearly deserted streets seemed a continuance of the bleak countryside, with its patches of hardening snow and the brittle branches of the pine trees. "Could we have the radio on?" said Olive Rainsford, a half hour away from home.

"Sure. Take your pick," said Henry. "Rock and roll, hill-billy, commercials, and news. Mostly commercials." They heard two mentions of the death of Keith Roberts, New York millionaire sportsman, in Blake Falls, North Carolina, while en route to Hobe Sound, Florida.

"Roberts was at one time intercollegiate doubles champion and captain of the Princeton University tennis team, later turning to golf and served as a governor of the United States Golf Association. He was also a collector of modern art and donated numerous paintings to museums," said the announcer.

"How did they know that in Blake Falls, North Carolina?" said Olive Rainsford.

"That came from the Associated Press," said her husband. "Probably Washington or New York."

"Nothing about Mary except that she was with him, so I guess she wasn't hurt," said Olive.

"She said she wasn't, didn't she?"

"I thought she was possibly being brave."

"Not that brave. If she'd been hurt she'd have told you."

"You *don't* like her, do you?"

"No."

"Why not?"

"You were right this morning when you guessed why they always stopped to spend the night with us. She was making an annual check on our marriage. And she didn't wish us well."

"Then why on earth are we going to all this trouble?"

"You answer that, Olive."

"In a situation like this we had no choice."

"You had no choice, or gave yourself no choice. You acted on a decent instinct. If it'd been me, I don't know. I think I'd have tried to get out of it."

"No, you'd have done the same thing."

"Well, maybe."

"We neither of us like Mary, but when we're needed we do

what we can. We've got to that age, where we don't have to
like our friends. They just have to be our age."

He smiled. "I couldn't have said it better," he said. "We
don't have to like our friends. They just have to be our age.' "

"Well, you know what I meant."

"Sure. I most certainly do. The thinning ranks, and baby,
it's cold outside."

The name Blake Falls was beginning to appear more frequently on billboards and direction signs. "Don't leave me
alone with her," said Henry Rainsford. "Stick with me every
minute."

"All right," said Olive Rainsford.

At the hospital the head nurse took them to her room. "We
didn't have a room for Mrs. Roberts, so I was only too glad to
let her rest in mine," she said.

"Very nice of you," said Henry Rainsford. "The death certificate and the undertaker?"

"All being taken care of, Mr. Rainsford. Ah b'lieve Mrs.
Roberts' brother in New York City did the talkin' with Dr.
Mercer, he's our chief of staff. Dr. Julian K. Mercer? Ah'm
sure you must of heard tell of heeum."

"The name is familiar, yes," said Henry Rainsford. "So the
local undertaker will put the body on the train, and so forth?"

"Yandell Brothers, they're the best in town."

"How is Mrs. Roberts?"

"Taking it very well. Didn't want a sedative, and I took her
in a cup of chicken broth and a lamb chop at ha' past two.
She's been on the telephone a great deal of the time, naturally,
and Ah b'lieve her brother is taking a four o'clock plane
from New York. Then he has about an hour's drive from
Charlotte. About an hour."

"She sounds much better than when we talked to her," said
Olive, half to her husband, half to herself. "Nurse, you've been
really wonderful with her."

"My name is Miss Coleman. Ah'm the head nurse. C, o, l, e,
m, a, n. Well, that's what we're here for, to do the best we can,
and Mrs. Roberts *was* in a state. Didn't *know* a soul, and every-

thing happened so suddenly as those things do sometimes. Uh-oh, that's my light blinkin'. Is there anything else I can tell you before you go in?"

"I don't think so, thank you," said Olive Rainsford.

"Then if you'll excuse me, that light means I'm wanted on the phone. I'll come by when I can."

Mary Roberts rose from the white iron chair and silently embraced her visitors. "You were so good to come. And it was such an imposition, but I was panic-stricken. As if I'd got in trouble in a foreign country. Are you exhausted, Henry?"

"No."

"I reserved a room for you at the hotel. You don't want to drive back tonight, do you?"

"We just got here, so we don't know," said Olive Rainsford. "We want to be sure everything's all right with you."

"Ralph is flying down, Keith's brother, and he said something about chartering a plane."

"And going back to New York tonight?" said Henry Rainsford.

"Yes, I don't see any point in staying here. Actually Ralph has a friend in Charlotte and this friend's company has a plane that they'd let us use, if it's here when we're ready to leave. Otherwise we'll charter one. I don't think I could bear to spend the night here."

"Well, you seem to have things pretty well under control," said Henry Rainsford.

"Thank you, Henry. I didn't want to let myself go to pieces, and when I knew you and Mary were on the way I began to make some sense. This Coleman woman has been very efficient, and Dr. Mercer, the head doctor, he couldn't be more charming. One of those real Southern charmers. *Knows Bob Hawthorne.* Went to P. and S. with Bob, and as soon as I told him I knew Bob, why the sky was the limit. Have either of you got any cigarettes? They have a machine out in the hall, but this would be the day it broke down."

"Here's an extra pack," said Henry Rainsford. "Well, what

would you like us to do, Mary? Do you need any cash, for instance?"

"Luckily I have about a thousand dollars in traveler's cheques, and they turned over the cash Keith had in his pockets, so no, I'm all right for money, thanks. I would like to go for a walk. The hospital smell. I've been here all the time. Henry, would you take me for five or ten minutes in the fresh air?"

"We'd love to," said Olive Rainsford.

Mary Roberts looked at her. "Uh-huh. I was thinking if there were any phone calls for me—oh, I'll just open the window. I guess I don't really want to go for a walk. Oh, do you know who called and was so nice you couldn't believe it, Henry?"

"No, who?"

"Miles."

"Miles Larkin?"

"Heard it on the radio, and then saw it in the afternoon papers. Miles Larkin was my first husband, Olive. I don't think you ever knew him. *He* knows somebody that has a company plane. One of the cigarette companies. And within five minutes after Miles hung up this perfectly charming gentleman called up from Winston-Salem—that's somewhere around here— and said everything was at my disposal. Car and chauffeur. Plane. Lawyer if I needed one. Imagine Miles, after all these years. I guess you'd better put down the window, Henry. It's gotten colder. I never knew that Miles had any connection with the cigarette business, did you, Henry?"

"He hasn't, as far as I know, but Miles is a pretty well-known man, in financial circles."

"And yet with *all* his money, what's it got him?"

"Oh, I brought your little case," said Olive. "It's in my bag, in the back of the car, Henry. It's a blue leather case about so big."

"I'll get it," said Henry Rainsford.

"Don't make him go," said Mary Roberts.

"Oh, yes," said Henry Rainsford, leaving.

"Go on about Larkin, Mary. You were saying that with all his money?"

"First I want to tell you how much I appreciate your coming all this way, Olive. The nicest thing about it is that Henry and I were never anything. You know? I'm sure you know who he's had affairs with and who not. So it isn't as if I had that claim on him. It was boy and girl and nothing more with Henry and I."

"Yes, I knew that, Mary."

"Then you see why it's nicer that he came all this way, and you, of course. Both of you. Just as nice of you, because you and I've never been very close. Henry's a very lucky man, and I'm so pleased for both of you."

"I'm a very lucky woman, and Henry's a fine, wonderful, decent man."

"Yes, I was very lucky, too. To have Henry for my first love, and then Miles as my first husband. Even if it didn't work out as a marriage, it was a good relationship. Well, the proof of it today. After all these years Miles came through, and he didn't have to. He could have just sent flowers. Or nothing. After all, he had good reason to dislike Keith." She smiled. "Henry had good reason to dislike Miles, too. Did Henry take you away from your husband?"

"No, I guess I took him away from his wife. His wife, and New York, and Wall Street, and all that life. Didn't you know that, Mary?"

"Well, I must say you're frank about it. Yes, there was naturally some talk at the time, but nobody can criticize the results after ten years. It is ten years, isn't it, didn't you say last night?"

"Ten years, that we've been married. Twelve years we've been together."

"You did the right thing, the intelligent thing, whisking him off to Virginia. I've always thought that, and I remember having a lot of respect for you when I heard it. It was the one sure way to keep him interested. A whole new life, away from those same people in those same surroundings. It wouldn't have worked with Keith, of course. Keith was determined to make a lot of money, and the place to do that was New York, and for the first years of our marriage that was uppermost in his mind, the prime consideration. I'd left Miles, a very rich man, and Keith was determined to make it up to me. Finally the day came when I said, in effect, 'All right, Keith, you have enough. Now let's enjoy life and stop thinking about making money.' And that's what we did. For twenty-five years he'd had a certain goal, a certain sum, and when he reached it I made him call it quits and do the things he wanted to do. His paintings, his golf, and his books. He was a great reader, you know. Terribly interested in things like psychiatry and psycho-analysis. Loved to study people, and in his will I happen to know he's left a very substantial sum to a thing they have at Princeton, a mental research thing."

"Oh, really?"

"Isn't this a depressing little room? Do you suppose Miss Coleman *lives* here? She's Southern. I imagine her family live somewhere near. Do you suppose this is her father and mother? And this. Her brother, I would imagine. A resemblance there. But you'd think they'd have nicer furniture for a head nurse instead of this hospital stuff. Heavens. She graduated in 1938. I wouldn't have *my* diploma hanging where everybody could tell my age. I wonder what's keeping Henry?"

"Oh, opening the rear deck, and unlocking and locking my bag," said Olive Rainsford. "Maybe taking time out to smoke his pipe."

"Henry and his pipes," said Mary Roberts. She put her hand on the telephone. "I have a feeling that I ought to be calling somebody, but I don't know who. I've called everybody that I had to call, family and so on, but then there are so many almost-family, you know. People like Charlie Bennington and Tom Whalen. That bore, but he adored Keith and every year they went to the National together for a week of golf."

"They'll have heard by this time."

"Yes, Miles did."

"So did we, on the car radio, several times."

"Oh, what did they say on the radio?"

Henry Rainsford entered and placed the blue leather case on Miss Coleman's iron desk.

"Thank you, dear," said Mary Roberts.

"You're welcome. I was thinking, Mary, you seem to have everything under control."

"I hope you're not thinking of leaving."

"Well, that's what I *was* thinking. Not if you need us, but you are going back to New York tonight, and everything's being taken care of. And I'd much prefer my own bed to a room in the hotel. Ralph should be here around six o'clock."

"Oh, how do you know?" said Mary Roberts.

"I've been talking to Dr. Mercer. He spoke to Ralph just before he left Idlewild. Or maybe it was La Guardia. Or maybe it was Newark. Anyway, one of the New York airports. Ralph got hold of Charlie Bennington's plane, and that's what you're going back in."

"See, Olive? I should have called Charlie."

"So, I think we'll plan to go back to the farm when Ralph gets here."

"Oh, don't wait. If Dr. Mercer's in the hospital I'll feel all right. I have confidence in him. You two go. I insist. You've done enough for me, and I'll always, always appreciate it. Just knowing you were coming made all the difference."

Henry and Olive Rainsford bade her farewell for the second time that day, and now their car was headed for home. "Do you want the radio on?" he said.

"No, do you?" said Olive Rainsford.

"No."

"When you get tired I'll drive," she said.

"All right. That'll be pretty soon."

"Let me drive now and you have a nap," she said.

"No, I'm good for the first hour."

"Well, the minute you begin to get tired, say so," she said.

"And you doze off if you feel like it."

"I'm not tired, and I want to keep you company."

"Why?"

"Oh, you know why," she said. "It's been a very unrewarding day."

"Yes," he said. "But it's over now."

"And we're going home."

"And we'll have a fire," he said.

"Yes, and you won't have to work on your speech."

"And we won't have to like our friends."

"No matter what age," she said.

"These bastards never dim their lights," he said.

The Free

Art Schwartz was finishing up the raisin pie, and his wife Rhoda was running her hand through her back hair, reading the newspaper spread in front of her, smoothing the ash from the end of her cigarette on the saucer, now and then taking a little sip of her coffee.

"Somebody at the kitchen door," said Art Schwartz.

Rhoda shrugged a shoulder, took off her glasses and put them on the table, and went to the kitchen.

"Hello," she said. "Oh, hello, Red."

"Is Art in?" The man was Red Moyer, town police officer, and behind him was George Pease, another policeman.

"Yes, he's in. Just finishing supper. Come on in," said Rhoda. "It's Red Moyer and George Pease," she called.

"Come on in," said Art Schwartz. "We got enough coffee, Rhoda?"

The dining-room seemed instantly smaller as Moyer, with Pease lagging behind, came in. They were in uniform and with all their equipment—extra-wide belts, pistols and holsters, handcuff and chain-twister holsters, blackjacks, double rows of cartridges, extra-large belt buckles, black leather jackets and silver-plated shields—they seemed to take up a lot of room.

"No coffee, Art. We're here to make an arrest," said Red Moyer.

"Did Rhoda do something, or me?"

"You," said Red Moyer.

"What did I do? You got a *warrant!* What's the charge?"

"Murder. Suspicion of homicide, in the warrant," said Red Moyer.

"You're crazy. Who was I suppose to kill?"

"Miriam Denby. Come on, Art. Get your hat and coat," said Red Moyer.

"When was I suppose to kill her? And what with?"

"You'll find out. Come on, get going."

"Wait a minute, for Christ's sake," said Art Schwartz. "I got a right to see what it says in the warrant."

"You shot her in the head with a .38, between one o'clock and ha' past five this afternoon," said Red Moyer.

"I did no such thing," said Art Schwartz.

"I guess you weren't with her this afternoon," said Red Moyer.

Art Schwartz looked at his wife.

"Were you with her?" said Rhoda. "That's all I want to know."

"She's gonna find it out," said Red Moyer. "Yes, he was with her, Rhoda. We lined up four people that seen him with her."

"You don't care if I killed her or didn't kill her. Is that it, Rhoda? All you care is if I was with her."

"You promised. You swore an oath," she said.

"She wanted a hundred dollars," said Art Schwartz. "But I didn't kill her."

"Come on, Art," said Red Moyer.

"Quit hurryin' me," said Art Schwartz. "I gotta talk to my wife."

"Your wife," said Rhoda.

"Is that final?" said Art Schwartz.

"I told you how it would end up. I gave you one chance after another," said Rhoda.

"And you think I killed her?"

"I don't know whether you killed her or didn't kill her."

"And if I did kill her, you wouldn't stick with me. Okay, Red."

"You better take your coat. You'll need it," said Red Moyer.

"Why? Don't you want me to catch cold? So long, Rhoda. I would of stuck with you. *J.R.* You remember that, or don't you? Just remember *J.R.*"

"I kept *my* promise," she said.

"Yeah, sure. Sure. Come on, Red. *Look at George,* with his hand on his gun. Christ, you're bloodthirsty, George. I think George wants me to make a run for it."

"Try it," said George Pease.

"*George* was a very good friend of Miriam," said Art. "Where were *you* all day, George?"

"Lay off, Art," said Red Moyer.

Within a week Art Schwartz was a free man. A frightened, but conscience-troubled woman came forth and testified that she had seen Miriam Denby place the revolver to her head and fire; three witnesses testified that at that moment they were shooting pool with Art Schwartz; a girl friend of Miriam Denby's reluctantly testified that Miriam was going to threaten suicide if Art did not give her the hundred dollars. The district attorney had no case, and knew it.

The people of the town were glad; only a few of the pious had been able to convince themselves that Art Schwartz would commit a murder. He was bad in some ways, very bad about money things, lacking in respect for some authority; but two of his grade school teachers had wanted to take the stand in his favor if the case had come to trial.

"You can go home now," said the warden.

"As far as you're concerned, yeah."

"Stay out of trouble, Art," said the warden. "You're not a kid any more. You ought to get a regular job."

"I make more shooting pool. That's what I'm best at."

"Shooting pool is no way to earn a living. With a good eye and steady nerves, you ought to be able to learn some trade."

"What?"

"Well—something that takes good eyesight and steady nerves."

"Right. Shooting pool," said Art. "It's what I'm doing. Thanks, warden. I appreciate what you done."

"Your father and mother were good people, Art."

"Yeah, but not my uncle, and he raised me."

"I know, I know. Well, good luck, and keep out of trouble."

"Or I'll be seeing you, huh? So long, warden. Now where?"

"Go home. Straighten that out first," said the warden.

"The warden is right, Arthur," said Wallace Webster, Art's lawyer. They were walking down the stone steps in front of the prison. "Straighten that out first."

"Mr. Webster, the warden wants me to learn a trade, and you both want me to straighten it out with my wife. I'll learn a trade about as quick as I'll straighten it out with Rhoda."

"This could be the turning-point in your life, Arthur. You could make a whole new start in every way."

"Wait a minute, Mr. Webster. I was just found innocent, wasn't I?"

"It amounts to that. The charge was dropped. You weren't found innocent or guilty, since there was no trial."

"I know, I know. But don't that make me just as good as you are, or the warden, or anybody else? I was arrested, but for something I was found innocent. So I'm just the same as if I wasn't arrested."

"Well—yes."

"So then why should I be the one to change my ways? I'm even better off than some people. I was charged with something and then they *prove*d I wasn't guilty."

"Have a cigarette, Arthur," said Webster. They were sitting in the front seat of Webster's parked car.

"Thanks," said Art Schwartz.

"You're out of this thing a free man, and that's as far as my duty goes, as lawyer to client. But your old ways got you into this position, Arthur. Your wife didn't stand by you as I think she should have, but it must have been a shock to her. It all came at once. The police come to your house and arrest you, and in the course of the conversation it develops that you'd been seeing a woman you'd promised to give up."

"Yeah, that's all she thought of, Rhoda. Not if I was on my way to the chair, guilty or innocent. She didn't even ask me that."

"No. You were guilty, in her eyes, of breaking your promise."

"And she cared more about that than if I fried."

"Momentarily, maybe she did. Momentarily. She's a woman."

"Yeah, there's plenty of proof of that, Mr. Webster. Some I didn't tell you. I'm all the one that has to change, I'm the one that the whole town knows I was with that crazy Miriam before she shot herself. I know what you were gonna say a minute ago."

"What was I going to say a minute ago?"

"Simple. If I get in some other kind of trouble, this goes against me, innocent or guilty."

"That's taken into consideration, rightly or wrongly. And my point is that although you didn't commit a homicide, your old ways got you into a situation where you could be charged with suspicion. Logically, you ought to be able to convince yourself that the best protection for your future is to change your ways. Your domestic life is your first problem, and as to your second, I'll help find you a steady job. You have brains, and you have other aptitudes, so even if you start at low pay, you ought to get ahead fast."

"That's what we used to say in Fourth Street Grammar. 'You'll get ahead—you need one.' "

"They even said that in my day," said Webster. "Well, shall I take you home?"

"Oh, hell, sure. The rent's paid, and I paid it."

"Be careful, Arthur."

"Why? In case I lose my temper? Mr. Webster, you never saw me shoot pool. If I scratch, I don't let it get me down. I make my living off guys that want to smash their cuesticks. They scratch, or miss a cock-up, and they want to smash their cuesticks, and it takes them a whole frame to get their stroke back."

"I used to play a little in college. I had a high run of eighteen."

"Not bad. You went into the second frame."

"I had a good break shot in the second frame, I remember, but then I guess I got overanxious. The record for high run in our fraternity was somewhere in the thirties. Thirty-two, something like that."

"Uh-huh. My high run is twice that. Sixty-four, but a college boy that can run thirty-two, he could of been a good pool-player if he stuck to it."

"He didn't. He's a surgeon in Allentown. Maybe you could have been a surgeon."

"Yeah. Rhoda gave me a book last year. The cover for a book. Do It Yourself Brain Surgery, or Brain Surgery Made Easy. I forget exactly. We didn't have no books to fit the cover *on*. When they had me in the clink was the first time I ever wanted to read a book. Then I did have the desire to read a book."

Webster smiled. "Maybe you should have stayed in a little while longer."

"And get to be a reader, yeah. And strain my eyesight. My wife can't read print this high. If she don't have her glasses on she can't read the big headlines. No thanks, Mr. Webster. I got two things I don't want to fool with. My eyesight, and my coordination. You never saw me shoot with a gun, either. I can break those bluerocks all day, if I got somebody there to pull them. Or unless the guns get too hot. I'd like to go up against some of those rich guys at the golf club. I hear they shoot for three-four hundred dollars a match."

"You're looking for easy money again," said Webster.

"Why is it easy money? What's wrong with that, if I'm good at it? Shooting pool I have to give everybody fifty to thirty-five, fifty to twenty-five, fifty to twenty. I'd have to give those men at the golf club a ten or twenty handicap, a hundred to ninety, a hundred to eighty. Or I might even lose to some of them even up, but I'm willing to take the chance. Very little easy money around when you got a reputation like I have."

"Well, maybe it isn't easy money, but it's still no way to make a living."

"Mr. Webster, I don't think you ought to tell me how I should make a living if I don't cheat. And where I play pool they got their eye on me every minute. It's skill, and a little figuring the percentages. And *you* used to play pool, so you know if you play pill pool you often lose before you even get a shot. And maybe I have a good night playing pool and then blow it all in a crap game."

"Maybe, but not often, from what I've heard, Arthur."

"No, not often."

"Here's your house. If you change your mind, I'll see if I can help you get some other work."

"Thanks. Thanks very much, Mr. Webster."

"You're welcome. Shall I send my bill here, or to the pool-room?"

Art Schwartz grinned. "My office, the first table at the Pastime Billiard Parlor. Office hours seven to closing."

"You're incorrigible, Arthur," said Webster, and drove away.

Art Schwartz entered by the kitchen door and quickly ascertained that the house was unoccupied at the moment. "Good," he said to himself. "I won't have to talk to her." But he was only half finished packing his suitcase when Rhoda appeared.

"I was over next door and I saw you come in," she said.

"How come you're off today?" he said. "You didn't quit your job?"

"I traded my day off with another girl."

"Well, you want to have a look at what's in the suitcase? You won't find anything belongs to you."

"No."

"You can keep the stuff I paid for, I don't want it. The TV and the radio. That kitchen stuff. All I want is my clothes and my guns."

"Where are you going?"

"I'll get a room some place."

"The battery's dead in the car."

"The battery's dead?"

"I didn't use it while you were away, so it ran down, I guess."

"How do you know it's dead if you didn't use it?"

"I tried to start it this afternoon. I was going up to meet you when you got out, but it wouldn't start. The horn didn't blow, so I guess it's the battery."

"You were going to meet me when I came out of the clink? Why?"

"I decided to."

"Why did you decide?"

"I talked to Mr. Webster."

"Oh, he decided. Not you. I *thought* he was kind of stalling up there."

"You don't have to spend that extra on a room. The rent's paid up till the end of the month. I'll go to my parents'."

"That's where I thought you'd be now."

"No, I been here all the time."

"Yeah. With J.R., probably."

"With nobody but my sisters and one night my brother. I got afraid to be here alone."

"Don't tell me Joe Rieger wasn't here at all?"

"He called up, but that's all. He knows that's finished."

"Then what'd he call up for?"

"Oh, he wanted to take me out. He wanted to start up again, but now he knows it's finished."

"Don't brush him off on my account. I'm a free man, you're a free woman."

"That's what my parents said, and my sisters and brothers."

"For once I agree with them."

"For once they agree with you. They said I did the wrong thing, I should have stood by you, no matter what."

"Don't say 'no matter what.' I'm just as good as anybody, you know. I was judged innocent, legally. No case against me."

"You kept on seeing her after you gave me your promise. I kept *my* promise."

"I wasn't talking about that. I was talking about the murder charge."

"I was talking about your promise. My parents were against me, but my friends weren't. Everybody in town knows you had her pregnant."

"Everybody but me. That's why I wouldn't give her the hundred dollars. I wasn't the only guy she was going out with, so why should I be the chump? George Pease, the cop. Stan Wilson at the Pastime. I got her to admit it that she didn't know *who* got her pregnant. That's why she shot herself. I told her to go to hell and get somebody else to be the chump, not me. And I got out of that car and I wasn't sure if she was gonna shoot me in the back. First she wanted me to marry her, and then she wanted me to give her a hundred dollars. But I didn't even know for sure if she was pregnant. She didn't look it, and maybe she was gonna take George and Stan for a couple hundred, too. Well, I would of given her the hundred dollars if I thought she was that desperate, but I didn't *know* that. When I got back to the Pastime I asked Stan if she put the bee on *him,* and he said no, not yet, but that same morning she called him up and said she wanted to see him. You know, she didn't threaten to kill herself. She threatened to kill me, and I don't threaten as easy as that. She said if I didn't promise to marry her she'd kill me, and pulled out this .38. I said go ahead and shoot and see where that got her. Then she said she had to have a hundred dollars and threatened me again, but I told her to go to hell and got out of the car. You should of heard the names she called me. Screaming and yelling and crying. And I walked down to the main road and took the bus."

"What did she do? Just sit there, I guess, and work herself into a state. Three men she was sleeping with and didn't know which one was the father. And all three married."

"There was four men," he said.

"I know."

"How do you know?"

"He told me."

"Oh," said Art Schwartz. "Well, it could of been him or it could of been me, or it could have been Stan or George Pease. Why would he tell you he was mixed up in it too?"

"Joe Rieger?"

"Yeah, now we got his name out in the open. Why would he tell you?"

"He was scared. That's why he called me up."

"Oh, come on, Rhoda."

"That's half why he called me up. First I told him I wouldn't go out with him, and then he wanted to know if you were going to mention his name in court, in the trial. There was a rumor around that Mr. Webster was going to subpeeny all Miriam's boy friends. So Joe was trying to find out if he was going to get a subpeeny so he could leave town. I told him I didn't know anything and he didn't believe me, so I understand he left town."

"Well, he'll be back now."

"Who cares?"

"He'll be back."

"She must of been desperate." Rhoda suddenly picked up an odd-shaped book, the only volume in a glass-fronted case that was half filled with china figurines of animals and brass and wooden knickknacks. She put her tongue on her thumb and rapidly turned the pages. "There. There she was when she was a cheerleader. I was a soph and she was a senior. She certainly was pretty. This is our Annual, my sophomore year. Here she is in High Jinks, the musical comedy show. Too much makeup on, but you can see how pretty she was. Here's all about her, the four years she was in High. 'She walks in beauty, like the night.' Miriam Denby, 204 South Fifth Street. Basketball. Field hockey. Gamma Gamma Gamma. Assistant cheerleader. High Jinks. Honor Roll, sophomore and freshman years. Not when I was there. She was bright, but she didn't study. Junior Prom Committee. Senior Ball Committee. Plans to enter college, probably State or Drexel. She didn't, though." Rhoda closed the book. "From High she went to work for Davison's. I guess she was one of the first models they ever had. If not *the* first. Part of the time she was a saleslady and part of the time she modeled."

Art Schwartz closed the lid on his suitcase. "When you get done talking about Miriam, how about you and me having a talk?"

"I'm ready whenever you want to. I was just talking while you did your packing up."

"Yeah. Well, you understand, Rhoda, I paid the last rent I'm gonna pay."

"I know."

"And other expenses. I don't pay any more of them."

"I don't expect you to. If we're not living together, I don't want you paying my bills."

"Well—that's all right then. You're not gonna have me hauled up for non-support?"

"No."

"Understand, you could make it tough for me if you got a lawyer. I might as well tell you that, because you'll find it out sooner or later."

"I knew it already. I heard about non-support. My sister had her husband up for non-support one time."

"Stella?"

"Yes. Ted had to put up some kind of a bond or he'd of been sent to prison. Mr. Webster wasn't the one that made me decide to meet you when you got out. It was Stella."

"Stella?"

"Well, look at Ted and her now. Three kids, and Ted's as good a husband as any woman has. They had their troubles, and they got over them. Ted drinks a little, once or twice a year he don't come home on payday. But that's better than some have it. And Stella said, 'You go and be there when Art gets out,' but then the car wouldn't start. I guess that's an omen. I wouldn't of known what to say anyway, and I'd of *died* if you walked away from me in front of Mr. Webster. So the car not starting was an omen. Where were you thinking of getting a room?"

"I don't know. Some place. I could probably rent a room from Stan Wilson."

"You'll be in the same kind of trouble again if you do. Phoebe Wilson's as bad as Miriam, if not worse."

"Everybody knows that."

"Then what do you go there for? Why don't you just stay here till the end of the month, and I'll go to my parents'. You can find a better place than Phoebe Wilson's."

"What are you being so big-hearted for?"

"For God's sake, Art! I got nothing but my whole family telling me how wrong I was, not standing by you. My father, my mother, my sister, my brother, and I even got it from Ted."

"But not your friends."

"Well, somebody had to be on my side."

"You go stay with your parents, they'll give you hell all the time?"

"Well, a person takes so much and then you get used to it. Oh, I don't intend to stay there, either. I'll get an apartment with one of the girls at the store."

"What one?"

"I don't know, but they're always talking about it. The single ones, and the ones that are separated, you hear them talking about getting an apartment. And if I have the TV and some of those other things I could probably fix it so I wouldn't have to pay the first month or two rent."

"And you could have guys to the apartment."

"Well, if I was divorced, or separated, and that's what we're gonna be. You're not gonna wait very long, Art. I doubt if you'll wait till tonight, if I know you. Phoebe Wilson, probably. She's on your mind."

"Well, that's none of your business any more."

"No, I admit it. You got a perfect right. Phoebe. Some other tramp. Go where you please. You're free."

"Well, so are you."

"*I* know, Art. *I* know."

"Yeah. What other phone calls did you get while I was up the hill?"

"What makes you think I got any?"

He laughed. "That was a wild guess, but now I *know* you did. Who?"

"You mean fellows?"

"You know God damn well what I mean."

"I'm not gonna get anybody into trouble. I didn't date anybody, so why should I tell you who called me up? No. You got your suitcase all packed, Art. If you want to stay here, I'll go to my parents. If you don't, why do you prolong the agony? You want to stay here?"

"With you."

She shook her head. "Oh, no, Art. Hunh-uh. What's through is through. What's over is over."

"All right, we're back to you being Rhoda Bevan and I'm Art Schwartz. I never saw you before."

"No. It has to be more than that with me. That's all right for Phoebe, and Miriam, but not me."

"It was more than that with Joe Rieger?"

"Yes, for a while. I told you. We don't have to go over all that again. I thought I was in love with him and he thought he was in love with me, only we weren't. It was you and that damn Miriam."

"Joe was with Miriam."

"I didn't know that then. I was just getting even with *you*."

"You did."

"Well, are you staying?"

"No." He picked up his suitcase, and started down the stairs, with her following. In the kitchen they halted.

"I could offer you a piece of raisin pie. Cup of coffee," she said.

"You eat it."

"I don't like raisin. You know that. You want to take it with you?"

She opened the cakebox and brought out an uncut pie.

"You want me to go along the street carrying a raisin pie in my hand?"

"Well, then eat it, and I'll save the rest for my brother."

He looked at the pie. "All right." He put his hat on one of the kitchen chairs, but kept his overcoat on. She poured him a cup of coffee and sliced him a wedge of pie. He began to eat, and the telephone rang. The telephone was in the living-room, adjoining the kitchen.

"Hello," she said. "Oh . . . Yes . . . All right." She hung up and returned to the kitchen.

"Who was it?"

"It was for me."

"I know that much. One of your boy friends, judging from the conversation. This time you said yes, huh?"

"What if I did?"

"You did, didn't you?"

"Yes," she said.

"And you said 'All right.' That means he's coming here? When?"

"I'll tell you who it was, for your own good. It was George Pease, and he's gonna be here at six o'clock."

"George was one of those that phoned you when I was up on the hill?"

"Yes, and I said no, but now I said yes. So eat your pie and go, Art."

Art ate the rest of his pie. "I never liked that George Pease, from the time we were kids. I'm out of cigarettes."

"Here." She handed him a pack, and he lit one.

"I remember the night we were sitting here and they came to arrest me. I thought a lot about that, up on the hill. Red Moyer, kind of embarrassed. Red never thought I did it. But there was George, hoping I did it, and hoping I'd make a run for it. And as soon as I was put away, he calls up my wife." He stood up.

"Where you going? Where you going, Art?"

"Getting something I forgot." He went to the living-room, closing the door behind him, and she sat at the kitchen table, afraid to admit to her mounting terror. The door opened quickly and she looked at him.

He was grinning. "The pump gun," he said. "My old Ithaca, 37-S. Five shots."

"Don't, Art. Please?" she said.

"We just wait. Just sit calm and wait."

The Compliment

George Remsen saluted his wife with a home-from-the-office kiss and placed the refolded newspaper on the sofa beside her work-basket. She rather liked the custom, one of the few old ones remaining since the children were married and the Remsens had taken a hotel apartment. All through their married life George Remsen had brought the afternoon paper home to Jan. The custom had originated as an economy, but now George Remsen's economies consisted only of large ones: giving up a house in town that had too many servants and too many stairs; hiring limousines for weddings and funerals instead of maintaining a car and chauffeur (both car and chauffeur had seemed to spend most of the time in the garage on East Seventy-eighth Street, with other chauffeurs and similarly useless cars); giving up, not reluctantly, those annual trips to Europe; and in general ruthlessly abandoning the habits and possessions that George Remsen had worked so hard to achieve. The hotel apartment cost seven hundred and fifty dollars a month, but in floor space it was almost identical with the walkup in which the Remsens had begun married life for a tenth the price.

Jan Remsen watched her husband as he picked up his half-dozen letters and culled the impersonal items and put them to one side. He held up one large, square blue envelope. "This looks as though it ought to be interesting, but I'll bet you it's a benefit. A hundred dollars a ticket to see some damn play I wouldn't go to on a pass. And inside there'll be a card saying 'Do come. This is really a worthy cause. Signed, Mary McA.'

Then we have to go through the whole list of patronesses to figure out who Mary McA is. Well, let's see." He slit the envelope with Jan's plain silver opener, and her attention was rewarded by his instant interest. He quickly turned to the signature, frowned, and commenced to read. "It's from a girl I used to know, years ago," he said.

"*Not* from Mary McAndrews. I rather guessed that."

"No, before I ever knew Mary McAndrews. In fact, before I knew you. Hazel Dobson, from Batavia, New York. She's visiting someone in New York. Can't quite make out the name. Congratulations on my success. Very nice. Friendly. Buzz-buzz-buzz. Ah! Has a letter I wrote her in 1916, when I was eighteen years old, before I joined the Army. Wants to keep it, but would like to bring it and show it to me. Will lend it to me if I want to have a photostat made. But it's such a remarkable letter that she wants to hold on to it. No strings. Doesn't want to be a nuisance. Well, she wouldn't be a nuisance anyway. She was a terribly nice girl. Thinks you would be as interested as I'd be. Let's call her up and ask her to come over tomorrow?"

"All right," said Jan Remsen. "Is there a phone number? Do you want me to invite her?"

"Here, see if you can make out the name. I can read the number, and it's a Butterfield 8 exchange. Yes, you call her. She'd feel better about it, knowing Hazel. Hazel Dobson Chandler. Mrs. Dwight Chandler. Go ahead, give her a call."

Jan Remsen dialed the number and said, "May I speak to Mrs. Chandler, please? This is Mrs. George Remsen . . . Mrs. Chandler? Janet Remsen, yes. George and I would love it if you could stop in for a drink tomorrow afternoon, say about six? And please bring the letter . . . Oh, is that so? I don't think George ever knew that, or at least he didn't tell me. Well, I'll be expecting you, *we'll* be expecting you. Thank you." Jan Remsen hung up. "She sounded very nice."

"What was it that I never knew or never told you?"

"That she used to know Tom."

"Your brother Tom? I didn't know that. I guess she's just trying to tell you that she's all right. Reassure you. Nothing between *her* and me."

"Wasn't there?"

"I would have married her in a minute when I was twenty-one or -two, but she had other fish to fry. Other irons in the fire. In other words, it was all one-sided, on my side. But she was one hell of a girl."

"How old would she be now?"

"Sixty-two. Exactly my age."

"I'm reassured," said Jan Remsen.

"There was never anything. Nothing but a nice friendship between a very attractive girl and an awkward boy that needed someone to talk to," said George Remsen.

Jan Remsen looked at her husband, and the quick reassurance was gone, but she said nothing.

Hazel Dobson Chandler was announced at ten minutes past six, and Jan Remsen stood at the open door of the apartment to greet her guest as she got out of the elevator. "How do you do? Sometimes we don't hear our doorbell. It's only one of those buzzers," said Jan Remsen. "George will be here any minute."

"I'm *very* glad to meet you after so many years. I always felt as if I knew you," said Hazel Chandler.

"Where did you know Tom? At Cornell, I imagine."

"Yes. My brother Frank was in Kappa Alpha, a class ahead of Tom. Frank was killed in the war, in 1918, and I remember I had a very sweet letter from Tom after the war. Speaking of letters, Mrs. Remsen, I hope you don't think I'm some sort of crackpot, but I saved this letter of George's because I always felt that he was going to be a great success. I always felt that. You know how you do, with some people?"

"Yes. Will you have a cocktail, or shall we wait for George?"

"I'd just as soon wait, if you would."

"We could have tea, but George never takes tea."

"I'd rather talk. You see, I'm not sure, on thinking it over, I'm not at all sure I want to show George the letter. I'd rather show it to you first."

"He'll be here any minute. He's never later than six-thirty."

"It isn't terribly long. You can read it in five minutes, and then you decide whether to show it to him or not."

"I can't wait to read it," said Jan Remsen.

"Well, here it is," said Hazel Chandler. "You'll see why I hesitate."

Jan Remsen read the letter, the first few lines to herself, then, at Hazel Chandler's urging, aloud:

> Ithaca, N. Y.,
> Oct. 15, 1916

Dear Hazel:

Just a few lines to tell you I received the copy of *The Genius* by Theodore Dreiser and wish to express my thanks altho' I do not see how you managed to get hold of a copy. They are at a premium here & perhaps I should accept the book with thanks and "no questions asked." It is pretty raw in some places, at least as much as I have read so far but very true to life. I have never read anything by Dreiser before this but have great respect for your judgment, therefore will read the book and when I complete it will let you know what I think of it. Am not very good at book reports but I like a book that is true to life in preference to the average novel or many of the classics. Do not have very much time for reading these days as it is hard enough to keep up with my studies but they say it gets easier after freshman year. However, if it does not begin to get easier I may give up college and enlist. Saw your brother Frank last week, getting ready to go up to Canada and enlist in the Canadian Army. He said your parents are very upset. Can't say I blame them in a way as Frank is very bright and should stay here until he graduates, then enlist if he still wants to. I do not know what came over me because I suddenly said to Frank "Why are you planning to enlist in the Canadian army and get yourself killed over in France?" He became very angry with me for which I do not blame him as it is not my place to make such remarks but it was out before I realized what I was saying. If looks could kill I would be lying dead in Ithaca, N. Y., not Frank in France. I hope he gets over being angry as I always admired Frank & he is entitled to enlist if that is his wish. It would be different if I enlisted as I am not very optimistic as to midyears, therefore I could better myself in the army. However, am planning to stay here as long as I can until we "get in it." That will be sooner than most here think. I fail to see how we can avoid getting in it much longer. The Germans know who's side we are on or they would have to be very ignorant. If you look at it the way a German would they ought to declare war on us before we have any more opportunity to get ready for it. If I were a German I would take heed from all this talk about "preparedness" and declare war.

Hope you do not think I am a cheap skate afraid to waste a 2-cent stamp but I did not finish this letter altho' that was over a week ago. Saw Frank before he left and apologized. "That is alright, George," said Frank. However, I wish I had not said it in the first place as I should learn self-control instead of speaking without thinking, not that I think Frank is going to be injured. I am sure he will return safe & sound. Glad we parted on friendly terms as I may be over with him sooner than you expect, judging by the way things are going both scholastically and diplomatically (bet. U. S. A. and Germany). I am getting into the right frame of mind to enlist. I do not like mud or cooties but I will be ready when the time comes. The war will not last very long because there are so many modern inventions that as soon as we get in the tide will turn. When it is over I have decided that I will not try to get back in my class here but will try to get a job in one of the banks at home to learn the business, then go to N. Y. City. Would like to take the business course at Harvard but the next best thing is to get a job in one of the banks, then N. Y. City. The only time I was ever in N. Y. City I said to myself that I would be back some day and here that day is not far away! I am willing to put in two yrs in the army and two yrs in a small bank, then N. Y. City, here I come! That's the place for me. I appreciate your efforts to encourage me to take an interest in literature, etc., but that is not my bent. Please do not be disappointed in me, but you know the old saying about a silk purse and a sow's ear. I have a knack for figures, could always add 2 columns of figures when the other kids were learning to add 1. Also discovered that it was fun for me to do the problems in pounds Sterling and francs, etc. altho' others in my class found it impossible or were much slower at it. Therefore do not see the good of wasting time & money studying a lot of stuff I will never have any use for. I will be better off in a bank after we have licked the Kaiser, then I can start making my "first" million. I have never told this to anyone else, even you, but I am convinced of it that some day I am not going to stop at my "first" million. I cannot explain why, but it is a premonition. Do not think me conceited as that is the last thing I want you to think. I value your good opinion more than that of anyone I know. Hope to see you at Christmas if your "date" calendar is not monopolized by a certain Deke from Hamilton.

> Yours sincerely,
> Your friend,
> George K. Remsen

Jan Remsen smiled and handed the letter to her visitor. "I don't see why he shouldn't read it," she said. "What would be the harm?"

"Probably none, if you think it's all right. After all, I haven't seen George in almost forty years and I don't know what he's like now."

"Well—he's as nice as the boy that wrote that letter, but of course not as naïve."

"Oh—well, I wouldn't have said naïve. It isn't often a boy of eighteen is so sure of what he wants to do, and then goes ahead and does it, as George did. And his premonition about my brother Frank. Notice he said in the second part of the letter that Frank was going to return 'safe and sound,' but George didn't believe that, did he? Do you think?"

"No, I think that's fairly transparent. Didn't want you to worry."

"And his predictions about the way the war would go."

"Yes, he certainly gave that some thought. And I see what you mean about his not being naïve. Naïve was the wrong word. But I don't see why the letter should upset him now. I still don't see that."

"It's just that my reaction to the letter, when I first reread it, was amazement that a boy of eighteen could predict so accurately. Then, as I thought it over, if *I'd* ever predicted things so accurately, I'd wonder what had happened to me that I'd lost the power."

"Oh, I see," said Jan Remsen. "But he didn't make any other predictions, did he? Or did he?"

"Yes, he did. The Deke from Hamilton that he mentions in the letter?"

"Yes?"

"That was my husband, Dwight. George made a prediction about him. That Christmas. He said, and I can hear him this minute, 'Don't get serious over Dwight Chandler. He's a natural-born crook.' Well, I was very cross, naturally, and put it down to jealousy, but George said it wasn't jealousy. Did George happen to tell you that he was a little bit in love with me years ago?"

"Yes."

"But I thought he was too young. You know how boys your own age seem terribly young?"

"Oh, yes."

"So I wasn't in love with George, although I considered him a really dear friend. Well, anyway, I was very cross and I stopped seeing him. I got so serious about Dwight that I married him, and three years later he was sent to prison. For embezzling. He embezzled twenty thousand dollars from his grandfather's lumber business, which was a partnership, and the partner saw to it that Dwight went to jail. My husband died in prison. A ruptured appendix."

"Oh, dear. And what happened to you?"

"Oh, I did various things. I taught school, and I ran a little bookshop and then I got a job as librarian. People were very nice to me, and I managed to educate my son and daughter."

"I'm just adding up years. You were married three years and then you had these other jobs. George could have helped you by then. Why didn't you ask him? Not that he could have done very much, but you know George."

"Yes, but you don't know me, Mrs. Remsen. George was the last person I'd have gone to."

Jan Remsen looked at her visitor. "I can understand that, Mrs. Chandler. Maybe we'd better *not* show him the letter. Not because he lost the gift of prophecy."

Hazel Chandler returned Jan's look steadily. "No, not because he lost it or ever really had it. He was just very good about people."

"Very good about people. And you don't want him to know you had such a bad time."

"He must know some of it, but he doesn't know how bad it was, some of the time."

"You're all right now, though, I hope?"

"Yes, I'm all right now. I have a job in the hospital and a little money from a legacy, and I don't need much."

"What *do* you need?"

"What do I need? Nothing, really."

Jan Remsen leaned forward and put her hand over the back of her visitor's hand. "You just want to see George, is that it?"

Hazel Chandler nodded. "Just to see how he is. How he looks."

Jan Remsen smiled. "That's the least I can do, Hazel."

"Why?"

"Think what I owe you for staying away all these years."

"That's the dearest compliment any woman ever gave me," said Hazel Chandler. "Thank you."

Sterling Silver

The woman with the white, white skin two cabañas away called out: "Norman, come here a minute, please. Nor-man?" From her tone we expected that a small boy would respond to the call, but the man who separated himself from the group on the sand was well in his forties, furry as to chest and belly and shoulder blades, all but bald above the forehead, and deeply browned by the sun. He wore a gold identification bracelet, Hawaiian print bathing trunks, web-strapped clogs, and carried a raffia hat shaped like an oldtime planter's Panama. He looked at his half-smoked cigar, then on his way to the cabaña he dinched it in the concrete flower-pot.

"What is it, Irma?" we heard him say.

"I wanted a Collins," she said.

"I know, but when the waiter comes around," said the man.

"He was just here, but I wasn't ready for one."

"I know, but by the time he gets here you could have ordered one and you'd have finished this one. Wuddia want? Another rum Collins?"

"Well naturally I don't want a Tom. Gin on top of rum."

"No. You want a rum Collins—"

"Exactly like this one. This was just right."

"Well, now how was that so I can tell them?"

"I don't know, but it had just enough sugar."

"In other words, not too sweet."

"Not *too* sweet, but you could taste the sugar."

"Two spoonfuls, about?"

"I honestly don't know, but *they'll* know."

"Which waiter brought you this one? Joe?"

"No, I didn't like the one Joe brought me. It was *too* sweet."

"Then it was Mark?"

"Is that his name? The thin one."

"That's Mark. All right, I'll go find Mark and he'll take care of it for you."

"Oh, I don't know," she said.

"What?"

"Well, it's close to ha' past one. There won't be any lobster if we don't get there before two. They were all out yesterday. You take another dip and then we can go up and have lunch."

"You mean cancel the drink? You don't want it?"

"I'd rather have the lobster. I was so disappointed yesterday. I just felt like lobster."

"We could have lunch served here, or I guess it's too late today, but it's only a buck apiece extra to have it served in the cabaña."

She shook her head. "I'd rather go buffet. I hate to see those dirty dishes sitting around after I eat. You have a dip."

"No, I'll put on my bathrobe."

"Don't do that, Norman. Change into your slacks and your Filipino shirt. Don't let's go up there in your bathrobe."

"All right."

He entered the cabaña and came out a few minutes later wearing a white ruffled shirt and orange-red slacks. "Y'all set?" he said.

"Yes, but let's wait till those two go up. I don't care to stand in line next to them," she said.

"Who are they?"

"They're in 24. Their name is Mr. and Mrs. Copeland."

"How do you know?"

"It says so on the cabaña list. Here." She handed him a card, which listed the numbers and names of cabaña occupants.

"What have you got against them?"

"If she's his wife, I'm Lady Mountbatten."

"Lady Mountbatten is dead."

"Well, so am I, if that's Mrs. Copeland or Mrs. Anything Else."

"You could say that about quite a few here," he said. "Live and let live."

"I'm surprised they allow Bikinis in a place like this," she said.

"Oh, it isn't a regular Bikini," he said.

"If you can see a woman's belly-button, that's a Bikini for my money."

"Well, you can't see anything now. She's all covered up, right up to the neck. Come on, Irma, or we won't get any lobster. Or *you* won't. I don't want any. The roast beef was good yesterday, and it satisfies my appetite."

"You haven't lost any since we've been here."

"No, but I haven't gained. I just don't want to go over one-ninety. That's what I gotta watch out for. One-ninety. God, you're lucky. You take in the calories. One of those rum Collinses is more calories than I take in in a whole breakfast. And how many did you have?"

"What are you, counting my drinks again?"

"Oh, Irma. Lay off. Let's go eat."

They were Mr. and Mrs. Norman Borse, Cabaña 18, and they had arrived from Los Angeles in a black-and-grey Rolls-Royce. There were some Borse brothers who had lately got their names in the newspapers in connection with several fairly spectacular real estate deals, and we assumed that he belonged to that family. At the hotel he was on familiar terms with four or five men, but his wife kept to herself. In the late mornings she sat in the cabaña, and after lunch, while he was playing golf, she presumably retired to their room. They dined late, together, and for about four hours in the evenings she displayed her Paris originals and jewelry in the bar, then he would go with her to their room, returning to take his place in a bridge game with the same three men every night.

"Irma, Irma, Irma," said my wife. "And where have I seen that face before? You're no help at all."

"Yes I am," I said. "I told you she was never in the movies

and never on the stage. That saves you a hell of a lot of trouble."

"Are you sure she was never in the movies?"

"She was never even a Wampas baby star. Not even a Meglin Kiddie. I'm sure of it. Think back on some ax-murderers."

"No, and she wasn't the Pig Woman, in Debussy's Lane."

"De Russey's Lane. I could easily find out who she was."

"How?"

"By asking him. But that would take the fun out of it."

"Have you spoken to him?"

"Yes, today. We were held up on the first tee and we made conversation. He asked me where I got my putter, and I'm playing in a foursome with him tomorrow."

"If I don't figure it out tonight, ask him tomorrow who she was."

"If I can. It may be an embarrassing question."

It was not. Norman Borse and I were partners in the golf match, and he immediately became a fraternity brother, with the right to overpraise a good shot, to suggest changes in my stance, to recommend a tailor, to convert me to a vitamin preparation, to inquire into my financial investments, to give me a guided tour of the development he and his brothers had created near Santa Ana. "You're a married man, I take it," he said.

"Yes," I said.

"Some evening you and your wife might like to have dinner with my wife and I. You staying a while?"

"Another week," I said.

"Yes, now I know which one is your wife. She was the charming lady you got out of the station-wagon that she was at the wheel. I been married to the same woman for twenty-two years. Three to go before I have to go for that big silver number. I have it all planned out. Do you remember the girl with the beret?"

"I didn't notice her."

"Oh, I don't mean today. I mean the one that first they ran a picture of her on the cover of *Life* magazine. The girl with the beret, she got to be called. Black beret and trench coat, and then her picture was in all the ads every time you picked up a magazine. That was my wife, Irma Hopwood."

"Oh, of course," I said. "Billboards, all over the country."

"That's it. Bradford Petroleum put her under exclusive contract. She was practically their trademark there for a while."

"Yes, I remember her very well. She was like Betty Furness and Westinghouse, on TV."

"Well, she's my wife, and what I'm going to do, I'm going to get one of those sculptors and get him to make a statue of her in the beret and trench coat and present it to her on our twenty-fifth. Solid silver, of course. I don't care if it costs me a fortune, it's something I been wanting to do for over twenty years. I'll bet she's the only woman in the United States that has a contract that precludes her from wearing a beret."

"Really?"

He nodded. "If she wears a beret and has her picture taken and it gets into like the society page, she's in violation of contract. Oh, hell, they wouldn't go to court now, but they could. And twenty years ago don't think they wouldn't. I guess at one time her face was as well known as the President of the United States. There's no doubt about it."

"I'm sure you're right."

"The Bradford Petroleum Girl. The Girl in the Beret. We used to count how many billboards we saw her picture on. On a five-hundred-mile trip it used to average around fifty, depending on what part of the country."

"I remember. She'd be standing there with her hands in her pockets and her feet spread apart. Very dashing. Beret and trench coat."

"And you know what they did, don't you?"

"No."

"They used to give her a bonus of Bradford stock. That's what they thought of her. Oh, she needs me like a hole in the head. I didn't start making mine till after the war, and what I got in the Seabees you can imagine, but I made her hold on to that Bradford and I don't know how many times they split it."

"Irma Hopwood, eh?"

"That's it. Hardly anybody knew her name. To this day they don't. The Bradford people didn't want her name known."

"Then what happened?"

"Oh, what you might call a combination of circumstances. I never knew exactly. But somebody in the Bradford organization conceived the idea that the public was sick of trench coats after the war, and then they began publicizing that big B, you know. You know, the black-and-yellow B you see on all their pumps and all. And I guess an oil company couldn't go on forever with the same girl advertising their product. Irma wasn't sore. She got bored with it, to tell you the truth. You know, a woman likes to dress up, but every time she had to pose for a new painting or some photographs, always the beret, always the trench coat. And she gets paid, you know. She gets a couple thousand dollars a year today to enforce the contract. And she has that beautiful Bradford stock, and it's oil stock, don't forget. Tax-wise, very nice."

"Yes," I said.

We were standing together on the fairway, waiting for the foursome ahead to hole out. "It's an advantage when the wife has money of her own," he said. "I got one of my brothers that everybody knows the only reason why his wife is sticking to him is the money. We weren't always millionaires, the Borse brothers. Al married very young and she'd of been all right for like if he'd of stayed where he was, making a nice living but never very big. He had a used-car lot on Cahuenga, and a nice home in the Brentwood section. But he came in with my other brother and I and inside of three years if you wanted to find her she'd be in Bullock's-Wilshire or I. Magnin's, spending. There, or trying to get the fat off her in some reducing salon. Which was all right, understand. A man makes a lot of money, his wife is entitled. But she got so she hated him. The more he made, the more he gave her, the more she hated him. Al's no

Gregory Peck, this I got to admit. He's undersized and he has a
high-pitched voice that he sounds like everything he said was
an argument. So all right, that's what he was when she married
him. It shouldn't be any news to her. Go ahead hit, you're
away."

I made my shot and got on the green.

"You'll get your four," he said. "You got a chance for a
birdie, but I'll be satisfied with a four." He hit his own shot,
and it went in the trap. "Short," he said. "That may cost us,
partner. It's when I get thinking about my brother." We walked
in silence to the green, and when it was his turn he blasted the
ball out of the sand and laid it an easy two-foot putt from the
cup. He winked at me. "This is a game of concentration," he
said. But on the next hole he returned to the subject of his
brother. "Al used to play this game better than I do, but he
never gets time for it any more. We used to play in Griffith
Park. That's where they invented the saying, 'A ball is not lost
till it has stopped rolling.' I was telling you about Al and his
wife. So anyway, how do you think he feels, knowing that
she'd walk out on him today if it wasn't for the money.
Whereas, I always have the consolation that Irma could walk
out on me any time. It's an advantage when the wife has her
own. It gives a man the feeling that he has more to offer.
Whereas, Al, the harder he works, he's only getting in that
much deeper. He makes it and she spends it, and every dollar
he gives her she gives him back five dollars' worth of hatred.
This is living? I don't see it. He don't even get any consolation
out of their children. She took away all the pleasure he got out
of the children. We came from a very strict family and it nearly
kills Al, the way they don't show him any respect whatsoever.
Like I was over at his house a couple weeks ago and he went
around looking for the evening paper, and Daphne was reading it. The older daughter. 'Never mind,' he said. 'The hell
with that,' I said. 'Give your father the evening paper.' Oh,
they hate me. They really hate me, but I get more respect out
of them than their own father. When I see what's happening
with his kids, I don't regret it not having any of my own. I

wouldn't hold still for the way they treat their parents nowa-days."

"It's a problem, all right," I said.

I liked him, he sensed it, and when our match was ended he took me back to the hotel in his Rolls and invited me to play again the next day. We arranged to meet at two-thirty, and he declined my invitation to have a drink in our cabaña.

My wife was sunning herself at the pool. "How'd it go?" she said.

"We won. He's damn good," I said.

"Did you find out?" she said.

"Oh, yes," I said, and told her about Irma Hopwood, the Girl in the Beret. She did not receive my report with as much interest as I had anticipated. Instead, when I had finished, she resumed reading her novel.

"What's the matter? Lost interest?"

"Not exactly," she said.

"Here I come home with a good story and forty dollars I didn't have when I left, and all I get is Cloud 90."

"Relax," she said, and from her smile I knew she had some-thing on her mind.

Norman Borse and I won again the next day, and as he was leaving me near the pool area he suggested dinner for four. I said I would speak to my wife and call him in his room.

"No thanks," said my wife, when I relayed the invitation. "Let's not get involved with Mr. and Mrs. Borse."

"Why not? He's not a bad guy, and she might be amusing for one evening."

"I don't like women that sleep with waiters."

"Who? Borse's wife?"

"She and the waiter called Mark. Yesterday I saw him going in their room. Today I saw him leaving."

"You're sure?"

"Yes, I'm sure. Are you playing golf with Borse tomorrow?"

"No, he's going to be in Los Angeles all day, but we have a date to play the day after tomorrow. He's flying back tomorrow night."

"He'd better not get back too early," said my wife. "Who are you playing with tomorrow?"

"It's ladies' day, so I'm skipping a day."

"Then let's drive around. You can show me that house you used to have."

There was a house in the foothills I had rented many years ago, a comfortable, isolated, overgrown cabin, with its own tennis court and a view of the desert—and rattlesnakes. We found the house, now no longer isolated but in the midst of a colony of modern ranch-type units. "That's it," I said.

"I imagine it had charm then, but not now," said my wife. "Why do they have to build so close together when they have the whole desert?"

"Probably the water supply," I said. "Expensive pipe lines."

"Yes, I suppose so," she said. "And yet it isn't a low-cost housing development. There's one family that have a Rolls."

"The people that own that particular Rolls don't live there," I said. "Let's turn around and go back."

"Why? Whose car is it?"

"Belongs to Norman Borse."

"Oh," said my wife. "Well, you're not surprised, I hope."

"No, you were right. But he isn't a bad guy, you know."

"Do you really know that?" said my wife.

"No, I guess I don't. But this is so disrespectful, flaunting the Rolls, and he was so outraged by the disrespect his brother's children show."

"I'm not on her side, but after twenty-two years he must be awfully obtuse."

"You think he knows about these things?" I said.

"That's the only way I could forgive him."

"Forgive him?"

"Well, excuse him," she said. "If he doesn't know she sleeps with waiters, he's too stupid to live. If he does know it, and still loves her enough to ignore it, he may be kidding himself, but as you say he's not really a bad guy."

"But you don't like him," I said.

"I don't have to like him," she said. "Neither does she.

She's just a sterling silver bitch that he has to live up to. A girl he stole from a billboard. Don't play any more golf with him."

"I was just thinking, I didn't want to," I said. "Why?"

"Because you don't really like him, and you'll come home depressed. He's not a bad guy, but that's all he is. Just not a bad guy, and that isn't enough when you're our age."

"And this place is too damn expensive anyway, for what you get."

"For what you get," said my wife.

The Trip

Harrison Deering was apprehensive of his coming trip to London, his first in many, many years. On his last visit he had seen royalty, in black satin butterfly tie and white waistcoat, playing the drums at the Kit Kat; in recent years he had seen the same royalty briskly walking in Park Avenue and several times having lunch at his, and Harrison Deering's, club. "I suppose I look as old as him," Deering would say. "Or maybe I should say he looks as old as me. But by God he had style, and he still has it. I don't know what London's going to be like without him." Harrison Deering did not mean to imply that he had been chummy with royalty. No such thing. His approach to London and Londoners was and always had been American-English: American, in that he had no wish to be taken for anything else; English, in that he was not a man to scrape up acquaintance with strangers on trains and on shipboard. He liked most of the English ways, since they were very much his own ways. But in London during his forthcoming trip he would be seeing other Americans like himself and *their* English friends, just as he had done on previous visits. He had no English friends of his own, and his best reason, or excuse, for going to London at this time was to confirm his hope that a great deal of the London he was fond of was still there. Royalty would not be playing drums at the Kit Kat—if there was still a Kit Kat. No one wore butterfly bows or white evening waistcoats any more. The firm that had always made Harrison Deering's shoes had moved from Oxford Street to some place else. Gertie Lawrence was dead, and Noel Coward was over sixty. Harrison Deering did not expect to be invited to parties by Fruity This or Porchy That or Jack What's His Name. Harrison Deering had never done anything for the Englishmen who came to New York, and he did not expect any Englishman to do anything for him. He was not going to London for parties; he no longer went to parties in New York. "I'm going to London because I have four thousand dollars to blow-in," he told one friend. "How long that would last me in Florida, I don't know. I could probably sponge off a few people and make it last a couple of months. But it's too damn cold in Florida and they won't admit it. I was there two years ago and I wore a sweater every day I was there. No heat in the houses. Rain. Cold. Cold that gets into your bones and stays there. And who do I see? The same damn people that are just as sick and tired of my face as I am of theirs. So I'm going to London. At least it'll be different."

"Yes, but different in what way, Harry?" said his friend.

"Well—they drive on the left-hand side of the road," he said. "Intentionally."

He gave other explanations and excuses for choosing London, but his private one was that hope of finding a scene of his youth that had not undergone alterations or, indeed, total obliteration, as was the case with so many neighborhoods in New York, Philadelphia, Boston, Palm Beach, and Long Island and the Main Line. "You should *see* what they've done to Princeton," he said. "I went there to a wedding last week, and they have a new station at the Junction."

"That's not new, Harry," said his friend. "It's been there ten years. The old one burned down."

"I didn't know that. Burned down? I didn't see anything in the papers about it."

"Oh, yes. It was in the papers, but that was ten years ago. I think it happened during the Christmas holidays."

"Hmm. Then they couldn't blame the undergraduates?"

"Much as you'd like to, you can't blame the undergraduates," said his friend.

"I have nothing against the undergraduates. At least they're not responsible for the rest of what's been going on there. *You* are, you alumni. That new library."

"New?"

"New to me. It looks like one of those department stores in Manhasset. The Sunshine Biscuit Company."

"Then I advise you to stay away from Oxford on your trip abroad. I understand they've put up some buildings you won't like at all."

"I had no intention of going to Oxford. I don't know a soul there. Not even at All Souls. Joke. My father once had some notion of sending me to Oxford, but considering the fact that I never got a degree at Harvard, he was probably very wise to give up the whole idea. And I never would have fitted in there. I was there for two days once, and they all seemed so much younger than I'd expected. I'm sure they knew a hell of a lot more than I did, but they were so damn young. There's nothing younger than a young Englishman, is there? Or as old as an old Englishman. God, when an Englishman gets old, he looks as if he'd been around since 1066. Wouldn't surprise me if some of them had been."

Harrison Deering was a widower among widows. He knew that his widows liked to think that they were taking care of him; protecting him from loneliness; seeing to it that he was invited out at least one night a week; remembering his birthday and his widowerhood at Christmas with rather expensive presents of fine handkerchiefs, good cognac, re-orders of his favorite pipe tobacco (he had a good-sized credit at Dunhill's on that account), and other consumable gifts that would not clutter up his small apartment. "A useless stallion with a brood of old mares," he would say to describe the situation. "Quid pro quo. I give them something to do, somebody to fuss over." He had only to say the word and any of two or three of his widows would marry him, but he did not at sixty-eight feel up to breaking in a new woman to his habits, and his habits contained the secret of his comfort and to be comfortable was as much as he could reasonably expect out of life. Six days a week he would get his own breakfast of orange juice, toast and coffee; rinse out the glass, cup and saucer, and occupy the morning with his moderate calisthenics, his newspaper, his shave and bath, his mail, a telephone call or two. So would go the morning until it was time to go to one of his two clubs. As a much younger man he had invested in life memberships in the clubs, so that he now had no dues to pay, and lunch at either club was cheaper and in more congenial surroundings than anywhere else that he knew of. After lunch he always took a fifteen-minute nap before the bridge or backgammon games. At the club where the game was backgammon he would be one of the same five chouetting, and at the other club he was one of a foursome who had been playing bridge together for fifteen years, with one substitution caused by death. There was some criticism of Charley Borden, who collapsed and died while playing a hand. The criticism was mild enough, but it was voiced, one player to another: it was simply that Charley had been told by his doctor not to play bridge, but he had insisted on playing, with the inevitable, extremely disturbing result. Harrison Deering defended Charley. "I admit it's a hell of a thing to do to your friends, especially when you know it's going to happen. But we all loved Charley, and I wouldn't like to think that *I'd* deprived him of a little fun those last few years. Damned sight better to have him keel over here, among friends, than out on the public street. Policemen going through his pockets to find some identification. Taxi drivers pointing to him. 'Look, a dead man.' No, God damn it, we owed that much to Charley." The man who joined the foursome in Charley Borden's place was about ten years younger than the average of the others, and a son of the oldest living member of the club.

Harrison Deering did not stay around for the late-afternoon drinking at his clubs. The distance to his little apartment was just long enough for him to stretch his legs and get a breath of fresh air, work up an appetite for dinner. Miriam Washington came in five afternoons a week at four o'clock and cleaned the apartment and cooked his dinner, which he ate at seven; and if he was spending the evening at home, he had the television set which two of his widows had given him, the interesting short-wave radio that another widow had bought for his bedroom, and always two mystery novels from the lending library in Lexington Avenue. The evenings passed quickly, and as he moved about in his apartment Harrison Deering, who had a nice bass, would sing, "Last night I was dreeeeeming, of you, dear, was dreeeeeming." He had never learned the entire lyric, but he always came in strong at the end with "Once more to —my heart." It was a song his father had liked, sung on a record by John McCormack, who was certainly not a bass, but Harrison Deering loved it, and often sang it when he was alone.

A trip to London was such a radical deviation from Harrison Deering's established routines that nearly a full year elapsed between the first spoken announcement of his decision and the date for sailing. At his widows' little dinner-bridges his friends would ask him how his plans were coming, and he usually had some small item of progress to report. In the beginning he would say: "Well, I stopped in at the Cunard Line yesterday and got all their literature. Did *you* know that the Cunard Line has an office at Fifty-sixth and Park? I s'pose you did, but I didn't." A similar surprise awaited him with the discovery that he did not have to go all the way downtown to get a passport. He collected information on the ship of the line, and the kind of accommodations to book, the advantages to be gained by out-of-season travel, and so on. His widows and some of his men friends—among whom were a few who went abroad every year—jotted down notes to give Harry Deering, and item after item showed him how very different things were these days. On one subject there was unanimous agreement: flying was out of the question. Flying had no style, and even among those friends who went abroad every year and were quite casual about their own arrangements, the trip that Harrison Deering was planning had to be done with as much style as modern circumstances would allow. Months ahead of time his widows planned a series of small farewell dinner parties, and Harrison Deering himself was going to splurge with a farewell luncheon for all those who had been so kind.

After all his friends returned from the summer hiatus and the sailing date was weeks away the imminence of the trip was on all their minds. Harry was now at the packing stage; that is, the logistics of packing. He worked out the number of evening shirts he would have to have on shipboard (no laundry on the *Queen Mary*, which he was taking on the eastward passage). He would wear his grey flannel to the ship and take a tweed jacket, using the grey flannel trousers as slacks. He was slightly disappointed to be advised that he would not need his tails, although this gave him extra room in his luggage. He looked well in tails and knew it, and while he was forced to agree that his friends knew present-day London better than he, he was going to put in one wing collar, one stiff shirt, one white evening tie and the appropriate jewelry in case a white-tie occasion arose, and without telling any of his friends he also made a note of his miniature medals: his 1916 Mexican Border, his Victory Medal, and his Croix de Guerre with bronze star. They would not take up much room, and he was ready if the right invitation came along. He might have to hire a tailcoat, but be damned if the lapel would be bare.

It went without saying that he would be stopping at Jordan's Private Hotel, and he was delighted to be told that they could give him the same room he had occupied in 1922. In his correspondence with Jordan's, which was carried on over a period of two months because neither Harrison Deering nor Jordan's used the air mail, he was assured, or reassured, that the room would be just the same except for the wallpaper, which he did not remember anyway. The room rates were considerably higher, but he expected that. He was completely reconciled to the expense all around; he did not actually speak of this trip as the last one he would make, but he planned everything with that thought in mind. He would have precious little left of his four thousand dollars when he got back to New York. Tommy Long and Erskine Rockwell, his American friends in

London, were going to keep him busy every minute, or nearly every minute, and he was already planning a big bash, as the young fellows said, for Tommy and Skinny and their wives in the Savoy Grill the night before he sailed for home. That would leave him enough for tips on the westward passage, and that was exactly the way he wanted it to be.

And then one day when the sailing date was less than a fortnight away, he went to the club, had his lunch and his nap, and to the card-room. Bobby McGowan was there at the usual table. Bobby, by two years the oldest of the foursome, was always first at the table, always a bit impatient to get the game started. "Well, Sir Harry," said Bobby. "Only a few more chances to take your money."

"Looking forward to taking yours and converting it into sterling," said Harrison Deering.

"The luck I've been having lately, you won't have any trouble," said Bobby. "You know, I rather envy you your trip."

"Come along. Do you good," said Harrison Deering. "You can get a passport in two or three days, and surely you'd have no trouble booking passage."

"Oh, my passport's good for another year, and I guess I could wangle a stateroom, but Marjorie wouldn't hear of it. Where the hell are the other two? Oh, here you are." He thus greeted John Banks, who seated himself and filled his pipe.

"No Williams?" said Banks.

"Not so far," said Bobby. "And I know he wasn't here for lunch."

"No, I didn't see him," said Harrison Deering.

"Well, we'll just have to wait," said Bobby.

"Getting all ready to shove off, Harry?" said Banks.

"Just about. Four more chances to take your money, and then off I go."

"Harry, call downstairs and see if Williams is in the club, will you please?"

"Oh, he'll be here," said Harrison Deering.

At that moment Jimmy Walsh, the club servant in charge of

the card-room, came to the table. "Gentlemen, I'm afraid I've bad news for you," said Walsh.

"What's that, Jimmy?" said Bobby.

"Mr. Williams. He fell over dead in a taxicab."

"Old Mr. Williams?"

"No sir, *your* Mr. Williams. Mr. J. L. The taxi brung 'im here because this is the address he gave. But he was dead. Too bad. A *nice* man. I'm very sorry, gentlemen."

"Oh. I see. Thank you, Jimmy," said Bobby.

"Yes sir. Can I get anything for anybody?"

"Yes. Yes. Three brandies, I guess," said Bobby. The others nodded their approval of the order.

"Three brandies, sir," said Walsh, and left.

"First Charley Borden, and now Jerry Williams," said Bobby McGowan.

"Exactly what I was thinking," said John Banks.

"Yes," said Harrison Deering. "Alone in a taxi. Heart, I suppose."

"Must have been," said Banks. "But his father's over ninety."

"Ninety-one, but I don't see what difference that makes," said McGowan.

"Well, I was thinking of longevity running in families," said Banks.

"Alone in a taxi," said Harrison Deering. "I can just see that driver, if he's a typical New York taxi driver. Sore as hell because he probably has to make out some police report. Lose fares. The last man poor Jerry ever spoke to. At least Charley had us with him."

"Yes, that's one way to look at it," said McGowan.

Walsh served the drinks and McGowan raised his pony. "To Jerry."

"To Jerry," said Banks.

"To Jerry," said Harrison Deering.

They drank their brandies and Banks rose. "I think I'll go downstairs and find out what happened. You fellows staying here?"

"For a minute or two," said McGowan.

"You'll excuse me," said Banks. "I don't think I'll be back."

"All right, John," said McGowan. "Goodbye."

"Goodbye, John," said Harrison Deering.

"Jerry was sort of a cousin of his, wasn't he?" said McGowan, after Banks had gone.

"I believe so, yes. There was some connection," said Harrison Deering.

"Yes, I think Jerry was about a third cousin, something like that."

"I believe you're right. Jerry's mother was a Thatcher, and I think old Mrs. Banks was a Thatcher, too," said Harrison Deering.

"Yes, she was. John's mother and Jerry's mother were I think second cousins. Not very close, but there was some connection. John took it rather hard."

"Well, remember it was John that got Jerry in this game. They were in a couple of things together."

"Oh, were they? Business things?"

"Yes. They both had money in a small electronics plant in New Jersey. I never knew much about it."

"No," said McGowan. "Well, Harry, I don't suppose I'll see you now before you sail."

"Jerry's funeral."

"Of course, of course. Then I will be seeing you."

"Yes," said Harrison Deering. "I'm not so sure about sailing. I may change my mind."

"Oh, don't give up your trip. You've looked forward to it for so long."

"I'm not afraid of dying, Bobby. It isn't that. But I'd be such a damn nuisance if I checked out in a London taxicab."

"Oh, that won't happen, Harry."

"No, maybe not. But after today . . ."

"I know," said McGowan. "It *is* something to think about."

In a Grove

In this obscure little California town, far away from Hollywood and not even very close to the Saroyan-Steinbeck country, William Grant once again encountered Richard Warner, as he had always known he would.

Johnstown—to give it a name—was one of those towns that vaudevillians used to describe as "a wide place in the road" and that had owed its earliest existence to the gold strikes of more than a century ago. But in the intervening years it had been all but abandoned until irrigation began to help agriculture, and Johnstown got a second life; unspectacular, unromantic, unexciting, and obviously unprofitable—the last place Grant would expect to find Warner, and yet, since his disappearance had been so complete, the kind of place that was just made for a man who wanted to leave the world in which he had once been widely known.

Grant stopped his car at a filling station. "Fill it up, will you please? The oil is okay, but will you check the water and tires?"

"Right. What do you carry, twenty-six pounds, the tires?" said the attendant.

"Twenty-six, right."

"You been driving a distance, they'll all be a little high, you know. You want me to deflate to twenty-six?"

"Yes."

"Some don't, you know."

"Well, I'm one of those that do," said Grant. "What's the name of this town?"

"Johnstown. Johnstown, California."

"Is that a cigarette machine in there?"

"It's a cigarette machine that's out of order. The nearest place is the supermarket. You can see it there on the edge of town. They call it a supermarket, but nothing very super about it. It's only what used to be the Buick agency, that's all it is."

"But they have cigarettes there."

"Oh, they have cigarettes. They have most everything you find in a supermarket, but I don't know who they think they're kidding, calling it a supermarket. It's no bigger than when it was the Buick agency."

"What happened to the Buick agency?"

"What happened to it? This was never a town for Buicks. You wait here a few minutes and you'll see a couple Model-A Fords, still chugging away. Maybe some International trucks, been through various hands, one rancher to the other. Way back, when I was a kid, one family had a Locomobile. You ever hear of the Locomobile?"

"Yes."

"Another rancher had a big old Pierce-Arrow. Those big ritzy cars, but I'll tell you something. You look on the running-board of those cars and every one of them carried canteens. Ed Hughes, that owned the Locomobile, I remember he had like a saddle holster he had strapped to the right-hand door, to carry a 30-30 rifle in. They didn't buy those cars for show. They bought them because they stood up. That was before they thought up this planned obsolence."

"Planned obsolence. Uh-huh."

"You know, 'Here's this year's piece of junk, come back and see what I allow you on it two years from now.' That's where all the trouble lies. Now what you got here is a foreign car, and it aint even broke in at forty-five thousand miles. This is an automobile. You don't mind if I take a look under the hood? I know, you said you don't need oil, but—"

"That, that just went by. That was no Model-A," said Grant.

The attendant had missed the passing Jaguar, but now waved to it. He smiled. "No, that was Dick Warner. He's a·

fellow lives here. You ever hear of the expression, as queer as Dick's hatband? I think that's who it originated with, Dick Warner."

"Dick Warner? How long has he lived here?"

"Oh—I guess fifteen, maybe twenty years by now. Why, do you know him?"

"Possibly. Where did this fellow come from?"

"Oh, well I'm not even sure about that."

"Is he a tall thin fellow? Brown hair? About my age?"

"Well, I guess he'd answer that description. What are you, the F.B.I. or something like that?"

"Hell, no. If I were the F.B.I. I'd go looking for the deputy sheriff, wouldn't I?"

"You found him. *I'm* the deputy sheriff, and I never had any bad reports on Dick, bad or good for that matter. He pays his bills, don't owe nobody, and his fingerprint's on his driver's license. Well, now he's making a U-turn. Maybe he recognized you."

"I doubt it."

"Heading back this way. Yeah. Moving slowly. Wants to get a good look at you. Mister, are you armed? You got a gun on you?"

"No."

"Well, Dick has, so get behind something. I am."

"There's not going to be anything like that."

"All the same I'm getting out of the way till I make sure. I'm going in and put my badge on. And my gun."

"Go ahead. I'll stand right here."

The Jaguar drove past slowly, the driver staring at William Grant. After the Jaguar had gone past the filling station it stopped, then backed up into the parking area. Dick Warner got out.

He was tall and thin and wore a planter's Panama with a band of feathers, a safari jacket with the sleeves rolled up, sun-tan slacks and leather sandals. "Is it you, Grant?"

"Yes it's me. Hello, Dick."

"Christ Almighty," said Warner. He put out his hand, and Grant shook it.

"No, just me," said Grant.

"What the hell are you doing here?"

"I was looking for a good place to hide out from the law."

"Then get going. There isn't room for two of us. Well, God damn it, Bill. Hey, Smitty, come on out and meet a friend of mine. This is Mr. Grant, Mr. Smith. See that you give him four quarts to the gallon."

"Now, Dick. Now, now."

"Mr. Smith thought you might be going to shoot me," said Grant.

"Now why'd you have to tell him that? I didn't know but you were somebody snooping around and Dick didn't want to see you."

"I hear you carry a gun, Dick," said Grant.

"Smitty, whose side are you on? You talk too much."

"This fellow stard asking me questions. He's the one with the big mouth. That'll be four-eighty, Mister, and the next time you come here there's another filling station the other end of town."

"You decided not to check the air for me?"

"I decided if you wanted to check the air you can do it yourself, and there's the hose if you need water."

"All right, Sheriff. You owe me twenty cents," said Grant, handing Smitty a five-dollar bill.

"Mr. Grant's a nice fellow, Smitty. You shouldn't take that attitude."

"I know what attitude to take without any advice from you, Dick."

"I know. Your gums are bothering you again," said Warner. "Smitty has a new upper plate, and he won't give his gums a chance to get used to it."

"I don't think it's his gums. I think he's just a disagreeable guy."

"Move on, Mister, or I'll give you a ticket."

"What for?" said Grant.

"Obstructing traffic. Failure to pay for parking on my lot. I'll think of a few things."

"He will, too, and his brother-in-law's the mayor," said Warner. "Smitty, this is no way to treat a visitor to our fair city."

"We don't encourage tourists. If this fellow's a friend of yours, Dick, you get him off my property pronto."

"All right. Follow me, Bill. And don't go through any stop-signs."

"I'll get out of here as quickly as I can."

"Thirty-mile zone," said Smitty.

"I think that dentist gave you the wrong plate, Smitty," said Warner. "Come on, Bill."

The built-up section was four blocks of one-story white stucco business buildings, which changed abruptly to a stretch of one-story frame dwellings, all badly in need of paint, and then there was country, bare in the rolling hills where the irrigation was not effective. Grant followed Warner for about a mile, until Warner blew his horn, slowed down, and made a right turn into a dirt road. A few hundred yards along that road Warner again slowed down and entered a dirt driveway that ended in a grove of various trees, in the center of which was a ranchhouse. Two horses in a small corral looked up as the cars approached, and a collie ignored Warner's car to run along beside Grant's, barking ferociously. Warner signaled to Grant to drive up alongside him.

"Stay in your car till I put Sonny away. He's liable to take a piece out of your leg," said Warner. He got out and the dog came to him, and he grasped the dog's collar and snapped a leash to it and attached the leash to a length of wire that ran between two trees. The dog could run only between the trees. "You're safe now."

"What do you feed this dog? People?"

"I don't have to. He helps himself. Particularly fond of Mexicans. Itinerant workers. Salesmen. Hollywood writers, he hasn't had any but I can tell he's willing to have a taste of you."

"I can tell that myself."

"Well, just stay out of reach."

"All right, Lassie," said Grant. "Maybe if I gave him a good swift kick."

"You'd never leave here alive if you did. Even if I let you get away with it my wife wouldn't."

"Oh, you're married."

"Good God, do you think I could live here if I wasn't?"

"Well, what the hell. Itinerant workers, Mexicans."

"Lay off the Mexican angle. My wife is half Mexican."

"What else do I have to look out for?"

"Well, at certain times of the day, down there near the ditch, rattlesnakes, but they don't come up here much. I've done a pretty good job of exterminating them around the house. Anyway, you won't be here that long. You're on your way somewhere, obviously. Come on in and meet my bride and have a cooling drink."

"And I forgot to get some cigarettes."

"We have plenty. The señora's a heavy smoker. There she is."

A girl, not readily identifiable as Mexican but wearing a multi-colored peasant blouse and skirt and huaraches, opened the door of a screened porch. "Hi," she said.

"I brought somebody out of my past. This is Bill Grant, used to be with me at Paramount. Bill, this is the present Mrs. Warner, Rita by name."

"Hi," she said. "And what's with that present Mrs. Warner bit?"

"We can only wait and see."

"You wait and see. Come on in, Bill. What would you like to drink? I got some cold beer."

"Thank you, that's just perfect."

"Where did the great Warner run across you? Or you across him? He never has any company. From Hollywood, anyway. Dick, you get the beer."

"All right," said Warner, and went to the kitchen.

"I'm working for TV now, and I came up this way scouting locations. Have you been in pictures?"

"No, but I know what scouting locations means. I went to high school in L. A. Fairfax."

"How did you stay out of pictures?"

"You think I'm pretty enough? I guess I'm prettier than some of those dogs, but I was never discovered. Except by his majesty."

"Where did he discover you?"

"You better ask him, he has a different story for everybody. He told a couple people in Johnstown I was his daughter. The son of a bitch. I *am* married to him though. You married?"

"Sure. I have a daughter around your age."

"Well, so has Dick, although I never saw her."

"I know. She lives back East."

"And he has a son. You don't have to be cagey about that side of him. Three ex-wives, a daughter and a son. A brother, a sister, a mother—all that I know. Did you know him a long time?"

"A long time ago I knew him pretty well. Then we had a falling-out. I can't remember what about."

"Well I remember," said Warner, bringing in a tray of bottles and glasses. "I fired you because you went on a three-day bender and never let me know where you were."

"I guess that was it."

"You made me look bad on my second picture as a producer."

"Yeah. You behaved like a jerk producer, that's right."

"Why do you say jerk producer? What other kind is there? You're one now, only in a worse medium. I've seen your name in the paper once in a while. The hell with that. What are you up here for?"

"What are you?"

"I asked you."

"I'm scouting locations."

"Stay away, will you? Go on up to Marin County. I don't want a bunch of those bastards coming to Johnstown. I went to a lot of trouble to get away from them, so don't spoil it for me, will you?"

"I won't promise. Anyway, I might make you a few dollars. I could rent this place for a couple of weeks."

"I don't need the money."

"Hey! Who don't need the money?" said Rita. "I could use a few bucks."

"On what? We have enough."

"I was wondering about that," said Grant. "You do have enough? This is a nice place and all that, but I remember when you were playing polo."

"I could still play polo if I wanted to, but who plays polo these days? For that matter, who makes pictures these days?"

"His majesty thinks the movies stink," said Rita. "That's why he never goes to them, and that's why he knows all about them."

"You don't smell with your eyes. The beautiful odor is wafted all the way from Culver City," said Warner.

"Culver City is where I work. I shoot a lot of stuff on the Metro lot," said Grant.

"Speaking of shooting, what was that conversation with Smitty?"

"He told me you carried a gun. Apparently he doesn't know anything about you, your background, where you came from."

"I've seen to that."

"But this is the strange part. He was willing to believe that you were ready to shoot it out with the first stranger that asked about you. That's an odd impression to leave after living here fifteen years."

"I've told Smitty what you might call conflicting stories. It's nobody's business what I did before I came here, or what I do now, if I stay within the law."

"What *do* you do now?"

Warner pointed to a wall that was completely covered with bookshelves containing paperback books and old magazines; western stories, detective stories, science fiction, popular delvings into the human mind.

"You write them?" said Grant.

"I steal from them and then write my own. I have five by-lines, and I make anywhere from five to fifteen thousand a year, turning out stories. I'm what we used to call a pulp writer."

"It must keep you busy, but do you need the money? I thought you left Hollywood with plenty of glue."

"Don't give this greedy little Mexican the wrong idea," said Warner. "We live on what I earn."

"Except when you want to buy a Jaguar, or send away to New York for some clothes," said Rita.

"My extravagances, my spirit-raising expenditures, they come out of my capital, the money I took out of Hollywood," said Warner.

"You let him get away with this, Rita?"

"She's devoted to me, you can see that. Sit on his lap," said Warner. "He's wondering if he can make you, so let him have a try at it."

"You want me to sit on your lap, Grant?"

"Of course. He's right."

She put down her glass and sat on Grant's lap. Grant took her in his arms and kissed her and felt her breasts.

"Cut!" said Warner. "Now go back to your chair."

The girl returned to her chair and picked up her glass.

"How do you feel, Chiquita? Would you have gone on?"

"What do you think, king? Of course I'd have gone on."

"Then why didn't you?"

"Because I knew you were going to say 'Cut.' "

"That isn't the answer you're supposed to give."

"That's the answer I gave, though. I told you I have a lot to learn."

"She has spirit, this girl," said Warner.

"Plenty."

"Oh, not only what you mean. She still has a mind of her own."

"I always will have. His majesty thinks he rules me, but he doesn't tell me to do anything I don't want to do. You can't hypnotize somebody against their will."

"Yes you can," said Grant. "But there's some theory that while they're under hypnosis they won't do anything they don't want to."

"I guess that's what I meant."

"Let me remind both of you that this has nothing to do with hypnosis. I am not a hypnotist."

"Maybe not, but you like to think you have hypnotic powers," said Grant.

"There you're perfectly correct."

"I'd like to know why you said 'Cut'? It wasn't just to show your power. It was because you were afraid."

"Nonsense," said Warner. "Afraid of what?"

"Ho! Afraid that Rita and I would get in the hay. She was willing to stop because she was getting embarrassed."

Warner gave a short laugh. "Embarrassed? Rita? Tell the man what you used to do for a living."

"I was a hooker," said the girl.

"A fifty-dollar girl that got tired of the grind," said Warner.

"And several other things," said Rita. "You don't only get tired of the grind."

"My wife doesn't embarrass easily, Grant."

"I guess not," he said.

"The complexities and deviations are all old stuff to her. What did you think of Grant when you first laid eyes on him?"

"Well, I knew by the car that he was probably some Hollywood friend of yours."

"Yes, but what else?"

"Well, he'd make a pass at me if he had a chance."

"So far nothing very complex," said Grant.

"Well, I knew he didn't like you."

"Now we're getting somewhere. Do you know why you thought that?" said Warner.

"That I couldn't tell you."

"All right, never mind. Tell us some other first impressions and reactions."

"I thought I wouldn't mind getting in bed with him."

"She doesn't see many men here," said Warner.

"Let her tell it," said Grant.

"But he wouldn't be much fun after a while. You're still the most fun, king."

"Why is he so much fun, Rita? Not just sex," said Grant.

"Don't knock sex. And it is sex. With this character everything is sex. Want to ask you a question, Grant. Did he lay all those picture stars?"

"He had his share, but not many of the big ones. He was afraid to go after the big ones. He was afraid he'd get a turndown and it would get around that he'd made a pitch and was unsuccessful. In Hollywood, honey, that's losing face. No, your husband didn't score with the big ones."

"I knew you were lying about that," said Rita to Warner.

"Grant is only telling what he knows. There's a hell of a lot he doesn't know."

"What Academy Award winner did you ever lay? Now don't give me any best-supporting actress. I mean the Number One. Or what star that got top billing, her name over the main title? Or a hundred percent of the main title."

"What's that?"

"Your name in letters as big as the title of the picture," said Grant. "The only one was Ernesta Travers, and she was giving it out to projectionists. She actually laid a projectionist while he was running a picture for her."

"You've got the story wrong, but no matter. I even forgot about Ernesta."

"I didn't know she was ever a big star," said Rita. "Have some more beer, Grant."

"All right, fine," said Grant.

"You, king? You want another?"

"If you get it, yes," said Warner.

She left them.

"Yes, what you're wondering is true. She was a hooker."

"Well she was a damn pretty one. Is. I have to be careful of my tenses. Is damn pretty, whatever she was."

"Would you give her a hundred dollars now?"

"Sure."

In a loud voice Warner called out: "I've got you lined up for a fast hundred dollars."

"With Grant?" she responded from the kitchen.

"Yeah."

"All right," she said. She brought in three bottles of beer, clutching them by the neck. She put a bottle in front of Warner, then sat herself beside Grant and poured beer into his glass. "Do I get to keep the whole C-note?"

"Certainly," said Warner.

"Do I get shot in the back?" said Grant.

"That's the chance you take."

"Just so you don't shoot him while he's in the kip with me."

"That's the chance *you* take, señora."

She looked at her husband. "Listen, how much of this is kidding and how much is kidding on the square?"

"I'm not kidding at all. If you'd like to make yourself a quick hundred dollars, Grant and I made a deal. Ask Grant if I'm kidding."

"Just like old times, back in the Thirties," said Grant.

"I don't know," said the girl.

"What don't you know?" said Warner.

"Well, what the hell?" she said.

"It's how you used to earn your living," said her husband.

"I don't deny that. But the first friend of yours ever came to the house and you promote him into a party with me," she said.

"Don't you want the hundred dollars?" said Warner.

"I always want a hundred dollars."

"Well, you necked him, you let him give you a little feel."

"Yeah, but I thought that was—I was just playing along with the gag."

"Grant wasn't playing along with any gag, were you, Grant?"

"To tell you the truth I guess I wasn't."

"And it was no gag when you said you'd give her a hundred bucks."

"No, I'd give her a hundred bucks."

"Well, you son of a bitch, if you meant it, I'll level, too," said the girl to her husband. She reached out her hand. "Come on, Grant."

Grant stood up. "You'll excuse us, I'm sure," said Grant.

The girl looked at her husband. "You can't be on the level," she said.

"Why not?" said Warner.

"God damn you. God damn you!" She ripped off the peasant blouse and, naked to the waist, put her arms around Grant and kissed him. "Come on," she said, and led him by the hand.

She lay on the oversize bed, and Grant shed his clothes and got down beside her. She looked at him. "Don't worry, I won't welsh on it now," she said. She put her arms around him and began running her little hands up and down his spine, slowly, caressingly.

"Perfect." Warner's voice was cold and calm.

The girl saw her husband in the doorway, then she screamed. "No! No!" The first shots struck Grant in the spine, he shuddered and died. The girl tried to hide behind his body, but Warner grasped his hand and pulled him aside and took his time firing the remaining four shots. Then he went to the telephone and dialed.

"Smitty, come on out here. I've got something for you," he said.

The Old Folks

The house stood a mile to the north of the main road, on land that was flat and covered with snow. It was a large, white house, with the pillars that made it describable as American Colonial, and set in among a dozen now leafless walnuts and elms. It happened that there were no buildings whatever between the main road and the house, so that the side road that eventually reached the farm and cut through it seemed like a long, private driveway. So it had been, in the previous century.

"That's home?" said the man.

"That's home," said the woman, who was driving the car.

"Looks good," said the man.

"Yes, it always looks good from here," said the woman. "After I've been there a while I want to go away, but it always looks good when I come back."

"Is all this yours? This land?"

"Heavens, no. Not any more. It was when my grandfather was alive, but now we only have two hundred and forty acres."

"As compared with what, when your grandfather was living?"

"I have no idea. Maybe a thousand acres. Maybe more. Beginning with the road we just left, and then quite a sizable piece of land on the other side of the house, where you see the barns and the silos. And to the east and west."

"That would be a lot more than a thousand acres, if I'm any judge."

"Probably. Grandpa was one of those people that liked to

be able to say that it's all theirs as far as the eye can see. Although I don't think I ever actually heard him say it. In fairness."

"What was he? An oldtime landowner?"

"No. Not if you mean did he make his money that way. He bought it all after he'd made his money elsewhere. Grandpa made his money in the steel business. This was where he lived after he retired."

"To become a country gentleman?"

"Exactly. He bought this from the widow of a friend of his. Grandpa knew the property from visiting here, but he had nothing to do with the development of it. Mr. Frick and Mr. Carnegie built big houses on Fifth Avenue, and Grandpa, not being that rich, bought a farm in Ohio. Now you get a better look at the house."

"Looks fine. Comfortable."

"I keep it up. I'm glad now that I did. There was a long time when I never saw it, and I was often tempted to sell, but now I'll never sell unless I really have to. I had good times here, and I was very fond of my grandfather. I'm very lucky to have this place to go to. By the way, my daughter and her husband won't be here till tomorrow. She telephoned as I was leaving to meet you."

"Are we terribly distressed about that?"

"Not unless you wanted to play bridge. It certainly won't interfere with any other arrangements. Nancy has no illusions about me. In fact she may be thinking she's giving her mother a break."

"By leaving the old folks to themselves?"

"Precisely."

"Well, she is. I'd rather be alone with you tonight than have to play bridge, or make conversation with Nancy and her husband."

"I'd rather be alone with you, too. I'm glad Nancy's going to be here part of the time. I'll concede that much to Ohio morality. But your first time here should be just the two of us."

"You're dead right. I can see how much competition I have from the house, and you can make up your mind whether I'd fit in."

"That's a very disarming trait you have. Suddenly you'll state the whole case when I least expect it. You *have* got competition from this house, and I *do* want to see if you'd fit in. But I wouldn't have had the honesty to put it all into words. You're a nice man, Arthur."

"Oh, hell. Why should you and I practice small deceptions? You and I? We know everything except whether we want to spend the rest of our lives together."

"At this moment I have no doubt at all, but I'm very different here from what I am other places you've seen me. I never feel I have to *try* here. You could see me for ten years in New York and never know that I have this side."

"What side?"

"This side. You'll see. The side that loves this house. You'll notice things."

"So will you."

She stopped the car at the front door. "Take your bag in and I'll put the car away. We won't need it again tonight. If you want to wash—under the stairway. I'll be right back."

"Why can't I wait, or go with you?"

"Because it's cold and it's almost four hours since you left your office. Go on, don't be polite."

"Is this one of the things I'm supposed to notice?"

"I hadn't thought of that, but I guess it is. If you'd like to fix me a bourbon and water, you'll find everything in the little room on your right."

He handed her the drink when she returned from the garage. "It's weak, I hope," she said. "I go for days here without anything to drink."

"What do you do on an average day?"

"On an average day I have a cup of coffee in bed at half past eight. I take my time about dressing and breakfast, so that I'm seldom really up and about before ten in the morning. Drive to the village, which is six miles away, and do whatever marketing there is to be done. Come home, and by that time the mail and the New York papers have arrived. Read both, and if there's any mail to be answered, I answer it, and the morning's just about gone. After lunch I go for a walk, then I come home and do my needlework, with the radio going, till it's time to have my bath. At seven I have my supper, and then I read and watch television—we get very good reception, but a lot of it's wasted on me. After the news I go around with a flashlight and see if everything's secure for the night. Glass of milk and so to bed. And that's an average day, at this time of year."

"Don't you see anybody?"

"Well, literally, yes. The people in the village, the postman sometimes, the cook and the maid, and my farmer and his family. I don't lose the power of speech. In the spring and early fall I may play golf at the little country club that we passed on the way out, but I don't enter into the social life. There are three or four women that I play golf with, but they never come here. My grandfather and grandmother discouraged that. When I was a girl I could have anyone I wanted to come here and play tennis, before there was a country club, and swim in the pool. But the fathers and mothers weren't invited. Grandpa and Grandma's guests were from Pittsburgh and New York."

"Where were your father and mother?"

"Traveling, or at a place we had on Murray Bay. But I was here more than any place else, every summer till the year I came out, and even then. I actually looked forward to my visits here, until boys began to enter my life. Then my mother bought a house in Southampton to launch me socially, and I promptly disrupted everything by eloping. Well, you know that. Number One on my hit parade."

"Why did you elope?"

"The real reason? The real reason was because I was so terrified of Southampton. I didn't think I was very pretty and I was afraid of being unpopular. Boys liked me, but the girls were horrid, and this boy got tight and when he suggested that we run away and get married, I did. Anything to get out of Southampton. Instead of which I got into it more deeply than before. All three of my husbands were Southampton types."

"Roy I know, but did the other two have any dough?"

"Oh, yes."

"But you never got any of it. Didn't you ask for alimony?"

"No. I should be embarrassed to tell it, but my first husband could have named my second husband as corespondent, and my second could have named my third."

"And Roy? Who could he have named?"

She shook her head. "He's married and living with his wife again. I won't tell you. At least I won't tell you now, and maybe I never will. Roy doesn't know, and that's why he's so bitter about me. But why should he know? Why should I tell him? I told him I was in love with another man, having an affair, and wanted a divorce."

"Why didn't you marry the other guy?"

"He didn't want to marry me. That was quite a blow. I told him that I'd asked Roy for a divorce and he said, 'Now wait a minute. I didn't ask you to get a divorce.' Which was perfectly true. He hadn't. I'll certainly never forget that little scene. We were on the train together on a Monday morning, coming in from Southampton, and I made my announcement. I thought it was going to be greeted with love and enthusiasm, instead of which my brave lover was terror-stricken. When I saw that I got up and went to another car, and I've never spoken to him since."

"But you went ahead with the divorce anyway."

"Of course. I'd told Roy everything but the man's name. I couldn't ask Roy to overlook my indiscretion, not after telling him I was in love with another man."

"Roy isn't the soul of forgiveness."

"No man would be, under the circumstances. Roy might have excused me for having an affair. The reason I say that is because I always felt that he was *waiting* for me to have an affair. But a silly affair is one thing, and telling your husband that you love another man is very different."

"Roy wouldn't have forgiven you for an affair. I know Roy. He thinks I'm kind of a traitor now, even if you are divorced."

"Do you mind?"

"Being on Roy's jerk list? Not a bit. Roy demands absolute loyalty from all his friends, you know that. If he sees you having lunch with another stockbroker he immediately suspects you of getting ready to transfer your business. If you go out with a woman he slept with twenty years ago he thinks you spent all your time talking about *him*. So I knew I'd be on his jerk list, the moment he heard you and I were seeing each other."

"Especially since he automatically assumes that every man I ever danced with was a former lover or about to be one."

"In fact, how did you put up with him for ten years?"

"I put up with him for five. The first five were pleasant, the second five—that's when I started coming back here again."

"Alone? I hope that doesn't sound too much like Roy."

"I was about to say, it did sound a little like Roy. Yes, I always came here alone—at least, not with a man."

"So this became your refuge. Your Shangri-la."

"I guess so. I always think of Shangri-la as that place that Roosevelt used to go to. This has a different connotation. This is a place where I was a princess, and knew it, the way children do know. And my grandfather and grandmother were sweet and kind. And *I* was nice. That's the important thing, Arthur. *I* was nice. I never had to be punished here. At home, which was Pittsburgh, with my father and mother, I got away with everything I could, and that was damn little. But as soon as I came here I was in a different atmosphere. I went to bed when I was told to, and I was on time for meals. I always wanted to get married from here."

"Why didn't you?"

"I spoiled that by eloping, and my other two marriages were civil ceremonies."

"What about the one in between, your second husband?"

"Mike? Well, he's Nancy's father, and I find that increasingly hard to believe. When I have to see him about Nancy—

money, legal things—it's usually in a lawyer's office. 'Good morning, Dorothy,' he'll say. Kisses me on the cheek, and Mr. Charlton, my lawyer, is so relieved that there's not going to be any fireworks. We sit there, Mike and I, and Mr. Charlton drones on about tax advantages and all that, and I find myself staring at Mike and his bow tie. He always wears bow ties. And his father's watch-chain. And I *know* the intimacies we shared. I know them, but I can't believe them. Six years together, which included the war years, some of them. Me pregnant part of the time, and other times following him from one place to another when he was in the Navy. Where's it all gone? Does it mean as little to him as it does to me? And yet I used to move heaven and earth to be with him. Black market railroad tickets. Black market gasoline. Bribing hotel clerks."

"And then the roof fell in. How did that happen?"

"The war did it. He came back from the Pacific and was in Washington and I went down there to be with him. But he didn't want to do any of the things I thought he'd want to do. I'd have people in for cocktails, *his* friends, not mine particularly, and then he'd give me hell because he said I didn't realize that he wasn't going back to that life. Well, I *didn't* realize it, because he hadn't *told* me. I was supposed to guess that. He was very disagreeable, and all I was doing was try to please him. Well, you can take just so much of that, and then you let ding. We had several bad fights, in which I was accused of failing to realize that there was a war on, and trying to make a Southampton out of Washington, and neglecting the baby. That really got me. Neglecting the baby. He'd come in and look at Nancy in her crib, sometimes play with her for as much as five minutes, and that was being a good father. No thought whatever about the 365 days a year I was taking care of her, without any help at all. Oh, well, Mike took it big, the war, and I was the convenient one to blame for the cocktail parties in Washington, and my grandfather was a merchant of death, having made his money in steel. And what did I know about the wave of the future. Well, nothing, but I didn't see why I should take the blame for Pearl Harbor or the sinking of the

Hornet. Or for that matter, Mike's friends. Under those circumstances I was a pushover for somebody like Roy. Yes, literally. He built me up, flattered me, was sympathetic. Got a nice colored woman from Tennessee to help with Nancy, and that was it."

"And now where is Mike?"

"Living in Providence, where he belongs. Married and has two children by his horse-face of a wife, who I'm sure regards me as a nitwit that he had to get over the way you do measles. He's active in politics, goes around making speeches in Italian. And writes me letters about Nancy, how she ought to take things more seriously and would I please cooperate. I don't know what I'm supposed to do. Nancy has a husband, a very serious-minded young man studying law at the University of Pittsburgh. I wrote and told Mike that it seemed more important for Nancy to be a good wife than to nip over and help Dr. Schweitzer. But Mike isn't one for the light touch. He wrote back and said that Dr. Schweitzer was doing a noble work and wouldn't take Nancy unless she had the right qualifications, such as a degree in nursing. Oh, a long diatribe, ending with the suggestion that since she was living in Pittsburgh, perhaps she could take some courses and volunteer to work with Dr. Salk. So I wrote him just a note and asked him who was Dr. Salk. You should see the answer I got. I wish I'd saved it. There probably isn't a mother or grandmother in the whole United States that hasn't heard of Dr. Salk, but Mike didn't stop to think of that. First he told me all about Salk, and polio shots, and polio. Then ever so gently he used it all as an excuse to—as a text for a sermon. My ignorance of Dr. Salk was typical of me and the kind of life I lived. They say that religious converts are the most bigoted, but for pomposity, for sheer pomposity, that sermon on Dr. Salk was the end. The reformed aristocrat turned progressive, liberal, whatever you want to call it. And his horse-face wife looking over his shoulder at every word he wrote. Well, why not? I'm sure Mike and his wife are descended from a long line of witch-burners, so it's perfectly natural."

"What did you see in him in the first place?"

"The exact opposite of my first husband. Mike was a quiet, conservative young man. Almost painfully shy, but not really. It wasn't shyness. It was just that he wasn't flamboyant, and that made him seem shy after my first husband."

"But you had an affair with this Mike while you were still married to the first one."

"Don't kid yourself about people like Mike. They have affairs, too. Just like you and me."

"How old are you, Dorothy?"

"I'm forty-three, and I know what you're thinking. It's quite a crowded record for someone forty-three, but I was nineteen when I married for the first time. I should be older, and most people think I am, but forty-three's the correct age."

"You may be a bit young for me. I'm coming up fifty my next birthday."

"Roy's fifty-two, although I don't know why that matters, except that he's that much older than you, or you're that much younger than he. If we reach the point where we really seriously discuss getting married, our ages will be important, but there are other things much more so."

"Such as?"

"Such as where we'll live."

"I have to make my living in New York."

"How much money would you have if you didn't work in New York?"

"Not much. I couldn't live on it."

"Do you mean your present style of living?"

"Oh, hell, no. No, I mean—well, I have an income of about seven thousand a year, apart from what I earn. We wouldn't get very far on that."

"What do you make all told?"

"Around fifty thousand a year."

"And you'd never be content to live here, with just your seven thousand and my income."

"I couldn't. Fifty isn't young, but it's too young to quit, to retire and live on an Ohio farm that isn't really a farm. What

would *I* do, Dorothy? You don't think I could live the kind of
day you described as your average day. I've been a go-getter all
my life. I worked my way through college in the bottom of the
Depression, and I was just getting on my feet when the war
came and I joined the Army. Four years less a month in the
Army, and I had to hustle when I got out. And I have re-
sponsibilities. I have my mother and two sisters. My sisters
work, but I'm probably going to have to take care of them
sometime."

"If you don't work yourself to death in the meantime. It's a
grim thought, but you have to think it."

"Oh, I've thought it. But the grimmest thought is that the
way things are constituted, you and I can't afford to get married. Not on your terms. Not if it means we'd live here. I'm
making fifty thousand a year, and I'm just getting by. If I
stopped working, it would make a difference to my mother and
my sisters. Fifty thousand a year, but I couldn't really afford
this visit on my own. I had to make it a business trip to Columbus. I'd never go anywhere, I'd never leave New York if I had
to pay my own way. I've been to London twice this year,
Seattle, Mexico City, Montreal, Phoenix, Arizona. But on company business. If a trip to anywhere costs more than twenty
dollars, and isn't company business, I don't take it. So you see,
Dorothy, I don't fit in, and this house *is* competition. Jumping
way ahead, if we were married and you insisted on living here,
I wouldn't be able to see you more than once a month."

"I see what you mean."

"I got out of the Army in '45 and as I say, started hustling.
I was thirty-five years old, and I met a girl I wanted to marry,
but she married someone else. I didn't have any money. What
I'd saved I spent during the war, on myself and my family. I
came out a major, but majors were a dime a dozen in civilian
life. I even had a Silver Star and a Purple Heart, in case anybody was looking for an ex-major with a Silver Star and a
Purple Heart. But they weren't. So I lost out on the girl and
began to hustle. Then suddenly I'm almost fifty, with a mother
and two sisters who aren't very well off, but I'm making fifty

thousand a year and riding in jets and staying at the best hotels. And you're trying to make some sense out of your life. We both are. You have this place, and you love it, and you'll meet some guy that you'll want to marry and that can afford to live here with you. But I'm not the guy."

"Oh, you're the guy. I fully believe that, Arthur. But I could never live in New York again. I wouldn't be nice. That sounds insipid, but you know what I mean."

"I know exactly what you mean, just from seeing you here this short time. It's a good thing we're not in love."

"No, it's a pity we're not in love and twenty years younger."

"I stand corrected."

In the silence she got up and closed the draperies.

"What are you thinking?" he said.

"I was thinking that nobody would feel sorry for us."

He smiled. "No, they wouldn't," he said.

"We have everything. We have money, we're free to marry."

"That's the way they'd describe it. I'm a fifty-thousand-dollar-a-year man, and you're an attractive divorcee. What's keeping them apart? Why don't they get married and settle down, instead of this silly middle-aged affair of theirs?"

"And they're not getting any younger," she said.

"They're not getting any younger, and——"

"And it's very unbecoming for people their age, when there's nothing in the way. It isn't as if she hadn't been around long enough to find out what she wants."

"And when is *he* going to stop ratting around?"

"She'll be a grandmother any day now. Out of consideration for her daughter—*let's not play this any more*. It isn't very funny after a certain point. What is your mother like, Arthur?"

"Oh, I don't know. She was a schoolteacher and so was my father and so are my two sisters. What were your parents like?"

"Not were. Are. They're still alive, living in Santa Barbara. Mother keeps hoping that Nancy doesn't turn out the way I have, marrying so young. But that's hardly an original thought. I hope so, too."

"Still alive? How did you happen to get this house?"

"Grandpa left it to me because Mother didn't want it, and he knew I did. Or knew I would, when I got older. And he was right, I do want it and I am older. But I wish I didn't."

"Don't say that. Anything that you've loved as much as you do this house, and as long, must be good. You *are* nicer here, Dorothy."

"But I'm a little afraid that from now on I won't be. I may come to hate this house."

"No, as long as you can live here you'll have a nice memory of yourself. In fact, you'll always feel that you have at least one more chance in life. And believe me, that's worth holding on to." He rose and stretched his arms. "I think I'll have a quick bath before dinner."

"Your bag's in your room. Have a nap if you're tired. I'll wake you at seven-thirty. It's just you and I for dinner."

"I know," he said. He put his hand on her cheek. "Nice Dorothy."

"Nice Arthur," she said, and covered his hand with her own.

A Case History

For ten months at the outset of his professional career Dr. Drummond had served as ship's surgeon in various liners that called at South American, Australian, and Asiatic ports. In his front office hung framed photographs taken on some of his voyages, pictures of himself in tropical whites posed with men whom he would identify as presidents of banana republics, opera and concert performers on tour, forgotten financiers, the inevitable Englishmen of title, and Orientals in native costume or western dress. At home, his den was furnished with drums and spears, shrunken skulls, lovely brassbound boxes, Chinese gongs, and more photographs. The brass was now tarnished, the wooden objects now brittle dry, the drumheads crinkly and the photographs fading after nearly forty years of sunlight, but almost nothing had been moved from its original resting place. Dr. Drummond had always been delighted when a new patient commented on the photographs in the office or a visitor to his house showed curiosity about the primitive weapons. "Yes, that's me, if you can believe it," he would say. "On my right is Sir John Humberland. He wasn't Sir John then. That's when he was Leftenant Humberland, of the Yorkshire, uh, Yorkshire some regiment, but of course you probably read about him at Tobruk. On my left, that's a friend of mine named On Ling, he was a financial adviser to one of the famous war lords. An Oxford graduate, spoke beautiful English, of course. That was on a voyage from Auckland, New Zealand, to Hong Kong, and an interesting thing about that picture, it was the only time those two got that close together. Jack Humberland was thought to be a British intelligence agent, but if he was he never got anything out of On Ling. On Ling would bow to him very politely, but he'd never sit down with him, never engage in conversation. I finally got the two of them together long enough to pose for a photograph, but On Ling didn't like it very much. You can tell by his expression.

"Now this is a young lady that we had with us on a trip from Havana to Santiago, Chile. Through the Panama Canal. Very attractive. Her husband was a chemist, worked for one of the big chemical companies . . . The man on her left. An American. I don't know what he did, if he did anything. He was three sheets to the wind all the time he was aboard. Glad to see him go, I can tell you . . . These, of course, you can guess where this was taken. Bali. That was before the Dutch made them cover up. I always manage to stand in front of this picture when the Reverend Hostetter's here for dinner, but I guess he must have seen it by this time . . . I bought this in Sidney. It's an authentic boomerang. Needs a bit of waxing, but I keep putting it off. My housekeeper before I had Mrs. Brophy took it upon herself to do a job on my collection, and she put her thumb through one of my drumheads, so I don't let anybody touch any of my souvenirs . . . That, that's a blow-gun. You've heard of them. They use them to blow poison-tipped darts. Some of the tribes use curare, others have their own particular poison that you won't find listed in the U.S.P. United States Pharmacopoeia . . . I shot that tiger from the back of an elephant, but I didn't have enough money to bring the skin home with me so all I have is this snapshot. Oh, it's all a long, long way from Gibbsville, P A, in miles and in years . . . These teacups, aren't they delicate little things? The last ones I have left out of a set. Lucky to have these two, after forty years and the clumsy women I've had working for me."

The doctor was a widower, childless, whose wife had died of liver trouble during the Second World War. The late Mrs. Drummond had money, some of it her own, most of it the income from a trust fund established by her first husband. When she died everyone agreed that Buz Drummond had fully earned the money he inherited; he had been nice to Sadie, done all he could to make her stop drinking though knowing it to be a hopeless task, and for a time he had practically given up his practice to take care of her so that she could have her wish, which was that she not be sent to a hospital. Sadie loathed hospitals; her father and mother and first husband had all died in the same hospital, on the same floor, in the same year, and she was bounden determined that the only way they would get her into a hospital was if they put her in a straitjacket. That, as a matter of fact, was done, but Buz honored her wish and did not take her to a hospital. As soon as she died he again became more active in his practice, and he kept busy until the younger men returned from the war; then he announced that he was taking no new patients, and during the late Forties and the Fifties he more or less retired to play golf and bridge and to devote his time to writing. He had missed out on two great wars, but he had seen a great deal of the world and he had a lot of good stories to tell.

The news that Buz Drummond was writing a book immediately caused some alarm, since the town had not fully recovered from the notoriety that followed the publication of several novels by a former resident. But on second thought Buz Drummond's friends were able to reassure themselves with the knowledge that first of all Buz was a gentleman, and in the second place, he intended to live out his life in Gibbsville. He was, moreover, an M.D., and there certainly were some written or unwritten rules to govern the degree and kind of revelations a doctor could make, even in the guise of fiction. After the early alarm Buz Drummond's friends, with few exceptions, began to take a friendly interest in his new writing career. Most of his friends would ask him how his book was coming, and he would reply that there was a lot more work to it than he had anticipated but it was *fascinating* work. Those acquaintances who were inclined to be apprehensive or suspicious—other doctors and former patients—were in accord on one thing: they knew a thing or two about Buz. But most people relied on his good sense, his good taste, his professional ethics, his decision to remain a resident of the town, and the now comforting knowledge that he had never really completed anything he had set out to accomplish.

His contemporaries recalled that after serving his internship in a Philadelphia hospital, Buz had come home for a round of farewell parties. According to his announced intention he was about to take off for South America on the first leg of a journey to last five years, during which he hoped to make a special study of tropical diseases and their cure. The high point of the bon voyage festivities was a dinner dance at the brand-new country club, for which two hundred were invited and Markel's orchestra played. The dance went off without unpleasant incident, other than the too-frequent repetition of a song called "Tell Me Little Gipsy," which had to do with fortune telling and an obvious connection with the adventurous young doctor's future. Buz got moderately tight, and the next day departed for Baltimore and his first berth in a fruit boat bound for Honduras. His closer friends had chipped in for a farewell gift—a doctor's emergency kit in an alligator-hide satchel—but he accidentally left it on the train.

When he returned to Gibbsville in less than a year his friends supposed that he was merely on a holiday between voyages, and they said so, thus supplying him with an explanation of his return. "Waiting to hear from the Dollar Line," he would say. Then, as the weeks passed: "Oh, that Dollar Line proposition fell through." Meanwhile his friends were getting postcards and little gifts he had sent them before his return, and several boxes of stuff arrived at his mother's house on Frederick Street. Then, in the autumn of '21 he opened an office on lower Lantenengo Street, in a neighborhood nicknamed Pill Row. He bought a Dodge coupe—one of the standard doctors' cars—and became a regular attendant at the meetings of the County Medical Society until he noticed that the only men who seemed to find time for the meetings were the young fellows just starting out, the arthritic old men, and the mediocrities of the profession. His own practice at first surprised him. His office hours were from one to three in the afternoon and six to eight in the evening, and he always had one or two patients, at least, in the waiting-room. Some of them were deadbeats, but they were patients; quite a few of them were the servants of his well-to-do friends; high school boys with their first gonorrhea; consumptives from the Negro section; old men and old women with real or imaginary illnesses to talk about; schoolteachers who, in the vernacular, doctored with him because he did not charge too much.

He lived at home with his mother, who was financially secure but not rich, and he watched his expenses, but at the end of two years he owed money at the bank. Like every other doctor in Pill Row he was offered a substantial sum by one of the local bootleggers in return for his liquor prescriptions, but professional gossip had immediately identified those physicians who dealt with the bootleggers, and Buz declined their offer even though it would have got him out of debt and with money to spare. The solution to that problem, the respectable solution, was to marry a girl with money. There were of course other solutions less respectable, and still others that were respectable enough but, for a young man, a too-early admission of failure. He could sign up with one of the coal or iron operators, he could be the official examiner and physician for the middle-class lodges that provided insurance benefits. But one of the older men advised against either arrangement. "You'll find out that for their God damn fifty-cent fees they think they own you, and as far as the big companies—the surgeons are the only ones make any money out of them. The lodges and the coal companies will crowd the other patients out of your office." A nice girl with money would also complete the picture of the up-and-coming young physician that Buz Drummond wanted very much to impress on the public mind; he was anxious to have the townsfolk think of him as a well-traveled man, but he wanted them to believe that the curtailment of his five-year trip had been a decision of his own, a desire to settle down to something constructive.

He found that his mother had been proceeding along the same line of thought, was just as far along as he. "You'll be thirty any day now," she said. "That's not old for a man, but

it's not young either. And there are two or three nice Gibbsville girls that aren't getting any younger either. Well situated
financially. Mary Bowen, but unfortunately she's a Catholic.
But there's Minnie Stokes, you've always liked Minnie. And
you'd go a long way before you'd find a nicer girl than Josie
Entwhistle. All the right age to get married, and just waiting
to be asked."

"You can rule out Mary and Josie."

"Well, then, Minnie."

"Minnie's the only one of those three. I've already had too
many arguments with Mary, about her religion. And Josie has
you fooled, Mother."

"Well, I'm not insisting on either one of them, but find
*some*body. Doesn't have to be a Gibbsville girl necessarily, but
people would be that much more pleased if you married a town
girl. And she doesn't have to be one of our friends. This town
has a lot of money and it isn't all on Lantenengo Street."

"Oh, I know that."

"Look at some of the names of the directors of the banks."

"I have."

"Well, don't let the grass grow under your feet," said Mrs.
Drummond.

Henrietta Moore chose this inopportune moment to inform
Buz Drummond that she was pregnant and was taking her
name off the nurses' registry. "I can go to Philly and have it
taken care of, but, honey, I'm going to lose a couple months'
work and I don't have much saved up."

"How the hell—"

"Oh, what's the use of complaining about it? I should of
known better and you should of known better, but we took our
chances, so I'm not taking any calls till maybe January or
February. That's thirty-five dollars a week I'm out, times twelve
weeks. Twelve fives sixty, twelve threes thirty-six and six to
carry is four hundred twenty dollars."

"You're better at arithmetic than you are at some other
things."

"You be careful I'm not too good at multiplication. Or addition. Catch wise?"

"Very witty, I'm sure. Well, you want me to raise five hundred dollars."

"I didn't say that. Five hundred is only what I'm out. Don't you expect to pay for the abortion and while I'm in the hospital? I need a thousand, Buz."

"A thousand dollars?"

"Do you want to do it yourself? You'll still have expenses. I want to be in a hospital. I don't want to start hemorrhaging in a boarding house. Listen, Buz, I'm not holding you up for anything, but I want to go to Philly and be in a hospital. I'd have a hard time getting it done here, in the hospital. I had my appendix out five years ago, so I can't use that old excuse."

"When do you have to have the money?"

"I have to let them know I'm coming at the hospital, two or three days' notice. A girl I trained with is the head nurse there."

"What hospital is it?"

"As if you didn't know. Every intern in Philly knows, and most nurses. And those society bimboes."

"All right, I'll get the money."

"You certainly are good-natured about it, I must say. *God!*"

Mrs. Drummond handed over a bond. "I'm not giving you this," she said. "This is a loan, and you must pay me back. I don't object to helping you when I know what the money's for, but you've told me two versions of why you need a thousand dollars and frankly I don't believe either one of them. I want the money back and forty-five dollars interest. I mean it, this time I do."

"You'll get it back, and I'm no child, Mother. I don't see why I have to account for every nickel I spend."

"There are a lot of nickels in a thousand dollars. And I'm no child, either, by the way. I think you're ashamed to tell me what you want the money for."

"Have it your own way," he said.

Henrietta Moore did not go back to work as soon as she had

said she would, but when she did go back, Drummond's first knowledge of it was through the nurses' registry. He telephoned to find out what nurses were taking calls and Miss Moore's name was mentioned. "Tell her to call Dr. Drummond," he said.

She telephoned him. "Good evening, Dr. Drummond. This is Miss Moore."

He was alone in his office. "So you're back at work?"

"Yes, I'm going on a case for Dr. English, starting night duty tomorrow. Why?"

"Are you calling from some place where you can't talk?"

"No, I'm in a booth at the drug store. I stopped in after the movies and I saw you phoned. I can talk all right—if I want to. Only I don't want to. The least you could do was send me some flowers, all the time I was in Philly. I could of had a septicemia for all you cared."

"But you didn't have. And I take it you're all right again."

"You asking for a date?"

"No, I'm not, Henrietta."

"That's good, because you wouldn't of got one. Goodnight, Dr. Drummond."

She was a good nurse, was asked for by the leading physicians of the county, and if they guessed among themselves which of their number had gone to bed with her, they got no confirmation from her. She was equally discreet in the matter of passing professional opinions of the doctors. She had never been known to commit the unforgivable sin of expressing any but the most impersonal, complimentary comment on a member of the medical profession. Nevertheless she managed to convey favorable and unfavorable impressions of doctors without uttering a word, without making a face, and men like Malloy, English, and the Woodman brothers easily guessed that Henrietta Moore's opinion of young Buz Drummond was not very high. Oddly enough it was her non-professional opinion of Dr. Drummond that had the greater influence on the leading men. They could make up their own minds about Drummond as a physician, but if he could not stay out of trouble with Moore, if he antagonized such a good-natured old war horse—she was thirty-two—he could not be much of a fellow. They had been through too many vigils with her, been awakened by her from too many naps in too many Morris chairs, had drunk too many cups of her coffee and glasses of her iced tea, not to feel something that was part comradeship, part affection, part gratitude. She had helped them put chains on tires and taken the reins when they fell asleep in zero weather, and all of them knew that when she got them out of bed at four o'clock in the morning the patient had taken a turn for the worse. In her career as a nurse she had even seen one or two doctors cry.

She took herself out of Buz Drummond's life and was soon enjoying the company of a jovial cigar salesman from Reading, but Drummond's coldness during her brief pregnancy and the let-down after the abortion had done something to her spirits. The cigar salesman was new and therefore did not know that it was unusual for Henrietta to need a shot of rye to pep her up. But then one day, on a confinement case, Dr. Malloy said to her: "Did I smell whiskey on you?"

"Yes, Doctor. For cramps."

"Pack your bag and go home."

"Are you going to report me?"

"Not this time, but believe me if you'd lied to me I would have. What's the matter with you, Moore?"

"I don't know."

"Come and see me at my office tonight."

"I'm not sick."

"Then whatever's the matter, drinking on a case won't do you any good. You know how I feel about whiskey. You've been taking Sen-Sens, but I could smell that booze the minute I went in the room. God damn it, Moore, I'm giving you fair warning. Do you need money?"

"No thank you, Doctor."

"Maybe you'd better get married. I'm going to tell this patient I need you on another case. But this is the last time. God damn it to hell. Whiskey!"

On Malloy's word alone her name could have been stricken from the nurses' registry (nurses who detected whiskey on doctors' breath kept silent), and the threat to her livelihood and to the work she loved was effective for a few weeks, but the cigar salesman complained of her lack of pep and she had a few shots of rye with him. When she turned up on her case to relieve the night nurse she was so badly hung over that the night nurse had to stay with the patient. "Any doctor could tell what you've been doing, Moore," said the night nurse. "I'll do a double trick, but you're gonna get caught."

"Oh, don't sermonize to me."

"Listen, if that's the thanks I get for protecting you, I'm supposed to report you anyway. You're drunk."

"Mind your own business and leave me alone," said Henrietta Moore.

The nurses had been raising their voices during the altercation and the patient's household later in the day reported to the attending physician, who quickly discovered that the night nurse was shielding Henrietta Moore. He telephoned her at her boarding house and there could be no doubt as to what had kept her off duty that day. She was incoherent, coddling, insulting. "Lay off me, Dr. Fabrikant. You lay off me and I'll lay off you," she said. Within the hour he had reported her to the Medical Society, and her nursing career was ended. In a couple of weeks she had vanished and no one in Gibbsville ever saw her or heard from her again.

Buz Drummond made an effort in the direction of Minnie Stokes. He took her to two programs of the cultural series—the Philadelphia Orchestra and the Denishawn Dancers—and to the Lions Club Ball. If it had been the summer season he could have played tennis or golf with her, and the conversational gaps would not have been so painfully noticeable; but Minnie Stokes was not deceived, no one was deceived. It was apparent that Buz Drummond had decided that Minnie Stokes would make him a suitable wife, and he was going through the perfunctory motions of courtship. Everybody was all for it: home town young doctor, home town rich girl. The only one who was not all for it was Minnie Stokes, whose self-respect and sense of humor caused her to vacillate from annoyance to laughter, and when he proposed to her she said, "No, Buz."

"I admit I haven't been very romantic, Minnie, but we've known each other all our lives. To suddenly act like Romeo . . ."

"Oh, it isn't that."

"Well then think it over. Don't say no right away."

"It'll always be no, Buz. At least *my* answer will always be no. I'm looking for a husband, but if we can't have love at least we ought to have some fun."

"What kind of fun?"

"Any kind. But you seemed to think the whole thing was cut and dried. Take Minnie to the concerts and a few dances, and then propose and get married. I know doctors are always thinking about their cases, but is that what you were so preoccupied with?"

"I suppose I was. It's my life work."

"Well, it's not going to be mine. That's what you can tell people if you want to. Tell them I wouldn't have made a good doctor's wife. As a matter of fact I probably wouldn't. Why don't you transfer your attentions to Mary Bowen? She's very serious, and she's free. And—well, why don't you?"

"What was the third thing about Mary?"

"She's well off. I somehow don't see you marrying a poor girl, Buz."

"That has nothing—well, why should I?"

"That's better. We couldn't even be frank until now, when it's too late. Shall I say something awful? This is the first time I've liked you since our first date. Buz, we're such old friends —why don't you marry Mrs. Loffler?"

"Mrs. *Loffler?*"

"She's only about thirty-five, and she has all that money from Mr. Loffler. Go on, marry Mrs. Loffler, and make her spend some of that money on someone besides herself. She's dying to, you know. She'd love to give parties and travel, and you like to travel, don't you?"

"How do you know she's only thirty-five?"

"Her class in high school."

"Seems older than that to me."

"That's because she's been wearing black since Mr. Loffler died, and you think of her as older because Mr. Loffler was older."

"Do you know her?"

"Worked with her at the Red Cross during the war. She's gained a little weight since then, but not too much. Love to hear her laugh. Daddy says she's worth over four hundred thousand dollars."

"From that musty old store?"

"And buildings. He owns most of the 300-block, or did. She's not afraid to spend money but she doesn't know how. She did over the Norton house when they bought it and she has very good taste. Well, *quite* good."

"I don't even know who she was."

"Sadie Gardner. Her father was Squire Gardner, where they used to take people when they were arrested."

"Of course, I remember her now. I had trouble placing her. Didn't she work in the telegraph office?"

"I don't know. I didn't get to know her till the Red Cross, during the war."

"She doesn't play golf or tennis, I imagine."

"No, she isn't in the club, and I doubt if she'd play if she were. But if you want me to I can have her here some afternoon and you can drop in, accidentally on purpose." Minnie put her hand on his arm. "Aren't you pleased, the way this is working out?"

"The way you're working it out. You're the one that should be pleased, Minnie."

"I am. I know you have to marry someone with money, but as long as it isn't me I'm in favor of it."

He put his arm around her. "I want to kiss you."

"All right," she said. She gave him a full kiss, then stopped. "That's the way we should have started, Buz. You should have taken me out in your coupe and parked."

"I didn't know that that's what you wanted."

"Oh, yes," she said.

"Do you now?"

She nodded. "If you'll take precautions."

"I haven't got any with me, but I could go downtown."

"No, then just let's be like this."

They were not long in advancing from lazy kisses to ardent demands on each other, and she amazed him with how much, how desperately she seemed to center her very will to live in the motions of her hips. She was going to be hard to give up now, with what he knew about her. It was not going to be easy to let her go.

Minnie's plan to effect a proper meeting between Drummond and Mrs. Loffler was dropped. He was evasive because he did not want Minnie in on his conquest of the widow, for no other reason than a kind of squeamishness; it would embarrass him to have Minnie see him polite and attentive—and crafty. Instead he made a habit of driving past the old Norton house, now the Loffler house, when he was out on calls, and as he intended, his opportunity came. On some days he passed her house a dozen times, and finally he saw her hurrying home during a shower. He stopped his car at the curb, opened the door, tipped his hat, and said, "Jump in, I'll take you home."

"Oh, it's Buz Drummond? I mean Doctor. How nice."

She got in. "You sure you know who I am? You don't think I'm someone else? I'm Mrs. Loffler."

"Oh, come on, Sadie. Gibbsville isn't that big. We've both lived here all our lives."

"You never spoke to me before."

"The other way around. I've spoken to you, but you've never spoken to me."

They were only a couple of blocks from her house, and they reached it in a minute.

"Have a cigarette till the rain stops," he said.

"Shouldn't you be taking care of your sick people?"

"They'll wait till this clears up." He gave her a cigarette and lit it for her.

"I was never allowed to smoke while Mister was alive. He said a cigarette was the sign of a fast woman. Maybe he was right."

"Then there are a lot of fast women."

"Yes, and I'll bet *you* know a lot of them."

"Me? I'm a hard-working country doctor."

"Oh, yeah? That's what they *all* say."

"Too busy for that sort of thing, I'm afraid."

"Oh, sure. Oh, of course. Mr. Innocent talking. How come you're still single?"

"I just told you. Too busy."

"Oh, yeah? Too busy with what? I'll bet all those lady patients, not to mention those pretty young nurses."

"Neither men nor women are at their best when they're sick, and nurses only lead to trouble, so I'm told."

"That's not what I heard. A young doctor with S.A. Sex Appeal. How many of those lady patients really have something the matter?"

"Well, take yourself, for instance. You're an attractive young widow, but you never sent for me."

"I doctor with English when I have to have a doctor, which is very seldom."

"There's none better."

"But you wouldn't call him loaded with S.A. . . . Rain's stopped. Come on in and have a cup of tea, or something stronger if you wish. Or do you have to go?"

"I'll have a cup of tea, just to prove you're wrong about the medical profession."

"I wasn't talking about the medical profession. I was talking about Buz Drummond."

"And you're not afraid of me?"

"What's there to be afraid of?"

She went upstairs to take off her wet shoes, but she came down in a complete change of attire, a flowery print dress with a short skirt that revealed her pretty legs.

"I like your dress, or do you call it a frock?"

"You could call it a frock. It's old. I didn't have it on since

Mister passed away. Just been hanging there waiting for me to wear it. You want tea, or liquor?"

"What are you having?"

"Tea. Liquor's supposed to be fattening, and I'm trying to reduce. Do you know anything I can take to reduce?"

"Yes."

"What?"

"Take in your belt a few notches, and when it fits you, that's how much you ought to eat every day."

"I don't wear a belt. You should see what I wear. I'm too stout. I'd give anything to take off ten pounds. Do you know what I weigh? I weigh a hundred and thirty-four in my birthday suit. That's too much for five foot three, don't you think so? A hundred and thirty-four with nothing on?"

"You wouldn't have any trouble losing ten pounds if you put your mind to it."

"The trouble is, the extra weight always goes to the wrong places, if you know what I mean. Well, I guess you do know, being a doctor. If I ask you a question—maybe I better not."

"Go ahead."

"Well I always wanted to ask it but Dr. English isn't—well, are you sure you don't mind? It's a personal kind of a question."

"I ask a thousand of them a day."

"Well, how do you feel when you have a lady patient, and you have to examine her, and she's somebody you know socially?"

"When you say examine her I presume you mean her Eustachian tube?"

"Like that."

He stood up. "Well, if I were going to examine your Eustachian tube—"

She held up her hands. "Go away, go away! I didn't ask you to examine me."

"Hold still!" he said, in the voice of command. She obeyed, though she was apprehensive.

"Now if I wanted to examine your Eustachian tube, Mrs. Loffler, what is the first thing I would say to you?"

"Well—I don't know, but something like 'Take off your dress,' or something like that."

"Why should I?"

"Well, because it's customary."

"Not in my office."

"It was when Dr. English examined me."

"Made you take your clothes off to examine your Eustachian tube? That old rascal, Billy English."

"He was a perfect gentleman. I wasn't a bit embarrassed."

"Mrs. Loffler, I might as well stop kidding you. The Eustachian tube is here, in your ear." He tapped his ear.

"Oh, *you!* And all the time I thought—I really thought there for a minute you were going to—well I wasn't sure exactly what I thought. You have a sense of humor. I must say I like a person with a sense of humor. You wouldn't think it, but Mister said a lot of funny things. He had that *dry* humor, you know. If some of the people in this town ever heard what he used to say about them."

"Do you miss him?"

"Well, I do. Not as much as I did, but I would have if we'd kept on living in the other house. This house he never lived long enough to get used to. But I miss him. After all I was married to him for eight years and you get used to a person. A lot of people criticized me for marrying a man so much older, but when two people get along, you forget about the age. And no woman could ask for a better husband. He lavished presents on me, really lavished them. I could go to Philadelphia and go hog wild in Wanamaker's, Strawbridge's, but it seemed to give him as much pleasure as me. Of course I didn't take advantage, too much, and in a business deal I guess Mister was one of the smartest men in town, if not *the* smartest. Starting out clerking in Boyle's dry goods store for four dollars a week. That's all he got. Four dollars. He had to open up in the morning and lock up at night. Twelve hours a day, six days a week, and no vacation the first two years. Old Terence Boyle liked him so much he wanted him to marry one of his daughters, but Mister wouldn't turn Catholic, and that was how he happened to go in business for himself. You know, it isn't generally known around town, but Mister was never very fond of the dry goods end. People thought he was, but he wasn't. He was more interested in buying and selling properties, real estate. But he kept store because—to show you how clever he was, he didn't want people to think he was a real estate man. A dry goods and notions man, people wouldn't think he was as smart as a real estate man when it came to buying or selling a property. Oh, he was very good to me. I never would of ended up in a house like this if it wasn't for Mister."

"Well, obviously you made him happy, too."

"If we'd of had children. But he ruptured himself when he was younger and he blamed that on why we never had children. It's a big house for just one person. I miss the war."

"The war?"

"Well, I don't mean the bloodshed and all those boys going away, but the Red Cross. During the war I used to go to the Red Cross four-five days a week and I made a lot of friends, but after the Armistice they didn't have the Red Cross any more and I didn't see as much of them. I'm thinking of learning to drive a car. A lot of women do now. Mister didn't like a woman to drive a car, but he never said I *shouldn't*. They're trying to sell me a Pierce-Arrow, but I want to start out with something smaller. The Fierce-Sparrow. Imagine me driving a Fierce-Sparrow? What make is that little car you brought me home in?"

"That's a Dodge."

"Are they hard to drive? Mary Bowen has that Paige, but that's more of a big car. Minnie Stokes gave me a ride in her car and I watched her manipulating all the things. She says it's much easier than it looks. You get so it becomes second nature, she says."

"Minnie has a Templar."

"Oh, I wouldn't want anything as sporty as that, but I like that size car. The Dodge sedan is a nice car. I noticed a lot of them around with women driving. Everybody says don't buy a Ford, because it has no gear shift."

"It has a gear shift, but you operate it with your feet."

"Well, you see how much I know about it. I'm pretty sure I won't buy a Fierce-Sparrow, because then I'd have to hire a man to drive it, and a woman my age driving around with a man all the time. It's all right for Minnie's mother and ladies that age, but I wouldn't feel right about it."

"Why don't you let me teach you to drive?"

"Oh—but how long would it take for that to get around? Can't you just hear them?"

"It would probably get around in two days, but do you care? I'm sure I don't."

"Well, will you give me a couple days to think about it? I'm not worried what they say about me, but—"

"Don't worry what they say about me."

"I was thinking of Mister. It's all his money. Or it was."

"You smoked a cigarette."

"I guess you're right. I'll ring you up, if you really mean it."

The estimate for the circulation of the news that Buz Drummond was giving Sadie Loffler driving lessons was fairly accurate. "Well, I just heard the latest," said his mother. "You and Sadie Gardner."

"Did you?"

"I did, and I guess everybody else has too if it's got to me."

"Have you any objections?"

"Depends on which way you look at it, I guess. But I guess you're looking at it financially."

"Your idea wasn't so good. Minnie turned me down."

"I know, but Sadie Gardner won't. She's older than you are, a good five years. She hasn't long to go before she's forty, and you're not going to get any children out of her."

"There's no proof of that, but anyway I've never longed to have children."

"Every man wants children, sooner or later."

"No, not every man. Not every man wants a wife, either. What's the matter with Sadie? Because her father was Squire Gardner?"

"If I have any objections to Sadie they're the same ones you'd make. Don't try to make me feel like a snob, when you're one yourself. A Frederick Street snob is worse than a Lantenengo. You and Joe Chapin, very much alike."

"I wish I had his money."

"Well, you won't have as much marrying Sadie Gardner, but it's a nice nest egg. You gave up very easily with Minnie, and she has more than Sadie Gardner Loffler, or will have."

"Minnie and I will always be very good friends, but I'd never propose twice to the same woman."

"You'd be making a lot more money if you'd become a surgeon. Why didn't you?"

"Can't stand the sight of blood."

"Don't be impertinent, Buz. A man that's rude to his own mother."

"All the rudeness has to be on the one side, eh, Mother? Is there anything else you want to say before I retire?"

"No. Yes. But you're so thin-skinned you might just as well go to bed."

"You pique my curiosity. What is it?"

"Did you ever have anything to do with a nurse named Henrietta Moore?"

"I had her on a lot of cases. Why?"

"If you're planning to marry Sadie Gardner, Sadie Gardner Loffler, make it quick. A story reached me that you paid this nurse a thousand dollars to leave town. And thinking back, you borrowed a thousand dollars from me just about that time."

"Jesus."

"There's something to it, isn't there?"

"What do you do when people come to you with stories like that about me?"

"I brazen it out, deny everything or else say I know nothing about your affairs, personal or professional. But alone, I think a good deal."

"Have you any more juicy tidbits?"

"Well, two in one evening. That seems to me a lot."

"Yes. Well, I guess I'd better get married before I get into more trouble. Isn't that what you'd suggest?"

"I suggested it a long while ago. Now I suggest you get married before it's too late. Squire Gardner's daughter probably has very old-fashioned, conventional ideas. They're great ones for respectability, people like Sadie. They're the ones that don't tolerate certain things that you and I might overlook."

"*You* might overlook, Mother?"

"Only because I have to, sometimes. My ancestors were among the people that made those rules, those ideas. Pity we didn't all live up to them."

"Didn't Father?"

"Well, he tried. Goodnight, son. I'm going to read a while."

"What are you reading, that has you in this mood?"

She held up her book, the spine toward him. "It's a library book, Miss Williams recommended it. Called *Winesburg, Ohio,* by a Sherwin Anderson. Sher*wood* Anderson. It's not for young people like you. It's for the old, like me. Full of plain, unpleasant truths. Very gloomy little stories that could have happened right here in Gibbsville. And did, some of them. Don't read it."

"I won't. I was just wondering what you were reading."

The book was in her lap when he came down in the morning and saw her sitting there, one side of her face contorted, but her appearance otherwise that of an aging lady who had stopped rocking her chair to let herself be overcome by a deep sleep.

2

Dr. Drummond's reappearances at the meetings of the County Medical Society were welcomed, since what he may have lacked in purely professional standing he possessed in civic prominence. He had money now, was not dependent on his practice to meet his bills. He was a doctor, he treated sick people, but as he said, he had time for other things. The more skillful members of the profession were perfectly willing to have Dr. Wallace P. Drummond represent the medical art at luncheons and banquets, and they conceded that he represented them well. Some of the ugliest men in town were among the most successful healers, but Buz Drummond's appearance on a dais was a great asset to the profession, to the enterprise of the moment, to the community, and to Buz Drummond. His light brown hair had grown darker, then patches of grey had appeared. He was clean shaven at a time when most doctors still grew moustaches. He was nearly six feet tall and flat-bellied. And since his marriage he had been going to a Philadelphia tailor. In this new phase of his life he discovered that he could talk on his feet, but no matter what he said or did not say, people liked to look at him while he told his introductory funny story, waxed persuasive in the inevitable appeal for funds, and ended with a winning smile and a modest disclaimer in advance of the applause that would follow. If most of this was directly or indirectly the result of marrying Sadie Loffler for her money, then it was worth it. There was no doubt that it was worth it to Sadie, to whom he was courteous in public to a degree that was a lesson to other husbands. She took pride in his new popularity and in being half of Dr. and Mrs. Wallace P. Drummond of Lantenengo Street. When he invaded the meetings of the County Medical Society he did so with a purpose. He wanted to be elected president of the Society, he was so elected, and he handed the honor to Sadie like a present. Thenceforth in print he was not merely Dr. Wallace P. Drummond, but Dr. Wallace P. Drummond, president of the Medical Society of Lantenengo County, his full style and title. He took care to remind the editors of the newspapers that the correct usage was Medical Society of Lantenengo County, and not the more abrupt Lantenengo County Medical Society.

No layman, of course, could successfully challenge Buz Drummond's authenticity as a doctor. There were those citizens who were inclined to be cynical about the well-barbered, well-tailored personality, but Buz Drummond could smell their hostility and in their presence he made a point of using medical language they could not possibly understand, a protective device employed by doctors everywhere to defeat lay criticism. Buz Drummond had few occasions to use it. In two or three years of the new prosperity he had made a remarkable advance from his earlier mediocrity, and some of the admiration for him that counted most came from other doctors. "Put Buz Drummond on it, he gets things done," they would say. He could telephone the mayor, the chief of police, the county judges, and even the governor and get an audience. He did not deal with lieutenants of local industry but captains only, and possibly because he looked like the canon of a cathedral, he was influential with the clergy of all denominations. No one paused to consider what the consequences might be for opposing Buz Drummond. In the beginning of his civic career no one said, "What if I don't?" The original power was all persuasion, when Buz Drummond had no latent power of reprisal against those who could have refused him. Then in a few years it was too late; too many men had yielded too many favors gracefully or unquestioningly, and now the power was real. He had prestige. Now he could quickly summon the support of the men who had inadvertently given him his power, and since it was true that he seemed to want nothing for himself, he usually got what he asked for.

Politicians so thoroughly convinced themselves that he was an ideal candidate for public office that they could not understand his refusal to run. The smartest politician in the county, Mike Slattery, said to his wife Peg Slattery, "I keep asking myself, what does this fellow want? I have a hard time understanding a man like that. Everybody wants something, and he was about ready to tip his mitt a year ago, but it's nothing in my line."

"Ready to tip his mitt, how?" said Peg Slattery.

"I mean he was ripe. All these good works and civic activity. Usually I can tell when they're ready to announce. With him it was about a year or so ago. But I asked him did he have his eye on anything, and he said yes. He had his eye on a big new wing for the county hospital. That was in the machinery, I told him. What about for him, what did he want? To stay out of politics, he said. To stay out of politics! That fellow's in politics up to his ears, every day of his life. I'm not afraid of him, but I sure as Satan want him working for me. The one thought did occur to me."

"What's that?"

"The man may just be stupid."

She shook her head. "No. That you can't say about him."

"Yes I can, and I do. The only man I came across in my reading that doesn't seem to want anything for himself is that little fellow in India. Mahatma Gandhi. And we can forget about him. He's not coming to this country, and if he did they'd lock him up."

"The little man with the goats, wears a shroud?"

"That's the man. I'd put Buz Drummond up against him and Buz would win every precinct. Here. Not in India, mind you. Oh, no. But those Hindus, they're a hundred and fifty years behind us, woman. We got free of England a hundred and fifty years ago, and that's all the farther they are now. When they get their independence that's when they start being like us, the way we started to be back in 1776. They won't need their little man then. They can start fighting amongst themselves, as we did. And do. You need a little fellow like Mahatma to lead the fight for independence, or a great fellow like George Washington with Jefferson's brains behind him. Men that don't want anything for themselves. But this is 1925, and we have our independence for a hundred and fifty years, and everybody's out for themselves. Those that don't are stupid, because this country is a nation of competition. Either Buz Drummond wants to be Mahatma, or he's stupid. Politically, I'm speaking now. And financially. Politically and financially he's stupid not to strike while the iron's hot. What else does a man like him want? Well, we have a dirty file on Buz. I started collecting items for it about two years ago."

"There was some story, but I don't remember it."

"Yes. There was one story got out. He knocked up a nurse, back a few years ago, and he gave her money to leave town. He sold a bond he got from his mother. A thousand-dollar bond.

The nurse disappeared from the face of the earth. If she's alive or dead we don't know. The tip on that story came from Billy English. It isn't much of a story till we find out more what happened to the nurse, and that seems hopeless. Then I began delving into a trip he took, working as a ship's doctor. He was supposed to be gone five years, but he was home in less than one. Why? Well, he met some young woman that fell for him and they had a romance on the boat. She was supposed to get off some place in South America, but when the boat sailed she was on it. Left her husband because she was stuck on Drummond. Some place in Australia the American consul came and took her off the boat and they shipped her back to South America with a nurse. She went out of her head."

"Over him? Over Buz Drummond? She must have been *crazy*."

"She was. That's what I said. That's what I just got finished telling you."

"I meant it differently."

"Then as I understand it he was on two other boats over in that part of the world, and on the second one an Englishman with a name like Cumberland took a shot at him."

"At Buz?"

"Yes, woman. Who're we talking about? Shot him in the arm. The official report says that Buz accidentally shot himself, but I don't always go by official reports. Buz had to stay in China or some place till the arm got better, and then he was quietly given the sack and shipped back home. How's that for Mr. Dr. Buz Drummond?"

"He doesn't know you have any of this?"

"Oh, good heavens, no. We spent a lot of money collecting this data. Most of the dirty files the data doesn't cost you a cent. But I had to know a few things about Buz when he began getting strong a year ago. What I told you cost us about eighteen hundred dollars. But wait. I'm not finished. The prize data didn't cost us anything at all, and it isn't a lot of stuff that happened when he was a young fellow, way out on the other side of the world. The prize is what's going on now, here in town."

"Wuddia want me to do? Say please? You're going to tell me, so go ahead. The prize data."

"*Who*—is Buz Drummond's girl friend?"

"Don't know, and didn't know he had one."

"None other than Miss, Minerva, Stokes, alias Minnie Stokes."

"That's old. She jilted him, oh, four-five years ago."

"Did she now? Peg, sometimes you're not as smart as I give you credit for. Dr. Wallace P. Drummond, alias Buz, and Miss Minnie Stokes have been carrying on together since before he got married, and right under Sadie's nose. Whenever Minnie jilted him, she turned right around and began having a passionate love affair with him that if this town ever finds out about it, I wouldn't be surprised if they stoned her. And what they'd do to him I can't in my wildest dreams imagine. Pillars of society, eminent practitioner of the medical profession. And underneath it all they're like a couple of alley cats. He puts his car in the garage at night, and there she is, waiting for him. The carriage-house, the old Norton place? Going on now for I guess five years. Just in the past year they stayed together as man and wife twice in New York and three times in Philadelphia. Dr. and Mrs. W. P. Drum, they go as. Oh, the sinning that goes on, Peg."

"You don't have to make a joke of it. I suppose it's useless to ask how you found out, and if you're sure."

"The meetings in the carriage-house, how that was discovered—well, not to make a joke of it but it was funny. Sadie Loffler had a maid, and *she* was using the room in the carriage-house to meet *her* boy friend. And one night she went up there and heard voices. Sneaked up the stairs in her bare feet and guess who she saw, using her hideout."

"Is that the Chapman woman, that works for Sadie?"

"Correct. She puzzled over whether to blackmail him or not but she asked the priest in confession, as if it was happening to a friend of hers, and the priest said he couldn't give absolution to a blackmailer. So she never said anything to Buz. But when I began making some inquiries she said she'd talk to me but no one else. I offered her some money, but she said she was afraid she wouldn't get absolution if she took money."

"Huh."

"Now don't start complaining about the dirty files. You couldn't run politics without them."

"I didn't say anything."

"You grunted. But I notice you always listen to every story I tell you."

"Well, I agree with you he is stupid."

"Sure he is. I could *make* him run for office if I had to. Usually the dirty files are used for the opposite effect, but if I ever need Buz Drummond, I've got him. And console yourself, Peg. I never used the dirty files to make a nickel in my insurance business. Not a nickel."

"Huh."

"There you go again," he said. "Can I get you a bottle of beer?"

"I'll have a bottle of beer."

"All right. But it's illegal. Ten years ago it wasn't illegal. Ten years from now it won't be. But now it is. That's law for you. And the Church changes its laws, too, Peg. What's your penance when you go to confession? Five Our Fathers and five Hail Marys. But you used to have to do sackcloth and ashes, in front of everybody. Think I'll have a Coke."

"You're a rascal. An old-time rascal."

"No, I'm not. I'm a man living in a world full of people, Peg. And I must be fond of them or I wouldn't study them so much. I'll bet you Lincoln and I would have a great time swapping stories together."

"Oh, tonight it's Lincoln. Who was it the other night, the Italian fellow?"

"Niccolò Machiavelli. Him, too. This is the most fascinating work there is, Peg. I wish I knew all those ones in the past, and the ones to come."

"Get the beer, will you, please? We can talk then."

3

Happy Sadie Drummond, fetching and carrying for people, giving of her money and her time, had wanted to go back to the days of the Red Cross, but the early years of her marriage to Buz Drummond made the Red Cross days (and marriage to Mister Loffler) seem like some sort of rehearsal. Every day she had something to do, somewhere to go, or new plans to engage her attention. Buz, she said, kept her busy. She had automatically become a member of the country club on her marriage to Buz, and she dutifully took some golf lessons, but she gave them up and did not even try to play tennis.

In the third year of her marriage her feelings were hurt, and she sulked and brooded until Buz had to give her a good talking-to. Minnie Stokes had invited Sadie to attend the meetings of the Wednesday Afternoon Bridge Club, not, at first, as a player but as one of the learners, along with a few younger girls who were just starting the game. In the second year Sadie had picked up enough of the rules and basic mechanics of the game to become a playing member, and one of her happiest times was in making preparations for the day when it was her turn to entertain the ladies. Her chicken à la king was all white meat; her dessert was not just ice cream but ice cream in molds, George and Martha Washington, cherry trees, hatchets, drums, stacked muskets, all appropriate to the third Wednesday in February; and she had not only a first prize and a booby prize, but favors for everyone. She completely ignored the custom of a five-dollar limit for first prize and two dollars for the booby. Her first prize was a silk-and-hand-embroidered-lace camisole from Bonwit's, Philadelphia; her booby prize, a pair of hand-painted salt and pepper shakers; and each lady received a cute little sterling silver bridge pencil with her initials engraved on it. "Oh, Sadie, you *shouldn't* have," said Minnie Stokes, the first-prize winner.

"Oh, I know, but after all why not? When a person has as

much fun as I did selecting the things. And everybody *came*. I didn't have to ask anyone to substitute." She had dreaded the prospect of having to ask a non-member to fill in, since any acceptable substitute was probably more truly eligible than she.

In the third year, as October came and went and November was half over, and Sadie had not been notified of the resumption of the meetings, she said to Minnie Stokes: "When are you going to start the Wednesdays again, Minnie?"

"Well, we still have the Wednesdays but with a different bunch of girls. More serious bridge players, you know. They all play for blood."

"Oh."

"Not as much fun, of course, but some of the girls thought we had too much conversation and not enough bridge. After Christmas we may decide to have another club, more like the old one."

"I see," said Sadie. She saw plainly when she saw a group of cars parked at Josie Entwhistle's house. Josie Entwhistle was one of the girls whose bridge game was of a caliber to give Sadie confidence in herself.

"Mean, nasty stuck-up things," said Sadie to Buz. "And I don't trust that Minnie Stokes. I think she kept me out. She always looks at me funny."

"Now you listen to me, Sadie," said Buz. "You told me over and over again you were never going to learn the game. And there's nothing worse than playing bridge with somebody that doesn't *care* about the game. Spoils it for everybody. Minnie's a very good player. She plays with men."

"Maybe that's her trouble. If she played with them in other ways maybe she'd find herself a husband, before it's too late. Her and her golf and her tennis and playing cards."

"Well, perhaps so. But you like Minnie and she's never been stuck up with you, you *have* to admit that."

"She didn't used to," said Sadie. "But now she looks at me funny."

"Something you imagine."

Happy Sadie Drummond could not long sulk over a snub by other women when her intimate life with Buz was so exciting, full of things that were so exciting that she could not tell them to any of her friends. Sometimes he would stay away from her for weeks at a stretch, but she knew, because he told her so, that abstinence so deliberate stored up desire. He introduced her to methods of pleasure that he himself had not heard of until his voyages to the Orient, and he assured her that periods of abstinence were essential to the creation of a desire strong enough to conquer her feeling of wickedness. "I guess I ought to feel more wicked than I do," she once told him. But instead she only felt a superior pity over the girl she had been as Mrs. Sadie Loffler. Most of the time she could hardly remember that side of her life with Mister Loffler, and she was glad that Buz had no jealousy of her first husband. It would have embarrassed her to reveal now the unrefined pleasures of her first marriage. Sometimes at a banquet, when Buz was making a speech, she would steal a look at the faces of the women in the audience and think of them with their Lofflers and of herself with this man who was her husband, and her sense of possession would become almost unbearable. It was especially lovely torture when she had reason to guess that a period of abstinence might end that night.

4

"One of these days," said Buz Drummond, "I'm going to have to do away with her."

"Why do you say that?" said Minnie Stokes.

"You'll see why," said Drummond.

"No I won't, so tell me," said Minnie. "You'll never do away with anybody, darling, but why do you think you have to say it? About once a year you say something like that."

"Some day, some year I won't say it, but just do it."

She shook her head. "Never," she said.

"Don't be so know-it-all. It's very exasperating," he said. They were lying on a bed in a hotel in Newark, New Jer-

sey, a city in which neither of them knew a single human being.

"You're more apt to do away with *me,* as a matter of fact."

"Why?"

"Well, I can make you very cross. You lose your temper with
me, but she only bores you. You might push me out of a window, but in anger. Or want to kill me when I can't go away
with you, but then I wouldn't be there, when you lost your
temper. But the only way you'd ever do away with her would
be like giving her small doses of arsenic or something like that."

"I've thought of that."

"I'm sure you have."

"But that isn't the way. There are doctors in this town—I
don't mean here, I mean Gibbsville—that are going to want to
be damn sure there's nothing suspicious about the way she
checks out, when she does check out."

"Yes."

"If she fell from the court house tower, in full view of everybody, there'd be doctors ready to do a post-mortem. If she ever
gets sick I'm not even going to give her an aspirin tablet. I'll call
in Billy English or somebody equally respectable, let him be
responsible from the word go. Of course I wouldn't have these
murderous thoughts if you'd marry me."

"Well, I don't intend to."

"She'd give me a divorce. I know she would."

"Yes, she probably would. If you told her that you were in
love with me, she would."

"What kind of a life is this for you, Minnie?"

"Hmm." She smiled faintly.

"No, really?"

"Oh—it's all right I guess." She knelt on the bed and kissed
his mouth.

"Well, it isn't," he said.

"No, of course it isn't. But you love me, and I love you. You
love me as much as you can love anybody, and I love you the
same way, which is more. You haven't got much love to offer,
have you, Buz?"

"Well, that's what you keep telling me."

"But what there is is for me, isn't it?"

"Yes. All of it. A nasty little eyecupful of love, according to you."

"You're sweet," she said.

"But let me tell you something. An eyecup full of arsenic is a fatal dose, and the same amount of love has just as big an effect on me."

"How do you mean?"

"I mean, well, don't you get it? Whatever love I have to offer is yours, whether it's enough to fill a bathtub or an eyecup."

"Oh, yes. I see. I guess I see."

"Why don't you marry me? I'll make you happy."

"Maybe you could. You make *her* happy."

"Oh, Christ."

"But maybe the trouble is—I don't know—I love you, and never, never anyone else. But I've always shied away from you."

"I wouldn't say that, exactly."

"Oh, heavens. This? If you asked me to I'd do this in the middle of the floor at a club dance. Not really, of course, but I've often wanted to."

"Yes, I can think of times."

"There were other times that you didn't know about, too. Other boys I've danced with have got the benefit of what I was thinking about you."

"Who?"

"Oh, I don't know. Ever since I stopped thinking like a nice girl I had some such thoughts about you. But then you were so *dull* when you came a-courting. Fate protected me."

"Oh, shit."

"Don't say that. I don't like that word. You can say anything else."

"Well, to go on. You've told me this before, that if I hadn't been so considerate of your virginity we'd be married today."

"Yes. I expected to be swept off my feet, and was ready and willing. The second time I went out with you I even wore underclothes that wouldn't interfere. But you brought me home from the concert and didn't even try to kiss me."

"I know, I know. But why was that a mistake? You've never been able to tell me why. Do you know why?"

"Oh, I do now."

"Money-proud?"

"Not exactly. It was just that—as if I'd been looking forward to an affair with Don Juan and he spent the evening discussing iambic pentameter."

"I didn't discuss iambic pentameter."

"Or anything else. You just put in the time with Minnie Stokes, making a cold-blooded, calculating effort. And that made me realize that you could be cold-blooded and calculating. Gave me time to get my breath. I wasn't in awe of you any more."

"I see. Should have taken it right out and given you a jab with it."

"Well, something like that. Anything would have been better than yawning through Mendelssohn's Scotch Symphony. That's what they played."

"How do you remember that, or do you?"

"Oh, I do, Buz. I remember everything about us, things you've forgotten or never knew."

"The question is, when are you going to be a mature woman and marry me? You're over thirty, and people aren't going to say nasty little Minnie broke up Dr. Drummond's marriage. Everybody's grown up—except you. There are no young kids in this triangle."

"Do you know what people can do?"

"What?"

"Well, I won't say it, but you know what they can do."

"You mean they can go fuck themselves?"

"Yes. Thank you for saying it for me."

"It's a word that occasionally passes your lips. Minnie, do you *want* to stay single all your life?"

"I'm not single now, to my way of thinking. I couldn't be more double than I am with you."

"But I'll be forty before very long, Sadie's past it now. The longer you delay, the worse it's going to be for her, if that's what you're thinking about."

"Partly."

"The question of children. You've been very careful, but you've never said you didn't want to have children."

"I'm resigned to not having them. And you *don't* want them."

"Is that why you're resigned?"

"Partly. Principally."

"What is life going to be for you when you're, say, fifty? Do you think now that you and I will still want to go on like this? You won't be able to stand it. Love won't last that long, Minnie."

"Maybe not."

"Well, what will you have then?"

"When I'm fifty? Oh—I'll have you. By that time this won't be so important."

"You don't know much about biology if you believe that. Are you aware of the fact that after the climacteric, the menopause, many women get more pleasure out of sex than they ever did?"

"I don't believe it. I've heard it, but I doubt it very much."

"Take my word for it, free. No charge. See, I'm not just after your money."

"Ah, Buz, don't say that. Sweetheart."

"Well, Christ, what else is there for me to think? The fact of the matter is that I don't need Sadie's money any more. Or yours. If I wanted to I could make fifty thousand a year, in perfectly legitimate business. If I wanted to go into politics I could make a lot more. A *lot* more. But I won't do it as long as I'm married to Sadie. Why should I? I'm respectable and respected now. I carry a lot of influence, and incidentally I've given Sadie a good run for her money."

"Yes, you have. Nobody can take that away from you."

"The squire's daughter has gone as far as she'll ever go, and much farther than she had any right to expect. She's not on my conscience, even if she is on yours. She is, isn't she?"

"On my conscience? Yes, I guess so."

"You know so. That's the whole damn trouble."

"No it isn't. The truth is she bores me, too, intensely. I have to put up with her friendship, which I don't want. You have no idea how many times I've been tempted to describe a night with you, in vivid detail."

"Why don't you sometime?"

"That would do away with her, more quickly than arsenic. But why don't *you?*"

"Describe a night with you?"

"Yes."

"I don't know, I never thought of it. I guess I couldn't do that."

"You couldn't do it to her, or couldn't do it to me?"

"I don't think I could do it to her, because I know how she'd look. And I couldn't do it to you, because I couldn't tell anybody about you. I used to talk about girls and everything about them, everything. Naming names. But I wouldn't even admit that you have nipples on your breasts. You and I are—us."

She put her hand on his cheekbone. "The eyecup turns into a bathtub," she said.

"Yes, and I still don't get my answer."

"My darling, whatever answer I gave you would be a thinking answer, and false. The real answer is a feeling one, and I don't know what it is."

"All right," he said. "What would you like to do? I have another pint of Four Roses, bottled in bond. Shall I send down for some ginger ale? Or do you want to take the next train back to Philadelphia? Or do you want to just lie here and see what happens?"

"I certainly don't want to take the next train back to Philadelphia."

"One of these days you will," he said.

5

It was the day after Thanksgiving and the year was 1939, in which there were two Thanksgiving Days: the officially proclaimed, or FDR holiday, and the second a week later on the traditional fourth Thursday. Sadie and Buz were in a Chestnut Street jeweler's, doing their Christmas shopping.

The clerk stood patiently while Sadie contemplated a silver dish. "I tell you what you do," she said. "You take it over and ask my husband what he thinks of it. That's him over at the leather-goods counter. And while you're gone I'll have a look at these other things."

The clerk said, "Thank you, Mrs. Drummond," and departed. He always waited on her for silver articles. She busied herself for a moment, then turned to look at Buz and the clerk. But the clerk was talking to another customer, paying no attention to Buz, and the other man was shaking his head. The man was at least sixty-five years old and did not have the look of a regular customer of the shop. The clerk shrugged his shoulders and returned to his post. "I guess your husband must have moved to another counter," he said.

"He did not. He's still there. The tall man wearing the brown overcoat."

"Oh, I beg your pardon. Oh, *that's* Mr. Drummond?"

"Dr. Drummond."

"My mistake," said the clerk.

It was only one of several incidents that did not seem to annoy Buz as much as they annoyed her. In this instance Buz had been unaware of the incident, but she was unable to keep it to herself. "Are you ever sorry you married me?" she said, back at the hotel.

"When you make a mountain out of a molehill. You could have pointed me out and prevented that mistake."

"Then you'd have seen me point and thought I didn't have any manners."

"Oh, what balls, Sadie. You're forty-nine years old, and I'm forty-four. We're neither of us young people."

"But you should of seen what he picked out to be my husband. And not only the age. Practically an old tramp, in off the streets."

"Well, what do you want me to do? Try to look older? Let my appearance go to hell? Well, I refuse to. And I also refuse to pamper you. Every woman has to go through change of life and you're just being selfish. I won't put up with it. You over-tire yourself with this damned Christmas shopping and you take offense at the least little thing. I'll give you something now to put you to sleep and I'll go over and have dinner at the Union League."

"Anything to get away from me, that's what it is."

"Right. I don't care for your company, and I'm sure you don't care for mine."

"One of these days I'll kill myself. You mind. I will."

"Will you indeed? Here, take this and go to sleep."

"What is it?"

"It's something to put you to sleep, and I hope you'll wake up not feeling so sorry for yourself."

"Why shouldn't I feel sorry for myself? Nobody else does."

"Now listen to me, Sadie—"

"I don't want to listen."

"If you don't listen I'm going to pack my bag and leave you, this minute."

"If you do I'll jump out that window."

"No you won't, so just listen to what I have to tell you. Are you going to listen?"

"All right."

"You promised me a month ago that you weren't going to drink except before meals. Did you have something at the hair-dresser's this afternoon?"

"No."

"Yes you did, or if not at the hairdresser's, somewhere. Now don't lie to me."

"I had a cocktail downstairs."

"You had three cocktails downstairs, or four."

"I had three, not four. And they were small ones, not doubles. They only give you a half a cocktail here anyhow. This place is a gyp."

"When we get home you're going to go see English."

"I am not, and anyway he's too old."

"Then somebody else, but you're going to make an appointment to see a doctor next week. So you decide which one you want to see."

"There's nothing the matter with me. You said so yourself, every woman goes through the change."

"Sadie, you *know* what else is wrong with you. I'm a doctor, remember. And even if I weren't, you couldn't keep it from me forever. You never used to take a drink unless I was there."

"Yes, but you're never there when I want one."

"I'd have to be there pretty much of the time, it seems to me."

"Are you calling me a drunkard?"

"I'm telling you that you're on the verge of becoming an alcoholic, and I'm telling you that your liver isn't going to be able to stand what you've been doing to it."

"It's the only pleasure I get out of life any more."

"Do you call it pleasure, sitting with Josie Entwhistle and getting drunk every afternoon?"

"I didn't see Josie all week, and what's the matter with Josie? She's one of *your* friends, the only one that's nice to me. The only one that ever shows any appreciation."

"You can't buy people's friendship." As soon as he said it he realized it was a mistake. Josie Entwhistle was the last of the Wednesday bridge players who continued to be companionable with Sadie.

"That was a nasty mean thing to say, and you said it to hurt me. You took all the pleasure out of my Christmas shopping. I wish I never would of married you. If I hadn't of been rich you never would of looked at me."

"That's insulting."

"Minnie Stokes wouldn't have you, that's why you married me."

The harm was done, and so he continued. "Well, I married you and I didn't marry Josie Entwhistle, if she's the one that gave you that idea. And she is." He had now spoiled her only companionship.

"I notice you don't deny it about Minnie Stokes."

"Josie Entwhistle has been jealous of Minnie all her life, long before you ever knew Josie or Minnie, and I'm not here to discuss Minnie."

"What are you here for?"

"To watch you go to sleep, and then have a few minutes' peace by myself."

At the word sleep she tried to fight it, but almost immediately her eyes closed. He watched her for five minutes and then went out. He walked over to South Broad Street and at the club he telephoned Minnie.

"I just wanted to hear your voice," he said.

"Is something wrong?"

"Yes. You're ninety-five miles away, and you always are."

"Yes, most of the time. I'm sorry, darling, but you caught me at a bad time. I'm going to dinner."

"Who's taking you out to dinner?"

"Mr. McHenry."

"Haven't you started to call him Arthur yet?"

"Well, yes I have, but it doesn't come naturally."

"It will."

"I don't know. Darling, I have to hang up. Shall I see you next week?"

"Come to the office, tomorrow evening?"

"No, I don't like that. You know I don't."

"All right. Next week. Monday night?"

"Tuesday night."

"Not Sunday night?"

"No, it'll have to be Tuesday at the earliest. Goodbye, darling. Sorry I couldn't be more help."

After Pearl Harbor he tried to get a commission, but he was not wanted. He was younger than some of the new majors and lieutenant commanders, lieutenant colonels and commanders, colonels and captains, but he was neither young enough nor good enough to overcome the Army's and Navy's indifference. There was a vague irony too to the fact that Sadie, with her fond recollections of the Red Cross of the First War, was asked to contribute money but not her services. The only people who knew her now were also tolerantly aware of her addiction to the bottle. "No, Buz," said Minnie Stokes McHenry. "We simply couldn't have her disrupting things."

"It might help her. It really might," he said.

"It might for a while, but what if she turned up drunk? Or had to be taken home? Then everybody in town would know, instead of just a few. No. I'm sorry."

"You've done a pretty thorough job of getting the Drummonds out of your life. Drummonds. It almost sounds like gremlins."

"She was never in my life, and you'll always be in it."

"What do you tell Arthur?"

"He has never asked."

"Can any man be that incurious?"

"He isn't incurious, but I told him I'd only marry him on condition that he not ask. I told him I'd had love affairs, but I wouldn't tell him how many or with whom."

"Some day you *will* tell him."

"Yes, some day I probably will, when I want to get some comfort out of my past, when I have to think back on how attractive I used to be. But I don't need that quite yet. A few years from now, probably."

"I hate Arthur McHenry."

"Well, I guess I hated Sadie but wouldn't admit it. If I'd given in to it I'd have been miserable, all those years."

"And might have married me. Do you remember one time I wanted to kill her?"

"I do. We were in Newark, New Jersey. You talked about it other times, too, but I remember that because there was something in your voice that day that—it was the one time I was afraid. You weren't angry. You were bored and weary, and I had a feeling it was getting you. You used to have a habit, you know, or you don't know but you did have a habit, when something bothered you."

"I'd lower my voice, speak more softly."

"No. This was completely unconscious. You'd start rubbing your scar, where the Englishman shot you. You were completely oblivious of it, but I noticed it."

"I'm sure Arthur McHenry has no such scars."

"He has no scars of any kind, that I've been able to find."

"Have you discovered any of your own?"

"Oh, a deep one, yes." She laughed. "But I can't rub it, and I can't blame anybody for it but myself."

"Tell your physician."

"I'll tell you. It's what hurts when I think of how much I loved you and how happy we could have been. But every time I have my palm read they always say my head rules my heart. You've never read much. Did you ever read anything by Joseph Conrad?"

"No, I don't think I did."

"He said a very strange thing for an author to say. He said that thinking is the great enemy of perfection."

"That's why I don't read novels. Statements like that. But he has a point, at least in love affairs."

"Well, he included love affairs, as I remember it."

"And so you have a scar, too, Minnie?"

"Uh-huh. But it doesn't show. It doesn't show."

"When it does what's McHenry going to do?"

"Oh, he knows what love is. He loved his other wife, too. You never really loved anyone but me, did you? Or I anyone but you. What did that prizefighter say? We were robbed."

"We wuz robbed. Don't be so prissy."

"And don't you be so bossy. I'm a married woman now."

"Yes. That's what you are, Minnie. A married woman. And you have the scar to prove it."

"Don't make it hurt, please. That's not what a doctor's supposed to do."

"Well, you tell me a good anaesthetic to use on myself."

"If I knew of one I would."

"I guess the best is what I tell some patients. Those that haven't got very long. 'Keep busy. Don't overdo, but keep yourself occupied.' It never made a one of them live a day longer than he should have, but at least some of them felt useful for a few months."

"You're useful."

"At the moment, I am."

"That isn't what I meant, Buz, but there are lots of ways, aren't there?"

"Oh, sure. As a matter of fact, what *did* you mean?"

"You thought I meant your practice, but I meant Sadie and myself. I don't know what either of us would do without you."

"You seem to be doing very well without me. Sadie is another story, one that we'll see the end of fairly soon. Two years, three years."

"Two or three years? I could almost laugh, couldn't you?"

"Sure. Often. But only almost. And in a way I'm glad you didn't wait."

"Why?"

"Well, my ethical problem is bad enough as it is, and if you were still single it would be much worse. Sadie is drinking herself to death, literally, and I know as her husband that she's doing it deliberately. Not in any mean or vindictive way, but because she has nothing to live for. Nothing. Sex is no pleasure for her any more. Dressing up. Giving parties. None of the things she enjoyed for a while. She doesn't want to look at herself in the mirror, and she doesn't, or when she does she cries. So she drinks. She gets what she calls sozzled. For about two hours a day, in the middle of the afternoon, she makes a little sense and I try to go home and see her then. But the rest of the time she's intoxicated, or sozzled. I could probably have her committed, but she's not going to respond to any treatment that I know of, including psychiatry. I could compel her to go to a hospital, but she has a genuine terror of hospitals, and in these times I have no right to put her in a hospital, with the shortage of nurses, and sick people sleeping in corridors. Can you imagine Sadie in a corridor? And would you put her in a private room when the demand is what it is today? Have you been to either of the hospitals lately?"

"Yes."

"Then you know. So I have Mrs. Brophy in the house. She's not a nurse and she's not young, but she's pretty strong and conscientious, and at least I know that Sadie isn't going to set fire to the house with a cigarette she left burning, or fall asleep in the bathtub. And if she has a bad fall, Mrs. Brophy always knows where she can reach me."

"What about Sadie herself?"

"Most of the time she doesn't know what's going on."

"Have you had any other doctors in to see her?"

"No, not yet. I know what they'll say. The younger men will say psychiatry, and pass the buck that way. One or two might recommend surgery, but why subject her to that ordeal when I know damn well that as soon as she comes home from the hospital she's going to start drinking again? I'm not giving her little doses of arsenic. My wife is a hopeless case. She's going to die from the things that are wrong with her organically, and even if they could be cured, she'd still die. There's a thing I've noticed about Sadie and others as well. There are some people that don't seem to be interested in themselves, seem to be more interested in other people. And we tend to think of them as unselfish and so on. But I wonder. Sadie, for instance, has always been outwardly generous and so forth, but I don't believe that she ever spent much time thinking about herself, about her own mind, her motives, her limitations. And if she did, possibly she didn't like what she learned, and therefore stopped. She was safe, comfortable, as long as she didn't do any thinking about herself."

"Escapism."

"Of course. But a case of escapism like Sadie's is a form of death. Not suicide, but death. Sadie probably died of shock years ago, when she got a good look at herself and didn't like what she saw."

"I never thought of it that way."

"Well, I never would have if I hadn't been married to a case of it. I think Sadie murdered Loffler."

"Oh, come on, Buz. He died in the hospital. That's why she hates hospitals."

"He not only died in the hospital. I also went to the trouble of looking up his death certificate. He died of normal causes. A heart condition. Billy English signed the death certificate. No post-mortem. No suspicious element in the whole business. But I think she hoped so much for his death that she got her wish."

"Oh, well that's a different matter."

"Is it? I think that's what she saw that she didn't like. I think that after Loffler died she took the one and only look inside herself and was horrified by what she saw. Horrified. Admitted to herself that she had wanted him dead."

"Is she a witch? Is that what you're implying?"

"A kind of one, yes. Fat, and not very bright, not skinny and clever, the way witches are supposed to be. You said something a few minutes ago about fortune-tellers. Were they skinny?"

"No, as a matter of fact the fortune-tellers I went to were both stout women. I only went to two. One in New York and one in Collieryville, but they were both heavy-set."

"Well, I saw them in China, the Hawaiian Islands and several other places when I was out there years ago, and they were all fat women. Rather jolly fat women, except when they were fat men."

"Are you making this up?"

"No. If it sounds that way it's because I've never put it into words before. Even now I'm not going to tell you everything."

"What is there to keep back?"

"Things I don't like to tell, and that you wouldn't like to listen to."

"Oh, in the sexual line?"

"Yes."

"Well, without going into detail, what kind of thing? Be objective."

"Well, medically objective, which is to say things she didn't know herself, she was a sadist. But not in the obvious ways. With a man like Loffler, a man that couldn't have known there was such a word and was probably frustrated anyhow, she could have been very dangerous."

"How?"

"Well, I don't think he'd had much sex life before he married Sadie, and he was fifteen years older than she when they got married. He was always fifteen years older, of course. When I married Sadie I discovered that I was expected to function every night of the week."

"But you didn't."

"No, I didn't, but apparently she had Loffler trying every night. When it got dark, you went to bed, and when you went to bed you had sex. That must have been quite a strain on Loffler, who wasn't accustomed to any at all during the first forty years of his life. I can see how this conversation could become embarrassing to you, Mrs. McHenry."

"Well, yes, it could. But I'm fascinated by the witch theory. Since it's come up, I admit I always thought Sadie was—strange. I remember one time at a dinner at the hotel. You were making a speech for the Community Chest, I think it was, and I happened to notice Sadie. She wasn't looking at you at all. She was studying all the women, one after another. Pride, I thought it was at first, but that wasn't it. I decided it was more like jealousy, trying to guess which of the women wanted to go to bed with you. Why wasn't she more jealous of me? Why didn't her instinct tell her about us?"

"Who knows? She wasn't jealous of women patients, either. She once asked me what a doctor thought when a woman patient also happened to be a friend of his. I told her that sick women were completely devoid of any attraction for a doctor. She accepted that. She also accepted my statement that doctors never fool around with nurses. Those were the days when she accepted everything I told her. These past few years she doesn't believe anything, but that's not only directed against me. She doesn't believe anybody. Mrs. Brophy, me, anybody. Oh, if I were just out of medical school I wouldn't say this, but Sadie is crazy. Take away all the language of anatomy and diagnosis and therapy and prognosis—and I'm married to a crazy woman."

"Then she's not a witch, Buz," said Minnie, smiling.

"No? In the tropics the chief conversational topic after sex and money is witchcraft, whether you're in Port-au-Prince or Honolulu. I never knew a ship's officer that didn't have some favorite witchcraft story. But you have a word like poltergeist, which comes from the German, meaning a noisy ghost. Those things aren't confined to the dark-skinned people. The banshees. *Macbeth.* And I know this much about my wife. When Mrs. Brophy has to sit with her at night, she won't do it without her rosary beads. Don't ask me why, but I guess Mrs. Brophy has heard her say things in her sleep."

"What are you grinning at?" said Minnie.

"Something that might amuse you. Should, if you haven't lost your sense of humor."

"What?"

"Mrs. Brophy told me that Sadie thinks there's a ghost in the garage."

"Us? You mean to say she knew about us?"

"No, positively not. This ghost has only been there in the past year or so. It's over three years since you and I've been up there. This is completely imaginary."

"Unless one of your maids is going in for hanky-panky."

"Which one? Agnes, the cook? Or Mary Chapman? Agnes couldn't walk that far, and Mary could walk that far but who'd want her to?"

"I guess Sadie has nightmares."

"Of course she has. Delirium tremens nightmares. But I thought it would amuse you, ghosts in the garage."

"What if that had ever got out about us? Think what a sensation we'd have caused."

"I often think of the sensations we caused, Minnie."

"Never mind, never mind," she said. "Well, this is the first good talk we've had in three years."

"Yes, and think how many years since we had such a good talk fully dressed."

"I won't think about that, Buz, and don't you." She got up and left him as the crowd began to gather for the meeting of the Lantenengo County Red Cross Executive Committee, Dr. Wallace P. Drummond, chairman.

6

A new doctor, wholly new to the town, created a place for himself that was made up in part of Buz Drummond's former position and in part his own. "I've only been practicing a little over thirty years," Buz said one evening at the Gibbsville Club. "Well, not quite forty. But already I'm obsolete, thanks to three things. Psychiatry. The wonder drugs. And the New Deal. If I were just getting out of medical school, knowing all I was supposed to know in 1921, I couldn't get a license to practice today. Not in this State. Most of us my age won't admit that, but it's true. You take thoracic surgery. I watched a man do an operation the other day that in my early days, if he'd have attempted it he'd have been expelled from the Gibbsville Hospital, kicked out of the Medical Society. It was a heart operation. Oh, our men operated on the heart, true, but this man went in and took care of the obstruction and then put a sleeve over the aorta—too complicated to explain to a layman—but the patient will live ten more years. In my day we'd have let him die, without any surgery. I started out with a Dodge coupe, but in reality I was one of the last of the horse-and-buggy doctors. Nowadays if a patient is too sick for an office call they send him to the hospital. Doctors are just too damn busy to make house calls, not to mention the fact that there aren't enough nurses to take care of private patients at home. Not to mention the bloody awful expense, and the fact that the hospitals have the facilities that aren't available at home. When I was starting out, though, if I sent a patient to the hospital the family would begin to wonder whether Pop had made a will."

"You mentioned the New Deal. Where does that come in?"

"Socialized medicine."

"But you're holding the line against that, you and the County Medical Society."

"Every two years we elect a new president—the same old new president. Me. But this year I'm not running again. I'd get licked, and I want to retire undefeated, bow out gracefully, if not graciously. You see, Arthur, the Society is still made up of men like me, who can outvote the new men, but every two years the new fellows are a little stronger. Officially the Society is opposed to socialized medicine, but the new young men are just waiting for a form of it that will be acceptable to them. And it won't be acceptable to me. The monthly meetings aren't what they used to be, a few nonentities getting together to talk shop, swap a few dirty stories and adjourn to the Elks for beer. We get a bigger attendance these days and some of the best men. And they're so damned serious. Oh, hell, Arthur, I'm on the shelf. Do you know that two doctors in this town have telephones in their cars?"

"No, but I'm not surprised."

"It doesn't surprise me either, except that I came across a discussion in the minutes of a meeting back around 1902, 1903. Old Dr. Wainwright, long since dead, led the discussion. The question was should doctors charge a fifty-cent fee for talking to patients over the phone. The vote was thirty-five to one against charging them. Today we charge two dollars, to those who can afford it. Wainwright brought up the point because he hadn't decided whether to put in a phone or not, and he wanted to be sure it would pay for itself. He was outvoted on the fifty-cent fee, so he didn't put in a phone. Now nearly every doctor in town has an office phone, a residence phone, an unlisted residence phone, and the answering service. And two of them, phones in their cars. How things have changed!"

"Yes."

"I was never very fond of Malloy. Too brusque, too domineer-

ing. But he was nice to me when I first started out, and I remember him trying to get me to stop smoking. A doctor must
rely on all his senses, he said, and one of the most important is
the sense of smell. Smoking ruins your sense of smell, he said.
The reason I bring him up is how can you smell a patient over
the phone, sitting in your car? I'm older now than Malloy was
when he died, but he practically belongs in the Dark Ages, and
where does that leave me? Sitting here in this club, waiting for
our bridge partners. Standing on the first tee, waiting for the
other members of a foursome. I have an M.D. on my automobile license plate, and sometimes I think I get it under false pretenses. However, last Sunday coming up from the club a state
policeman pulled me out of a traffic tie-up. He saw my license
plate and escorted me to an auto accident. I was too late for one
poor son of a bitch, but I stopped another from bleeding to
death. Not that a chiropractor couldn't have done the same. Or
a first-class Boy Scout."

"How are you coming along with your book?"

"Oh, you've heard about my book? Well, I've been making a
lot of notes. I have a dozen school tablets filled with them, and
I could go on filling them with the things I remember. The
trouble is I'm not sure what kind of a book I want to write."

"At least you know what kind you don't want to write."

"What kind is that?" said Buz Drummond.

"Like that piece of tripe Dr. Malloy's son wrote a few years
ago," said McHenry.

"Oh, but that was a novel. Fiction. He made all that up."

"But he certainly gave this town a black eye."

"That's what I don't understand, Arthur. If it was all made
up, what were people so sore about?"

"He gave the town a black eye, that's why. And not one
damn thing he wrote about actually happened."

"That's what I said. But you as a lawyer, and I as a physician, we know that things *like* them happened."

"Oh, hell, as far as that goes, I know some things that if
young Malloy ever heard about them . . ."

"So do I, Arthur," said Dr. Drummond.